The VENGEFUL BRIDEGROOM

Also by Kit Donner

The Notorious Bridegroom

Published by Kensington Publishing Corporation

The VENGEFUL BRIDEGROOM

KIT DONNER

ZEBRA BOOKS
KENSINGTON PUBLISHING CORP.
http://www.kensingtonbooks.com

ZEBRA BOOKS are published by

Kensington Publishing Corp.
119 West 40th Street
New York, NY 10018

All Kensington titles, imprints and distributed lines are available at special quantity discounts for bulk purchases for sales promotion, premiums, fund-raising, educational or institutional use.

Special book excerpts or customized printings can also be created to fit specific needs. For details, write or phone the office of the Kensington Special Sales Manager: Attn. Special Sales Department. Kensington Publishing Corp., 119 West 40th Street, New York, NY 10018. Phone: 1-800-221-2647.

Zebra and the Z logo Reg. U.S. Pat. & TM Off.

ISBN-13: 978-1-4201-0847-7
ISBN-10: 1-4201-0847-6

First Printing: September 2010

10 9 8 7 6 5 4 3 2 1

Printed in the United States of America

For my siblings
Kim, Jill, Lee, and Todd
On the way to growing up, you became my best friends
And for my other "siblings"
Kelley and Ron

Prologue

The Times
January 1811

DIED

On Monday, at 21 Westcott Gate, Bloomsbury, aged 54, Sir Reginald Colgate, much lamented by his son, the new baronet, Sir Matthew Colgate, and his daughter, Miss Madelene Colgate.

Gossip heard at White's (March 1811)

A duel was held early yesterday morning. They say a man was defending his sister's honor from a reprobate who had taken license with her affections. No reports of fatalities, one wounded.

Extract from a letter dated 17 May 1811
Miss Lucinda Westcott, Ludlow, Shropshire,
to Miss Jane Parlymle, Oxford

I regret to inform you that my health has not improved and my brother insists that we travel to Italy for a recuperative visit. I shall try to write.

London Lady's Social News
18 June 1811

MISCELLANY

Tuesday past, Mr. Nelson Gobler, of Kent, was to be married to Miss Madelene Colgate of Bloomsbury, but sadly is it reported the bride did not appear for the nuptials. It is believed Mr. Gobler returned to Kent to seek a local maid for marriage.

London Lady's Social News
October 1811

MISCELLANY

Unsubstantiated. A license of marriage was obtained by Aaron Winchester, Earl of Chesterbroke, for the hand of Miss Madelene Colgate. Within a week, the request for the license was withdrawn. No further details were given.

The Shropshire Gazette
December 1811

Mr. Gabriel Westcott has returned to his home at Westcott Close from a long sojourn near Florence, Italy, to regretfully bury his sister, Miss Lucinda Westcott, in the family plot.

From Miss Madelene's Diary
January 1812

I miss Father. No man will ever be equal to him in my eyes. It is hard to believe it has been a year. Matthew despairs of ever finding a suitable husband for me, but soon that will not be his main concern. He has been gambling rather heavily, and I think he is afraid to tell me of his losses. If our debts are great and our funds low, I worry Matthew may go to prison—

Chapter One

15 May 1812
St. James Street
London, England

"No question Miss Madelene Colgate is a beauty, but no gentleman in his right mind would want to marry the termagant," Lord Vincennes insisted.

Mr. Arnold Duckins, great grandnephew of the Marquess of Stalingsford, hurried to disagree with his lordship's pronouncement. "One with such beauteous features could only have the temperament of an angel. Those deep blue eyes and the long, dark hair. She could make Aphrodite jealous." He sighed and looked heavenward, hoping his dramatic flair would intrigue his companion.

Earlier, Duckins had noticed his target, Lord Vincennes, lounging by the bow window at White's, as he was wont to do every morning. To be most effective, Duckins took his time to bait the hook before he reeled in his fish.

Since gossip abounded Vincennes and his wife had a very acrimonious marriage, Duckins thought to walk a tightrope in introducing the topic of matrimony and a sure bet into the conversation. After exchanging pleasantries on the weather and the Prince Regent's latest excesses, Arnold had launched the subject of marriageable ladies, and in particular, one Miss Madelene Colgate.

As they watched the street peddlers pushing their carts up the street in search of those with funds to spare, they continued to dispute the merits of the young woman. In another corner of the club, the morning crowd enjoyed a hot repast of scrambled eggs, sausages, fresh salmon, and fried tomatoes in the lingering smoky air from the previous evening.

Duckins watched Vincennes's countenance closely to determine his best strategy.

His lordship shook his head and swallowed his coffee. "You, young swain, are charmed by any young thing with a pretty face. I heard tell not a year ago she jilted a man from Kent, and it wasn't the first time. Said he went home with a broken heart. Even the family's former servants have spoken about their mistress's blazing temper and to watch for flying objects when she's in a sniff. Seems the death of her father has only served to exacerbate this rash behavior. And to compound matters, prattle-bags waggle their tongues her brother has spent all of her dowry."

Vincennes presumably had an opinion on everything, and obviously not a fair consideration of Miss Colgate. Undeterred, Duckins continued, while staring out the pristine window, "Perhaps the death of her father struck her insensible, and she needs a man to set her on the right path. For the suitable man, I'd bet she'd prove easy to tame."

Vincennes snorted. "And *I'd* be willing to bet no man would have her, not until she learned to control her passions." He popped out his watch fob. "Must take my leave and see to my lawyer," he muttered.

Duckins wasn't about to let his prey slip away. "Would you be willing to wager Miss Colgate could be married off in three days?" he asked casually while fingering a coin from his pocket.

The older man stared at Duckins in consternation. "What say you? Are you suggesting a wager that you can find a man to marry Miss Colgate? I'd like to see the day."

"*In three days*," Duckins told him succinctly.

"Three days until what?"

"I'll find a husband for Miss Colgate within three days, and she'll go to the altar happily." Duckins smiled and waited to see if his lordship would nibble at the trap. The older man had plenty of money to lose, even with his impending divorce. Indeed, given his lordship's penchant for gambling on lost causes and his considerable wealth, Vincennes had been an easy choice for this venture.

His lordship heaved himself out of a cozy chair. "Impossible," he uttered, probably thinking the conversation at an end.

"Then you have everything to gain," Duckins replied lightly. He hoped Vincennes wouldn't notice he held his breath.

His prey appeared to study his options and Duckins, and then shook his head. "Bah, you probably are not even acquainted with the lady. How could you convince Miss Colgate to marry in such a short period of time? And who," he smirked, "would be the lucky bridegroom?" He waved his hand in dismissal, but narrowed his eyes on Duckins.

Duckins lifted his chin confidently. "I like a right challenge. I'll find the bridegroom, don't worry. One thousand guineas?"

Scratching the back of his head, Vincennes seemed to consider the offer. "A thousand guineas? Quite a sizeable amount." He hesitated, then nodded. "Done. I hope you have plenty of blunt to back up your claim. You'll need it."

Duckins stood and together they walked to the betting book and entered their wager, figures, and date.

After Vincennes shook Duckins's hand, his lordship sauntered down the stairs, whistling.

While Duckins lingered by the stairs waiting for Vincennes to leave the club and its vicinity, he noticed another gentleman rise from his chair and head toward the betting book. *Wonder what he'll be wagering on,* he thought.

Dismissing the stranger, Duckins trotted down the stairs to the club door. A quick glance up and down the street assured Duckins his movements would go unnoticed.

Sir Matthew Colgate grabbed Duckins by the arm as he strolled past and pulled his accomplice deeper into the narrow alley. It would not do to be found together. If his plan had gone accordingly, anyone seeing him and Duckins together might be suspicious of the wager just placed. It must appear to be an honorable and fair bet. If it were to be discovered that he'd arranged this elaborate scheme to dupe Lord Vincennes and any other gentlemen of the *ton*, he would either land in prison or have to flee the country.

"What is the news? Did he agree? Did you place the bet?" Matthew asked, snatching a look at first one end, then the other of Water Lane.

Duckins rubbed his hands together. "The wager is in the book, sir. Now it's up to you to convince your sister. As you say, I'm sure the old beard will spread the word to his associates. This wager should put a pretty penny in our pocket."

"Yes, thanks to your excellent work. You'll get your share when all is done. Remember, not one soul can learn of what has transpired here." Matthew's tone implied what would happen should he not keep their bargain.

Duckins nodded several times. "Of course, of course! Not a word to anyone."

Colgate watched his short companion hurry down the alley and back to the street, where he resumed a casual walk. Smiling broadly, the young baronet turned in the opposite direction, pleased with the events of the day. His plan was set in motion. He knew Madelene would agree. What choice did she have?

Crash. There went the cup and saucer.

Crash. A crystal vase.

"Mad, please listen to me!" her brother, Matthew, called, dodging the teapot she threw at him. "Not the teapot! It was our— "

The heavy china teapot missed her target and smashed against the parlor wall. *Crash.* The looking glass didn't survive the meeting with the teapot.

"—our grandmother's," he ended lamely.

Madelene breathed heavily, her shoulders heaving, as she looked for something more to throw at her imbecilic brother. "Impossible! I refuse! Find another solution! Marry a stranger? In three days or three years? Never! It will not do!"

Normally her favorite room in their town house, the front parlor, in lemon colors, had become a battleground where in all likelihood, no one would claim victory.

Her brother hovered by the door, his face downcast, his

shoulders hunched. His silence indicated he didn't *have* another solution.

Madelene shook her head in disbelief. *How had it come to this?* She found it hard to credit this marriage wager was Matthew's only solution. If only Father hadn't—or if only her fashion designs had made progress, but it was still too early for the kind of success and funds she needed in haste, particularly to save her brother.

Her brother finally found his tongue. "Mad, I know this plan must sound insupportable, but trust me. I have thought it all out carefully, and I am assured it will work." He still remained near the door, correctly assuming she wasn't nearly finished with him yet.

Madelene needed to sit down, her temper cooling slightly. If her anger continued unabated, she'd have to begin throwing larger objects, which would be difficult to lift. Instead, she pulled a white handkerchief from her pocket and began twisting it, imagining it was her brother's neck.

He must have sensed he was safe when she sat down because he joined her on the settee, albeit at the other end. "If you will simply listen for a moment, I can explain everything to you."

Staring wide-eyed at Matthew, she couldn't keep her voice from rising. "What is there to explain? How did you end in such a fix that the only solution to your problem is my marrying a complete stranger? Do you understand what you are asking of me?"

"Yes, I do know. Would that I could think of some other scheme, but time is critical. You see, since Father has been gone, I've been a bit extravagant with my gaming, believing my luck due to change. I have delayed my creditors for as long as I can. But the time has come, and I can put them off no longer."

Large brown eyes filled a pale youthful face, older than he appeared. Madelene heard pity, contriteness, and desperation in his words.

She closed her eyes to deny this scene, this moment. Their situation, indeed, did seem dire. Restless, she rose to pace the length of the room, stopping to view herself in the lone remaining looking glass and patting her curls. She had read recently in the *London's Lady's Companion* how strain could conceivably cause widow lines. She pursed her lips and took a seat at the window.

"Matthew, please explain how this wager at White's can possibly save our apparently soon-to-be penury existence? And however did you get this maggot in your head?" As the younger sister, she could still inject reason into the situation, although it often fell on deaf ears. Usually they got on well, but their relationship had been strained since the death of their father, and Madelene's pleas for caution had not halted her brother's path to apparent ruin.

She watched as Matthew leaned forward and rested his arms on his thighs, favoring his weakened left arm. The movement reminded her of the duel and how he had almost died, over a year ago.

"I'm not really sure how this idea came to me, but when I latched on to it, I immediately saw its possibilities."

She shook her head, tapping on the windowsill. "Oh, how many times I have regretted we lost Father too soon. He would never have allowed this to happen."

Matthew rubbed his brow. "Yes, yes, I realize that is the way of it. However, it does not change matters, Mad. You are the only one who can make things right." Her brother, always one to see the humor in any circumstance, used his serious tone. He was never serious.

With raised eyebrows, he pleaded, "But you will do this, Mad, won't you? I've already put my plan into action."

Her eyes widened, and she straightened her back. "What are you saying?" Was there no choice? No going back?

He scratched his neck before his words rushed out. "Simple. An acquaintance of mine placed the wager at White's that you will be married within three days."

A coughing spell nearly overwhelmed her before she could recapture her thoughts and derision. "I see. Please do not delay in telling me the name of the man you are planning for my husband. Do I know of him? Is he aware the marriage will be a sham in order to win this wager?" She rose to pace the room again.

"Ah, yes, he is aware of the circumstances." He rubbed his finger between his neck and his cravat. "And actually, no, you have never met him. His name is Mr. Leonard Brelford."

She raised her eyebrows in inquiry. "The name means nothing to me. So this Mr. Brelford is agreeable to marry me in three days? Without ever having met me?" Madelene closed her eyes briefly. The evening's events had given her quite the headache. Reseated at the window, she waited for her brother to continue.

Perhaps long ago she had dreamt of marrying for love, but that dream had been discarded not long after Madelene realized any man who would need her dowry for inducing a marriage proposal would be a man she would have no wish to marry. Thomas Winchester had taught her that particularly cruel lesson.

"Mr. Brelford has agreed. You know, Mad, there has been many a suitor who has spoken of your beauty and your wit."

Wherever did he think he was going with this excess of flattery? "Not in some time, because as you know, my dowry no longer amounts to much to encourage any new offer for my hand. Be that as it may, go on." She gritted her teeth.

"Ah, yes, Mr. Brelford, whom I met through a series of acquaintances, has agreed to marry you on a name-only basis."

"I presume the only motivating factor would be money won from the bet," she said more to herself than her brother. "How can you be sure that Mr. Brelford will keep his part of this bargain?"

Matthew hung his head. "Mr. Brelford seems to prefer—" His voice faded.

"Prefer what? A shorter bride? A bluestocking? A chit?"

"Men," he interjected and looked away toward the cold fireplace.

An evening in mid-May did not require a fire, but Madelene felt a chill. She rubbed her arms for warmth, contemplating his answer.

"Men," she said softly. *Prefers men.* It sounded quite strange. Preferred men to women? For what purpose? To gamble with, enjoy a cigar at their club? Boxing?

Matthew must have seen her confusion because he came to sit next to her and whisper in her ear.

Before he was through, Madelene jumped up as if burned from hot coals. "No, no, I will have nothing more to do with this plan of yours." She hurried to the door, tossing over her shoulder, "Tell Mr. Brelford that I cannot marry him."

"Madelene," he said to her back, "if you don't marry Mr. Brelford, we will lose this house. I'll have to go to the Continent, and you to live with Aunt Bess."

A moment passed or was it an hour, before he added, "You know, our father would want you to do this."

At the door, she swallowed hard and bowed her head.

His argument was persuasive for all the reasons she should continue with this farce. *Living with Aunt Bess? Move all the way to Scotland? Seldom to return to Town, if ever?*

This was her home. And what about her fledgling fashion designs? She needed more time to create a success behind the name of Madame Quantifours. But they needed funds now, and she couldn't leave Matthew in this state, his tone mired in self-pity and anguish, even if he had brought this misery on himself. If he didn't make it to the Continent, surely he would be sent to Newgate, if his debts were such as she imagined. She couldn't let her brother dwell in prison.

But all those reasons meant nothing as much as doing that which her father would have wanted her to do.

She turned to face her brother and said, "Perhaps you could review your plan with me again. I did not catch all of the particulars." She still had three days to plan the end of her arranged marriage.

Mr. Brelford opened the door to his rented lodgings to Matthew, who rushed in, hoping no one had seen him enter. Issuing no greeting, Matthew threw himself into a nearby worn chair, wiping sweat from his brow, relieved. No time to waste since he had a wedding ceremony to prepare. Everything was proceeding exactly how he had planned. At the earliest opportunity, he had hastened to share his news with his accomplice, although he heartily disliked Brelford's address at Covent Garden. A couple of footpads had gained Matthew's notice but fortunately the distance between his hack and 73 Swan Alley was quite abbreviated due to his earnest regard for his pocket and his life.

He took a deep breath and announced, "Brelford, my sister has agreed to our plan. I have sent a message to our Aunt Bess in Dumfries, where you'll stay for the short duration of your marriage. Oh, I'll send your share of the winnings to you as soon as everything is settled. I also made arrangements to obtain a special license."

Engrossed in his thoughts, he ignored his friend to count on his fingers all the tasks needed to be completed. "We'll have the ceremony at night. Remind you, no one can know until after the signatures are written in the parish registry. Better still, the following morning, we alert the *Morning Post*. There may be those who are betting Madelene won't be married and will do everything in their power to prevent such a thing happening. This calls for extreme secrecy." He began tapping on the arm of the chair in his enthusiasm. His ego convinced him that no one could put a halt to his stratagems.

He finally took notice of his friend, standing near a narrow cot with a half smile on his face. A smaller man in a cutaway coat of the latest fashion and shinier shoes than Prinnie would own, Matthew never had determined what his friend called his livelihood or where he had funds for his excellent taste in fashion, but little remaining for better rooms.

Matthew had grown accustomed to Brelford's lack of animation and brevity of speech. Indeed, his friend possessed the equanimity Matthew could never claim. They were quite opposites.

Hands clasped together, Brelford inquired calmly, "What is it that you require of me to do?"

Matthew launched from his seat for he could hardly remain still. "Good man. You must meet my sister, Madelene, three days hence, on the eighteenth of May. We'll head to the church from our house, hold the ceremony, then you and my sister will be off to Scotland."

The small man blinked rapidly, a faint smile on his face. "It, it sounds simple. Afterward. Are, are, you sure we will be able to obtain an annulment with little difficulty?" His pale face shone in what little light there was left of the one candle.

Matthew shrugged. "If the marriage remains unconsummated, there are legal grounds for an annulment. No one needs to be the wiser on the actual reasons. We can't have anyone crying foul on the wager. After the annulment, you can continue your secret life with no one the wiser."

With hands on his hips, Matthew paused for a moment to reflect on how all the pieces were fitting into place. Truth be born, he gave little thought to his sister or Mr. Brelford. They both had agreed to his plan of their own accord, knowing what was expected of them.

I am undone by my genius. Little does my sister know our financial straits are not as bleak as I may have led her to believe.

A twinge of conscience hit him unexpectedly. He had thought his sister's beauty and intellect would still bring offers of matrimony, but Madelene's betrothed for a brief time, Aaron Winchester, had educated Matthew on the true nature of marriage and dowries. No sooner had Winchester courted Madelene and proposed marriage then he abruptly ended their engagement upon learning her dowry was quite paltry. His sister's lack of matrimonial proposals was unanticipated.

With a change in his fortunes, Matthew decided he would fix everything after the marriage was annulled. He'd ensure what funds remained after paying off his debtors would be considered Madelene's dowry. With that responsibility put to rest, he could relax with his new friend. "Let's drink to our success."

Matthew accepted the brandy Mr. Brelford offered, which he threw back before slipping out the door and down a rickety staircase to a back street, where he had instructed the hack to wait. Relaxed and on his return to Bloomsbury, he was willing to admit the earlier scene with Madelene had shaken his resolve a bit. However, his sister, as usual, would make everything turn out tolerably well.

Overly pleased with himself, Matthew failed to notice a young man, more a picture of a thief than a gentleman, climb the stairs to knock on Brelford's door. The young man wondered how much blunt it would take to learn what Sir Matthew Colgate had planned. Mr. Westcott would pay a good wage if his news was of import.

Chapter Two

"Are you sure you want to do this, Gabriel? It all sounds quite outlandish." Former mistress, Miss Caroline Montazy, watched Gabriel Westcott from across her seat in the carriage.

Gabriel turned from looking out the window and studied Caroline. No one observing her dowdy gray carriage dress and plain mantle with a severe bonnet perched on top of her blond hair would recognize her as an Original. He smiled stiffly and leaned back against his seat.

"Caroline, have you ever known me to be careless in any of my arrangements? I have thought long and hard over this plan, and I am convinced I will succeed." He gestured to her costume. "You do look the part of my country cousin."

She scoffed. "The part I play in this little drama, I hope, will be brief. We must get you married to this woman before her brother discovers you are one step ahead of him."

"Exactly. We're almost there. Don't forget your lines, you must be convincing." His revenge almost at hand, he wondered why he didn't feel more satisfaction than he did. His goal almost realized, and yet he felt nothing. Sir Matthew Colgate would receive his comeuppance when he learned who had kidnapped his sister, Miss Madelene Colgate.

Caroline nodded. "Don't worry, I'll do exactly as you require. I simply wish you weren't going to such drastic measures to exact your revenge, especially on the girl, who appears to be innocent in any of her brother's doings." She peered at him more closely. "And that disguise. I can only hope the lady doesn't immediately become indisposed and take to her bed after one look at you."

Gabriel made no comment, satisfied his disguise would be a means to an end, even if he was unaccustomed to a heavy beard and spectacles. Their carriage came to a halting stop at a fashionable town house in Bloomsbury. Dusk had almost settled, creating a warm peach haze. As they descended the carriage, Gabriel vaguely noticed a peddler wheeling his cart of wood carvings down the street, and a maid on the steps of the next house over calling children in to wash for tea. Another ordinary day for most of the Town.

The town house, with standard façade of stucco over brick with a bowed window and flower boxes, looked empty, somehow deserted, until a young maid answered his knock. Before she could utter a greeting, Gabriel ushered Miss Montazy before him and followed her into the house, as if they had been welcomed there often.

"Good afternoon. We are here to see Miss Madelene Colgate. It is an urgent matter. Is she at home?" Gabriel removed his beaver hat and gloves and smoothed his hair while waiting for an answer, which came from the lady in question.

"Millie, who is it?" a lilting voice called down from the

first-story landing. "Please tell whoever it is that I have just returned from calling and can see no one at the moment. Perhaps they could leave their card and return another time."

She watched them look up at her in her carmine walking dress with feathered pelisse and red bonnet as she leaned on the gold railing. Perhaps they were friends of Matthew's. Dismissing them, she began to turn away.

"Miss Colgate. I'm Leonard Brelford, your betrothed. I've come with my cousin. Do you forget we are to be married today?" His voice echoed in the hallway chamber. The stranger calling himself her intended walked toward the stairs, stopping at the bottom of the grand staircase. He put one foot on the first step and rested an elbow on the staircase newel. His gaze never left her, pinning her to the spot.

Madelene dropped her bonnet and put her red-gloved hands to her mouth. *Not today. It can't be today.* Surely, it was to be tomorrow, the eighteenth of May. Today was only the seventeenth. She slowly walked toward the top of the main staircase to face him, the man claiming to be her husband-to-be.

Her first impression of the stranger was one of surprise. She would have preferred less bushy hair on his head and a clean-shaven countenance. His spectacles magnified his eyes in a strange way. *I know I must seem small-minded to desire my husband to have a pleasing persona, but truly, he does have an aura of a rather overbearing nature.*

She had hoped, irrationally, Matthew would find a new plan and extricate her from the present ridiculous marriage arrangement. Last night, he had even mentioned something about a valuable dagger.

But it must have led to naught. Unfortunately, she had been unable to find a solution herself with so little time.

She had one last hope. Perhaps she could reason with her false betrothed. "Sir, I would be persuaded not to sound unreasonable for your urgency. However, I must remind you that today is only the seventeenth, and my brother assuredly mentioned the wedding to take place on the eighteenth. You'll need to return tomorrow."

She gave him a beatific smile. "However, since you are here, we can discuss our plans in more detail for the marriage ceremony occurring *tomorrow*. Would you and your cousin, is it, kindly wait in the parlor? Millie can show you the way. I'll just be a moment." Again, she turned to leave. And again he stopped her.

In a few strides, he had climbed the stairs until he stood by her side, his hand outstretched in front of him. "Miss, your brother has changed the plans. I cannot believe he did not apprise you that we need to marry today. The sooner, the better."

She stared askance at this stranger before shaking her head, unwilling to admit to herself that his calm dispassionate voice unnerved her. "Mr. Brelford, I can assure you that we have until *tomorrow*. Matthew told me it was the eighteenth of May, and he would certainly not have forgotten to tell me if the date had changed." She gave him another beguiling smile, usually effective on most gentlemen. Her shoulder turned, his arm shot out to forestall her.

"Miss Colgate, it is to be *today*. Probably your brother did not wish to worry you. Sir Colgate informed me only this morning he thought it best to have the ceremony one day ahead. I've brought my cousin, Miss Caroline Montazy, to serve as a witness. Dare I hope your trunk is packed?" He scooped up her bonnet and thrust it in

Madelene's one hand, then grasped her other hand to pull her down the stairs.

She tugged to escape from his grasp, a futile effort. There had to be a way to delay what seemed the inevitable, if only for a day. "Please, sir, I must change and make myself more presentable. I must look a regular sight. And we should truly wait for my brother."

She could only stare at the back of his bushy head in frustration when he didn't respond but brought her down to the vestibule. Her red boots tapped on the black and white tiles as she followed him, her hand still gripped in his.

"Miss Madelene Colgate, it is my pleasure to introduce you to my cousin, Miss Caroline Montazy. Caroline, meet my bride-to-be." Madelene thought he certainly conducted these arrangements in a formal business manner, with no hint of warmth or pleasantries. A forewarning?

She nodded at the other woman, desperate to keep her wits about her. It was all happening so quickly. "It is a pleasure to meet you, Miss, Miss Montazy." Surely, her cheeks were a bright red to match her costume, while her heart beat at a frantic pace. She needed more time and something cool to ease her parched throat.

The cousin gave Madelene a warm smile. "I am delighted that you are to be part of our family, Miss Colgate."

"Yes, of course. I had just hoped . . ." She hesitated, still plotting a delay. "Mr. Brelford, I believe it would be best to wait for my brother to straighten this matter out. Why don't you and Miss Montazy retire to the parlor while I change into more appropriate attire?"

She turned to Millie, who was watching the proceedings wide-eyed. "Millie, would you bring some lemonade to the parlor?"

"No time to waste. Thank you, Millie," Mr. Brelford told the maid firmly. "I'll have one of the coachmen return for Miss Colgate's trunk." Miss Montazy stepped toward the door as Mr. Brelford looked at Madelene expectantly.

"No, wait." Madelene touched her sham betrothed's arm. *Vanity, thy name is woman,* she thought. "I cannot wear this dress to be married in! I have a lovely white gown I thought—"

Mr. Brelford perused her clothing. "Nothing wrong with your attire. We must go. Time is of the essence."

Married in red! It simply wasn't done, she thought in horror. But then she realized since no one was to know of their marriage until afterward, she doubted anyone would learn of her entirely improper wedding garments.

Mr. Brelford placed his arm at her back to escort her out the door.

"Mr. Brelford, you may, perhaps, be accustomed to others obeying you without question. I happen to not be someone so easily cozened. I'm sure you can appreciate how much it would mean for me to have my brother at my wedding. He's the only family I have left, and I believe it best to wait for him. I do not think he will be long." Of course, she had no idea where Matthew could be. But it might not be too late.

She tried to see behind his spectacles and bushy eyebrows in anticipation of his reaction.

His jaw moved slightly. "I see. No willingness to go to the slaughter, eh? Must I remind you that you have chosen your path, as has your brother, and now it is time to take it? I will not stand for any further shilly-shallying. You are wasting my time."

Madelene drew back her shoulders in defiance. She was unaccustomed to anyone treating her without deference, and he wasn't her husband, yet.

"No." She hoped she could conduct a defense over the

deafening sound of her own heartbeat. "Mr. Brelford, I plan to tarry in the parlor for my brother. If you will not wait with me, we will join you later. What church is it again? We will meet you there, as soon as opportunity allows." She clasped her shaking hands and walked toward the parlor, assuming her guests would follow her.

Once seated in a comfortable chair, she looked up to find Mr. Brelford standing near the door. "Please, sit down. And ask Miss Montazy to join us. We should really try to make this as pleasant as can be, especially since, we are, will be, ah, married." She choked slightly on that last word before attempting a smile, which faded when she noticed the dark look he gave her as he leaned against the doorjamb.

"Miss Colgate, I have advised you that I cannot delay. I have a schedule to keep."

With raised eyebrows, she returned, "You mention a schedule as if you are driving the mail coach. I do not understand your urgency, nor do I care to. Let us relax and become better acquainted." This did draw a brief smile from him, one she eagerly matched, until she saw him walk straight toward her. Her smile and courage quickly deserted her.

"While I can certainly appreciate your wit, my schedule has only to do with one passenger, which would be you."

Her eyes widened as she watched him draw closer. "Don't come any closer. There is no need to bully—" Before she knew it, he had swept her up into his arms and headed for the door. She even tried to grab the doorjamb as they walked through the doorway, but her strength was no match for his determination. Before Mr. Brelford strode out the door with Madelene squirming in his arms, Millie grabbed Madelene's pelisse, the bonnet she had dropped, and reticule, and threw it up on top of her.

As he carried her down the steps toward the carriage, she sputtered and spewed in his arms, very strong and brawny arms.

No escape. And he left her with no pride.

"Please, put me down. I can walk of my own accord," she demanded. This was most improper, but she would have no contradiction from the will of her soon-to-be-bridegroom, she realized.

At the carriage, Miss Montazy looked out the window while a footman held the door open for Madelene and her kidnapper. Mr. Brelford lifted Madelene into the carriage and dropped her on the squabs before climbing in after her. He placed his arm around her, probably concerned, given the chance, she might bolt.

With the wind knocked out of her sails, she fidgeted with the strings of her reticule on the way to a church, the name of which she had no notion. This stranger had caught her off guard, tossed her emotions into a whirlwind from which, it appeared, there was no alternative but to marry the man. She bit her lip while staring out the window as the carriage jerked into motion. She could only hope she had remembered to pack everything for a month's stay in the country.

Tears formed as she looked back at 21 Sullivan Court, the Georgian town house, and the only home she had known. What would Matthew do without her? He would be directionless without her or their father.

Madelene drew up her shoulders and shored up her confidence. She would go to the altar willingly, but she didn't have to like it. She would consider it a brief sojourn in the country until she returned, and life could resume as she knew it.

She had enough mettle in her to get through this unfortunate event and prayed the days would pass quickly. For some reason, even knowing she was helping her brother did little to bring solace to her heart.

"Millie! You must know where they have gone!" Matthew pleaded with the young woman who sat in the kitchen crying into her apron.

"But I don't, sir. I don't know the name of the church. I only heard they was to be married today." Her pasty complexion was pinked with raw tears.

Matthew braced his hand against the doorjamb. "You say he told you his name was Leonard Brelford?" He shook his head in disbelief.

"Aye, sir, that is what 'e done says. And his cousin was with 'im too. 'er name was Miss Caroline sumthin'."

He yelled, "Can you not tell me anything that might help?"

Millie only cried louder and harder. "I don't know nothin'. It all 'appened so fast." Her Cockney was more pronounced when she was anxious and had displeased him.

Matthew rubbed his face and wandered away from the kitchen to the parlor. Seated on the settee, he moaned into his hands. All of his plans for naught. While he had been making final preparations with the authentic Brelford, some stranger, calling *himself* Brelford, had swooped up his sister and taken her somewhere in London, or anywhere in England, or the seas, for that matter.

This stranger must have learned of their plan and spirited his sister away. That could be the only possibility. But why? And was this stranger actually going to marry his sister? Or just ensure the wager would end with his sister unmarried? He was sure to lose everything by the end of day tomorrow.

His only recourse was to find Madelene immediately,

for she had to marry the real Brelford, unless. Unless. The more he thought on it, it could just be possible that there was one other person who had placed a bet Madelene would be married, and ensured it happened. There was more blunt to be had betting Madelene would marry in three days than not. He determined to go to White's to search for answers.

The dagger. He had forgotten about the dagger. Matthew dashed upstairs and burst into Madelene's bedchamber.

It was gone. Madelene's trunk where he had hidden the valuable dagger was missing, along with his sister. No one knew he had hidden the object in her trunk but him.

Time was now his foe. He had to get the dagger back before anyone found it. Madelene would have no understanding of its value or importance because he had only mentioned the dagger in passing without any of the details.

Matthew had stolen the dagger from a young man, having intercepted him on his way through Covent Garden. Surprise on his side, Matthew had plucked the dagger from the youth's belt before the boy knew what had happened. On his return home, he congratulated himself the theft had not resulted in violence.

It had been just as the count instructed him on where to locate the youth and how to steal the dagger, with a promise of a handsome purse for returning it to its rightful owner, the count. Matthew had hidden the dagger in Madelene's trunk because many sought the valuable object, and he feared he himself would be the victim of thieves. He was to have returned the dagger to the count on the morning after next.

Now disaster loomed everywhere he turned. No Madelene, no won wager. No dagger. It didn't bear thinking about. He went to change his clothes for the club. Perhaps a look at the betting book and a bottle would help with this unfortunate change in circumstances.

Flames from street lamps wavered in the onset of darkness as the trio descended from their carriage and walked up the steps of the south front entrance to the Roman stone portico of St. George's Bloomsbury. The Corinthian pillars under a coffered ceiling, part of Hawksmoor's designs, accented the stepped tower with George the First's Roman-clad figure atop.

Madelene tried to stem her shaking hands by clasping them together. The stranger, who would soon be her husband, walked beside her with his hand on the center of her back, his expectation that he clearly expected her to flee.

In the carriage, she thought to rail at Mr. Brelford for his appalling behavior in carrying her off in such a manner, but he completely ignored her by talking quietly with his cousin.

With little to do, she had moved closer to the inside wall of the carriage to subtly sneak a peek at her betrothed. Could this man really prefer the company of men? Madelene found this difficult to believe, although she had never met someone of that ilk before. And why this should be the first thought to have occurred to her, she couldn't exactly say.

Madelene breathed a sigh of relief she would not know his touch because of his predilections. She could feel his heat emanating from her side, and she kept telling herself it would do no good to find this man the least bit attractive.

Out of the corner of her eye, noting his acceptable looks, she had hoped he would be somewhat more handsome than what her brother had described. He certainly was not unattractive.

Interestingly enough, the man before her bore little resemblance to Matthew's description. Her brother hadn't mentioned any bushy eyebrows or unruly brown hair or the spectacles and bushy mustache, which helped to hide his features.

He looked to have a strong chin and dark eyes, the color difficult to ascertain. Indeed, he appeared fit and healthy in his weathered broad-shouldered black coat and faded breeches. Her betrothed would benefit from a more stylish hair design and fashionable clothes. Little wonder at this marriage to gain an easier living, or perhaps he possessed unsettled debts such like her brother.

She supposed he could have been a laborer. The way he had carried her from the parlor to the carriage with little effort spoke of his strength and fortitude. But his manners implied an entirely different situation.

Not that his looks or beastly manners mattered a whit to her. He would be her husband for one month only, and in name only. After all, it wasn't as if she would need to spend all of her time in his presence. Indeed, they need not spend any time together. She was looking forward to visiting Aunt Bess, whom she hadn't seen since her father's funeral.

Through the doors, the vicar in formal robes greeted them in the dark silent alcove. Gold friezes shimmered in the candlelight, creating a soft, hallowed warmth around the small group. Father John guided them to the east apse on the right side of the church, mainly used for baptisms and a few hurried marriage ceremonies, their steps echoing on the wood floor.

Madelene shivered, in part due to the church's dampness, but more from her impending marriage of doom. She could hear the shackles clank closed ever so softly. What would it take to be free of him, of this marriage?

Only her brother imprisoned. It seemed she was the one to be imprisoned behind wedding vows.

She swiftly glanced at the man who held her arm and escorted her to their place before the altar. He certainly seemed determined to wed her. His face lit by candlelight was a complete mask. How little she knew about her husband-to-be. He must be desperate since he, too, was marrying an unwilling stranger.

Odd, her brother would benefit from this marriage as well as the man standing next to her. But Madelene? She would claim her reward within a month to return home to London and Matthew, free of his creditors.

She looked forward to the day she could continue her work on her designs for ladies of the *ton*. Even Matthew had no idea. Her secret shared with only Madame Quantifours herself, the establishment on Bond Street.

Madelene kept looking back to the large wooden doors, hoping and praying her brother would come dashing through and call a halt to this, this travesty, this mockery. Where could he be? He had to know she needed him at this moment.

When the vicar began the marriage rites, Madelene's heart pounded uncontrollably, almost to the point of feeling faint. Swooning, maybe that would work. But one look at the sternness of Mr. Brelford's visage made her think twice about creating any delay.

"I will." Her voice registered barely above a whisper in answer to "... keep thee only unto him, so long as ye both shall live?" Could this truly be happening?

It was done. There was no turning back.

She waited with bated breath at the end of the ceremony, when he turned to her, his new bride. His shadowed brown gaze held hers briefly. She tried to read emotion in his face, a hint of kindness or understanding.

Nothing.

With a hand under her elbow, he hurried her to the table with the parish registry and showed her where to place her signature.

Resigned, she signed *Madelene Colgate* before Miss Montazy called her over to congratulate her and welcome her to the family. In a daze, Madelene hardly noticed the walk back to the entrance and down to the carriage.

Settled into the carriage with its dark ruby squabs, the newly married couple began their journey north to Dumfries to see her aunt. Unbeknownst to Madelene, her new husband had an entirely different direction in mind.

Chapter Three

"What is this? You don't have the dagger, Colgate? You were to deliver it to my associate in Canterbury by tomorrow morning." The Count Giovanni Taglioni sat in his gilded chair behind his large rosewood desk as if he were judge and jury in the Old Bailey, his swarthy features forbidding with black eyes and a minute mustache. By the look on the count's unforgiving features, Matthew knew he had to offer a plausible excuse for the unfinished matter of the dagger.

The count's dark eyes narrowed on him, awaiting an answer that no doubt would displease him, very much. The air simmered with the smell of opium, although Taglioni appeared quite lucid. Perhaps his imbibing only waited for this business to be transacted. Various dark candles placed on white pillars around the deep blue parlor did little to welcome visitors, while the light at the count's desk proved especially unilluminating. Attired all in black, Taglioni was known not to suffer fools lightly.

Could it only have been three weeks ago when Matthew had stood before the count in this dark chamber in the large glittering town house in Mayfair? How the count had even found him to request his assistance still puzzled Matthew. Their meeting had taken place at the late hour of midnight, as the count directed in the note he sent to Matthew, asking him to come to 5702 Trumbull Place and to be vigilant of anyone watching his movements.

"Please do not worry, my lord. The dagger is very safe. I simply need a few more days to collect it, and then I will deliver it as planned." Perspiration beaded Matthew's forehead, which he attempted to mop with his handkerchief.

The count viewed Matthew with half-masted eyes. "I will be generous and give you more time. You have exactly a fortnight to return the dagger, as originally planned. I'm assured you won't disappoint a second time."

Matthew nodded and rose shakily, anxious to depart this claustrophobic atmosphere.

"Colgate. One more thing. Have you considered my offer for your lovely sister, Miss Madelene?"

Clasping his hands in front of him, Matthew bowed his head slightly. "Ah, yes, my lord." He paused. "Although my family is honored by your request, I fear that my sister has already accepted another's hand in marriage."

The count snickered, reaching for his snuff. "I believe you misunderstood me, Colgate. I was not offering *matrimony* for your sister, since I understand she has no dowry. I am also not willing to settle for no as an answer. You see, I have decided to take your sister, Madelene, back to Florence with me. That is the best solution for all. See that you provide the dagger and your sister within a fortnight."

Matthew nodded and found his hands trembling. He would think of something. Better to let the count believe he would follow his orders. By the time Matthew returned the dagger, Madelene would be safely married and living in Scotland, far from the powerful count. He hoped.

Mr. Brelford did not seem inclined to converse as their carriage rocked down the cobblestone streets of London and out into the dirt and stone lanes of the country. Madelene couldn't remember the route she and her brother had taken years ago to Dumfries, and the opaque night only curtained the view outside her window.

With little else to occupy her, Madelene fell into an uneasy sleep.

"Miss Colgate, we are stopping here for the night." She vaguely recognized her husband's voice through a haze of sleep and felt his strong hand on her shoulder.

Voices of the groomsman and ostler could be heard outside as Madelene rubbed her hands and her face to bring herself into wakefulness. Her neck pinched where she had rested it near the window, and her back ached from the bumps and jolts along the way. She was glad to escape from the confines of the carriage and to gain distance from her—the stranger whose nearness disturbed her.

Madelene followed him into the Cock's Crow Inn where Great George, the innkeeper, showed them into a private dining room for a light repast. Great George must have been named for his size and bellowing loud voice, for she had no doubt his voice could be heard miles down the road.

Exhausted beyond thought, she removed her bonnet and stifled a yawn behind her red glove. Feeling the need to be wit-filled taking their first meal together, Madelene stretched her arms above her head and walked the perimeter of the room a few times to undo the stiffness remaining from the carriage ride. She noticed the clock on the fireplace mantel showed nine o'clock.

The door banged open when Great George swept into the room, hurrying his servant girl with bread, cheese, and wine for them. Bowing to Mr. Brelford, he told them, "We haven't had travelers for a day or so. We're right glad of your fine company. Mary, there, will fix up a room for you." He twisted his rotund self out the door, yelling over his shoulder, "Pork pies on their way!"

All the while, Mr. Brelford remained silent, in deep thought standing by the window. Her legs unsteady, exhaustion hung on her shoulder, Madelene couldn't decide which she was in more dire need of, food or a bed. She certainly had little energy to ponder her predicament other than self-assured Mr. Brelford had arranged for two rooms, which would enable her to have a good night's rest.

"Help yourself to the food, Miss Colgate, ah, Mrs. Brelford. You must be hungry," Brelford told her politely, then turned his attention to the window again. Madelene wondered what he saw in the darkness.

She glanced over at this stranger, still too new an acquaintance to call "husband." "Please sit. I find I cannot dine whilst you stand. Share the bread with me?" she asked her husband evenly.

He cast a cool gaze her way before joining her at the small table.

Gabriel had never been hesitant before in any situation, but now he had wedded his enemy's sister, he took time to contemplate his actions and wondered whether the revenge he demanded from Matthew Colgate could be enjoyed at the altar of Madelene's innocence.

And then there was the Count Taglioni, whom he had met a few times while in Florence due to Gabriel's friendship with the count's niece, Alessandra. He didn't approve

of the count then, and his opinion hadn't changed since
Taglioni had arrived in London. When Gabriel learned
the count showed more than a passing fancy for Miss
Madelene Colgate, it proved unsettling.

He knew what had to be done. Now he could hardly
accept she was his wife, and little did she know her surname to be Westcott and not Brelford. She had signed the
registry before him, and he made sure she had been called
away before he signed his true surname.

By the time Madelene's brother, along with the rest of
the *ton* and the count, heard the news of the marriage, he
and Madelene would be long gone from Town.

Yes, Miss Colgate had indeed captured his attention at
the time of their one and only meeting. He remembered
her deep blue eyes shooting arrows at him on the dueling
field for wounding her brother.

Her dazzling blue eyes certainly had left her mark on
him. She never understood it might have been worse for
her brother. Gabriel could have killed Matthew. Later, he
realized while caring for his sister, Lucinda, in Florence,
he wanted his revenge to last longer.

And Matthew Colgate provided the perfect opportunity
by arranging a wager that someone would marry his sister
in three days. Of course, his own pocket would increase
in coin from winning the bet, but he continued to want
the young man to suffer. Suffer he must, since there was
no way Matthew could know his sister's location and the
status of her welfare.

A niggling thought that perhaps Matthew might be relieved and unconcerned his sister could not be located
bothered him briefly, but he dismissed it out of hand.
What brother would not care about his sister?

Yes, everything was falling into place, just as he had
planned. Gabriel would decide when the time was right

to return Madelene to her brother. When he divorced her, it would bring shame on the Colgate name and both brother and sister would be unwelcome in polite society. They would be ruined.

As for him, he could easily find a replacement bride, but there was more to consider than simply finding a wife. He would also need a mother for his children.

Madelene. His wife. The beautiful Madelene that no man could tame. Rumor had it she had broken many a heart with her own heart unengaged.

Gabriel knew his heart to be safe from her wiles, but after seeing her on the dueling field, tending to her brother, he had wanted her. Wanted to possess her. He wanted her to look at him with as much tenderness as she had given to her brother, undeserving though Gabriel himself might be. Perhaps only then would his lust for revenge be satiated. Perhaps.

"Mr. Brelford, you seem quite lost in thought. I would prefer we converse to break the silence." She reproved him with a smile.

He scratched his beard, deciding how best to answer her request. "What had you in mind to discuss?"

"How long do you anticipate our journey to Dumfries? I'm sure Matthew told you about our Aunt Bess? I remember she's rather hard of hearing but quite kind. I hope the weather will be pleasant during our stay, until, of course, we're able to return to Town and seek our annulment." She smiled tentatively at him and hurried a glass of wine to her lips.

"Yes, Aunt Bess," he murmured and continued to stare at her. *Truth will out soon enough.* He supposed he should admire her pluck since she had been hastily wed and removed from her only known home and family. And where was the famous temper he had been warned about?

The woman before him painted a picture of docility and femininity and seemed as devious as plum pudding.

Gabriel sighed in relief when Great George burst into the room with the hot pork pies.

"Eat up! Eat hearty! Mary says your room is quite ready," he informed them, his smile broad and warm. He bustled out the door, whereupon silence again spoke the loudest in the room.

Gabriel watched Madelene eat quickly and wondered if she had given any thought to her wedding night. When the time was right, they'd have their wedding night, he thought with an inner smile.

"Mr. Brelford, I think I'll retire. No need to accompany me, I'm sure Great George or Mary will show me the way. Have a restful sleep, and I'll see you in the morning," she told him, her words hedged in exhaustion. When she rose to quit the room, Gabriel also stood.

"Mrs. Brelford, I'll accompany you. We are, after all, sharing the same room as man and wife."

"Oh, but I thought. You see." She halted in obvious perplexity. A frown marred her lovely brow. "That is, well, this is quite impossible. My brother—"

"Your brother isn't here. Surely you understood the vows you recited earlier today?" He cocked his head at her, narrowing his eyes. "You don't wish for me to heave you over my shoulder and carry you up to our room?" He almost smiled at the thought of her reaction or the amusement it would bring him.

"I should think not." A look of indignation blew past. She sighed. "I guess I have made my bed," she finished in resignation.

Interesting, she didn't finish the thought. He watched her straighten her shoulders, turn toward the door, and begin climbing the rickety wooden stairs.

He admired her resolve. He also admired her backside, as her traveling gown clung to her hips and other places while she preceded him. Steady, he told himself.

At the top of the landing, outside their room, Mary greeted them and curtsied before hurrying past them and down the stairs.

His new bride hesitated before entering the bedchamber, warmed from the fire Mary had started for them. Few pieces of furniture adorned the room other than a large tester bed with a frayed blue counterpane and a table and chair in the corner of the room. Dull white curtains covered the windows.

When Gabriel entered the room, he noticed her trunk and his carpet bag near the bed before throwing his greatcoat over the chair. He turned to look at Madelene, wondering what she was thinking and feeling. And why it should matter to him. This game he had set in motion had many moves yet to make.

She stood with her back to him, warming herself at the fireplace.

"Mrs. Brelford, I'm going to return to the common room to discuss our travel arrangements for the morning with Great George. I would suggest using that time to prepare for bed," he instructed her before departing the room.

"Mr. Brelford—" She held up a hand to stop him.

At the door, he turned to look at her. "Yes? Is there something amiss? Do you need something?" Gabriel couldn't wait to be rid of the moniker not his own, hoping annoyance did not show in his voice.

"No, it's of no consequence," she told him, shaking her head. He walked out and closed the door. His boots thumped down the stairs.

Madelene slowly sank down on the floor next to the fireplace, hoping the warmth might seep into her bones and spirit. She still could not believe she was actually here, in an unfamiliar village, married to a stranger. It was an impossible position. If only her father could have saved her from this mockery of a marriage. Matthew should never have placed her in this situation.

Even knowing it was only for a short time did little to stem her resentment. She now had a husband to obey, which did not suit for a moment. Until she could discover another alternative, she'd have to endure these events thrust upon her. Somehow, she'd find the will and pray the month would pass quickly.

Frustration poured through her; she had to do something. When she looked down at her red walking dress, she suddenly despised it. She tore off the bodice and skirt and shoved them into the fire, wanting to burn the evidence of her wedding dress. Why couldn't this all be a terrible dream?

Destroying her wedding dress would do naught to the marriage itself, but she felt a little better watching the cloth catch fire.

Until smoke began to billow out from the fireplace and suffuse their bedchamber. Clad in only a white short-sleeved shift, fine lawn tuckers, knee-high silk stockings, and shoes, and overtaken with fits of coughing, she tried to pull the garments out of the flames.

To no avail. Smoke quickly filled the room, and realizing she couldn't stop the conflagration, she ran toward the door and jerked it open, bumping right into her husband.

Chapter Four

Gabriel pulled Madelene out onto the landing and raced inside to contain the smoke and flames, Great George not far behind him. Together, using the bed counterpane and water from the washbasin, they smothered the flames in minutes. Although the fire and smoke caused little damage, the bedchamber would be uninhabitable until the smoke had dissipated. Once reassured all embers were dashed, Gabriel opened the two small windows and followed Great George down the stairs.

He found Madelene sitting on a bench with Mary in the common room. His wife clutched a draught, unable to keep from coughing, almost doubled over from a spell. A rough woolen blanket wrapped tight around her shoulders hid her disheveled state of undress.

His mouth grim, Gabriel stood on the opposite side of the table and leaned toward Madelene. "Was marriage to me so intolerable that you wanted to kill yourself, or are you simply a fool?" He bit his words out.

Madelene blinked at him and frowned. "Is there another choice?"

Surprised, Gabriel stepped back, and his anger at her

subsided, slightly. "None. Your wedding attire has effectively gone up in smoke, which I can only assume was your intention and not burning the inn to the ground."

She didn't answer him immediately, taking a long swallow of what he hoped was weak ale.

He continued, his voice less stern. "I'll obviously have to watch you more closely, to avoid any further disasters."

When confident Madelene had overcome the worst of the smoke inhalation, Gabriel sought Great George to request bath water for his wife to remove the effects of the smoke, ignoring his own untidy combination of perspiration and soot.

The innkeeper and Mary went to fetch the tub and water in the kitchen while Gabriel sat down next to Madelene, still concerned over her condition.

"Madelene, please assure me that you are suffering no ill effects that a bath and sleep won't cure," he requested, staring into her dazed dark blue eyes.

She nodded slowly, obviously still bewildered about what had transpired. "I'll be fine. It all happened so quickly. I had no idea."

Removing a fine white handkerchief from his pocket, he started to wipe the soot smudges from her forehead, then thrust the handkerchief in her hand. He must remember to show no signs of kindness in order to achieve his goal. "If you promise to stay put for a few minutes, I'll remove our baggage from the room so you might find something to wear."

When he soon returned to the common room carrying the red-ribboned bonnet and matching gloves saved from the fire, he overheard Mary inform Madelene her bath was ready in the kitchen, where she would not be disturbed.

Showing Madelene the remainder of her bridal costume,

he said wryly, "Apparently, you were unable to destroy all evidence of your marriage garments."

Shrugging, she replied, "Perhaps Mary would like them, for I have no further use of them."

Mary's sad little face broke into a smile. "Oh really, miss! That would be ever so lovely! I mean, missus," she exclaimed and hurried over to touch her new belongings. "I've never had nothing this nice before. Oh to be sure, I thank you, miss, and you, too, Mr. Brelford!" Grasping her bonnet and gloves to her chest, the little maid scurried from the room with her treasures.

Madelene rose unsteadily and found her husband's hand on her elbow. Too tired to pull away, she let him lead her to the kitchen where her bath awaited. The smell of cheap wine and old fish hung in the air. She noticed while sinking into the nearest chair that Mary had left clean towels for her.

Unfortunately, her husband showed no interest in vacating the little kitchen, which was becoming warmer and warmer as much from the bath water as his nearness. She couldn't quite determine why she felt unnerved by her temporary spouse. Indeed, he had no interest in her as a woman, if her brother was to be believed. Then she should have no concerns over their sleeping arrangements for the night.

But she did. Truthfully, Madelene's new husband disturbed her, whether she wanted him to or not.

Enough of this woolgathering. There was nothing for it. When she swept a long curl away from her forehead, she noticed her gray grimy hands and frowned. Without further delay, she stood, gathering her faculties about her.

When Mr. Brelford made an effort to remove her blanket, Madelene dashed a few steps away, crossing her arms over her chest in protection and holding her blanket even tighter. What could he be thinking? Did he wish to play the role of lady's maid?

"Mr. Brelford, would you kindly leave me alone to bathe? I am accustomed to bathing without an audience," she told him politely. She raised her eyebrows and jerked her head toward the door.

Mr. Brelford's lips twitched before replying. "There are a lot of things you'll need to become accustomed to in the future as my wife. However, for the present, I'll return to our room and have Mary wait outside, if by chance you have need of her."

Ignoring his words, she watched him leave before casting off her remaining undergarments and stepping into the wooden tub, slowly sinking into the warm water. The bath soothed her and removed most of the travel and smoke grime. She prolonged it as long as she could until the water became cold and unpleasant. Earlier feeling sleepy, Madelene felt refreshed, and her mood vastly improved.

Wet hair draped over one shoulder, she climbed out of the tub to shrug into a wool robe when she heard a loud shout. With her borrowed robe clasped tightly in her hands, two young men burst into the kitchen yelling for Great George.

Her heart pounded in dismay but she took a deep breath, determined to brave her way through the situation.

"*Gentlemen!* As you can see, Great George is not, at the present time, located in the kitchen. Now, if you'll be on your way in the direction from whence you came." She tilted her chin, daring an argument.

They halted in stunned silence and surprise when they saw her in a state of undress, ogling her in their dusty traveling clothes. The older-looking one in a threadbare greatcoat and long, dark unkempt hair sauntered forward.

"And what do we have here? Are you one of Great George's new maids? He must know where to find them. What are you selling tonight, my lovely?"

Mr. Brelford pulled him back by his coat collar. When had he arrived? "Gentlemen, please return to the common room for Great George, and I would appreciate it if you would stop gawking at my wife," he told them harshly as he strode over to Madelene.

She almost bristled at his possessiveness. Surely she could have handled the strapping young men with logical persuasion. But her husband thought she needed rescuing.

Wait. Something didn't seem quite right. He was her husband and yet, not her husband. In the candlelight, she couldn't see him clearly but assumed his countenance looked as harsh as his words. They both watched as the two intruders, eyes bulging from their heads at the sight of Mr. Brelford, bumped into each other trying to be the first through the door.

Her husband stood near her, ready to defend her, already acting the role of protector. But when he turned to her, she caught her breath, and she was the one stunned into silence, briefly.

What was he doing here? And where was Mr. Brelford, her husband? Why did he wear her husband's clothes?

She shook her head. These circumstances did not bode well. The man standing before her was Gabriel Westcott. Her brother's enemy. Hers as well.

Chapter Five

She could only stare at the man standing before her. He had been wearing a disguise. Mr. Gabriel Westcott stood before her without his spectacles, beard, and bushy eyebrows, clad in the same well-fitting fawn shirt, pantaloons, and boots. His dark brown curly hair matched his deep brown eyes taking her mind briefly from her indignation, and she caught her breath. She had not remembered his attractiveness.

His lean jaw and determined mouth declared no quarter given. A hard man indeed, based on the intent look he now gave her. What could he possibly want with her? Why was he here and not Mr. Brelford? This nightmare seemed to have no ending.

Mary burst into the room. "Oh, miss, I beg your pardon, missus, but Great George called me away to serve customers. I didn't mean to allow—" Mary finally noticed Mr. Westcott. "Sir, I don't know who you are, but you take yourself right out those doors. You shouldn't be in here! Out with you!"

Mr. Westcott held up his hand. "Mary, I am—" He

cleared his throat. "I am Mr. Brelford. No, correction, I am Mr. Westcott."

The little maid stared and stared and kept shaking her head. "You don't mirror Mr. Brelford, and who is Mr. Westcott, I should know? Great George! Great George," she yelled while fleeing the room.

Mr. Westcott started after her. "I have had a conversation with Great George." But his words were lost on the maid.

Alone again, Madelene and Gabriel looked at each other.

"Madelene, I know this must be a shock to you, my appearance unexpected—"

Her mouth dropped open. He had truly rendered her speechless. How had she married Mr. Brelford, who turned into Mr. Gabriel Westcott?

Madelene thought of Matthew. He would never have colluded with his own enemy to marry off his sister.

Mr. Westcott interrupted her deliberation. "Madelene, did those culprits disturb you? They haven't hurt you?" His tone quiet and concerned as he looked her over to assure himself she remained unharmed. He obviously missed the fire in her eyes.

Narrowing her eyes, Madelene backed away from him and held a hand out in front of her. "You *can't* be my husband. You! You *tricked* me! How could you do this? I demand you return me to Town this moment. We will immediately obtain an annulment." Her eyes widened. "Unless you falsified our marriage license."

Oh, the horror and shame she would bring on the Colgate name. Was she actually married, and to Gabriel Westcott? Her fury at his deceit needed vengeance. She looked around the kitchen for something to use as a weapon, but nothing looked close enough. And any movement might reveal more than she wanted to show, grasping her robe more tightly to her chest.

"Madelene, now is not the time for this discussion." He walked toward her as she retreated until she felt her back at the wall. "We can discuss this sensibly in our room. In private." He held out his hand in supplication.

Her thoughts in disarray, anger heated her reply. "I want my *own* room. *Then* I want you to return me to my brother in the morning," she commanded.

He grabbed her arm and started pulling her toward the kitchen door. "And what about your brother? He'll need to return his won blunt, and you'll be back where you started. Surely a year with me is worth the price of saving your brother and your home," he explained logically.

She hesitated and frowned, shaking her head. "A year? No, that was definitely *not* the plan. I remember my brother telling me it would only be for a month, no longer." Had she really been tricked into marrying her family's enemy? For a whole year?

Something else suddenly occurred to her. If her husband wasn't Mr. Brelford, then Mr. Westcott could conceivably prefer women, which meant Madelene wanted to avoid their bedchamber at all costs.

"We need to discuss this upstairs. Try to pretend you're a willing wife." He grasped her hand and pulled her out the kitchen door and up the stairs.

The new inn arrivals hovered around their tankards, uninterested in the comings and goings of Madelene and her husband. A casual look around the main room confirmed Great George and Mary nowhere in sight. No one was near to help or hear her story. Sighing, she followed him up the stairs.

Mr. Westcott opened the door to their second bedchamber of the night. This smaller room held only a narrow bed, a few blankets, and cold air. The first room must have been the more requested of the two. No fire lit the fireplace, in all likelihood to prevent a repeat of the earlier incident.

Madelene saw her trunk safely installed next to the cold fireplace and rubbed her hands together, realizing she needed to quickly put on warmer clothes. Mid-May was much colder than usual this time of year.

Digging into her trunk, she found a soft pink night rail and matching jacket for sleeping. The garments would provide covering but not much warmth. Unfortunately, she couldn't put her hands on her cotton nightgown without unpacking everything.

She began, "I would appreciate it, if—"

"No, I won't leave you alone. However, I will turn my back as you undress, if you can assure me that if I light another fire, you'll step nowhere near it," he said with a trace of amusement in his voice. Not waiting for an answer, he knelt before the cold fireplace and placed short sticks and logs on the metal shelf, preparing to light it.

Crack! He never saw her come from behind and hit him with the bed warmer.

Gabriel Westcott! Of course, Matthew thought. *That blighty bugger! That swine!* Westcott had his bloody hands on Madelene! He should have realized as he stared down at the bettor's book. It was the only answer. *Westcott must have thought to make me a fool by forcing Madelene to marry him and receive sizable winnings from the wager at the same time.* Westcott must still blame him for his sister's broken heart.

It wasn't his fault. He had tried to keep young Miss Lucinda Westcott at arm's length, but she proved harder to convince than a thief to give up a grand living. Because they had one night of indiscretion, Lucinda believed he should marry her. However, the young woman didn't realize she simply couldn't convert Matthew, the bachelor, to Matthew, the husband.

By a trick of fate, Lucinda actually believed his banbury tale that he only had a few months to live from a disease with no known cure. She was all tears and ineptitude with death, but agreed it was better they never see each other again.

Convinced matters with the young woman were settled, Matthew couldn't have been more surprised when Lucinda's brother issued a challenge. Matthew had to face him on the dueling field.

He closed his eyes thinking back on the day of his greatest humiliation: when inebriated, he couldn't shoot straight.

Granted, the man could have killed him, but only wounded him. Westcott had offered Matthew mercy, which he readily accepted. Matthew could hardly believe his eyes when Madelene almost created a disaster grabbing his pistol to shoot his enemy. Thankfully, the man was as quick with his reactions and the shot rang wide.

Westcott claimed victory, even if they both walked away. Matthew thought the man was satisfied by the blood he had drawn and his injury which had taken a long time to heal. Madelene had seen to his recovery but his left arm still hung by his side, virtually useless. She couldn't fix everything.

After the duel fiasco, to his great relief, he'd heard the rumor Mr. Westcott and his sister had left for Italy for an undisclosed period of time. There were too much gambling and other hedonistic pursuits to enjoy rather than be disturbed with one small chit and her feminine sensibilities. He assumed her brother would see to her.

When someone told him recently Lucinda had died around the Christmas holidays, stunned, he felt a moment of pity for this particular girl, but nothing more. He knew many willing women who could satisfactorily occupy his time and not his heart, especially when they learned he was a baronet.

Time was his for the wasting until his coffers had run dry, and he had had to devise a plan where he could save the family home, his reputation, and provide for his sister. Damn! His plan would have worked, if Westcott hadn't interfered.

Matthew began making inquiries about Westcott's estate and where he might possibly locate the man and his sister. If he found his sister, he'd find the dagger. When he had the dagger in hand, he could collect his handsome purse from the count, as well as secure his safety from any number of the count's minions.

"Well, Colgate. Hard to believe, but I see you found someone to marry your sister." A loud voice carried across the lounging room.

Matthew glanced over and saw Lord Vincennes walking toward him. How did he know?

"Saw it in the *Post* tonight. Says she married a Gabriel Westcott. I believe he is in shipping." His lordship leaned more directly into Matthew's line of vision. "Isn't he the same man you dueled with last year and gave you that useless arm?"

Matthew gave his lordship a false smile. "Turns out, they fell in love on the dueling field, but told no one. Not even me. Lucky that, eh?" He hurried out of the room without waiting for a response to a man who had lost quite a few guineas on Matthew's wager.

* * *

Madelene found a dark blue traveling gown and dressed quickly. She planned to be on her way back to London before Westcott awakened. He deserved the headache he would have later, because, after all, he had tricked her into marrying him. And there were times when a lady simply had no recourse but to save herself. Before she dressed, she confirmed the blow dealt him had not been fatal.

She decided the best plan would be to post a letter to Matthew explaining what had happened, and to journey to visit Aunt Bess for a brief spell. Later, her brother would help her obtain an annulment from Westcott as he had promised with Mr. Brelford. One man or the other couldn't make a difference.

With a few pounds in her reticule, which she believed enough to hire a coach to take her to the next town north, Madelene started for the door without a backward glance at her fallen husband.

A sudden hard yank on her cloak threw her to the floor, where she landed on her backside with a thump. Her husband sat next to her, staring at her oddly.

"Surely you're not taking leave of your husband on your wedding night? If this is the way you treat all your suitors, there is little disbelief why no man has actually made it to and from the altar with you." He winced when he shook his head.

Madelene watched him feel the back of his head for injury. Mercy! She had nearly escaped and been on her way. She wouldn't turn her back on this man again, a hard lesson to learn.

She tried to free her cloak from his tight grip, hoping he was too weak to offer a defense. Unfortunately, his determination was probably greater than his strength, because she soon realized she wasn't going to be leaving their bedchamber in the very near future.

Perhaps another go at persuasion. She turned to him with quivering lips. "Mr. Westcott, you must see that this will never work. We loathe each other, and we certainly do not wish to be married to each other. We can be reasonable about this—"

"Absolutely not. No amount of begging or inducement will shake loose my resolve to keep you as my wife. I will not entertain any bargains you may have hatching in that noggin of yours, so let's not hear anything more about it," he told her darkly, as he rose stiffly from the cold floor.

She continued to sit on the floor stewing before he grabbed her under her arms and hauled her to her feet, ripping her cloak off and throwing it over the trunk.

"Mrs. Westcott, thanks to your efforts of lighting the first room on fire and a hit on the head, I find myself very fatigued. I would advise you to join me in bed."

Madelene's eyes opened wide. "No, Mr. Westcott, this is not what I had planned—"

She found herself unceremoniously thrown onto the bed where she landed in a heap on the far side next to the stone wall.

"You're correct, this is not what I had planned either, but your shenanigans weary me. Get some rest, and we'll start in the morning for my home in Shropshire."

She watched in surprise as Gabriel fell on to the bed and onto her traveling gown, anchoring her to him. Her heart beat fast as she worried what he might do to her. Indeed, she was his wife, and she *had* caused him a spot of trouble this night. Did she have enough fight left in her to save her innocence?

He leaned back against the pillow and studied her

lazily with one eye open. "Do not waste your time trying to escape. Rest assured, I will know when you try to leave this room. And if you do somehow manage to escape, I'll find you, wherever you go." His last words, a threat and a promise before sleep claimed him.

Madelene heaved a sigh and looked around the room to determine how far away the bed warmer lay. Definitely out of reach. She pursed her lips in defeat. Obviously, she should have hit him a lot harder, a fact she'd remember for next time. A glance over at her husband showed him fast asleep. Close enough that she could feel his heat, touch his strong jaw, and know his indefatigable will.

She wouldn't give up and would make him regret ever taking her to wife.

Someone shook her shoulder. "Not now, Millie, I need a little more sleep," Madelene muttered.

"The name's Westcott, not Millie, and it's time for you to rise, Mrs. Westcott. We have more miles to cover on our journey." He returned to the washbasin before going to the door and calling down for more water.

Patches of sunlight shone through the mottled window, illuminating the small room. Madelene slowly sat up, pushing her hair behind her, and looked around the room. It was true. All true. It wasn't a nightmare. It was more of a daymare.

What would the new day bring, her first full day as Mrs. Gabriel Westcott? Hopefully, an opportunity to escape.

She rose from the bed and looked down to find her traveling dress wrinkled. Her eyes not fully opened, she crossed the room to her trunk when Westcott stopped her.

"No time for changing. Perform your ablutions, and I'll have your trunk taken down to our carriage."

"But I can't," she began, then shook her head. She needed to conserve her energy, having decided she would do whatever it took to leave Mr. Gabriel Westcott and this marriage far behind.

After a quick breakfast, they sat silently in their carriage continuing west, both occupied with their own thoughts.

Gabriel had known Miss Madelene Colgate would not be easily subdued, but he wanted her and wouldn't let her go.

Madelene hated Gabriel for tricking her into marriage and removing her from her home and family. As the carriage wheels bumped along, taking her farther from London, she kept telling herself, "Escape, escape, escape."

Chapter Six

"You want me go with you to Shropshire?" Mr. Leonard Brelford looked over at Sir Matthew Colgate with surprise, his drink forgotten in his hand.

"Yes. You're the only one I can depend on to help me." His friend stood by the Fleeting Stag's fireplace with his brandy, staring distantly down at the amber light.

"I see," Brelford said, but he didn't. "You plan to save your sister from this Westcott bloke and bring her back here so I can marry her as we had planned?" he asked, dreading the answer. Although he much admired his friend, he had been greatly surprised and greatly relieved when someone else had married his sister.

Colgate frowned and shook his head. "No, no. I have to travel to Shropshire to collect something my sister mistakenly stored in her trunk. I have to take it to Canterbury within the month, and I am uncertain how long this endeavor may take." He dropped his voice, clearly concerned someone might overhear their conversation.

"But your sister. Surely you're worried about her welfare."

"Of course," Colgate responded. "However, the man

who married her is known to me to be an honorable one and will see to her needs. But I promised a person of great power that I would recover this valuable dagger and deliver it to his family. In turn, I will receive a great deal of money." He finished his brandy in one long swallow.

"I see." Brelford paused. "A dagger. Why was this dagger in Miss Colgate's trunk again?" Certainly it sounded like a far-fetched plan, which still didn't sway Brelford's admiration and affection for Colgate. If only he could show him how he really felt, the young man would have no further need for the female sort.

Colgate grunted before replying. "I had it on good authority someone planned to steal the dagger from me, which is when I decided to hide it in Madelene's trunk, until I could safely hand it over to the—rightful owner. If I cannot return the dagger, I cannot even consider what might happen."

"I see," Brelford replied, not quite understanding Colgate's lack of interest in his sister or his recklessness in willing to bargain with a nefarious person. Surely money was the root of all evil. "How long will we be gone and when shall we get started?" he asked, rising to his feet. He had preparations to make for their trip.

His friend looked over at Brelford with a smile. "Early tomorrow morning. Meet me at my house in Bloomsbury. We'll leave from there, perhaps be gone about a week or more."

Brelford nodded, then asked, "Have you thought about what you're going to do if Miss Colgate sees you? She might want you to bring her home."

Colgate waved his hand in the air, as if what his sister might want was inconsequential. "If we're quick about it, she'll never know we were there. That's my plan."

"And have you considered what to do if she or her new

husband has already found the dagger before we arrive?" Brelford's left eye began to twitch, which always happened when he became nervous or distressed.

With his empty glass in hand and a fierce look in his eyes, Colgate replied, "I mean to collect that dagger with or without my sister's help. No one will stop me."

Brelford could not resist chiding him. "Isn't her new husband the man you fought a duel with and lost? Grateful he didn't kill you. Leastwise, that is what you told me soon after."

"I don't plan to lose twice to the same man," his young friend told him before heading in the opposite direction for more libation.

Another night, another inn. Bed warmers and any other potential weapons had been deliberately removed from their bedchamber. He grinned remembering how puzzled the staff looked when he requested any sharp objects be removed from their bedchamber, or any tools to start a fire. The idiosyncrasies of the gentry.

At the door to their room, he gestured for her to enter before him as he leaned against the doorjamb, glancing around the room. Nondescript, sparse of furniture with little décor or niceties, their bedroom resembled most inn accommodations.

She seemed nervous tonight, skittish, probably believing tonight would be the night he would truly claim her as his own. A desire he could not deny.

His body ached with wanting his nubile bride after spending much time in close proximity to her during their journey. He could smell the rosewater scent on her skin and shiny black hair. The previous night, he had glimpsed fair skin and graceful ankles in her borrowed robe and knew a fierce desire to possess her.

But he wanted her to want him with the same ferocity. After they consummated the marriage, it wouldn't be long before he would be satiated with her and anxious for their sham marriage to end. Then he could begin his search for a more suitable wife.

Appreciating the fact they both wanted their journey to be over, Gabriel thought to ease Madelene's mind. "Since I can't trust you not to effect a plan of flight, we will sleep in the same room and in the same bed, as we did last night. However, I have no intentions on your body. You're much too skinny for my taste, and your feet are a bit scrawny, almost like a child's." He ignored her blazing blue eyes and turned to remove his coat and boots before starting to wash.

Perhaps this will give her something else to think about. He heard Madelene's footsteps on the creaking boards as she paced the room. Gabriel dried his face and turned to watch Madelene stop long enough to pull off her bonnet and gloves, her lips in grim impatience.

"Madelene, you must be exhausted. Tomorrow we should reach Westcott Close, which will certainly be a relief to both of us."

She turned to face him with her hands on her hips. "Sir, the only relief I will know is to return to my own home, and for an annulment to take place in the greatest of haste, if I am, indeed, Mrs. Gabriel Westcott." She paused. Her words boiled in fury.

Gabriel sat on the bed and sighed. "You are truly my wife. After you signed your name to the registry, I had Caroline call you away in order that I might sign my correct name. I planned for you not to know my true identity until we were far from London."

As he stretched his legs out on the bed, he realized again the painful cost he would have to pay to have her near him. "Please join me, or I will have to carry you over here."

She must have believed he was serious because in no time, Madelene had washed, slipped into her bedclothes, and hesitantly climbed onto the bed. His eyes closed, he promptly rolled over and pinned her next to him. He actually felt more exhausted than he appreciated, because in little time, he let sleep overtake him.

The hour grew late. Madelene lay stiffly in bed, noticing the stars from the window and wondered what tomorrow would hold when they actually arrived at his estate in Shropshire. She blinked, remembering. Skinny? Child's feet? Even with a cuff to his shoulder in indignation, he merely grunted, stretched, and continued slumbering. She finally drifted into slumber worrying why it seemed important he desire her instead of being relieved he didn't.

She dreamt someone stroked her arm, then the curve of her cheek, and next her lips, the touch as soft as silk. She smiled, thinking this must be what bliss felt like, and snuggled deeper into the side of another warm body.

Body? She sprang into wakefulness and tried to pull away from strong arms that held her tight against him, her husband. Her husband? She was still unaccustomed to thinking of Mr. Westcott as her husband.

She struggled briefly until daring a glance at Mr. Westcott, who, with eyes closed, appeared to be sleeping. She watched him suspiciously, but his controlled breathing indicated he continued to slumber.

Had she imagined his touch? Or perhaps, Mr. Westcott

himself dreamed he held another woman in his arms? She steamed, thinking her best revenge would be to roll him off the bed. But one glance of his strong physique gave a halt to that idea. If only she could stay awake, then he couldn't touch her again without her knowledge.

But I can't stay awake, and it really had felt quite lovely. With little choice, she fell asleep in his arms, missing the smile on her husband's face.

Madelene couldn't believe they had almost arrived. She felt like she had been riding in a coach for months instead of three days. A few miles back, Mr. Westcott had decided to exchange the carriage ride for a horse, anxious as he was to arrive at his home.

Earlier on the journey, Mr. Westcott had offered that he had inherited his uncle's estate several years earlier. His wife Aunt Adelphia had raised his sister and him but she had been gone some time. After a sojourn in Italy, he now divided his time between his town house in London while managing his shipping affairs, and on his large estate on the border of Wales.

Madelene had heard about the death of his sister and thought it best not to mention it.

From the carriage window, she enjoyed the view of early summer's green passion as they approached the village of Ludlow in Shropshire. The carriage rumbled on past the village, down a few more dusty roads, until turning into a long, graveled driveway. Passing through a large stoned archway, Madelene could see the terraced landscapes with a magnificent neoclassical home sitting atop a small hill.

She leaned out the window to delight in the subtly altered hills and valleys, naturalistic plantings of trees and breathe in the sweet if dusty spring air. There even appeared to be a serpentine lake nestled through a band of trees on the horizon.

Could this magnificent estate truly be her home for a short while? Madelene had heard rumors Mr. Westcott earned his money in the Far East trade, and he must have been successful in order to keep up such a large home in the country and a home in Town.

The clacking wheels on the cobblestones announced their arrival. When the carriage stopped in front of the grand stone steps, Mr. Westcott appeared and opened the carriage door to greet her and assist her from the carriage. As she walked up to the manor's entrance, Madelene noticed more weeds than late spring flowers. She mused it would be a lovely place with the proper care and attention.

The house had almost a forlorn feeling, as if it had been neglected for too long and forgotten like a spinster's heart. She couldn't understand why it had not been better maintained.

As Mr. Westcott unlocked the large wooden doors and beckoned Madelene to enter, she heard the driver wheel the carriage around and clack out of the courtyard.

Following her husband inside, Madelene stepped farther into the small but high-ceilinged hall, admiring the grand staircase in the center, with a flight of steps flowing down on each side as if curtains parted for a stage. Although the wooden rails hadn't been polished in some time, the railing had not lost its majestic splendor.

Studying her surroundings, she noticed through an open door to the right a drawing room with covered furniture, a large fireplace, and covered paintings on the walls.

No servants to greet them. Odd, that. Her husband made no comment or offered an explanation.

Unable to keep her curiosity contained, she inquired to the back of his head as he pulled linens off the few straight chairs standing sentinel in the hall. "Mr. Westcott, where are the servants?" Back at their house in Bloomsbury, they had had a full entourage of servants until their father passed on. Then with Matthew's gaming losses, they slowly, one by one, released all their servants, housekeeper, butler, until they retained only Millie, who cooked and cleaned for them.

"The house has been shut for over a year, and the servants released. I could not be certain when I would return. I plan to visit the village tomorrow and bring our old housekeeper, Mrs. Henchip, and the assortment of cooks, gardeners, and groomsmen. We'll simply have to handle matters ourselves until then. My man, Windthorp, should not be far behind. Tomorrow night in all probability." His tone nonchalant as he headed for the mahogany doors to the right of the staircase.

Madelene hurried to follow him, lost in a fog of uncertainty. No servants? Who didn't have servants to open their house for them and prepare for the master's homecoming? Was this Mr. Westcott's oversight, or had he merely been in a hurry to marry her and win the bet? Perhaps his investments had recently soured or he had empty pockets and couldn't pay their wages? No matter. She had never before been without a servant.

"Mr. Westcott?" she called to him, in her attempt to halt his progress.

He turned around to look at her with hands on his hips. "Yes?"

"Mr. Westcott, this simply will not do. We could return to the village, spend the night at an inn, then return here tomorrow with the servants." She thought it a sound and plausible idea, a pleading smile on her lips.

Her husband obviously thought differently because he looked at her cryptically as if to see if she intended humor, then shook his head. "Madelene, this is now our home. I'm sure one night without servants catering to your whims will do you no harm." He turned and continued farther into the house.

Her boots tapped down the corridor as mistress followed master. It certainly appeared her new husband had not considered her needs in the slightest. Mr. Westcott had not heard the end of this untenable position in which he had placed her. What could he possibly be thinking? She had no intention of performing any duties. It wouldn't do. She wasn't a servant, she was a baronet's sister. He needed reminding.

In his commanding stride, his long legs easily swallowed the length of the hallway, which permitted no dallying on Madelene's part for peering into the richly colored rooms they hurried past. Late-afternoon shadows followed her following him, first down a short set of stone steps to two thick doubled oak doors, and then another short flight into the kitchen, the oblong room still warm from the day's sun.

If he presumed that she would be cooking for him, she would start walking home. She began, "Mr. Westcott—" before he interrupted her.

"Let's check the storeroom to see if Mrs. Henchip left provisions. I had sent her a note earlier this week," he told her, proceeding into an open door to the left.

Unable to continue the conversation without an adversary, Madelene looked around at the stone kitchen. It was quite large with only the last remaining sunlight filtering from the ceiling windows and well stocked with tinned pots, stills, spits, and serving dishes. The room felt quite stuffy as she crossed her arms and leaned against the large wooden table, waiting for her husband to reappear.

In short shrift, Mr. Westcott managed to find bread, cheese, and a bottle of wine for their repast and pulled two wooden stools to the table.

Madelene warred within herself, trying to simmer her anger. They were eating, in the kitchen? Foraging for their own meal? This was totally unsupportable, and nothing could condone what she considered neglect.

She drew up her shoulders, planning to reject any of her husband's offerings. If anyone found out about this, she would be an object of ridicule for weeks, maybe months, for the gossipmongers. As all of her arguments gathered like a storm in her mind, her stomach growled, reminding her of the need for nourishment, along with being overcome with simple exhaustion. Disheartened, she reluctantly joined him at the table.

Tomorrow. She'd state her position in no uncertain terms that he would have to provide staff to assist her, including a lady's maid. He couldn't expect her to dress her own hair. Or maybe he did. Maybe this was some sort of devious punishment. Was he capable of such? She didn't know him very well to guess the answer.

Madelene began to realize that none of her assumptions about her husband had proved very accurate. But she did understand that he needed to know *her* expectations, including they would be sleeping in separate beds tonight.

"Please, Mrs. Westcott, eat, you must be famished," he told her almost kindly, watching her with hooded eyes. Was it only three nights past she had requested the same of him?

She hesitated, then perched across from him and took a sip of wine, which slid down her parched throat. Next, she ate the bread and cheese, and almost moaned with delight, trying to refrain from devouring her food in an unladylike manner.

They continued to eat in silence until Madelene could no longer hold her tongue. She cleared her throat. "I intend to continue in this marriage only as long as the demands of the wager are met. Since you have odiously consigned me to this marriage, I do not believe it should be out of the question to request my own room." She forced her stare into his surprised brown eyes. Surprised at her audacity? She held her breath, waiting for his answer. She didn't know how she would respond if he negated her request.

Mr. Westcott shrugged his shoulders as if her demands were inconsequential and deserved no answer, while sipping his glass of wine as if he had all kinds of time on his hands.

Why did he not respond to her request? She had to gain some reaction from him. "How long do you intend to keep me here?" she blurted out.

He watched her intently before replying. Relaxed on the hard stool, his coat long since discarded, his white shirtsleeves rolled up revealing tanned, strong forearms, her husband leaned slightly away from her. "I have not yet decided. Your tenure here is based on many factors, which I do not choose to delve into tonight." He broke off another piece of hard crust and offered it to her. She refused with a shake of her head.

"I don't suppose I have any say in the matter?" she asked coolly. Before he could respond, she continued, "I must remind you that my brother will discover you have deceived him, and he will come to take me home."

That threat appeared to have no bearing on Mr. Westcott's enjoyment of his repast. He cocked his head slightly with a short smile. "Come, our first meal as man and wife in our home, and you choose to be disagreeable? Besides, I wouldn't count on your brother saving you, when he'd have to return all the blunt he won in this bet."

Madelene opened her mouth to disagree, then just as quickly closed it. She thought of the words she could toss at him in defense of her brother or his cowardly plan to force her into marriage, but decided to finish eating. Tomorrow she would show Mr. Westcott her true mettle.

Westcott's friend and servant could have used more help in toting the new lady of the house's trunk from the courtyard to the first floor. After pulling it up the stairs, one step at a time, he was convinced she had packed gowns lined with lead. But he wouldn't find any assistance tonight. Just the three of them.

His steps quickened, pulling the trunk down the carpeted hall. He realized he didn't have much time if he wanted to finish before the master and mistress retired to bed.

The mistress. She looked like her shoes would never become muddy in the rain, someone extremely hard to please, her mouth in a perpetual pout, as much as he could see from his vantage point above the stairs. How long must he endure her presence? As long as it took, he imagined.

His muscles sore, he had to rest and stretch his back for relief before dragging the trunk the rest of the way to her bedchamber. To his exasperation, the trunk stuck on the thick carpet in her bedroom as he tried to pull it farther into the room. Finally, one last heave, and he pushed it next to her bed and turned to leave.

He paused. It couldn't possibly make a difference. It would only take a moment to discover what lay in the trunk. He fell to his knees, greedily unclasping the locks and flinging the lid open. His mouth turned grim at the sight of beautiful, soft, colorful gowns made for morning, walking, traveling, afternoon, calling, and evening wear. The satiny materials swished in his hands as he began fishing in the clothes for anything of value before he felt something hard and familiar.

Grasping the hard end, he carefully pulled the short-hilted dagger out of her trunk and stared at the sharp object in his hand in disbelief. Why was the dagger in *her* trunk? Not one to question the gods for his lucky fate, he quickly stuck the dagger in his belt, slammed the trunk lid, and ran out of the room, remembering to close the door. Providence had shined on him, which could only mean right was on his side, and perhaps soon, he could return to his home in Florence.

Finished eating, Mr. Westcott gathered the plates and placed them on the sideboard before returning to the table and handing her two lit candles. "If you will light our way, I'll carry the water."

She bit her lip, mutely accepted the candles, and led the way out of the kitchen. In his long strides, he soon overtook her to collect one of the candles and with pitcher in hand, headed to the large stairway on the ground floor. He ascended the staircase, probably assuming she would meekly follow. But Madelene remained at the bottom of the stairs in defiance, her lips pursed. She didn't want to learn if they were sleeping together tonight.

Mr. Westcott looked down at Madelene waiting in almost complete darkness, quiet settling about the house. "Mrs. Westcott, your bedchamber is on this floor. Would you please attend me?" His tone brooked no argument.

She waited briefly to show him she wouldn't do his bidding willingly or quickly, then gathered her skirt and climbed the stairs. Exhaustion pulsed through her and helped her decide that sleeping on the floor or stairs could not be entertained as a sleeping option.

Madelene walked down the carpeted hall to where they met in front of one of the many doors on the floor. She tried to face her husband bravely, with her shoulders back, defiance in her stance, but he maddeningly ignored her.

He opened the door and gestured her inside.

Madelene hesitated, then walked past him into a bedchamber of bright pink and green colors on silk drapes and the rich counterpane. A pleasant perfume of lilacs assailed her senses. She had never expected anything so very charming. As she turned around in a circle, she realized this room was a lovelier room than she had known even back in Bloomsbury.

"Mr. Westcott, I didn't know what to expect, but this room is quite breathtaking," she told him.

"I hope you will be comfortable here. It was my sister's room. Earlier this year, I had all the colors and furniture changed for my new wife," he told her shortly before walking over to the small table and pouring water in the basin.

"Do I understand you planned to marry me as early as January, before the bet was even made?" She could hardly credit this news, for it was illogical.

He stopped and looked at her, his brow furrowed. "Ah, I had planned to offer for a young lady this year to take as my wife. I had no notion it would be you. I'm sure you'll be most comfortable here."

His plans mattered naught to her, and a beautiful bedchamber changed nothing. He had still married her for the needed funds. Madelene deliberated what to say when he interrupted her thoughts.

"In the morning, we'll begin setting the house to rights." He walked toward her and stopped in front of her, studying her intently.

She lifted her chin, determined not to show lack of character or fear of his closeness, although she couldn't quite manage her bottom lip not trembling. He was so very close—

But he didn't kiss her. And she was glad. She didn't want to know what his kisses tasted like. This man, out of necessity called husband, had brought her to a neglected estate with no servants. Madelene was unprepared to call her grievances trifling.

Probably tomorrow, he would have her cooking dinner or making soap or some such nonsense. Not Madelene Colgate. Madelene Colgate Westcott, she amended reluctantly. She hoped he noticed her steady glare at him.

His brown gaze seemed to search her face for something, but she couldn't fathom what.

"Sleep well, Mrs. Westcott," he told her before heading to the door. And then she was alone.

Was he actually leaving her bedchamber? Did he intend to return? That man certainly provoked more questions in her mind than he answered. After their hasty journey and sleep on lumpy thin mattresses, she felt the headache coming on. She gazed longingly at the large tester bed and wondered whether she had enough energy to change into her bedclothes.

When she saw her trunk by her bed, she frowned. Where had it come from? Mr. Westcott had certainly not carried it here, because he had been with her since their arrival. Someone must be here with them, but Mr. Westcott had chosen not to enlighten her. How very strange.

Simply too much to think about. I'll worry on it tomorrow, she thought sleepily. Madelene laid on the bed fully clothed, prepared in case Mr. Westcott would return and claim his husbandly rights. She wasn't exactly sure how she could keep him at a distance, particularly after a quick glance around the room showed an absence of bed warmers. She'd have to think of a better weapon for protection from her husband. An odd thought; she had never thought she'd need protection from her husband.

The thought of a husband brought back ugly memories of Aaron Winchester, a man who had professed unceasing devotion to her until Matthew had advised him that her dowry was more a pauper's purse than a king's. At first, he claimed this news meant nothing to him, that he couldn't live a day without her beside him. He had used all the right words, and all the words she had waited forever to hear. Aaron had kept the farce right up until a week after the banns were announced.

She didn't remember the banbury story he told her that night. She may have heard the words "his mother refused to consider Madelene for his wife, and he had acquiesced because after all, it was his mother." He couldn't look her in the eye, coward he, and suddenly his presence caused a sickness within her.

She had held her tears, determined not to show any distress at his words until he had left her life. The pain had felt like a slice through her heart, and she was filled with a saddening comprehension that no man would want her without a dowry. She later learned he planned to marry a young woman from a wealthy family in the north. Aaron, vain and obsequious, was more concerned over the style of his cravat then a possible Luddite protest or the never-ending war with Napoleon.

Madelene read in the *Post* the marriage of Lord Winchester to Miss Cecily Bryncome. Her father was Samuel Bryncome, owner of several mills in the north. His mother must have been pleased. Madelene refused to consider that he wouldn't have made her happy, wanting, instead, to nurse a broken heart. It was better to feel something rather than a continued state of emptiness, she had thought at the time.

Months later found her in an unanticipated marriage, bonded to a man who again only wanted her for what money she could bring to the bargain.

I'll close my eyes for only a moment.

Madelene sat up in bed with a start. Something had awakened her. With her knees clasped to her chest, she listened for any slight noise while keenly watching the doorknob.

Nothing.

A few more minutes. Still nothing.

Apparently she had imagined the noise.

She sighed in relief, blinking awake. If Mr. Westcott retired for the night, wherever that may be, she could conduct an exploration of the ground floor, which would be helpful when it came time for a quick departure.

Carrying the still-lit candle, she walked over to the door and opened it slightly to peek out. A window shutter banged, startling her, and she slammed the door shut. Holding tight to the doorknob, Madelene had to slow her heartbeat thundering in her ears to listen again outside her room. The wooden floor creaked outside her bedchamber. Surely this house wasn't haunted or some such nonsense.

Several minutes went by and all was quiet. Terribly relieved, her pulse returned to normal, she opened the door again wide enough to see the dark hallway. Taking a deep breath, she decided to head back down the stairs. All doors exiting the house would be high on her list of places to investigate.

She stepped into the dark, her candle illuminating a small window of light, and pulled the door closed. Her eyes were still adjusting to the narrowed light when she tripped over a body in the hallway.

The candle flew out of her hand as she pitched forward. *"Staire attento, Signora!"* commanded a low voice as Madelene yelped in surprise.

She slammed to the floor. Stunned. Out of breath.

Her candle, doused by the sudden toss, rolled down the hallway. In peril for her life, Madelene quickly turned onto her back and braced herself on the carpet. Her heart galloped in her chest, her breathing stopped.

Madelene swallowed hard, then gazed up at the stranger, a short, thin man who stood before her, holding his hand out to assist her.

She screamed.

Her scream must have frightened the stranger because he retreated against the wall and into the shadows. Madelene heard footsteps on the stairs and heard Mr. Westcott's voice.

"Madelene, what is wrong? Are you hurt?" he asked roughly and slightly out of breath from running up the stairs in breeches and boots, his shirt missing.

In those brief moments, his comforting presence had slowed the beating of her heart and given her strength to rise to meet him. "Thank goodness. This person was outside my bedchamber," she said, pointing to the figure in the shadows. "He probably plans to rob us or create some kind of havoc—"

He looked into the shadows, then surprised her by laughing. Walking over to the stranger, Mr. Westcott pulled him further into the light of a flickering hallway sconce.

"This is Alec, my friend. Alec, this is my, my wife, Mrs. Westcott."

Madelene peered at this new house occupant. She could not make out his face in this poor light, particularly when he wore a dark hat low over his face. Slim of build, he dressed in a black shirt, vest, breeches, and boots, from what she could see in the wavering glow.

After patting her hair back into some semblance of order, she nodded at Alec. "Mr. Westcott had not mentioned you before, and I certainly didn't anticipate tripping over anyone outside my bedroom door. Do you have a place to sleep here in the house?" She looked to Mr. Westcott for direction.

"Alec has watched the house these last few months. I met him during my recent stay in Florence. When he wanted to leave Italy, I offered him my home for as long as he needed one." Mr. Westcott slung an arm around Alec before continuing, "He agreed to come with me to England as long as he could be of service to me."

Madelene looked from one man to the other. "I believe I understand. However, I am still in confusion over one matter. What was Alec doing outside my bedchamber door?" she asked, her hands on her hips, her tone piqued.

Mr. Westcott hesitated before responding, "I've asked Alec to be your guard."

Chapter Seven

"My what?" she shrieked. She couldn't have been more surprised than if Mr. Westcott had told her she was free to leave and return home.

Her husband nodded to Alec, who slipped silently down the hallway.

"Madelene, we'll talk about this in the morning. We both need some sleep." His voice did indeed sound tired.

She opened her mouth to object, then closed it with a grim expression. Then she opened it again.

"Sir, I am aggrieved, simply aggrieved, that you would find the need to have someone guard me during my stay in your home. I don't know whether to be offended that you don't trust me not to escape or ask if you would like a diary of all my movements, which surely would make for dreary reading."

She sensed he almost smiled before asking her, "Do you plan to escape before the year of our marriage is over?"

Replying evenly, she told him, "I cannot say yes, and I cannot say no."

Mr. Westcott nodded. "Until I know the answer is

definitely no, Alec will ensure you don't forget you're married and heigh off back to London."

She scowled at him, knowing she didn't have a choice in the matter. Her annoyance was probably wasted, since in this dim light, he probably couldn't see her clearly. Soon enough, she would get rid of Alec and be on her way.

"Then, I guess that is the way of it." She conceded by retreating to her bedchamber.

Gabriel stared after her. Something was amiss; surely she had given in much too easily.

Late that night, Gabriel still couldn't sleep. What had his new bride done to his thoughts of revenge? He had determined to harden his heart against any womanly wiles she could use on him, but it was the unconscious ones she used that could prove his undoing. He must forget her dimples when she smiled, the long arch of her neck, her graceful way of walking and remember Lucinda. Madelene was here because his dear sister wasn't.

He tossed and turned, wondering if his plan to make Madelene suffer for her brother's atrocity to his sister might envelop him as well.

Although Mr. Westcott was absent in the morning, his faithful friend and her ever-watchful shadow, Alec, looking much the same as last night, rose to his feet when he met her outside her bedchamber. Completely ignoring his presence, Madelene wandered downstairs toward the kitchen, since it was the only room she knew how to find.

She couldn't very well complain to Alec, who had followed her, of eating in the kitchen again, since he understood little English. Shrugging, she told herself it wouldn't be long before she could take breakfast on the ground floor. But until they at least had a housekeeper, she needed to manage on her own.

She knew she must look a proper sight because she had not had her hair done properly in over three days, but there was simply nothing that could be done. However, she did believe her pink morning dress showed her pale complexion exquisitely.

Perhaps a bit vain, she would admit to herself, but even if Mr. Westcott noticed her appearance and thought her handsome, it changed nothing. There had to be some way to extract her from this marriage and the wager. She sighed. *I have certainly never felt so conflicted in my life.*

Wherever could Mr. Westcott be? She hoped her husband was in the village hiring staff, especially a lady's maid, since she was in most urgent need of one.

In the kitchen, Alec motioned to the coffee cup and the hard, crusty bread. When had the young man prepared this pauper's meal for her? The rumblings in her stomach convinced her the answer wasn't important. *Oh, for French bread and smoked salmon,* she mused. Her mouth turned down in wishful thinking as she sat on the lower chair provided for her. *Do criminals receive more than bread and coffee for their breakfast?* Indeed, she *felt* a prisoner.

At a loss for something of importance to do, Madelene sipped her coffee while looking around at the large kitchen. It reminded Madelene of the bricked kitchen in their old town house and their beloved cook, Mrs. Top-kind, who had taught her many culinary skills. Madelene loved the smell of the kitchen when the cook baked sweet cakes or puddings.

Lovely times with Mrs. Topkind helped make her forget her mother's loss at the age of ten but now brought tears to her eyes, remembering. They were so happy then, she, Matthew, their father, their cook, and the other servants. But time had a way of changing the present and future, and the past must stay buried in memories.

Enough of this sentimentality! Remembering her new station in life, she was confident Mr. Westcott would hire suitable staff and a good cook. As she chewed the hard bread, she noticed her Italian guard staring into the fireplace, a mute inconvenience and quite bothersome.

There had to be more to this story than a sudden friendship blossoming in Italy. She wondered about Alec's history. What was he really doing here?

As she reflected upon this intruder, a thought occurred. Perhaps, if she could make friends with Alec, he might help her to get away and return home. A little niggling thought about a bet and wedding vows were easily brushed aside. It just might be possible. After all, she could leave nothing to chance. But could she make herself understood?

Madelene brightened at the thought and prepared to beam kindness and charity like a patron of St. Agnes Home for Lost Children.

"Ah, Alec, do you like it here, at Westcott Close?"

The young man turned around to look at Madelene and frowned, as if to understand her question. He shrugged in reply.

She tapped her foot, wishing she could at least recall a smattering of Italian when she studied at Filmore's School for the Proper Raising of Today's Young Ladies to Become Shining Examples of Womanhood. Nothing came to her.

It didn't take long for Madelene to realize befriending her guard would take more than a friendly smile and hand signals to communicate. Her plan needed more thought and less impulsiveness.

She tapped her fingers on the table. And what about

Matthew? Surely, he must be consumed with worry about her whereabouts and her condition.

There was simply nothing for it. She imagined Mr. Westcott would try to contact her brother and assure him of her continued good health. She shook her head, realizing she had no idea what her husband had planned for her, and if her brother fit into those plans at all.

Here against her will, she had to find a way back to Town and her brother soon, or Mr. Westcott would—well, she might not be able to obtain an annulment.

And that would simply never do. She finished her coffee and rose wondering when Mr. Westcott would return, resigned knowing she would receive no details from Alec.

With time on her hands, she determined to have a look at her surroundings, since her opportunity last night had been thwarted. Not looking over her shoulder to see if Alec shadowed her, she walked up the steps and into the main house, strolling past each room on the ground floor, taking a cursory look.

She found a blue-and-gold parlor, a drawing room, a music room, and a library of primrose, copper, and celery with more books than even her father had owned, and his books could have filled almost one wing of a lending library.

What it must have been like to entertain in these great rooms while his sister and aunt were alive. Or had they entertained? She didn't know much about her husband's history. Had they all been happy, like her family, before the death of their uncle?

Scolding herself, she determined to think only bright thoughts, instead of gloomy ones. Returning to her exploration, she noted with a bit of dusting, polishing, and shining, these rooms could be prepared in no time. The house was surely large enough to accommodate a party with dancing. She smiled thinking how a dance would enliven her stay. It had been ever so long since she had attended a ball.

A local ball. It sounded wonderful; she couldn't remember the last ball they had been invited to or the last new gown.

Closing her eyes, she reminded herself she wasn't planning to stay long enough to play hostess at an affair at Westcott Close, for it could surely never be her home.

Fresh air might just be what I need to invigorate myself and clear my head. She walked to the front of the house and opened the large doors, which led onto a smooth-stoned porch. Before continuing outside, Madelene remembered to gather a parasol from the hall in case the sun might be too harsh. One must never be too cautious, for pink skin was not at all attractive.

Once outside admiring the view of the terraced gardens, she heard a voice shouting.

"Yoo-hoo, Mrs. Westcott!" cried a high-pitched voice behind her.

Madelene heard the call again before turning to greet her unannounced guest, still unaccustomed as she was to hearing herself referred to as "Mrs. Westcott."

In puzzlement, she watched a short rotund woman in black-and-purple raiment with matching turban wave at her, then amble her way up the driveway, which took no short amount of time.

Finally arriving and out of breath, the older woman dropped down on the bottom stone step, as if her legs could carry her no greater distance.

"Ooh, this is much farther than I thought!" She huffed and puffed, while fanning herself with one glove.

Madelene stood askance watching the woman and

wondering who she was and what she was doing at Westcott Close. Her only summation was this old woman must be from the village, which was how she knew Madelene's name.

The older woman breathed deeply, winded from her walk, and looked up at Madelene, wiping her brow. "Oh, dearie, dearie me. Well, that be the way of it. I thought a brisk walk from the road might do me some good, but clearly, I am not wearing my sensible bonnet. The day is a bit heated, is it not?" She affixed her turban to ensure it remained on top of her head. "Very good. Yes, well, I must make my introductions. I'm here as your new housekeeper. Mrs. Lavishtock Another moment, while I catch my breath," she gasped.

Nothing could have surprised Madelene more. She walked down the few steps and leaned against the stone wall above her visitor, studying her more closely. The older woman's sparkling blue eyes dominated a wizened old face, her cheeks rosy red. She had a kindly demeanor that seemed to say that all your troubles could be handled with a smile.

"*You're* the new housekeeper? But where do you come from? I understood a Mrs. Henchip was to be our housekeeper. You see, Mr. Westcott, my husband, went into the village to collect her and other servants for the house. How come you to be here?"

Mrs. Lavishtock rocked her head back and forth. "Yes, well, I heard Mrs. Henchip was feeling poorly, and I was told you'd be a-needing someone to look after you, I mean the house. So I came along to be of help," she replied in a singsong voice, reminding Madelene of a Welsh nanny she had had so many years ago.

Madelene could not quite keep the astonishment out of her voice. This seemed quite improper for their housekeeper to suddenly appear, as it were, on their doorstep. "I have no doubt we would appreciate your service, but I must speak with my husband, of course."

Mrs. Lavishtock braced her hands on a higher step and pulled her bulky self to a stand. Ignoring Madelene's comment, she asked, "Do you think someone could collect my things I left down the way? The carriage left me off at the main road, but I couldna carry my things and me." Not waiting for a reply, she tottered past Madelene and into the house while Madelene could only watch in surprised bemusement.

Collecting her thoughts, she followed Mrs. Lavishtock into the house. Although a seemingly friendly soul, Madelene didn't know what Mrs. Lavishtock was about and meant to seek answers. She found their potential new housekeeper resting on a linen-covered chair in the front parlor.

"Ah, Mrs. Lavishtock, I'm afraid there is no one but myself and a young servant. You'll need—"

Mrs. Lavishtock smiled broadly at Madelene. "Ooh, you are a pretty one. No wonder—dearie, would you mind fetching me a glass of water? 'Fraid I cannot move until I have something very wet. Yes, I think tea would be best."

Madelene looked out the hallway for Alec, but strangely, he was nowhere in sight.

She sighed, quickly discarding her parasol. "Of course, Mrs. Lavishtock. You rest, and I'll go—*bring* you tea." Madelene left the parlor and walked down to the kitchen, trying to remember the last time she had served anyone in this manner. Usually, someone served *her*.

Indeed, though, she thought with a smile, she didn't mind, for Mrs. Lavishtock seemed harmless, and kind, and rather old. How much trouble could the older woman be? Especially if she knew the ways of housekeeping and could provide suitable menus and see to the staff? Was she capable, and where were her references?

She needn't worry, for Mr. Westcott would handle everything upon his return. Madelene started to breathe easier. Perhaps Mrs. Lavishtock could be a confidante, that is, unless Mr. Westcott brought a lady's maid home for her. She needed someone to talk privately with in this completely foreign house.

"Here you are, Mrs. Lavishtock," she said graciously upon her return and handed the cup and saucer to the older woman. As their potential housekeeper swallowed her tea in seemingly one gulp, Madelene stood awkwardly nearby, uncomfortable to sit on the covered furniture and wondering what to do next.

"I'm afraid, Mrs. Lavishtock, you'll need to wait until Mr. Westcott returns home so you can discuss the position with him. I do not know this house at all to show you around, except to the kitchen. Would you like to see the kitchen?" She smiled, gesturing down the hallway.

"Och, then let's be to it. You show me to the kitchen, and I'll start gettin' acquaintain' with things until the master returns home."

Although Mrs. Lavishtock needed Madelene's assistance to pull her out of the chair, once on her feet, the housekeeper appeared well enough to manage on her own, and prepared to follow Madelene to the kitchen. Conscious of the older woman's slower pace, Madelene matched her lumbering gait, keeping slightly ahead to direct her.

Before she reached the stairs to the kitchen, Madelene saw movement out of a nearby window and thought it might be her husband returning. Anxious to see what staff he had brought home, she motioned the stairway to Mrs. Lavishtock.

"The kitchen is down these stairs. I'll be with you shortly. I believe my husband has returned home."

She hastened down the corridor to see her husband. With trepidation, she opened the front door and saw Alec already on the porch. A carriage rocked past the porch toward the stables.

A thought occurred and immediately worried her. She couldn't make herself an important part of the household, knowing that any day, she would depart. She shrugged. What would it matter? For the present, she must continue the pretense of the mistress of Westcott Close.

Madelene ventured out to the porch when she saw Mr. Westcott riding through the stone archway into the courtyard.

"Greetings, Mrs. Westcott, how are you enjoying your first day at Westcott Close?" he called to her as he superbly dismounted, threw his reins to a new footboy standing nearby, and ran up the stairs with his hat in hand.

Before Madelene could respond or greet her husband, they heard a loud thump and a wailing. Her husband brushed past her and into the house with Madelene following close behind. The cries appeared to be coming from down the corridor, where she had left Mrs. Lavishtock. Oh, no. Mrs. Lavishtock.

At the top of the kitchen stairs, Madelene and her husband stared in disbelief.

Mrs. Lavishtock lay on her side at the bottom of the stairs holding her ankle, moaning, "Och, I think it's broken, I think it's broken."

Poor Mrs. Lavishtock. She glanced at her husband, worrying her lip. If Mr. Westcott thought a strange woman with a broken bone in his kitchen a trifle odd, he kept his thoughts to himself. Madelene couldn't stop castigating herself for having left the older woman alone and not helping her down the steps. Grimacing, she trailed her husband down the stairs to kneel by the elderly woman, whose turban had begun to slide down onto her forehead.

Mr. Westcott stooped to lift the old woman to a more comfortable sitting position. "Now, let's have a look at that ankle. I'm not a doctor, but I've seen broken ankles before."

Mrs. Lavishtock paid no attention, all the while moaning, "Oh, my ankle, my ankle."

Mr. Westcott positioned himself in front of the older woman and gently lifted her leg, careful not to raise it any more than necessary. He was entirely solicitous to this stranger, which surprised Madelene.

Wanting to help in some way, she hopped down the last few stairs to sit beside Mrs. Lavishtock and hold her hand as both women watched Mr. Westcott examine the black-stockinged leg. When he removed her sturdy black shoe, the woman moaned again, then leaned against Madelene.

Mr. Westcott looked up into the woman's angst-ridden face. "It's not broken, but perhaps sprained. I will have a physician look at it." As if suddenly remembering something, Mr. Westcott looked at Madelene with lifted eyebrows. "Mrs. Westcott, would you, perhaps, introduce us?"

Madelene met his eyes, smiled and, said faintly, "Mr. Westcott, meet Mrs. Lavishtock, our new housekeeper?"

Chapter Eight

Mr. Westcott and Madelene had settled Mrs. Lavishtock into the housekeeper's rooms near the kitchen when the physician arrived to examine the patient. After taking measure of her pain by the housekeeper's moan every time he touched anywhere near her ankle, the physician turned to Madelene and her husband and assured them it was only a sprain.

This news greatly relieved Madelene, who still blamed herself for the accident. The physician put liniment on the ankle and wrapped it, warning Mrs. Lavishtock to stay off her feet for the next few days. Before the doctor left, he whispered to Madelene that a bit of spirits might hasten her healing or help her to sleep. She nodded and smiled at him, thanking him for seeing to their housekeeper.

At one of the less harried moments during the doctor's visit, Mr. Westcott and Madelene found themselves with a housekeeper, with nary a word exchanged of experience or references. Madelene had whispered to her husband they couldn't very well throw the old woman out on her injured ankle. Mr. Westcott had nodded his agreement, but asked her if she could handle the housekeeper's duties until Mrs. Lavishtock was able.

Madelene twisted her mouth ruefully. She had no intention of performing the duties of a housekeeper and opened her mouth to object.

Except at that moment, Mrs. Lavishtock had told them how grateful she was to them that they had given her a position in their household, and as soon as she was on her feet (in no time), she would prove their confidence in her.

Madelene closed her eyes and said a little prayer her husband would offer to return to Town and find Mrs. Henchip or someone as a temporary replacement for Mrs. Lavishtock.

Only he didn't.

As Mr. Westcott and Madelene closed the door to the housekeeper's rooms, they could still hear Mrs. Lavishtock mumbling about being an inconvenience, and it wouldn't be too long before she would be earning her keep.

After everyone had left the room, Mrs. Lavishtock looked up at the ceiling. "It looks like our plan has worked. I'm to be their new housekeeper. I can watch her while I'm resting. Don't worry, I'll make it all right. I'll see to her."

After a long day of cleaning, moving furniture, filling fireplaces, and stocking the storeroom, Madelene and Mr. Westcott sat in the newly polished dining room for their first meal of chewy venison and tasteless stewed tomatoes. Madelene managed a few bites and determined to have a word with the new cook in the morning. Even the raisin pudding stuck to her spoon. Her old cook had taught her spices should be used liberally for practically every dish. Given their untenable repast, Madelene wondered if Mr. Westcott couldn't find a more capable cook so far from Town.

As she contemplated a plan to repair the cook's menus, she realized Mr. Westcott had yet to say one word to her about the new servants, her duties, or his plans for re-opening Westcott Close. She watched him surreptitiously over her wineglass, noting he appeared to have a lack of appetite. However, she couldn't determine the source, whether it was the meal or something on his mind.

A knock on the door alerted them to a guest. "Excuse me, Mr. Westcott, I wanted to advise you that I have returned. You requested I inform you immediately upon my arrival." A tall, thin man presented himself inside the dining-room doors.

Mr. Westcott looked over at the stranger and nodded. "Windthorp, it is good to see you." He paused. "Windthorp, my wife, Mrs. Westcott. I had mentioned her to you and the occasion of our marriage." Her husband turned to look at her. "Mrs. Westcott, this is my valet, Windthorp. He would have been here to meet us; however, he had to undertake business transactions for me in Town." Mr. Westcott looked once again at the quiet man at the door. "Please wait for me in the study. I'll be with you shortly."

Madelene inspected the tall man with an almost gallows-like visage and small dark mustache. The new arrival never looked in her direction, which did not deter her from taking his measure. His skeletal form barely fit his clothes, and his demeanor was anything but light-hearted. Indeed, if possible, she felt a thinly veiled mood of disapproval emanating from him. She tried not to shudder at this darkness, the only word she could think of to describe him.

Windthorp. Mr. Westcott's valet and obviously Man of

Affairs. Madelene wondered what secrets he kept for his employer.

After Windthorp departed as silently as he had entered, Madelene tried to fashion a conversation with her husband. However, in mere moments, Mr. Westcott excused himself to join his servant.

Madelene sat back in her chair, relieved to watch his departure. Mr. Westcott always seemed to judge her and find her lacking.

Later that night, as she donned her night rail, she worried if her husband would make an appearance in her bedchamber. When would he require his husbandly rights? And how much longer could she endure not knowing his plans for her and wanting to escape this place to return to her own home? Home—a place she knew, and where she wasn't a stranger living in a strange house with an enigmatic husband. How the Fates played games with her life.

She felt caught in a web of circumstance and could find no way out. Would her brother find her and take her home? Before it was too late?

Not yet ready to retire to bed, Madelene contemplated her husband as she sat on the window ledge, gazing on the spring night. All was still, except for a shallow breeze now and then rustling the leaves and a lonely frog croaking from the lake.

Mr. Westcott. Who was he really, and what did he want with her? He had shown her many courtesies since they had been married, and he wasn't exactly the unkind man she had thought him to be. Even if he had placed a guard on her, which did not suit at all.

But it still didn't change the circumstances, which found her married to a man who could not possibly love her and for whom she could not possibly care. How would it end, she mused. Was theirs to be a marriage of comedic or tragic proportions?

She stared a long while at the stars lighting the night, the moon hiding behind misshapen, floating clouds. Since she couldn't depend on her brother finding her, and soon, Madelene would have to handle the matter of returning to London on her own. She would save herself.

With no easy answers in sight, she sighed and crawled into bed with the merest of linen draped over her in the heat of the May night. Deep in sleep, she never heard the door open or the little paws padding across the floor and Brussels carpet.

Madelene did, however, awake when something began to lick her face. She promptly sat up and screamed. The little dog barked in her face before jumping off the bed and running beneath it, howling in fear.

A few minutes later, Mr. Westcott burst in the door dressed only in his robe. "What is it?"

Madelene swore she could hear someone laughing in the hall.

The little dog continued barking under the bed. Mr. Westcott must have realized instantly what had caused the commotion because he knelt down by the bed, lifted the bedclothes, and looked underneath. "Falstaff, come here, boy. Falstaff," he commanded in a soft but firm voice.

Madelene watched this tall, almost assurredly naked man cradle the scruffiest little dog she had ever seen. The little black-and-white ball of rough fur had black eyes with lopsided ears—one flopped over and one stood straight. Although she couldn't claim fondness for animals, the little fellow did seem appealing, happily licking the face of Mr. Westcott, who minded not a bit.

Her husband looked at Madelene and smiled. "This seems to be a habit with us. You scream, and I run to save you from Alec or Falstaff, a harmless little dog. He is as terrified of you as you are of him."

Madelene sputtered a defense, but it fell on deaf ears.

He walked over to the door and handed Falstaff to Alec at his usual post. Madelene could hear them talking but couldn't distinguish their conversation. All that mattered was the dog had left her bedchamber.

Mr. Westcott closed her door and returned to her bedside. Eyebrows raised, Madelene watched him warily. Surely, he wouldn't— She waited for him to bid her good night but instead, he sat on the opposite side of her bed, simply staring at her. Her lips suddenly felt dry. Why didn't he leave?

She didn't know where to look except out the window, unnerved by his steady gaze.

"You look lovely in pink."

"Oh," Madelene breathlessly responded upon looking down to find the sheet didn't cover her nearly as much as it should. Her nightclothes revealed too much for propriety's sake, and his intense scrutiny made breathing difficult. *Perhaps if I could change the subject—what was the little dog's name again?*

"I know this marriage is not either of our choosing, but we can make the best of it, can we not?" His voice was soothing and soft, and dangerous.

Without giving her a chance to reply, he told her, "I want you." His expression was earnest as he brushed back his dark brown wayward hair.

Stunned, she gaped at him, not prepared for a frontal attack but remembering her indignity. "Sir, I cannot entertain such a thought. This was my brother's plan, which you interrupted for your own goals. It was to be a marriage in name only."

She paused, and unable to look him square in the eye,

looked in fascination at the pink-frosted counterpane. "I thought I was too skinny and had scrawny feet?" She muttered under her breath as she tried to maintain some hint of defensive decorum. Madelene reluctantly pulled her gaze from the covers and returned his study.

His smile did not quite reach his eyes. "I tried to convince myself that I found you undesirable, but I can't persuade myself of that anymore." His quiet sincerity struck her somewhere between her heart and her brain.

This wasn't to happen. She was going to leave him. He was to be a braggart, a wastrel; hard and despicable toward her. Make her suffer. He simply could not be pleasant to her, for she didn't want to like him any more than she already did.

His gaze never leaving her face, he rose from the bed and walked to the other side, closer to where she sat, and perched next to her. The air felt stifling even with the open window.

Maybe she should run. Run where? How far would she get? Her senses told her to fight off any advances, but his eyes asked her to surrender. Perspiration slipped between her breasts. Was it indeed the night air or was the heat exuding from him?

She should fear him, hate him, throw ugly remarks at him, but she couldn't, mesmerized by the sight of her impassioned husband. She couldn't move. Where was her courage when she needed it?

Gabriel lifted her hand, laying by her side, and brought it to his lips, almost in homage, almost afraid he would hurt her. She quivered at the warm contact and closed her eyes, casting any immodest thoughts aside.

This was her husband. The angel and the sinner warred within her. Indeed, she did want to feel his lips on hers. Wanted to know what this strange feeling inside that she only felt when he was around was. An aching, breathless, wordless feeling, she had never felt before, never lived before.

He slid a strong hand up her bare arm and wrapped it around her shoulder to pull her close as he leaned in to kiss her exposed neck. Startled, she froze, her heart pounding, worried about what he might do next or what he might not do. *What is he doing with his tongue? Does he realize he was making me addle-pated?*

"Madelene, I need you," he whispered in her ear.

She coughed, then gulped hard, unsure of how to respond. A fleeting thought—if she gained his affection, would it leave *her* unharmed?

Eyes closed, she turned her head and met his kiss. A kiss she knew would brand her soul. Knew it was like nothing she had ever felt or tasted before. If this was all wrong, why did this overwhelming feeling of rightness assail her?

When he pulled away from their kiss, she blushed at her inexperience and boldness, thinking she could not tempt him after all.

But he appeared to have trouble breathing, too, until he swept her into his arms and on his lap, planting kiss after kiss on her cheeks and eyelids before taking her by surprise with his demanding mouth. Tasting of his warm, brandied lips, she moaned when he teased her mouth open and mated his tongue with hers, where he appeared determined to take her breath and anything else she had to give him.

But not her heart, she thought frantically. *My heart is safe from him. It must remain so.* She lost her thought as he fell back across the bed, pulling her more securely on top of him, matching and molding his hard body to her soft pliable one, so easily fitting all the right places together. Her thin muslin-clad body to his—oh, goodness, nakedness, his robe vanished.

Her husband brushed her hair over her shoulder while holding her head in his hands as he lavished kiss upon kiss to her desperate lips, pressing her warmth more deeply against his hardened arousal. She ached everywhere he touched her and everywhere he didn't. She couldn't stop the little sighs that escaped. He had completely captured her spirit, or had she given it to him freely? She no longer cared or remembered.

His lips brushing the tops of her breasts sent tingling shocks through her. She felt on fire. She wanted more.

But while his lips continued their all-consuming assault on her willing body, rational thought returned. Madelene pulled away from his heat and anchored her hands on either side of his head, looking down at him and breathing deeply, her senses regained.

He looked at her with confused passion in his warm brown eyes as if to question why she had stopped this willing journey they both desired.

She closed her eyes for a moment to regain breath and virtue, then asked softly, "Is this part of your revenge of my brother?" A moment of silence later, she regretted those words as soon as they found a way to poison what lay between them.

Gabriel stared at her for a moment before rolling her onto her back and removing himself from the bed. The heat between them chilled whatever distance they had traveled tonight.

She watched him walk to the door, his robe securely tied, his back to her. Ready to walk out and forget what had just passed between them? She gulped with unshed tears because she knew she had hurt him, something she suddenly discovered that was the very last act she wanted to commit. But it was too late.

Closing her eyes, she heard the door open.

"I almost wish I could say yes, but I would be lying to both of us," he told her enigmatically, then closed the door softly.

Madelene continued lying in the same place for a long while. He was unlike any man she had ever met. While her mind might have retained her righteousness, her heart hurt for what he had left behind. She knew what she must do. She had to leave.

Chapter Nine

Restless, unable to sleep, Madelene decided to depart the house and her husband at the earliest opportunity, which appeared to be this moment. She could not dally any longer, uncertain of what lay ahead if she remained. There was no time to worry what her husband would think when he found her absent in the morning and whether he would follow her, as he had promised.

She hurriedly dressed in her traveling clothes, resolved to leave most of her belongings behind. Perhaps she could pay one of the groomsmen to take her to Ludlow, assuming the servants had not earned Mr. Westcott's allegiance in one day. It would make for the quickest departure so she could leave this unfathomable man behind who wanted everything from her, but could give nothing in return. Madelene had to keep the candle of her anger burning, for it would be the only way she could save herself.

Ready to do all that mattered to escape, she clutched her reticule while listening at the door. What to do about Alec? Her only solution appeared to be knocking him out temporarily. Her recently acquired bed warmer would suit her purpose, as before, but she might need to hit him slightly harder. It might make him think twice about guarding anyone in the future.

She cracked the door open to discern if Alec sat in his usual spot. Strange, the young man was missing. Perhaps he had to look after the little dog. Not daring to waste any time relishing her good fortune for a clear path to her impetuous escape, Madelene slipped out the door and headed down the back stairs to the servants' hall she had discovered earlier that day.

Soon enough, she left the servants' entrance and made her way over the graveled walkway in the direction of the stables she had noted when they arrived yesterday. With only her memory to guide her, for the darkness blanketed her sight, she was barely able to register her own hand in front of her.

Any moment she expected to be stopped, and she had no clear reason why she'd be dressed in traveling clothes other than flight. Her heart pounded in her throat when every click, every crunch, every jingle could mean she had been discovered.

On her short trek from the house to the stables, she reflected upon her fortune of finding a groomsman who would take her to the village, but dismissed the idea out of hand. Too many questions. Her only solution, if successful and undetected, was to either saddle a horse or hitch a gig. She preferred neither, but desperation allowed few options.

While in the country for brief visits to cousins, she had ridden a horse a few times but never actually saddled one, and by no means could she claim any talent as a horsewoman, her only skill being never having fallen off a horse.

Definitely safer with a gig, assuming Mr. Westcott kept that kind of transport. Then perhaps if she could make it to the village, someone could help her obtain passage on the next coach to Town.

Gathering her courage close like her black cloak, she appreciated the night that kept her identity a secret. As she rounded the square building, hugging the shadows, she stopped abruptly when she heard a voice.

"Cappie, I'm going up the house for dinner. Fanny was to keep something warm for me. Can you unhitch Silver? Stuffy Windthorp's just back from the village," a deep voice called. The groomsman with the baritone voice didn't appear interested in hearing a reply since his steps continued onward, growing more and more distant the closer he walked to the house and away from the stables.

Madelene hid in the shade of the stalls, waiting to see if the fellow called "Cappie" made an appearance. All remained still.

She rounded the side of the stables and saw a small gray horse hooked to a gig. The gray looked over at her, neighed softly, and swished her tail.

Could she dare? Any minute she expected the groomsman Cappie to find her near the carriage. With no time to lose, she dared to pull Silver by the bridle out into the courtyard. The wooden wheels clacked on the cobblestones, but she continued tugging the horse and carriage step by step, farther down the lane, until she felt safe to climb up into the gig. Her heart in her ears, she heard no outraged cries or thundering steps running to catch up with her.

A few minutes more. A few more minutes and she'd be free. While her burden began to lift from her shoulders, she refused to consider the bruises beginning to show on her heart.

Afraid to even breathe, lest she alert anyone nearby, Madelene finally nudged the gray into a trot when she determined herself to be far enough from the stables. She was concerned for the little mare, who had only just returned from the village and had more work to do this night, but she couldn't turn back now.

Mrs. Lavishtock watched from the housekeeper's window and shook her head. *Not now, girlie, not now. This doesn't feel right.* She had to do something.

Barely able to discern the outline of the lane, Madelene could only hope Silver knew the way better than she could guide her. Once through the stoned archway onto the road to Ludlow, she breathed a sigh of relief.

She had done it! She was on her way home. As the little gig continued down the road and farther away from Westcott Close, she wondered what Matthew would say when he arrived home. Would he be angry or extremely relieved she had returned unharmed from her little misadventure called marriage?

Yes, her marriage. Her husband. Without a doubt, Matthew would understand her need to be home, but she could never discuss her husband's breathless kisses and his heated touch. And the pull she felt even now.

Madelene knew she couldn't go back. She might have hoped her anger would trigger a great deal of hatred toward her husband, but her enmity appeared in short supply. He had made her want him, and this would never do.

She had every intention of getting an annulment.

If only her husband had stayed away from her. Perhaps they could have been friends and enjoyed each other's company until the time came when she would have to leave. They could have parted on convivial terms.

Madelene closed her eyes. She couldn't fool herself. She and Mr. Westcott could never live under the same roof and remain only friends. He had taught her that lesson with one passionate soul-locking kiss. She found herself wishing he would not be angry with her after learning she had escaped. But she would never know.

Silver trotted down the road, the night warm and silent, only her thoughts or regrets to accompany her on the journey.

Except a mile from Westcott Close, the carriage jerked and bumped as if it hit something. The gig suddenly pitched to the right. Madelene dropped the reins to hold on to the sides of the carriage to prevent falling out. But the next jerk of the carriage pitched her into the side, where she hit her head on the frame. The little gray must have felt something amiss, because she stopped and started to back up, then halted.

Leaning heavily toward the right and holding fast to the side of the carriage, Madelene looked down to discover the reason for her misfortune.

A wheel had fallen off. *Oh, the devil's foot!*

What to do? Maybe she could hook the wheel back on the carriage? Better to investigate what could be done first.

After untangling her skirt and cloak, she crawled out of the gig and fell onto the nearby embankment. Sitting on the small hill, she tried to catch her breath by breathing in the sweet grass. More than a little frightened, she rubbed her head where she had bumped it. Thankfully, the bump was her only injury, when it could have been much worse. But it still pained her.

She sat on the green-grassed rise next to the road to debate her next move. Of all the addle-pated ideas, when she could have been safely sleeping. If only the gig hadn't lost its wheel, but then at the present, she had no use for castigations. She sighed.

Past midnight, the only people out this late would be either highwaymen or neighbors heading home from a dance. She hoped to meet one of the latter and certainly not one of the former. Madelene couldn't stop shuddering, although the night remained seasonably warm. When she looked down the dirt road, first to the right, then to the left, the road remained empty but for a few oaks lining each side.

How quickly her night had gone from excitement to disappointment. No help for it, she would simply have to turn back. Obviously, she hadn't planned for any contingencies, consumed by her urgent flight.

Lost in thought, Madelene finally noticed Silver walking back and forth, trying to break free from the gig. Concerned the little gray might hurt herself, she knew she should probably unhitch the carriage. Once off the rise, she walked over to Silver to try and calm her. Grabbing the bridle, she stroked the horse's neck. "Good girl, good girl," she whispered.

"Are you going somewhere?"

Madelene recognized the voice immediately and stilled her hand and her heart. Surprised, she couldn't move.

Her husband. How had he found her? And so soon? Perhaps there was still time for a highwayman to happen along. She thought she'd rather face that fear than the wrath her husband had surely planned to rain on her head.

Still holding onto the horse's bridle, she walked to the other side of Silver to find Mr. Westcott on a big black horse, staring down at her. The man and horse blended into the darkness, adding to his mysterious appearance. As if a dark wish had been made by someone who was not her guardian angel. She could only surmise her husband must be completely vexed with her.

Her courage in tatters around her, she replied, "Not at the present time. We have appeared to have lost a carriage wheel," she told him, feeling slightly nauseous while waiting for his anger to show itself, and watched in alarm as he dismounted and walked over to her. His eyes remained steady on hers the closer he came.

"Are you hurt?" His voice sounded more troubled than irate.

His rough voice confused her. *Why did he ask as if he cared about the answer?*

Madelene rubbed the bump on her head. "I bumped my head, but—"

He reached over and brought her hand down before removing his glove and examining her head for himself. His nearness was quite unnerving. Standing breaths away, he gently touched the general area. "Yes, I do feel something there. You will probably feel the results of your expedition in the morning, nothing more." He left her side to walk back to inspect the gig and the wheel lying on its side.

Shaking his head, he returned to unhook Silver from the dead weight of the gig, as Madelene continued to hold the horse's bridle and coo to Silver. She watched as her husband returned to his saddle to retrieve a rope, then walked back to tie it to Silver's lead.

Clearing his throat, he said, "Mrs. Westcott, you can either ride or you can walk, but I can assure you, riding will be much faster and certainly easier on your feet. I'll send Cappie back in the morning to retrieve the carriage and the wheel."

Madelene had watched the scene unfold with her heart in her hands waiting for his anger to boil over and burn her. Perhaps he had something else in mind? Like more of his kisses? Surely he wouldn't consider that punishment; at least *he* couldn't be sure *she* didn't have those thoughts.

Mr. Westcott threw himself on the back of his black steed and looked down at her with raised eyebrows, waiting expectantly for her decision. He would give nothing away by his demeanor.

She knew she had little choice in the matter. Pride would make her walk, but fatigue proved her downfall. When she finally found her voice, she replied, "Mr. Westcott, I, I would prefer riding back to the house." With great trepidation, she drew closer to his restless horse and spoke louder, looking up to her husband with what she hoped would be a sincere apology written on her expression.

No sooner had the words left her than Mr. Westcott leaned down with one arm and swept her onto the horse, settling her between the pommel and his own very warm, hard body.

Since she had intended to sit behind him, she struggled before he whispered in her ear, "Surely you can endure being this close to me for the short duration it will take to return home. I promise not to take advantage of your nearness." The last words almost had a smile in them.

She looked up at him, trying to read his thoughts, as Mr. Westcott heighed his steed. With Silver meekly following behind, they started toward home.

Mr. Westcott looked down at her upturned face and told her gruffly, "Madelene, do not look at me in that manner or you will receive what you told me earlier was only a substitute for, what did you call it, revenge?"

Swallowing hard, she looked out into the night. It was an uncomfortable seat until he lifted her onto his thighs, which made the ride somewhat smoother. And brought her ever so close to him and every hard unrelenting part of him. He might not want to take advantage of her presence, but since he enveloped her in his heat, with his arms around her, she felt drawn to him. Wanted to feel his lips again, one last time.

She whispered to him as he leaned toward her. "I am greatly relieved you found me. I—"

"We'll talk no more about it. We have a lot of work to do tomorrow." They continued their brief journey home in silence while Madelene wondered how her husband had known where to find her. Had Alec seen her?

"Mr. Westcott, please don't punish Alec. I imagine he told you how to find me."

He didn't answer, as if considering her plea. "I'll take care of Alec. No need to worry punishment awaits him. I don't think either of us expected such a clever girl, or that you would want to depart my company so soon."

Did he refer to her in such admiring terms? This night was most definitely not ending the way she had imagined.

No further words were spoken until they returned to the stables. A groomsman, who must have heard the horses' hooves on the lane, appeared to handle the horses.

As they walked toward the main house, Mr. Westcott inquired, "How is your head? Is there anything I might offer for it?" Appearing most solicitous, he held her arm, sensing her unsteadiness on her feet and probably because he was more familiar with the path.

"No, I think sleep might be my only cure. Thank you, again," she added as an afterthought.

Later in her bed, as she considered the evening's events, and particularly Mr. Westcott, she heard someone at her door and sat up abruptly.

"Mad, Mad, are you in there?"

Chapter Ten

Who called her name? It sounded like her brother, but it couldn't be. She frowned at the bedroom door.

"Mad, it's me, Matthew. Open the door!"

In no time, she had flung herself off her bed and raced to the door, her heart on the other side of happiness. She could hardly believe it—he had finally come for her! He was going to make everything right and take her back where she belonged.

Anxious to greet her brother, she wrenched open the door with a welcoming smile. Before she could issue a greeting, Matthew had brushed past her into the room. She started after him, but another figure stepped in front of her to halt her progress.

She quickly closed the door, relieved Mr. Westcott had sent Alec to bed, assuming she wouldn't try to escape twice in one night.

She turned to greet her brother. "Matthew, I'm so happy now that you're here! You've come for me, just the way I knew you would!" She swept across the room to hug her brother, who didn't quite return her affection with equal enthusiasm. Not caring to dwell on the matter, she remembered the other man and turned toward him.

"I, I am Matthew's sister, Madelene Colgate, er—Westcott," she finished lamely to the short, quiet man standing by the closed door.

Matthew left her embrace to begin looking around the room and in her cupboard while murmuring offhandedly, "Mad, this is Mr. Leonard Brelford, the man you didn't marry." His caustic humor not lost on her.

Her eyes widened and her jaw dropped. "*You're* Mr. Brelford?" Everything started to make more sense, until she realized what her brother had just said. She turned to admonish him. "Matt, how unfair of you! I had no hand in what happened. This was all because of your plan," she began before he held up his hand.

"You don't need to remind me. We don't have much time, and we have come on a serious matter," he told her abruptly.

She could only stare at him in confusion. "Yes, I'll leave my trunk here and just gather a few things."

Matthew and Brelford exchanged glances.

She looked from one man to the other, frowning. "What are you about? Surely you have come to rescue me from this marriage. Are we to have an annulment?" Madelene paused. "I don't wish to sound rude, but I really have no desire to marry anyone else," she told her brother, while sinking onto the edge of her bed.

"Mad, where is your trunk? It is most imperative I see it. I, I hid something in there that I've come to retrieve."

Madelene shook her head. "What are you talking about? My trunk is over by the window. But I can assure you it is quite empty. I can have my things sent for later—"

Matthew looked over at his friend and rubbed the back of his neck. Then he threw himself into a nearby chair.

"Mad, it, we, we, can't take you back with us, not now. There is something more important we need your help with." His face showed the same fear as when they first spoke of the marriage wager. His chalky white skin and sharp eyes convinced Madelene his reason for being here was indeed serious.

But she could hardly accept his mission had nothing whatsoever to do with her. Perhaps if she explained her predicament to Matthew, he would have a better understanding and would reconsider.

"Matthew, it has really become impossible—"

"Madelene, we simply have no time for further discussion." He began to pace the room

Stunned, she looked from one gentleman to the other. "You aren't taking me back to Town or to Aunt Bess's? But I don't understand, why—"

He obviously did not wish to waste time with a prolonged explanation. "You have the dagger, and I need it or it could be absolutely disastrous."

If she had thought the situation bleak, in that moment, it became exceedingly unsolvable. *Dagger?* She faintly recalled Matthew mentioning a dagger recently. Why ever would he think she had it?

Her heart in her stomach, she rose from the bed, still unable to accept that he had not come all this way for her, but for a *dagger*. Shoulders back, she told him evenly, "Matthew, I do *not* know of any dagger. Why would I have it in my possession? And why is it so very important?"

"I hid it in your trunk, planning to remove it before you left for Aunt Bess's." He demanded, "Where is it? We must return it." He couldn't stop pacing, even checking the trunk to make sure it was empty.

"But I have told you, I don't have it." She couldn't think

how to convince her brother, nor could she offer a plausible idea of its location, if it had indeed been in her trunk.

Could someone here have searched my trunk and stolen it? Who?

In that brief moment of silence, they heard voices in the hallway outside her bedchamber.

"It must be Alec or Mr. Westcott. Perhaps they might know . . ." She trailed off, her eyes widening, as she watched her brother and Mr. Brelford launch to the window in an obvious effort to escape detection.

She raced to the window to stop them. "Matthew, Mr. Brelford, surely we can solve this dilemma." Diplomacy and a rational mind might sway her argument.

"I'll be back for the dagger, Madelene. I must have it within a fortnight," her brother told her roughly. Then they were gone. Out the window.

Madelene leaned out the window, still believing she could halt their escape. She had to convince her brother to take her with him. He needed her help. As always.

She heard a soft knock, then the door open behind her.

"Madelene, Alec told me that he heard men's voices in here," Gabriel said in a tight voice. "I assured him it wasn't possible."

She glanced at Gabriel, eyes bright with unshed tears, and shook her head, then flew past him and out the door.

Whatever is she running to—or running from? Hasn't Madelene had enough adventure for one night?

He and Alec followed close on her heels with Falstaff running behind them, barking at the excitement.

At the top of the stairs, Gabriel grabbed her arm, but she threw him off and hurdled down the stairs to the front door, allowing no time for explanation, her nightclothes billowing behind her.

Curious to see Madelene's flight in her nightclothes at this time of night, he helped her unlock the large front doors and pull them open. Together, they ran outside onto the front steps to watch two riders whip past them down the lane, toward the main road.

Gabriel thought one rider looked familiar. Of course! One of the riders was Madelene's brother, Matthew Colgate. *What was he doing here? Has he come to take Madelene from me?* His jaw tightened. *What else could it possibly be? And yet, she remained here. What could have gone wrong?* From his knowledge of Madelene's brother's character, Gabriel had no doubt Matthew planned some type of nefarious business.

His only concern was for his wife, who continued to stare down the driveway, long after any sighting of the riders was possible, having lost them to the night. Gabriel stood next to her, not touching her, but wanting to be near.

He knew he needed to remain aloof to this woman, needed to prove to himself she was only a means to an end. A beautiful means.

But he brushed these thoughts aside when he caught her as she swayed and brought her gently down to the steps with his arms tight around her. She stared into the darkness, seemingly in a daze. He didn't know what to do or what she needed. He could only hold her.

Without warning, Madelene bent over, hugging her stomach, as if in pain. But he didn't, wouldn't let her go. She shook in his arms as a terrible sorrow seemed to overwhelm her, racking her body with unspent grief. She wrapped her arms tightly around her waist as if to ward off the pain or keep it in, he couldn't tell which, and couldn't know whether she even knew he was there, by her side.

At first, he didn't hear her.

"Father, what can I do? I didn't think it would ever hurt this much. How could Matthew do this to me?" she whispered. Tears streaked her face and pasted strands of her hair to her cheeks.

He could give her no answers but simply rocked her in his arms while brushing her hair from her face. He didn't say anything. There wasn't anything *to* say. He was the reason she was here and not at home with her brother, where she belonged. But he couldn't regret what had brought them together and vowed to somehow make this right.

Gabriel lost track of the time sitting on the stone porch with Madelene in his arms on this late spring night. He held her until she fell asleep, exhausted, probably, from her curtailed flight and her brother's mysterious abandonment.

In the hushed silence of the early-morning hour, Gabriel swept his arm underneath Madelene and carried her up the stairs to her bedchamber. As if she could be broken, he carefully laid her on her bed and stood looking down at her. Pale cheeks rubbed pink, the curve of her sweet but sad mouth, her long dark hair brushed over one shoulder.

He knew of only one way to ease her pain, but he couldn't do it. He just couldn't.

Nothing more could be done, so Gabriel left Falstaff lying on the floor by her bed. The little dog would provide a modicum of comfort and watch over her.

Chapter Eleven

Usually Madelene would be pleased at the pretty picture she made with her robin's-egg muslin dress and beribboned hair, but she was still lost in a fog of bewildering sadness. Her own brother didn't want her, and his betrayal struck deep. Indeed, Matthew didn't seem concerned in the slightest at her situation.

And the man she had married? An enigma. She might never know why he had chosen her as his wife other than the obvious reason—to increase his own coffers.

Last night's surprising conclusion was still an act of tragic proportions. She could not begin to understand or conceive what the next act would reveal.

The dagger. She brightened slightly at the thought that if she could find it for Matthew, he would allow her to return with him. Her new resolution: to find the dagger, the center of her brother's torment, for he had never sounded so strange nor so desperate before. What trouble had found him, or had he found, was more likely the question.

Voices in the rose drawing room drew her to the entrance. Peering into the open door, she found Mr. Westcott and a strange man engrossed in their conversation, which ended abruptly at her arrival. She gave her husband a half smile and turned to walk down the hall. After all the commotion she had caused him last night, Madelene was quite wary of her husband's reception.

But he forestalled her. "My dear, please come in. I'd like to introduce you to a friend of mine, Mr. Hayden Bush." Mr. Westcott crossed the dusted and cleaned rose Axminister carpet and extended his hand to greet her warmly. She accepted his hand as they returned to their guest, who sat on one of the red brocade chaise longues, a wooden cane by his side.

"Bush, I'd like to present my wife, Miss, rather, Mrs. Madelene Colgate Westcott," he announced to his friend in an almost proud voice.

Madelene hesitated, waiting for their guest to respond, and when he didn't, she told him, "Mr. Bush, I'm glad to welcome you to our home." She hoped her sentiment didn't ring as false to their guest as it did to her own ears. Her heart had no optimism to playact a loving couple.

Their guest, Mr. Bush, turned his head and looked in her direction with an unfixed stare and a smile. His handsome face surprised her for some reason, his green eyes vacant. She couldn't help but return his smile, even if he couldn't see it.

Their guest wore deep brown pantaloons and matching top coat, his dark hair brushed in the latest style. Someone obviously looked after him with great care. She wanted to touch his hand or his face, her motherly instincts urging her to reach out to him.

"Westcott, is your wife as beautiful as she sounds?" His pleasant voice alight with humor.

Madelene dropped her jaw at the unexpected compliment, but Mr. Westcott laughed.

"She certainly is all that and more." Her husband must have noticed her disconcertment because he turned to her to explain. "My dear, my friend Mr. Bush lost his sight during a childhood sickness. We've been neighbors and friends for most of our lives."

"Yes, Westcott brings me news from Town of anything important, such as whether we are making any headway with that Napoleon or the latest *on dit* of acquaintances. Purely for amusement, I assure you."

During his reply, Gabriel seated Madelene in a nearby chair before returning to prop himself on the desk near the marble fireplace.

Mr. Bush continued, "Westcott, you, as usual, are the lucky one to have found the lovely Mrs. Westcott to take you as a husband. It must have been quite a task to get him to the altar, would you not say, Mrs. Westcott?" Clever man and no doubt keen of hearing, he directed his question to her, knowing her location in the room.

Startled, Madelene thought the man could not have been more mistaken. His question left her uncomfortable, and she furrowed her brow, trying to think of a suitable reply. An answer that would save both of their prides. What had Gabriel told his friend?

When her husband came to her rescue she sighed in relief. "Nay, Bush, it was I who was most interested in ensuring Miss Colgate met me at the altar. Indeed, I am most fortunate that she agreed to be my wife." His words almost convinced Madelene he spoke the truth or to tease her. Which could it be?

She hurried to add, "Mr. Bush, I understand it has been some time that Westcott Close has been occupied. You and my husband must have much to discuss."

Their neighbor nodded. "Yes, I've missed our talks on politics and our chess games."

Madelene frowned, thinking she had heard incorrectly.

But her husband laughed. "Mrs. Westcott, it is simply Bush's idea of humor."

"Oh, of course." Madelene bit her lip, trying to think of something clever or witty to say. Before another awkward moment passed, she rose and asked their visitor, "Has my husband offered you some refreshment?"

Mr. Bush stood, leaning on his cane ever so slightly. "Thank you, Mrs. Westcott, but I had breakfast before I left home. I appreciate your hospitality."

Madelene smiled slightly. "As I'm sure my husband has told you, we are in the midst of settling in and opening the house. I hope when we have everything in order you could perhaps join us for dinner?"

Nodding, their guest told her, "It would be the greatest of pleasures, Mrs. Westcott. I look forward to the event with much anticipation."

Prepared to depart the room, Madelene walked to his side and touched his arm. "It was a pleasure to meet you, but now I must now beg your leave to see to our housekeeper. She had an unfortunate spill yesterday." She turned to leave the room when a lone curl slipped onto her forehead, reminding her of what she needed to ask her husband.

"Mr. Westcott, I didn't have the opportunity to ask you last night. Did you remember to bring a lady's maid with you from the village?" As soon as the words left her lips, Madelene worried Mr. Bush might wonder why she had not brought her own lady's maid to the marriage. She added hastily, "You remember, my lady's maid had taken ill before we left Town." Her pleading eyes met his.

Thankfully, he confirmed her subterfuge. "Yes, I do recall your lady's maid could not attend you. However, Mrs. Westcott, I did neglect to ask at the village. There hasn't been the need for a lady's maid here in some time. Perhaps one of the housemaids might serve until we can find someone more suitable?"

Another day with doing her own hair? The result, she concluded, was she must continue to wear her hair in a simple fashion, since the latest hair trends were more intricate than she could manage on her own. And she felt too young to wear a mobcap, even if she was a married lady.

She responded in an even tone. "Of course, I will see what can be done. Mr. Bush, will you join us for lunch?"

"Thank you, Mrs. Westcott. I will only darken your doorstep for a few minutes more before I return home."

"I disagree. You've brightened our household with your presence. I look forward to your next visit," she replied, then departed for the kitchen, determined to have a word with the new cook, reluctantly remembering last night's disasterous dinner.

When she closed the door behind her, Falstaff appeared from nowhere to confront her and began barking. Surprised, Madelene refrained from her purpose down the hall. Small though he might be, on all fours, he was yet another guard for Madelene.

She sighed. He wouldn't hurt her, would he? After all, he was such a small little thing, and his tail wagged, which she thought a positive sign. Madelene tried again to walk down the hall, but he continued to growl at her.

Unwilling to wage battle with something with sharper teeth, she hesitated.

"Ah, Mr. Westcott," she cried softly before raising her voice. "Mr. Westcott!"

Her husband jerked the door open to find Falstaff looking at Madelene, who stood braced against the wall.

"Falstaff, come here!" he commanded, and the little

dog ran over and sat at his master's feet, banging his tail on the shiny wood floor.

Mr. Westcott smiled. "I see our Falstaff is bothering his mistress again." He looked over at her. "My dear, you will love him after you get to know each other better. He's actually quite harmless, except, of course, to rats." He bent down to scratch Falstaff behind the ears.

With a sigh, she informed him, "I sincerely doubt your dog and I will ever have a mutual affection for one another. I would greatly appreciate it if you would make sure he stays out of my way in the future." Confident the matter closed, Madelene put her shoulders back and marched down the hall.

Gabriel whispered in Falstaff's ear. "She's a bit of a shrew, but has a soft heart. Go follow her, she might give you a biscuit!"

At the word "biscuit," Falstaff tore down the hall, past Madelene, and toward the kitchen, seeking his promised treat.

As Madelene followed her nemesis, she decided the kindness her husband had shown her was all for his friend's benefit.

Reflecting on the night past, she realized he must have carried her to her bedchamber, because she couldn't recall arriving there of her own accord. Her brow furrowed in deep thought. She wondered if her husband's thoughts toward her were as unsettling as hers toward him.

Mr. Westcott. He certainly was a puzzlement. She sighed and shook her head. Indeed, he would not be *her* mystery to solve.

Concentrate. That was what she must do. She needed to find the dagger Matthew had mentioned and take it to him. But where to start? She didn't know where to look for the dagger, and she didn't know Matthew's whereabouts.

He was in trouble yet again. And like before, no matter what he had done, she had to fix it.

So, where indeed could this dagger be? If the dagger had not been stolen on the way to Shropshire, which she sincerely doubted, then someone here must have taken it.

Only two possibilities: her husband or Alec, not including the whole household. Which one and why?

While pondering her brother's dilemma, she stopped at the housekeeper's door to listen. When she heard Mrs. Lavishtock issuing loud snores, Madelene continued to the kitchen where she found a housemaid crying on a small stool near the cold fireplace.

"Why ever are you crying? What can be the matter?" Madelene reached the servant's side and touched her arm.

The housemaid leapt to her feet at her mistress's touch and dashed tears from her cheeks. "Oh, miss, I mean, mistress, I didn't mean for you to find me like this."

"Why the tears? Please tell me what has happened. Has anyone treated you ill? Have you been left all alone in the kitchen? Did Mr. Westcott not bring a cook with him yesterday?" Madelene didn't know where to begin to see to the situation.

The housemaid wrung her hands, avoiding Madelene's concerned gaze. The slender maid with reddened eyes, a small round face, and white complexion hesitated before replying. "Well, ye see, Mrs. Compton, the new cook, had words with Mrs. Lavishtock last night, and rather undone, Mrs. Compton left early this morning. Leaving me alone here, and I don't know what to do effen someone doesn't tell me."

How strange. What could Mrs. Lavishtock have said to the cook to anger her? With no help for it, Madelene shook her head, thinking about the time lost looking for the dagger while she saw to household matters. "We shall handle the kitchen until a new cook can be found. What is your name?"

"Fanny, ma'am."

Madelene rolled up her sleeves and found an apron hanging on a hook. "Then, Fanny, with the two of us, we shall put everything to rights. No need for more tears. I know my way about the kitchen. Clean yourself up, then carve the chicken remains from last night. We'll make sandwiches, then we'll start dinner preparations. Of course, this is only temporary until we have Mrs. Lavishtock's services and a new cook."

Fanny's little face brightened at Madelene's instructions, obviously glad for direction.

"Ruff, ruff." Him again. Madelene looked down to see Falstaff sitting next to her feet, his tail still flapping. She was quite relieved he no longer growled or barked at her. A decided improvement in their relationship.

"Oh, Mrs. Westcott, the little dog likes his biscuits. Would you like to give it to him?" Fanny hastened away before Madelene could reply.

The little dog stared hungrily as Fanny handed Madelene a hard biscuit. Cautious, Madelene knelt to lay the treat in front of the dog and jumped away to avoid any contact with sharp teeth.

Falstaff grabbed it up and ran into a corner of the kitchen, apparently to enjoy it and to prevent anyone from taking it from him or having to share, Madelene thought in bemusement.

With Fanny's help, Madelene soon had soup warming at the fireplace and a rabbit on the spit for their evening meal. Fortunately, Mr. Westcott had brought back a month's worth of supplies along with the now-departed cook. As she wrung the lettuce for a salad, Madelene smiled. While she enjoyed cooking, she loved baking even more. Maybe there would be time tomorrow for a plum cake.

Madelene's eyes widened. How could she be thinking about baking when she had to find the dagger? And although she wasn't planning to become a permanent member of the household, she couldn't very well neglect it until she left.

Perhaps it would not be too long before they found a cook. She must remember to advise Mr. Westcott of the need to return to the village to find another, less easily nettled cook.

A brief visit with Mrs. Lavishtock brought relief to learn the housekeeper thought to be up and about tomorrow and able to supervise in the kitchen. Her ankle appeared to be giving her less pain, for which Madelene was grateful.

While in the kitchen working with Fanny, Madelene did not see Mr. Westcott all day and she wondered what kept him occupied. To her frustration, she had no time to search for the dagger. The day hurried into late afternoon before she realized it. With only a short time to dress for dinner, she left the kitchen in Fanny's capable hands. The young woman needed only more confidence and, in time, would make a fine cook.

In her bedchambers, Madelene stretched her arms, her back sore from the day's work. She had not had to work this hard before, perhaps ever. Although her bed looked inviting, she needed to make herself presentable for the evening meal. Quickly bathing in cold water, she found the least wrinkled gown of soft pink that matched her cheeks; a dress she had always thought becoming.

Viewing her appearance in the looking glass, she was

very proud of the curls she managed to arrange at the sides and top of her head. Perhaps Mr. Westcott wouldn't notice the back of her head, which she felt might look a bit wraggled.

On the way down the main staircase to join her husband for dinner, she noticed the glass chandelier glowing with white candles and illuminating the gold-damasked walls and black tile in the high-ceilinged foyer.

But it was the man at the bottom of the staircase that caught her breath. Mr. Westcott waited for her with a warm smile on his handsome visage, wearing black pantaloons and a black cutaway coat, and looked ever so appealing. His stare unnerved her as she descended the stairs, which caused her to blush even more, remembering their kiss from the night before.

On equal footing, she placed her hand in his and watched as he bowed to place a soft kiss on her hand. Her eyes widened when he turned her hand over and placed a kiss on her palm. She jumped in surprise and laughed at her foolishness.

"My dear, you certainly look fetching tonight. I am a most admiring audience of one," he complimented her, escorting her down the corridor and into the dining room.

One of the footmen, Hazelby, she recalled his name, seated her at the table while her husband sat at the head of the table. She might be pleased with his courteousness, but she had difficulty forgetting, at times, that she was a prisoner. Like now. "I haven't seen my guard, Alec all day?" she mentioned, unable to keep annoyance from her voice, dampening the bright new start they had made this morning.

"Alec has other duties to occupy himself." He sipped his glass of red wine, then added, "I had hoped we had moved past our rancor and division. However, as you know, unless you are able to give me your word that you will not try to dash back to London and find your brother or annul this marriage, then I or Alec will be your companion."

She watched him resume eating his dinner, the matter obviously closed.

Since she couldn't say yea or nay on the matter, she picked up her fork to begin eating.

Silence reigned briefly while they dined on the first course of pea soup. "This is a great improvement over last night's repast. And to what can I credit the change?" Mr. Westcott's voice most pleasant.

A very good question. Madelene wondered if her husband knew how hard she had worked in the kitchen to arrange their dinner and whether it was relevant to mention it. She played with her fork before replying, "I gave one of the new girls, Fanny, a few pointers and suggestions, which I learned from my old housekeeper. Apparently the cook you hired did not get on well with some of the other staff." She dared a look in his direction, wondering what his reaction would be.

"Madelene, I must commend you and Fanny on a superb meal and offer my sincere apologies for not selecting a suitable cook in the first place. I did learn earlier we needed a new cook and have been assured we shall have a new one come the morning. Mrs. Lavishtock has also informed me in a most cryptic manner, I might add, that she would be in the kitchen tomorrow and you were to, how did she say, 'rest your pretty head on my shoulder.' Apparently your culinary skills will no longer be necessary. But I will need your assistance in other areas. We must discuss what needs to be done here at Westcott Close."

She blinked in surprise at his oratory, then sighed in relief. Her husband was pleased with her? Since her father and brother had considered her merely an ornament in their home to feed and polish, they had no real use for her. Madelene sat a little taller in her chair with a contented little smile on her lips.

Now if she could bring the conversation around to the dagger. If he didn't know of its existence, then it could only be Alec. How best to broach the subject? And what would his reaction be? Would he help her if he knew he was helping her brother?

Hazelby served the second course of greens and cauliflower before returning with the sliced rabbit. They continued their dinner in awkward silence, with Madelene considering and discarding ideas of how to pursue finding the dagger.

When the footman brought the apple tarts up from the kitchen, Madelene started feeling a bit light-headed. *It is probably the wine,* she thought.

Madelene doubled over from a sharp stab of pain in her stomach, a hot flush drenching her skin. She needed the privacy of her bedchamber before she became grievously ill. Her chair pushed back, she looked at her husband.

"Mr. Westcott, I find that I'm—" and she fainted.

Chapter Twelve

Gabriel rushed to Madelene's side, raised her shoulders and head from the floor, and put his arms around her. He immediately noted her flushed face and felt her clammy hands. What was wrong with his wife?

"Hazelby, send one of the footmen to the village for the doctor, and hurry. Mrs. Westcott is very ill. And send Fanny to me," he commanded before lifting Madelene in his arms and carrying her up the stairs and down the hallway to her bedchamber.

Fanny arrived not long after he had laid Madelene on her bed and removed her shoes in an effort to make her comfortable. When he felt her cheeks with the back of his hand, the heat nearly burned him, sending him to the basin for cool water. Returning, he placed the cool cloth on her forehead, hoping it might help to bring relief.

Standing nearby, but looking helpless and frightened, Fanny waited for instructions. Gabriel knew the maid wanted to help, but even he could not be sure what needed to be done. While he might appreciate her presence, he wouldn't allow the young woman to take his place at his wife's side. He needed to be the one to stroke her face, arms, and hands with another cold cloth.

Gabriel looked at the door several times while waiting for the doctor's appearance. *Please, please let my wife return to her former self, with no lasting harm done her,* he prayed to whoever might be listening.

In great concern, Gabriel watched as Madelene returned slowly to consciousness and rolled from side to side, holding her belly and moaning softly. When she needed to retch, he held the bucket Fanny had provided. Over and over again, he brushed her hair away from her face and talked in a low voice to her. Fanny stood by his side, watching and wringing her hands.

When Dr. Goodman arrived, Gabriel refused to leave the room, but stood by the fireplace, his heart in his throat. She had to get well. She had to. Was her sickness his fault? This situation reminded him of the time his sister was sick, and he could do naught for her. Was history to repeat itself? He would do anything if she would just look at him with those heated blue eyes and tell him he was a liar, a fraud. But if she asked him to free her of these matrimonial bonds, could he say yes?

Goodman immediately sent Fanny for a mixture of warm milk and salad oil to continue inducing all the contents from her stomach. After a few hours, when her stomach was nearly empty of anything she had eaten, the doctor declared her much improved. Goodman, Gabriel, and Fanny all watched with trepidation until Madelene fell into a deep sleep.

Gabriel walked over to the doctor, standing by Madelene's bedside, and said quietly, "She seems to be doing better. Do you know what happened and what caused her to become so ill?"

Goodman narrowed his eyes at Gabriel. "Mr. Westcott, I am of the opinion that she may have been poisoned."

Poisoned! It was the last answer he expected. Gabriel took a step back and grasped the bedpost in bewilderment. "I, what, how can you be sure?"

"I've seen these signs more often than I'd like. Probably a simple vegetable poison. However, she is a lucky little thing. She didn't ingest enough of the poison for any permanent damage," he intoned while reaching for his bag. "She will be extremely thirsty when she awakens. I would have barley-water and milk broth prepared for her. And I assume I don't need to instruct you to have someone watch her during the night."

Gabriel's mouth grim throughout this ordeal, he nodded but took no notice of the doctor's departure. His watchful gaze never left Madelene as she slept. Although Fanny wanted to remain, he sent her to bed. He wanted to be alone with his thoughts and his wife. Could what Goodman said be true, or could he be wrong about his diagnosis? Could someone have deliberately poisoned Madelene or was it an accident? Who might want Madelene dead?

In examining all possibilities, he wondered if Madelene would have ingested just enough poison to make herself sick but not cause death. Gabriel refused to give this more than a passing thought. Not the Madelene he knew. She loved life too much.

Unfortunately, it certainly now appeared he had to keep her safe from harm from her brother, the count, and a new unknown entity. With too many questions and no answers, sleep finally arrested him, although it was more like a catnap, because even with his eyes closed, he remained attuned to every breath she took, every sigh she made. He thanked God he would have a chance to make it up to her.

The next morning, Madelene awoke, her mouth dry. A glass of water would be welcome. She sat up slowly and noticed she still wore her gown from the previous night, although it had been severely loosened. Brushing the sleep from her eyes, she saw Gabriel sitting next to her bed and frowned. What was he doing here? Watching her as she slept?

She must have disturbed his sleep because he jumped from his chair and went immediately to her side, concern and alarm showing in his deep brown eyes.

"How do you feel?" he asked, taking her hand.

"I'm a little tired but very thirsty," she told him sleepily. She did not have the forbearance to ask why he was in her bedchamber.

He retrieved a glass of barlcy-water and handed it to her.

When she sniffed her glass and raised her eyebrows, he said, "Dr. Goodman thought it best if you drank barley-water for a day or so. Do you have any remaining ill effects from last night?" His sharp glance told her that he would find the answers one way or the other.

"From last night?" She closed her eyes to remember. "I recall taking dinner with you before I felt remarkably ill. I've never felt that way before." She opened her eyes and blushed, remembering her sickness and how he watched her retching into a bucket. "You and Fanny were here, to help me, then the pain went away. That is all I remember until now."

Gabriel told her briefly of the night's events and of the doctor's visit, but neglected to her inform her of the reason for her sickness. She needed more time to convalesce.

"Why don't you rest? If you're feeling better, I'll have someone bring you something to eat."

She nodded and sank back into a deep sleep.

A great burden lifted from his shoulders. He smiled and bent over her, removing a lock of hair from her cheek and smoothing it back. He longed to stay close to her, but he had a lot to do, namely finding what or who had poisoned his wife. In the meanwhile, he'd post Alec at her door, this time to prevent anyone from entering instead of preventing her from leaving.

Gabriel looked at the occupants of the bright yellow parlor waiting to be addressed. They were all there as requested: Windthorp, from his past military experience, standing at attention at the window; Mrs. Lavishtock worrying what looked to be a beaded necklace; Alec, slumped in a chair with hat over his face; the new butler, a young man by the name of Graham, sitting in earnest attention near Mrs. Lavishtock; and Hazelby, standing near the door. He had gathered them together because he trusted them all and needed their assistance.

Sitting behind a large desk, he began, "Thank you all for attending me. What I have to say is of the utmost importance." Gabriel paused before continuing, knowing his words would be heeded most assuredly. "As you may know, Mrs. Westcott was taken ill last night. When the physician examined her, he concluded she may have been poisoned."

Some of the servants gasped and Mrs. Lavishtock moaned.

"Oh, why couldn't I have prevented it?" she asked no one.

Eyebrows raised, everyone turned to look at the housekeeper, including Gabriel. "Mrs. Lavishtock, why ever do you feel responsible for my wife's condition, unless you know how she may have been poisoned."

"No, no, I know not how. Perhaps if I had been in the kitchen, I meant to say, I might have prevented this disaster."

Tapping a pencil on the table, he replied, "Be that as it may, it doesn't change what happened. Our meeting today is to ensure nothing like it happens in the future."

He stood and walked around to sit on the edge of the desk. "It may have been an accident; however, we can't assume such. I have my suspicions someone may want to harm Mrs. Westcott. Namely, a Count Taglioni."

The name of the possible perpetrator meant nothing to the little group, save one. And that person kept the knowledge to themselves.

Graham stood, his tall lanky frame easily dwarfing everyone in the room. "Begging your pardon, sir, but who is Count Taglioni? Shall we know of his description in order to keep an eye out for him?"

Gabriel smiled at the young man. "Very good, although I'm sure all of you would easily recognize a stranger in our midst at Westcott Close. Taglioni is a rather tall man with black hair, black eyes, and swarthy skin. He's from Italy and speaks both English and Italian."

He rubbed his brow and looked at Alec. "Alec, you'll remain at Mrs. Westcott's door for the time being, letting no one in, unless, of course, they are familiar."

"Mrs. Lavishtock."

The housekeeper pulled herself off the settee. "Yes, Mr. Westcott?"

"You are in charge of whatever Mrs. Westcott takes for food and drink."

Her mouth dour, she bristled slightly. "I know my job, and I'll take care of Mrs. Westcott. She won't be poisoned again from *my* food."

Gabriel ignored her defensive position. "Very reassuring. The rest of you," he turned to the other staff, "please see the doors are kept locked and keep on your guard for anything out of place. Inform me of anything unsettling, and I will deal with it. Remember, Mrs. Westcott must be protected from any danger. I am confident with all of you looking after her, she will be safeguarded. That is all." He strode to the door as the staff, solemn as in church, followed after him. Gabriel didn't inform the staff he planned not to let Madelene out of his sight.

Late that night, after Fanny assured Gabriel that Madelene slept well, he left his own bedchamber and climbed out his window. He had done this many a night when his sister, Lucinda, was ill and wanted his company.

Neither his parents, nor later, Aunt Adelphia knew he crawled out his window onto a tree limb, and climbed his way over to her window, next to his. He would sit on a big branch across from her window, and she would lean on the sill so they could talk.

Tonight and every night from now on, he planned to keep watch over his wife from his favorite spot in the tree, until she would sleep beside him. He could see directly into her bedchamber and watch as she slept. Nothing or no one would take her from him.

* * *

Madelene awoke the next morning to find Alec by the window. She sat up and blinked awake. "Do your duties now require you to be inside my bedroom instead of outside?"

The young man with the ever present low-brimmed hat put his hands in his pockets and slouched a few steps toward her, his eyes ever alert.

Madelene fluttered her hands, trying to dismiss him. "You may go. I feel much better and can look after myself."

"I will help you to escape," he told her.

Madelene blinked several times and frowned. Alec, Mr. Westcott's friend, wanted to help her to escape? This offer made little sense. "I don't understand. Why would you want to help me?"

"Poison. Mr. Westcott, he's dangerous." The young man retuned his gaze to the window.

Madelene took a moment to reply, believing she had heard incorrectly. Her husband poisoned her? Incomprehensible. "You must be mistaken. You believe *Mr. Westcott* tried to poison me? But why?" Her mouth felt as dry as flour.

Alec hesitated. "He loves another." He walked to the door, then turned back to her. "Tonight, ten o'clock, outside the kitchen. We'll walk to Ludlow, then hire a coach for Town."

He slipped out the door, leaving Madelene to wonder about his words. Gabriel wanted her dead? He loved another? If that were true, why had he married her? All the kindnesses he had shown her were for what purpose? What to believe? Alec's words almost made her ill again.

With the young woman's voice haunting her, anger stirred in her breast. Nothing mattered anymore, certainly not this façade of a marriage. Nothing mattered but finding the dagger for Matthew and returning home. Her maid Millie would be happy to see her, and she could return to her modiste business. Soon Mr. Gabriel Westcott and his machinations would be forgotten.

She rose from bed to dress for the day, determined to concentrate only on the night ahead, not wanting to examine the ache in her heart too closely.

When Mrs. Lavishtock informed her that both Alec and Mr. Westcott had left awhile ago, she breathed a sigh of relief. Her hunt could begin unobstructed; however, it soon became apparent this would not be an easy task.

If either Alec or her husband had stolen the dagger from her trunk, she surmised their bedchambers might be the best place to start. It was her only estimation, unless they carried the object on their person. After peering into many rooms on the first and second floors, she found what had to be Alec's bedchamber, since it was the only one with personal belongings. A quick search of the almost barren room took little time to reveal the missing dagger was not to be found there.

Mr. Westcott's bedchamber was the next room to search. She had noticed the door down the hall from her own and assumed it was his. With spurred heels of conviction, she opened the door and saw it was her husband's room. The largest tester bed she had ever seen occupied the center of the room. She appreciated the vivid backdrop of white walls and curtains to the dark mahogany tables and chairs. A door to the right indicated access to other rooms.

After she stepped inside and closed the door, she heard, then noticed Falstaff standing on the edge of the bed, barking at her.

"Oh, good gracious. How do you happen to know where to find me?" she asked more to herself than to the dog. "Shh, shh, please be quiet." She waved her hand to calm the excited little dog, wishing she had thought to bring a biscuit with her.

Falstaff stopped and sat down, watching her with his head tilted. Was it her imagination or did that little dog follow her? Oh, what a fertile imagination she possessed. At least he had stopped announcing her furtive presence in his master's room.

Relieved, she turned around to face the door, and saw matching cupboards on either side.

Perfect.

She opened the first one to a warm musky scent of Gabriel's clothing of fine coats and linen shirts.

Falstaff commenced his sharp barking. "Ruff, ruff, ruff."

"Can I help you find something?" Her husband's voice taunted her from behind the cupboard door.

Chapter Thirteen

Madelene pursed her lips and turned to face her husband, searching for a plausible explanation as to why she had her head in his closet. She slowly shut the cupboard and leaned back against it.

"Mr. Westcott, I thought you were in the village." She prevaricated while she waited for something to come to her. A warm smile on his face indicated he was not displeased with finding her here. Or was this a game he played with her?

Mr. Westcott bent to pick up Falstaff, who happily licked his master's hand. If she didn't know better, Madelene would be entirely suspicious of that dog. Her husband stood watching her as he petted Falstaff before setting him back on the floor.

"Madelene, I admit to being surprised finding you here but yet in the same moment, I find myself delighted. You were probably searching for space for your things, when you move into this room with me. I can also deduce you are feeling much better." Satisfied with his own explanation, he walked over to his bed and leaned against the edge with a perfectly charming look upon his face.

Sometimes kindness could be terribly more difficult to thwart than anger or annoyance. Madelene swallowed hard. She opened her mouth, then closed it. Then opened it again. "I, I—yes, I looked to see how much room there was here. I conclude, yes, satisfactory, no doubt. Yes, well, I'll be on my way," she told him, hoping she didn't sound too skittish, her eyes locked on his warm brown gaze. Deciding retreat was the best plan, she edged toward the door, but Mr. Westcott reached it before she did and shut it.

Perhaps Falstaff could distract him, but of course, that little dog was nowhere to be found. Probably hiding under the bed. She thought life would be made ever so much easier if she could determine whether Falstaff was friend or foe.

When Mr. Westcott pinned Madelene with his hands on either side of her head against the door, thoughts of the little dog flew from her mind.

"Please don't go, there's more I'd like to show you," he murmured against her right ear.

She pressed her hands to his chest in a little protest, while averting her face. She wanted, needed his lips to come no closer. She might be doomed if—

"Madelene," he sang in her ear as he brought her arms down to her side and behind her. Captured willingly in the embrace, her breasts meshed into his hard chest, Madelene was ever so near his seeking lips. The heat of his touch, the feel of his unrelenting body, could make a rational person go distinctly addle-pated, she thought dizzily.

He swept in for a soft kiss, which burned into a demanding, fiery branding. Madelene might have swooned if he hadn't held her so tightly. *Oh, why does he make me want this—want him? What is it about this man?*

Think terrible things. Think terrible things. Pestilence, fire, rain, wetness, wrong direction. He didn't want her as his wife, only for his bed. A place where she wanted to be. Hunger. To be filled with his touch, his heat, to be a part of him. Her plan to not desire him was proving ineffective.

He surely didn't kiss like Winchester. This man wouldn't allow her to hold back but demanded everything. She gave as much as he did, seeking to be closer to him than anyone could, while still fully clothed. When she placed her arms around his neck, she pulled herself up to meet his lips more fully, her breasts achingly snug against his chest.

He left her lips to taste the spot beneath her ear as his hand sought one soft breast, teasing, plying and rubbing her nipple through the thin muslin gown.

Madelene moaned, kneading her hands through his soft hair, pulling his mouth to her breast as he strained to gently bite her nipple. Oh, he was doing things to her that he had no right, not for his right as a husband, but because he loved another.

Remembering those painful words, she pushed Mr. Westcott away from her, her chest heaving, her breath difficult to catch.

His brow knitted, his eyes haunted hers. Why? Again?

"I cannot, you—leave me be!" Catching him off guard, she wrenched the door open and fled from his bedchamber to the safety of her own. She knew she must leave tonight. And this time, she would not fail. They could never be together. Fate, surely, had something else in mind for them.

Perplexed, Gabriel watched her flee down the corridor and shook his head. How could one minute she seem so willing and the next be anxious to escape from him, as if she couldn't tolerate his nearness, his touch? *My lovely wife Madelene, perhaps I should let you go home.*

Madelene's small bag packed, she sat on her bed waiting for the clock to near ten. She had taken dinner in her room, and Mr. Westcott had not disturbed her since their embrace earlier. With Alec's help, she knew she could slip away easily enough. But in the event anyone decided to look in on her, say Mr. Westcott, she bundled her pillows and coverlet to look as if she slept.

Inexplicably, she felt torn between leaving and staying. Perhaps she was a coward for wanting to flee this man who had turned her world topsy-turvy. But she would be safer in her own home.

And then there was the matter of the dagger. Matthew wouldn't be happy to see her without it. There was no help for it, she simply couldn't find it.

It was time. She quietly opened the door and slipped down the stairs, her boots muffled on the carpet. All quiet.

She thought to bid farewell to Mrs. Lavishtock but could not find time to prolong her departure when she knew Alec waited for her. Indeed, since Mrs. Lavishtock slept soundly, Madelene hesitated to disturb her.

Opening the servants' door off the kitchen, she observed a dark figure sitting on the stone wall when she opened the door. The figure looked at her and jumped off his perch.

Ready to return home, Madelene gathered her deep blue traveling gown and cloak to step outside when she felt a strong pull on her coat.

Falstaff growled and tugged on the edge of her cloak.

Frustrated, Madelene pulled harder. "Let go, Falstaff," she whispered severely. The little dog was committed to stopping her, or at the least, ripping her cloak, while Madelene was determined he would not have his way. He was a strong little fellow, for certain. Anxious to depart, she hoped the noise he made would not awaken those she wished to continue slumbering.

With a faint rip, Madelene tore her cloak from Falstaff's sharp teeth and shut the door quickly behind her, locking the little guard in the kitchen. As they made their way in the darkness of the night, without the moon to guide them, Alec and Madelene could hear Falstaff barking incessantly. They needed to act in haste, given the dog might have disturbed the residents of Westcott Close—in particular, the master.

Several minutes of hurried steps later, Madelene found following Alec a travail in itself. The young man could easily climb the small hills and stoned fences that separated Westcott Close from their neighbors, while Madelene dragged herself along behind him. Not a mile had gone by before Madelene begged to rest by the dirt road to the village.

"We do not have much time. With the dog barking, he might alarm Mr. Westcott, who will be after us soon. Mr. Westcott has been kind to me, and I do not want him finding I helped you to leave here," Alec told her in his voice-laced accent.

Madelene frowned, looking in Alec's direction with curiosity. Still too dark to really study his features closely, this monologue was the longest she had heard uttered from the young man. His English appeared better than passing. This young man was certainly full of surprises, which made little difference to Madelene.

"How much farther?" Madelene asked, rubbing her left foot.

The young man guffawed, indicating his annoyance

with her. With hands on hips, Alec told her, "About another mile. We must go on. I'll be glad when we're at the inn and you'll be sent on your way." He started down the road again.

Resisting the temptation to linger, Madelene grabbed her bag and hurried after her escort. If he had any manners, he would have offered to carry her bag. But wishful thinking couldn't make Alec act the part of a gentleman.

The quiet night gave her time to think about her rash actions. She wished she had remained safely in bed at Westcott Close; but then she also wanted to get as far away as possible from the unrelenting Mr. Westcott. Little did he know, if she remained, he would soon steal her heart as well as everything else she had to call her own. And still she couldn't understand why the man wanted to remain married to her, especially since she had no wealth to her name, *and* he loved another.

Onward they continued with no words spoken between them. After another mile and disliking the awkward silence between them, Madelene tried to start a conversation, but his grunted answers made it difficult to continue the effort.

Every now and again, they stopped to listen if pounding hooves followed them down the road. Strange, with all the noise Falstaff made, she would have thought someone had alerted everyone to the missing mistress.

Studying Alec's back, Madelene thought black must be his preferred color. All of his clothing—his worn boots, breeches, and coat with a few holes barely patched—were black. She found herself wondering again who he was and what Mr. Westcott had done to warrant such loyalty on this young man's part.

Alec pointed out a shortcut across the meadow. In the darkness, they could have been traveling in circles; at least, that was what Madelene's feet told her. As they walked over the dry grass, in the still blackness, Madelene could hear a faint sound of water. She stopped to listen with a keen ear. Sure enough, as they walked closer, she could hear the rushing water.

"Porter's Creek. I came this way a few days ago. The water might be up to your ankles," Alec told Madelene over his shoulder, continuing his trek over the countryside.

"What? My ankles? I had not planned on getting wet this night, Alec. Alec?" she called to him more loudly. His small figure melded into the night, making it difficult to follow him. She caught up to him fighting the low branches of the trees blocking their path.

Through the small copse of trees, she stopped at the side of the creek and watched Alec trudge through two feet of water, seemingly indifferent to wet feet. That is, until he fell in when he reached the deeper part of the creek. The water was over his head.

Shocked and frozen, Madelene could only stand waiting for Alec to show his head. Anxious moments later, she saw his head bounce up, breaking the water. He did struggle a bit trying to keep his head above water but floundered again. Finally, he gained purchase by paddling over to the more shallow part of the creek and clawed his way on his knees to the bank. Breathing heavily, he rested on the muddy ridge while Madelene sighed, thankful she wouldn't have to rescue him, especially since she couldn't swim.

Madelene called over to him. "Alec, how do you fare? Should I go for help?"

He shook his head but didn't answer her because he was preoccupied looking for something. She watched him search his coat pockets, then his breeches. Empty-handed.

Patting the top of his head, he must have realized he had lost his hat as well during this unexpected bath.

Madelene walked over to the spot on the opposite shore, trying to gain his attention. She yelled louder. "Alec. We need to find a shallower crossing. I can't swim, and you can't leave me here."

He ignored her, still looking anxiously through his pockets and around where he sat.

Madelene shook her head and looked down at the creek bed. Then she saw it.

Something shiny on the creek bed gleamed through the small pebbles.

Could it be? Could it be the dagger?

From each side of the creek, they both lunged for it. Undeterred by her gently bred manners, Madelene pushed Alec hard, sending him into shallow water. She reached the dagger first and grasped the hilt, pulling it from its watery bed. Water soaked her boots in short order, but she ignored the discomfort, staring in disbelief at the silver knife in the palm of her hand.

"The dagger! This is the dagger my brother wanted! You stole it from my trunk!" Madelene's eyes blazed with anger at the young man, then she stopped and stared. Alec rose to his feet, water streaming from his shirt and breeches, and suddenly he seemed more like a she, a young woman with short hair, even in the shadowed dark.

Perhaps it was the wet clothes, but with the dagger still held tightly in her right hand, Madelene's mouth dropped open. How? What? Yes, even in the grim light, her soaking left nothing to the imagination. He was a she.

"You, you're a female!"

As Madelene tried to make sense of the change in circumstances, Alec gained the upper hand and grabbed the dagger. But in her effort to escape, Alec had difficulty picking up her feet in the muddy water to get to the other side of the creek.

She had only turned when Madelene caught the tails of her coat and yanked hard, pulling them both into the wet stony stream. Alec, dagger in hand, thrust toward Madelene's shoulder, but Madelene knocked the dagger out of her slippery grasp, sending it flying back into the water.

Both fell headfirst into the water, reaching for the dagger again. As Alec grappled with Madelene, she shoved Madelene's face into the mud along the creek bed. Fighting back, barely able to breathe, Madelene pushed the smaller girl off and threw her back into the water.

On her knees, Madelene wiped her face with muddy gloves and tried to swish her way over to where she'd seen the dagger land.

Before she realized it, Alec had pulled her legs out from under her, and Madelene sat down hard in the water. The cooling water drenched her gown and cloak.

Molten anger gave Madelene strength to grab Alec by the waist and throw her into the mud, sitting on her. The dagger now lay out of both their reaches as Alec tried to buck Madelene off while Madelene tried to maintain her seat.

"I must have that dagger!" Madelene demanded.

"No, it belongs to my uncle," Alec retorted, waterlogged.

"Well, well, well. This is a sight to behold." They both stilled, hearing Mr. Gabriel Westcott's amused voice.

Chapter Fourteen

Madelene and Alec looked up in surprise to where the dark figure stood by the side of the creek. How long had he been watching, Madelene wondered, and then decided knowing the answer would make little difference. While Madelene stared at Mr. Westcott's dark form, Alec took the upper hand and knocked her to the muddy ground before jumping to her feet.

Exhausted from the long walk and the wrestling match, Madelene sat along the side of the meandering creek, thankful for the warm night, unable to stand in her soaked condition. Her husband must have noticed, because he splashed over to her and pulled her from her wet seat and onto the embankment.

The dagger. She glanced to where she had last seen it, but it was gone. Frowning, she looked at Alec, who watched her husband. Turning to look at Mr. Westcott, she saw him fingering the dagger they both desperately wanted.

Dagger in hand, he walked over to Madelene and Alec. "I'm extremely surprised to find my wife and my young friend traipsing through the meadows and creeks at such a late hour." His mocking tone informed Madelene her journey was at an end for this night.

"If it were not for all the noise Falstaff made to alert me of your departure, you may have made it all the way to Ludlow. However, it does appear that a contention has arisen over this," he said, indicating the dagger. "And until I decide what will become of it, it will remain in my possession."

Mr. Westcott glanced at Alec, then smiled. "I see your gender is no longer male, which is a relief."

Madelene looked from her husband to the wet young woman. "You *knew* she was a female?"

His amusement turned to a serious nature. He replied, "Alec requested I keep her secret. As her friend, I honored her request." He looked at Alec and shrugged. "There's no help for it now. Let's go home and dry out." He stuck the dagger in his belt and held out his hand to help Madelene off the embankment.

Finally able to catch her breath, Madelene looked down and realized what a sight she made after her altercation in the mud. Heaving a heavy sigh, she thought she had never looked so bedraggled. All those times she had been so meticulous with her appearance, and now reduced to muddy warring with an Italian thief.

Her favorite cloak soaked in streaks of black water; one glove missing; short boots ruined; and a missing bonnet. How could one night have ruined everything, including her hope to escape back home?

As she pulled the muddy strands of hair from her face, she looked over at Alec, standing in dirty wet clothes, and began laughing. Madelene couldn't tell who had received the worst of the battle. At least now she knew the location of the dagger.

Shaking out her cloak and gown for little good it did,

she decided a little persuasion was necessary to win the prize. Surely it wouldn't take much for him to understand the story of the dagger and her brother, or what she knew of the story. She opened her mouth to begin but Mr. Westcott interrupted.

"No delaying tactics. We need to get you both back to Westcott Close and out of those wet clothes. As for the dagger, and what shall become of it, we'll talk on it more tomorrow."

Shoulders slumped, Madelene silently agreed perhaps tomorrow would be best, as well as for discovering answers to Alec's presence and surprising transformation. In her current condition, a warm bath was the only thing on her mind that could provide relief from the scratchy drying mud.

Thankfully, Mr. Westcott had driven one of his carriages. How could he have known where to find them? A riddle for another day. Somehow her husband appeared to anticipate her every move, and she didn't exactly welcome the thought.

On their return, Madelene had to admit to herself tonight's journey had been hopeless from the start, especially in trusting the young Italian man, nay, woman. Alec and Madelene sat opposite each other in the carriage for the ride home, which took no time after seemingly taking hours to escape from Westcott Close. Ignoring the little Italian thief, which was how Madelene thought of Alec, she stewed in her rancid wet condition, while Gabriel whistled, sitting on the box next to Grimes, one of the groomsmen.

After a warm bath Fanny had drawn for her in the kitchen, Madelene, alone in her bedchamber, felt she had never been dirtier, nor cleaner, for that matter. She shook her head, hardly crediting it was she who had actually participated in a mud fight. But it was with all good intentions.

Madelene looked at her bed but felt too restless to fall asleep just yet.

Something drew her to the window in those early-morning hours. The stillness. The rustling.

She moved the curtains to the side and—

Mr. Westcott?

Madelene leaned farther out the window to see if her eyes deceived her.

There he was. Watching her with a warm grin.

"Mr. Westcott, whatever are you doing outside my window? I can only promise if I plan to escape again, it would certainly not be down a tree!" She leaned her elbows on the sill, hardly believing it was indeed her husband in the tree.

Her husband sat comfortably in the knot of the solid oak outside her window. Watching Madelene, he told her, "My sister, Lucinda, and I used to have all manners of conversations in this way. My old Aunt Adelphia was very strict and would hold to these impossible bedtimes when we were young."

He raised his hand to grasp the branch above him as he continued. "Our aunt would think we were fast in our beds, but Lucinda and I would sit and talk about the stars, about our fate, and how much we hated our aunt, our father's sister."

"Lucinda—"

"Yes," he said quietly.

She would have offered condolences or a measure of solace but didn't know what he needed most, and why it should matter to her.

Gabriel offered, "Are you in the mood for discourse tonight, since it appears you are not any sleepier than I?"

Madelene drew herself up, still at the window, unsure what to do next. She really ought to be in bed. But his charming nature sneaked its way into her beguiled senses. She leaned once more upon her windowsill. When would be the time to explain about her brother? Somehow she sensed it wasn't this moment.

"I didn't have trees to climb when I was younger, and *my* brother wanted nothing to do with his little sister."

"It seems your brother has not yet learned how to handle a female." His features too close to the tree revealed little of his true thoughts.

Madelene rested her chin in one hand on the windowsill, her wet hair quickly drying in the mild night air. "My father, I imagine, indulged Matthew to an extent, perhaps to make up for the loss of our mother. Indeed, it always seemed he was getting into scrapes, and Father had to help him again and again. Then when Father left us, Matthew relied on me to—"

"Deliver him from evil?" Gabriel broke in.

Madelene smiled at his suggestion. "I truly wouldn't say evil, only a few minor predicaments."

"Is that how you planned to live your life, playing your brother's keeper?"

"No, I, I presumed I would marry and, eventually, Matthew would mature into adulthood, marry, and have a family."

"When did you anticipate he would mature? After the ripe age of eight and twenty?"

She sighed. "I don't know. I hope soon."

"Did you ever wish upon a star?" he asked, changing the subject, looking up into the night, as if he could see through the thick leaves to the sky. "My sister would make many wishes, but never tell me what she wished for."

Madelene looked up into the dark sky, squinting to see if she could find just one star. Yes," she answered, not looking at him. "I wished my father wouldn't die."

The quiet night filled the empty space between them before he replied, "Some things, I suppose, cannot be wished for." Silence. "Let us think of something more cheerful." In a relatively short time, he latched on to that something else. "Why don't you come out with me on this tree branch? I can assure you that it will hold both of our weights." He held his hand out beckoning her.

"No, no, I am much too old to be climbing trees," she told him in her most ladylike manner, then realized what she must be inferring about him.

But he only laughed. "Yes, but I don't want to be old tonight. Nor too young either." He lithely rose to his feet, holding on to the top branch over his head with both hands. He stepped back and forth on the large branch to show her it was steady. "So, will you come out on a limb for me?" he asked, his eyebrows raised and an encouraging smile on his lips.

She tried to summon all her reasons for refusing him: the marriage, her failed escape, the missing dagger, Alec, having a guard, and even Falstaff was included in her litany of things for which to seek retribution.

And yet she warily sat on the windowsill and swung her legs over the side, careful not to catch her light green night rail and gown on the rough stone surface of the side of the house, her bare feet brushing the roughness.

"Put one foot on the branch, your left one, then your right. See how easy it is?" he asked her while watching her every move.

Knowing he would keep her safe and feeling a bit

daring, she edged a little farther out onto the thick lower branch, holding on to the higher branch with her hands in imitation of Gabriel. *Gabriel. When did I stop thinking of him as Mr. Westcott?*

A step away, Gabriel reached out his hand to grasp hers to pull her into the knot of the tree.

Her foot slipped. She screamed as her feet left the branch, and she dangled high above the ground with only one hand holding tightly to Gabriel's.

Any minute. Any minute, her bones would meet the hard ground. Fear pounded in her head and in her heart.

Seconds later, Gabriel easily pulled her up with one hand, grasped her waist, and pulled her tight against him. Breathless, Madelene clung to him as a miser to his penny, until she could slow her heart down. She couldn't stop trembling as they stood on the large branch, Gabriel's arms holding her tightly.

When she felt safer with her feet under her again, and her trembling had subsided, Gabriel surprised her by sitting down and pulling her with him. He sat at the worn cushion of the tree and with nowhere else for her to sit, sat her on top of him.

Facing him. Almost as if he had planned this, Madelene thought hazily, before he cupped her head and brought her close to him for a brief kiss.

A kiss that soon threatened to take away the breath she had just regained from her near fall. His strong hands entangled in her hair, then roped around his hands. She couldn't get away from him. She couldn't get near enough to him.

On this delightfully warm night, it had suddenly become sun-burning hot. They shared one kiss after another, with no end and no beginning. With her eyes closed, Madelene reveled in his searing touch and caressed his face, learning his eyes, nose, lips, and jaw as a blind person might.

He held her close next to his bare chest, his breeches his only clothing. She greedily ran her hands down his muscular chest and over his shoulders, learning every valley, every nuance, every soft and hard place a man has. Delighting in having her fill of him beneath her hands, she playfully nipped him on his shoulder.

"No fair, my woman. It's my turn."

He drew her slightly away from him to test the weight of her breast in his hand. Over her night rail, he caressed her nipple before moving the slip of silk aside. He needed to feel her softness and bent his head to nip and tug on each pink nipple until he no longer had any coherent thoughts. He wanted her with a madness, his manhood threatening to rip his breeches in life-preserving need.

But she found him. With no direction, she found his hardness and soon had his pulsing staff in her hands. Little did she know the agony she caused him. And the pleasure she gave him. The feel of her warm hands holding his member—he didn't think he could take much more of her fondling.

"Madelene, you do destroy me!" he whispered in her ear.

She smiled and continued stroking him, liking the feel of his hardness in her hands, knowing she gave him delight. She marveled at how something could feel so soft and so hard at the same time.

Somehow her innocent hands knew what to do. His breath came in short bursts, moaning as he kissed her harshly, his tongue mating with hers, accepting no withdrawal, no defeat. With all of his might, he broke from her sweet lips to growl and spill into her hands.

Both sat breathless, Gabriel stunned into disbelief at how

easily she controlled his desires. Madelene swallowed hard. What had she done? And in a tree? Oh, gracious goodness, she'd have penance to pay for this.

But . . . but . . . Gabriel took her hand and wiped it on his breeches. Then he kissed her tenderly while stroking her arm, causing a frisson between her skin and her silk sleeve. She shuddered but not with cold—with the passion he had only begun to stir in her.

She wanted something more, but didn't know how to ask for it. He knew. He swept his tongue over her plump lips while caressing her belly, then meandering his way down to the mound at the top of her thighs.

"Oh!" Madelene wanted to pull back in shock, but Gabriel wouldn't let her.

Slowly, oh, ever so slowly, he gently slid his finger into her wetness before delving further. She jerked anxiously, wanting to get away, yet pressing herself closer. He was setting her on fire, which both frightened her and excited her.

The pleasure from his hand was incomparable to anything she had felt before. She rolled her hips impatiently, and with great tenderness and expertise, he stroked her till she cried against his shoulder, a thin bead of perspiration across her forehead. Her fingers dug into his arms as she allowed the sensations to run through her like a river, ebbing unhurriedly out through her fingertips and breath.

He held her and rubbed her back, waiting for her. The delight of simply holding Madelene in his arms brought him more pleasure than he could have imagined. It wasn't to have been like this. What had this woman done to him?

Her sweet sighs reminded him comfort was only a branch away. After they righted their clothing, Gabriel helped Madelene stand. He rose to his feet and nimbly walked around her and to her window. With one hand on the windowsill, he grasped her hands with the other. She walked tentatively toward him, her eyes never leaving his. His eyes never left hers.

He climbed into her room and turned to assist her over the window ledge. Standing in her bedchamber, next to the window, they stared at each other, in new awareness. Gabriel began to want her again, quickly and easily, just staring at her flushed face, brilliant eyes, and hardened nipples peeking through her nightdress.

He couldn't. It was too soon. Madelene looked in a daze, and appeared speechless. To save his sanity and desire for another day, he took her by the hand and led her to her bed, where she sat on the edge, watching him. Who was this vision, this passionate woman who had captured his imagination, his Helen of Troy? Would she lead him to his doom?

Finally, he leaned over to kiss her softly on the forehead before taking his leave, and looked back once at the door and saw her unwavering stare. He smiled and quietly shut the door after him.

Madelene remained still, safe and back in her room. Who was this man and what had he done with Madelene? She wasn't the same person anymore. Could she be repaired? Could she still get an annulment? Did she still want one? Maybe, maybe, they could have something more. Something neither had planned for.

Chapter Fifteen

Back in his own bedroom, Gabriel stretched on his bed, wide awake from his unexpected visit with Madelene. This was proving to be an impossible situation. She wanted to run away—to what or from whom? Maybe after tonight, he could convince her to stay. Her passionate response to him made him realize it might be harder to let her go than he had originally planned.

And now the new complication of the dagger. Alec had informed him that the dagger given to her by her uncle had been stolen from her while she stayed in London. How how it reappeared in a creek?

He picked up the dagger lying by his side to examine it. When he returned to his room, he had retrieved it from a hidden spot behind a brick in the fireplace.

The dagger many people sought. He turned it over in his hands, noticing the hilt's silver shine in the candlelight, but the luster had worn off in places. Empty scrolled indentations marked where gems might have slept, long since nicked off.

The dagger itself showed signs of rust, although the edge was still quite sharp. Rather unprepossessing, he thought. His fingers traced every hole, scroll, design, and pock, worn clean, on the hilt, until his finger nudged a tiny slivered button. The handle turned easily in his hands and out dropped several loose diamonds onto his chest.

Gabriel sat up, astonished, before gathering all the glittering stones into the palm of his hand, watching them shine even in the meager candlelight.

This was what they wanted—not the dagger, but these precious gems, worth a fortune.

But why did Madelene want the dagger, for her brother? However, if Alec was to be believed, it belonged to her.

Gabriel knew he would have to disappoint both women because he felt confident the diamonds were stolen and needed to be returned to the rightful owner. He decided to keep the dagger safe and not mention the diamonds to anyone. When he returned to London, he'd make inquiries or have Windthorp make them. The difficult task would be to convince both women to give up their quest.

In the morning, he would discuss the dagger with Madelene to learn of its importance to her. He frowned. Knowing Madelene, nothing would stop her from trying to help her brother. Little did she understand that getting into trouble was Matthew Colgate's one sure failing.

And Madelene, he had no doubt, would have questions about Alec. Would she understand?

He sighed and shook his head. He had to find a better hiding place for the diamonds, until something further could be done.

During breakfast the next morning, as Madelene sipped her tea and reviewed the lady's fashions in *The London Lady,* she watched her husband out of the corner of her eye. He had delved into a soft-boiled egg and kippers, seemingly enjoying his repast. How to begin the conversation about the dagger?

He began. "Mrs. Westcott, I will, in all likelihood, need to return to Town soon. I'm planning to purchase a new ship for the West Indies."

Insignificant news to her. *The dagger, what about the dagger?* "I see. Mr. Westcott, would you care to discuss the events of last night?" she asked, determined to steer the conversation in another direction.

He smiled broadly. "I would be delighted. You are of course referring to our assignation in the tree?"

She started to cough. The man could be so obtuse. "Actually, I was thinking of an earlier time."

"Yes, now I recall. My wife and my friend wrestled in the creek."

Madelene pursed her lips. He was deliberately being infuriating. "Mr. Westcott, I had a very good reason why I was, I—you found me in the creek. You have the dagger, and I need it."

She finally had his attention. He put his fork down, sipped his coffee, and inquired, "And for what reason?" His brown gaze seemed to peer into her soul to question her honesty.

Becoming fidgety, she ran her fingers across the lacy tablecloth. "My brother needs the dagger. He had placed it in my trunk for safekeeping. If you could only give it to me, then I could see he gets it."

"Your *brother* needs it. Tell me, do you know what he plans to do with it?"

Unable to meet his gaze, she cleared her throat before replying, "He, he told me, he needs to return it to its rightful owner."

"And who would that person be?"

She found the courage to return his look and shook her

head. "I don't know. Matthew didn't tell me. But you will give it to me?" She no doubt sounded desperate. In fact, she *was* desperate.

Her husband pushed back his chair and rose to his feet. "Mrs. Westcott, I must think on your request. It is not as simple as you might believe or what your brother told you. Would you please advise me when you have the answer to my question what you were doing at that time of night, not in your bed? If you'll excuse me."

After he departed, she realized she still had not asked her husband about Alec.

Ever hopeful for her husband to graciously deliver the dagger to her, Madelene kept watch for Matthew's return, or at the very least, a communiqué from him. Still, she was prepared if her husband wasn't so generous. Her discreet and unsuccessful search for the dagger soon convinced her that her husband must carry it on his person.

Therefore, the only solution was to steal into his bedchamber at night and search for the dagger while he slept, for she had recently discovered, he now kept his rooms locked when he didn't occupy them. He obviously did not trust his wife. A prudent decision, she had to admit.

And how could she forget her very own thorn, Alec? If the young woman found the dagger first, Matthew's life might be forfeit.

Alec. Someone who troubled Madelene a great deal. She had yet to ask Mr. Westcott the reason why this young Italian girl lodged here, and so far from London or her home in Italy. An even odder question remained behind her purpose to dress as a young man and hide her identity. Only a few people had been alerted to Alec's true gender, including Mrs. Lavishtock, who seemed to know everything before it was told to her.

No matter all the mysteries surrounding the young woman, Madelene would have the dagger; of this, she was quite determined.

Gabriel had returned from a late-afternoon ride with Alec, when the butler Graham stopped him in the hallway with a note before he could breach the stairs. Leaning on the newel post, he scanned the contents.

The missive from Hayden Bush requested Gabriel's presence at his home at the earliest opportunity. Given Bush seldom required his assistance, Gabriel told Graham to have one of the groomsmen saddle another horse while he washed the dust from his ride. He would leave immediately.

Madelene curled up with Jane Austen's novel, *Sense and Sensibility,* in the library, which was where Graham found her to deliver another note.

Anxious to receive word from her brother, Madelene leapt from the chair to take the missive and rip open the seal, perusing the few lines the note contained. She sank back into her chair in complete puzzlement. Her brother had indeed sent a message instructing her to meet him at the Pickled Goose on the outskirts of Ludlow. He made no mention of the dagger, only the urgency to see her and to tell no one her plans.

Deciding to change for the assumedly brief journey, she rose from the chair with the missive in her hand. How could she plan to leave the house with no one the wiser? Especially her husband?

Mr. Bush. She informed Graham to explain to Mr. Westcott that Mr. Bush had requested her presence unexpectedly and to arrange a carriage. She did not intend to be away long.

Mr. Graham scratched his chin, then shrugged. It made no matter to him that the master and mistress were going to the same place, but separately.

Dressed in her favorite white muslin trimmed in pink and a deeper pink spencer to match, Madelene, with the assistance of a footman, climbed into the carriage, instructing the groomsman as to their destination.

Practically sitting on the edge of her seat for the journey to Ludlow, Madelene worried her reticule strings. What would he say when she told him about the dagger's whereabouts?

After thirty minutes of a bumpy, jolting ride, the groomsman finally slowed up the horses and brought them to a weary halt. Looking out the window, Madelene saw they stopped in front of an inn, with a swinging sign, The Pickled Goose.

The groomsman assisted her down the carriage steps, murmuring he would wait for her. She walked across the threshold, eagerly looking around the common room. No signs of her brother. Indeed, the tavern room remained empty without a whisper of another being.

"Hello? Hello? Matthew, are you here?" Silence.

She saw a door to the right and walked toward it, her reticule tight in her hand, her heart beating frantically, in hopes she would find her brother in a reasonable condition.

She pushed open the door and walked into what looked to be the dining room, dimly lit, with several small tables and chairs. She peered around the room for sight of her brother.

He wasn't there.

She caught her breath. Someone sat in darkness, not too far from a feeble fire in the fireplace.

"Thank you for joining me, Miss Colgate," the congenial, Italian-accented voice welcomed her, the figure remaining in the shadows.

"Who, who are you? Where is my brother?" Madelene stood near the door, ready to run in the opposite direction of the danger she felt emanating from him across the room.

"You have not heard of me? I'm Count Taglioni. Ah, a slight ruse to bring you to me. Your brother isn't here. I wanted to see you. Please have a seat."

Who was this count and why did he want to see me? "Thank you, but I prefer to stand. I don't know why I'm here, but my intention for this visit is to be brief." Madelene hoped the harshness in her voice penetrated to the man across the room. She had no interest in any charades this man had planned. Her hand on the doorknob, she began to turn it.

The dark figure stood, alerted to her intent to depart. "*Your* intentions, my dear, mean little to me." Like a hunter stalking his prey, he walked toward her, and she finally caught sight of a tall man with a pale face and dark mustache. The look in his black eyes made her take a step back; nausea assailed her stomach.

Her back to the door, she watched as he drew closer, a sweet smell emanating from him. She began to reach into her reticule for her handkerchief, when he stilled her hand with his own.

"Madelene, my dear Madelene. I have watched and waited for you for some time."

"Whatever could you want with me?" She concentrated on his waistcoat, unwilling to look into his face.

"Many things, but first the dagger."

Madelene looked up in surprise. "The dagger?"

"*Sì*. I have left a ransom note for your husband to bring the dagger here in exchange for your safe return. We will have a little time to wait. This will be an opportunity to get familiar with each other."

Madelene gulped. She had to get out of the room, away from the count. But how?

Chin up, Madelene looked him squarely in the eye. "I do not know of any dagger, and have no intention of becoming familiar with you in any way. I am extremely undone that you have brought me here on false purposes."

"You lie *molto bene. Siete una bella donna.*"

She closed her eyes against his stare, much too close for her sensibilities. A gloved finger ran down her cheek.

"So lovely," he whispered.

Whereupon she retched all over the front of Count Taglioni's well-tailored coat.

Chapter Sixteen

After a brief conversation with Bush, Gabriel quickly remounted and headed home, spurring the gelding to his top speed. His insides tight, he felt something was wrong and knew it could only be Madelene. Who sent the message he was wanted by his friend, and for what reason?

His purpose at the moment was to see Madelene safe. He threw himself off his horse before it barely came to a stop and threw the reins to one of the footmen.

Taking the stairs two at a time, he ran down the hall and yanked open Madelene's bedchamber door.

It was empty.

His jaw tightened when he realized a terrible possibility. Could Madelene herself have sent him the note? Had she run from him again? He sat heavily on the edge of her bed.

"Mr. Westcott. What are you doing here and where is Mrs. Westcott?"

Gabriel looked at Fanny standing in the doorway.

"You don't know?" he asked her.

"No, Mr. Westcott, sir. I thought she was to meet you at Mr. Bush's home. She left not long after you, and has not yet returned."

Gabriel stood up and stalked past the maid. He would uncover the events of the night. If Madelene indeed had left him again, he hesitated about following her. He couldn't keep her here and couldn't keep finding her and bringing her back, if she truly wanted to be free of him.

What else could he do? Weary from the rides and his wife's shenanigans, he roamed down the stairs, seeking port and answers.

Mrs. Lavishtock knocked on the door to the drawing room before entering at his direction. Standing near the empty fireplace, Gabriel watched as his housekeeper entered the room. With her hands on her hips and a glare in her eye, his servant looked entirely miffed at him. What had *he* done?

"Mrs. Lavishtock—"

"Mr. Westcott, why are you not out searching for your wife?"

Her question took him by surprise, and her attitude irritated him. "Mrs. Lavishtock, what I do or don't do is none of your concern. However, would you happen to know Mrs. Westcott's whereabouts? She has gone missing again. I've decided to give her what she so obviously wants, her freedom." He took a long swallow of port.

Mrs. Lavishtock harrumped at him. "She is a young, newly married woman and confused. She needs time."

"Which I have given her." He waved his hand in the air as if to discard her notions. "If I were to look for her, would you have an idea of where she might be?"

"I heard her tell the groomsman to take her to an inn on the outskirts of Town."

"Perhaps she has a mind to take the coach to London?" All this surmising was a complete waste of his time.

Holding her hands in front of her, she ignored his

question and told him calmly, "Why don't you give Mrs. Westcott a reason to stay?"

"Whatever can you mean? She is infinitely safer with me than with her reprehensible brother."

"If you believe this, then you must go and bring her back."

He made no comment but put his glass down to head for the door, his decision already made. "She has no reason to fear me, I thought I had made that quite clear," he muttered to himself, heading once again for the stables.

Outside the drawing-room doors, Mrs. Lavishtock told the back of his head, "She has reason to fear for her heart."

Something white on the floor caught her attention. She limbered over and squatted to retrieve it, moaning on the way down, and way up. It was for Mr. Westcott. Perhaps she should open it, if it might help find Mrs. Westcott.

Madelene's feet ached. Her once pink slippers, now muddy brown, provided no protection from the pebbles and stones she trampled on her way back to Westcott Close. Rummaging in her reticule, she managed to find a couple of peppermints, which she hoped would settle her stomach.

She couldn't help but smile remembering the look of outrage on the pale Italian count's face. He left the room immediately, locking the door behind him. Unperturbed at his anger, she searched the room and found an open window, her escape route. As soon as she managed to creep past the open windows, she looked for the carriage that had brought her here, but it was gone.

With no other choice, Madelene scurried down the road, keeping to the side, where she could duck into bushes if she heard the count's carriage behind her.

The bright moon's rays showered her with light, and she almost would not have been frightened, if every sound didn't mean an animal eyed her for his next meal or highwaymen might rumble along to do her harm.

She must be brave. Surely Mr. Westcott would come for her. He always did. After several minutes turned into an hour of trudging along the road, she had seen no sign of an irate count, wicked highwaymen, or a growling animal. Madelene began to breathe easier, but knew she still had a long way to go.

Madelene heard the rattle of the carriage wheels before she saw it. Since it came in the opposite direction, the carriage couldn't contain the count. She had to take a chance the travelers would assist her. Her white dress shone in the moonlight like a beacon alerting ships to the rugged coast. While waiting for the carriage to draw closer, she walked a few feet over to a boulder to sit and rest. Exhaustion weighing her very veins, she could go no farther.

When the carriage neared, Madelene looked up and recognized the carriage, realizing the driver was none other than her husband, Mr. Westcott. Relief poured through her like sugar melting in hot tea. He *had* come for her. But while she was delighted to see him, it was obvious from her husband's unsmiling expression that he did not share the same feeling.

Would he believe her story? Madelene pursed her lips. *She* probably wouldn't believe the events of this night. The third night in a row. Wonders that he came for her. She had to try to make him believe.

Mr. Westcott stopped the carriage near Madelene, who walked over to the side and looked up at him in profound relief. "Mr. Westcott, I'm quite glad you've found me."

His stern gaze never left her tired and assuredly unclean face. "Mrs. Westcott, are you not heading in the wrong direction, away from Town? Your purpose, I assumed, was to catch the mail coach to London."

"No, I was brought here under false pretenses. This count arranged for me to be ransomed in order that you might bring the dagger here."

"The count? Count Taglioni? Has he hurt you?" His voice unnecessarily gruff.

"No, but he wants the dagger. He planned to exchange the dagger for me. The note—"

"A ransom note? I found no evidence of such at Westcott Close. Did something go awry with your planning? Or with the count?" He easily controlled the two horses, both restless to continue their journey.

Madelene's mouth dropped open. She had presumed— the count told her—what to believe? Should she take him back to the Pickled Goose to confront the count? He had probably already departed the inn.

She felt the strain of looking up at him discussing how she came to be here. "Would you take me back to Westcott Close, where we can discuss this, and I'll show you the note that lured me here."

He appeared to consider her request, then jerked his head toward the carriage door.

The next morning, Mrs. Lavishtock and Madelene sat in the kitchen waiting for the bread to rise and discussing the courses for dinner. Madelene recalled last night's events when Mr. Westcott had dropped her at the front steps and continued on to the stables. Not another word had been shared between them. He wouldn't allow her to explain.

"Why didn't you go riding with Mr. Westcott today and

not that Italian chit?" the housekeeper asked Madelene as she rolled and dusted more dough.

"Mmmm," Madelene answered absentmindedly while feeding Falstaff little bits of venison from last night's dinner.

Mrs. Lavishtock shook her head. "There's something not quite right about that young woman. Did Mr. Westcott ever explain her presence here?"

Before she could reply, Mrs. Lavishtock hurriedly added, "For sure, it's none of my business, but she does seem a bit comfortable with Mr. Westcott. After all, going riding with him this morning and playing chess last night. I know it isn't for me to say, but I would think the master would be spending more time with his new wife than some stranger that what passes herself off as a young boy, who is really a girl." The housekeeper braced herself on the wooden table and pulled her hefty bulk to stand, finished with her summation.

At the fireplace, the old woman checked on the gravy heating. "If you keep feeding that dog, he will get himself a belly. Strange dog. He seems to have taken a liking to you after all." She turned back to stir the black pot.

Madelene continued to sit at the table, almost in a daydream. Mrs. Lavishtock was not normally so loquacious, offering her thoughts on Madelene's private affairs. Although she should really reprimand Mrs. Lavishtock over her gossiping, Madelene had quite a few other problems to solve, one of which involved her brother, and the other, convincing her husband she really had not tried to run away. It certainly would have helped the situation if she hadn't lost the note instructing her to go to the inn. To fix one, she had to fix the other.

Was Alec, in spending so much time with Mr. Westcott, any closer to getting the dagger? Perhaps the young woman needed to be curtailed in her habits with *Madelene's* husband.

Well, there was no help for it, Madelene thought.

She would simply have to seduce her husband.

How does one begin the art of seduction? She pulled little Falstaff onto her lap, where he happily nested. Thoughtfully, she stroked his soft fur while she planned, feeling comforted by his warm presence.

Tonight. It had to be tonight.

She had received a desperate letter from Matthew that morning, which she knew could have only come from him because he mentioned Mr. Brelford accompanied him. The only other person who knew about Brelford was her husband.

Matthew planned to meet her tomorrow night on the other side of the lake. She had to find and bring the dagger with her, if she wanted to save his life.

Again. She would certainly be glad when her brother could finally extricate himself from his own troubles, or rather, discontinue his reckless ways altogether. Rescuing him was a full-time obligation. Indeed, he was her brother, *although* she did love him *and* she would do anything for him. No matter what.

In anticipation of her evening, Madelene took a light repast in her room. She needed all the time she had to buff up her courage and make herself presentable. This was an important night.

There was no going back. After tonight, she would be unable to obtain an annulment. Madelene tried to convince herself that her sacrifice was for her brother. Then why did she keep remembering Gabriel's kisses and his touch and want to know them again?

Her only conclusion was that the man she married was not the man she remembered from before—with fury and hatred in his eyes, standing over her brother's wounded form.

Dress and hair prepared, all she could do was wait. And wait. Every few minutes, she would listen at the door for Gabriel's footsteps, to no avail. Falstaff slept beside her bed, keeping watch over her.

As time crawled, Madelene viewed herself with a critical eye in the looking glass. Perhaps a bit pale, and she'd have to practice her "fetching" look. She believed he found her handsome enough; he had articulated that sentiment on more than one occasion.

But after last night?

For this evening, she wore a pale yellow night rail and wrap. Oh, she simply must stop her hands from shaking and her heart from wanting to jump from her chest.

Finally, she thought she heard the heavy thud of footsteps stop at her door briefly before continuing past. She sneaked a peek out the door to make sure it was, indeed, her husband.

Because she had to wait a little longer while he prepared for bed, Madelene began to pace the room. Falstaff lifted his head with his eyes open slightly to see what was happening, then decided to go back to sleep and laid his head back on the floor.

All this nervous anticipation must have affected her appetite. When her stomach growled, she decided to go to the kitchen for something to sustain her. She needed nourishment, not knowing how long the seduction would take.

In the pantry, Madelene took a bite of a sweet lemon cake and licked her lips. This would certainly contain her hunger. A drop of wine might also serve the purpose of bolstering her courage.

"Ruff, ruff!" That could mean only one thing. Falstaff

must have followed her, thinking of enjoying whatever she was eating. The little dog was hungry all the time.

Shaking her head, she debated whether to eat the cake before Falstaff discovered her and she'd have to share her tidbit. Deciding she needed the food more than the dog, Madelene ate a few more mouthfuls before shutting the pantry door and turning to find not only Falstaff on the steps but Gabriel as well.

Mortified, she put a hand to her mouth to help cover her seeming overindulgence and managed to swallow the dry pieces.

"Ah, I'm glad to see that your appetite has returned. I was worried when you didn't appear for dinner," Gabriel told her easily, a small smile on his face.

Madelene nodded and coughed, trying to draw breath.

He must have noted her distress because he descended the stairs and filled a cup with water from a nearby bucket and handed it to her.

She downed the water before she could reply. "Thank you," she managed before coughing again. "Yes, my appetite did return. My apologies for disturbing you . . ." She trailed off, watching him watching her.

The dagger, remember the dagger.

Her bare feet rooted to the floor, Gabriel was close enough for her to tilt her head back to receive his kiss.

But he didn't. He had something more devastating in mind, such as licking the sugar from her lips, which seemed to take longer than necessary. Nothing else touched but their lips until she heard him murmur.

"You do disturb me and my appetite, for you." He grabbed her waist and pulled her close, determined to finish what he started. If he thought her lips as sweet as honey, it was nothing compared to the luscious taste of her tongue as she returned his passion, lick by lick. He felt her arms around his shoulders, her breasts pressed against his chest through thin muslin. One hand cupped her back while his other hand slid down her arm to her hand.

He wrenched his lips from hers to take a deep breath, his eyes never leaving hers, and brought her hand up to lick the remaining lemon stickiness from each finger. His eyes held her startled but passion-filled blue eyes, and he felt her shiver as he took each graceful finger into his mouth to suck each sweet, sugary speck.

When he playfully bit one of her fingers, he heard her giggle, bringing a smile to his face.

Tonight she would be his. She was his wife. He would not tolerate any longer this beautiful woman not lying by his side every night. He didn't question how long it would last, his desire for her. He only wanted her to want him as much as he wanted her. For the moment.

When he had removed the last of the sticky residue, he planted a kiss followed by a quick lick on each of Madelene's palms. She inhaled quickly, wondering what other surprises this night might hold, considering the seducer was the one being seduced.

Still holding her by the waist with one hand, he brought her closer for another searing kiss, tasting her lips over and over again, almost as if he was drawing breath from her. She returned his passion in equal measure, pressing her thinly clad body to his muscular form, seeking to match every contour, every roundness, every hardness and shadow to his. Her hands encircled his waist, touching the dagger's sheath hooked to his pantaloons.

"You taste sweeter than any cake Mrs. Lavishtock could bake," he murmured into her hair, while glancing around the room. "Ah, I have just the thing to complete our feast," he told her, loosening his hold on her.

Madelene blinked and slowly backed away, frowning.

What had happened? First, she was eating cake, then her husband arrived to—what did he have planned? Obviously, Gabriel had a lot more practice at the art of seduction than she.

Before she had recovered from his passionate assault that burned like a brand on her skin, he grabbed her hand, tossed a peach, a nectarine, and a bunch of grapes into a bag, and pulled her to the door and out the servants' entrance.

Falstaff's tail thumped softly outside the open kitchen doors, which led to the rest of the house. He knew what happened next. Mrs. Lavishtock bent her full form slightly and handed Falstaff his biscuit. She would have patted him on the head if she could have reached that far, but the dog tore off, eager to enjoy his reward. Smiling, she lurched back to her bedroom, satisfied with the night's outcome.

Refreshing after the heat in the kitchen, the warm breeze faintly cooled the lovers, tickling Madelene's hair. Gabriel broke into a run, pulling her in his wake. The meadowed grass felt delightfully cool beneath her bare feet, and her nightwrap billowed around her.

Where was he taking her? And why? At least he had the dagger with him. If she could distract him, she should be able to sneak the dagger from its sheath. Although he had definitely kissed her into insensibility back in the kitchen, she wouldn't let it happen again. Here in the fresh night air, with her senses collected, she would be the seductress and gain what she sought.

Gabriel led her across the nearby meadow into a clump of old sycamore trees, their leaves dashing the moon's light. He appeared to know the way without any illumination, having probably walked this path many times before.

To make sure she didn't trip over any large stones or downed branches, he walked the dirt path in front of her, grasping her hand. Odd, Madelene thought, how safe she felt with him and knew he would never let any harm befall her.

"Shh!" He quickly turned around and shoved Madelene behind the nearest tree and stepped behind her until he pressed against her.

"What?"

"Shh, it's Hayden Bush. I failed to remember he likes to stroll around the lake on his way home from visiting his godchild, Lucas Monroe. The Monroes live on the road to the village," Gabriel whispered in her ear, his lips close to her cheek.

In the quiet, they could hear Hayden Bush whistling as he ambled closer to their hiding spot, then passed them. They listened to his whistling and footsteps fade away.

Leaving their hiding spot, Madelene asked, "I'm curious. Since Mr. Bush is blind, we really didn't need to hide from him, and since he is your friend, we could have bid him good evening." She had to shout to be heard over his shoulder because he had continued down the meandering path.

When he stopped to reply, she ran right into the back of him. He turned to catch her before she lost her balance. "My dear, I did not want Mr. Bush to hear us about and have to make excuses for our reason for being here. And he enjoys his solitary walks."

Hmm. That still didn't explain why they had to hide behind a tree with her husband wedged tight up against her. She sensed he had something other than eating on his mind, remembering vividly how his hard body pressed against hers.

A few more yards and they arrived at the large lake, mirroring the now bright moon's light. Holding hands, Gabriel and Madelene stood on the slight knoll, admiring the dark beauty of the water. Madelene caught her breath, whether from their trek or the nearness of her husband was difficult to determine.

Gabriel dropped her hand to walk down the grassy knoll and found a flat area cleared of brush and weeds. Following him, Madeléne knew she wanted to discover a well-kept secret only lovers knew.

Standing across from each other, he reached over and slipped the muslin dressing gown from her shoulders and spread it on the soft grass. With a flourish of his hand, he said, "Your bed awaits you, my lady, my wife." His warm brown eyes beckoned her to accept the hand he held out to her, which she did, stepping to the thin gown and sinking onto their makeshift bed. Little bits of grass poked through her night rail, but not uncomfortably so.

Not letting go of her hand, he gently pulled her all the way down until she lay looking up at the stars. Before he joined her, she saw out of the corner of her eye that Gabriel removed the dagger from his waist and laid it aside, along with his pilfered bag of fruit.

"Much better," he told her, sliding down to lie next to her. "This is one of my favorite places on the estate. I used to come to this lake with my sister. She would read one of Mrs. Radcliffe's novels while I fished, or we'd swim."

Madelene smiled, thinking of the picture of Gabriel and his sister together. If he missed his sister as much as she knew she would miss Matthew, her heart ached for him.

"I wish I could have known your sister. I think I would have liked her," she told him honestly.

She felt rather than saw his body tense and could only wonder if it was at the mention of his sister or remembering that her brother had a hand in her dishonor. Their siblings had brought them together, to this moment, for some inexplicable reason.

Gabriel raised himself on one elbow to look down at Madelene looking up at him inquiringly. "Let's have no more talk of yesterday for tonight, shall we? I would rather us enjoy the moment." His voice was light and devoid of melancholy.

But she couldn't dismiss Matthew from her mind. She had to find a way to help him, or she would be left alone in the world, not unlike Gabriel. Surely her husband would understand whatever methods she needed to use to help her brother.

He rejoined her on the blanket, both now seeking the stars as Gabriel stroked her arm rhythmically, caressing her into a sweet haze. But she had to know; she couldn't forget.

"Gabriel?" she asked softly.

"Hmm?"

"Why did you marry me? Was it truly to enact revenge on my brother?"

Taking her gaze off the stars, she turned and watched a shadow cross his face, then it was gone.

Nonchalantly, he said, "Perhaps or perhaps I fell madly in love with you when I saw you on the dueling field."

She drew a quick breath, remembering, and closed her eyes. The dueling field, a day she would never forget. The early-morning hours with Gabriel Westcott facing her brother, Matthew Colgate, with pistols. Mr. Westcott believed Matthew had dishonored his sister, and he demanded justice.

Matthew had admitted to Madelene that in a drunken

stupor, he had taken advantage of the young woman. But he insisted the young girl had pursued him. What or who to believe? She knew her brother to be in the wrong and greatly feared for his life when she heard of the duel. She wanted to speak to Mr. Westcott to convince him to call off the duel, but her brother would not hear of it.

The day came, and Matthew instructed her not to come to the field. His instructions went unheeded, for she had to watch, desperately scared and wretched. Madelene couldn't convince her brother not to show because he told her in no uncertain terms that he could never live with that blemish on his character. If he was worried about blemishing his character, Madelene thought, he should have left Mr. Westcott's sister in her innocence.

As she waited and watched with a physician, a Mr. Arnold Duckins, Matthew's second, and another man, Mr. Westcott's second, Madelene could hardly believe when Mr. Westcott had only shot Matthew in the arm, when he could have taken his life. Her eyes blinded with tears, she raced across the field to see to her brother's welfare.

Matthew clutched a bloody arm and looked up at his opponent with terror written on his face. "Is this the end of it?"

Mr. Westcott fired into the air. "For now."

Gratitude and anger warred within Madelene, and anger won. She saw Matthew's pistol lay close by and grabbed it, aiming it in Mr. Westcott's direction.

Fortunately, Mr. Westcott's reflexes were sharper than Madelene's aim, and the bullet whistled harmlessly by his head.

"Madelene, no, leave be!" Matthew yelled to her.

She shook her head, then slowly sank next to her brother, her tears no longer imprisoned.

A year later, Madelene lay with her husband and former enemy, Mr. Westcott, and opened her eyes.

He had turned on his side to face her, his deep stare pinning her to the spot. She looked up and beyond him to the dark night, leaving his gaze without leaving his side. "I hated you. You almost killed my brother." Her voice was soft, catching at actually saying the words to someone for whom, she had harbored a resentment for so long.

When Gabriel sat up, giving his back to her, she had to join him to hear his reply.

Devoid of any emotion, he said, "I could have killed your brother. But I decided I wanted a more lasting revenge."

Madelene tried to control a shiver, hating his words. Could she bridge their grievances? "I know Matthew was wrong for what he did to your sister. I know he regretted his action. It seems since Father has gone, Matthew acts like a weathervane, his whims and actions directed by the wind." She paused and swallowed hard.

What was he thinking? Feeling? Madelene moved to kneel in front of him, wanting to read his expression. "Are you punishing me for what Matthew did?"

Gabriel sat for a long while staring at his hands, then he lifted his head and gazed into her eyes. "That was my plan."

Tears could fall so easily at his words. Her heart in her throat, she continued, "Was? Do you have some new plan that I'm to be a part of?" She hugged her shoulders to feel the warmth where his words had chilled her.

"It is too soon to know." His fierce gaze bored into her. "But I do know that I want you, Madelene. I want you to be my wife in more than name." She looked past the intense desire in his face to some unnamed pain he could not hide.

She might be afraid of what the future held, but

tonight, she saw only Gabriel, her husband. At his touch, she knew he would leave his mark on her heart, hidden from others, especially him, doomed to last her entire life.

She could pretend her sacrifice might satisfy Gabriel's need for revenge, and perhaps the desire they shared could bring them a semblance of happiness. Perhaps he was the man who could see beyond her blue eyes and black hair and no dowry and want her for herself. She wanted to know.

Sighing, she realized that she wanted him as much as he wanted her. It would be no true sacrifice, but a willing mate he would find in her.

Before she gave him the answer he sought, she peered into the dark.

"What are you looking for?"

"Your little dog. He seems to be able to read your mind, and I wanted to make sure he was nowhere in sight."

He leaned over her in a gentle leer. "Do you wish to read my mind?"

She lay back on their common blanket and held up her arms. "No, I want you to show me."

Chapter Seventeen

Gabriel stared in surprise at Madelene's bright blue eyes and lovely smile, her silky black hair flowing past her shoulders in a tangled cloud. She had never looked more beautiful, and she was truly to be his. Although he could take more precious moments to wonder at her words, he slowly leaned down and captured her lips lightly with his. He wanted the night to last as long as the old sycamore trees had stood in time. They would keep the lovers' secrets.

As he lay next to his wife, he realized he enjoyed thinking of Madelene as his wife and not his nemesis's sister. She was much more. Braced on one elbow, he traced her face with one finger and watched her eyes flutter closed. If he listened intently, he could hear the wings of the fireflies, the murmuring water of the lake, the rustling leaves, and an ancient frog croaking his love song.

He leaned down to kiss her neck, inhaling her lilac water perfume, brushing her soft cheek, her forehead, then her lush lips again. When he pulled her into his arms, she gazed up at him with a heated desire in those spellbinding blue eyes that caught his breath.

In false heroism, Gabriel had told himself, he had married Madelene to save her, but could she possibly save him? She wrapped her arms around his neck and pressed her breasts against his chest, but it was not enough.

Their kiss upon kiss answered hurriedly, longingly, and like they might never share another moment together. With a shimmering knowing look in her eyes, she broke their embrace to pull her night rail over her head and threw it on the grass nearby, shivering, but not from the cold.

She returned to his embrace, reaching for the buttons on his pantaloons, but he would have none of that. Although he knew she could feel his hardness straining against the fabric, his pleasure would have to wait.

She reclined on their makeshift bed, frowning. He planned not to keep her mystified for long. Stretching time as if there was only this night, he tenderly kissed his way down her pale form to her full breasts. He licked and lathed one pink nipple, then the other as only a lover could, paying agonizingly patient attention to each one as Madelene undulated beneath his ministrations.

"Soon," he whispered to her. "Soon."

Continuing his pleasure journey, he kissed his way down to her flat stomach until he reached the top of her thighs. As he stroked her slender thighs, she slowly opened them for him. He nudged a knee between her legs while grasping her bottom to bring her close to his mouth.

Exposed, she cried and tried to roll away, but with his greater strength, he would have his way. By the time his tongue had slipped into her wet folds, her body shook from surprise and intense pleasure. He took delight in caressing her with his tongue, with the knowledge that only he could give her the beauty of this moment. Again and again, he heard her moan to stop and continue, and almost smiled.

Concentrating all his efforts, he heard her shortened breath and knew she was near. When she shuddered with her release, he let go and gathered her in his arms, wanting to hold her, to make her feel safe and wanted and beautiful. He lay back on her nightwrap, pulling her with him, so she lay on top of him.

Her skin heated, her mind drugged with passion, she wanted to become a part of him. She wanted to give him pleasure but needed his help. Her arms braced on either side of his head, he shrugged off his pantaloons, causing her to inhale at the feel of his hardened member brushing against her thighs. Still overcome with passion, Madelene cradled his member in her hands before Gabriel guided himself into her wetness, stretching her and filling her. With his hands wrapped around her waist, he showed her how to move in just the right manner to give them both pleasure.

First slowly, then moving her hips more quickly, she felt his body tighten as she grasped his strong arms to steady herself. When he reached between them to touch her again, she cried out, disbelieving there was more to learn, more to feel.

She needed his strength, needing something, someone to cling to, lost as she was at the feeling of oneness with him. She had never been this close to another person. There could never be anyone else. The pleasure he gave her was exquisite, and she wanted to capture it with her hands, her body, her heart.

Soon, soon. He watched her as she watched him consumed in their journey, their chase, their reward. He waited for her, and when he knew she was ready, he pressed deep inside her, both wanting their passion to last longer than would ever be enough.

She fell to his chest, panting, and felt his heart beating

rapidly under her cheek. When she had recovered her senses, she rolled off him to nestle by his side. Their heavy breathing slowly subsided as Gabriel gathered Madelene close to his side, kissing the top of her head, hoping, believing, they could be happy, no matter the circumstances that had brought them together.

In the lush peacefulness of unexpected solace, they didn't notice a figure steal away into the dark trees, keeping more secrets.

Her rumbling stomach awakened Madelene in the early-morning hours. She raised herself on her elbows and noticed the fruit on the other side of Gabriel's slumbering form. Slowly, so as not to awaken him, she eased herself out of his embrace and reached over his chest for the peach.

Its sweetness almost made her moan as she sat eating the peach, unaware that juices had meandered down her wrist to her arm and from her lips to her neck. Almost finished, she was disappointed to not have another one to feast on. She looked down and noticed Gabriel staring up at her with warmth and amusement in his deep brown eyes, a satisfied smile held his lips.

"Enjoying your fare, my wife? I see none left for me. There must be something—" He swooped in for a few precious licks on her neck and a long tongue slide up her arm, which made her giggle. Playfully pushing him away, she rose and headed to the side of the lake to clean her hands, completely aware that she had halted his pleasure in doing so.

Madelene had no sooner stooped to put her hands in the lukewarm water before Gabriel came behind her and scooped her up and splashed into the knee-deep water.

She began to scream, struggling in his arms, as he dropped her unceremoniously into the dark lake.

"I can't swim," she yelled to him, floundering in the water.

He watched her and shook his head with a cockeyed grin. "Madelene, it's not deep. You can stand."

Flinging her wet hair out of her face, she pushed off from the lake floor and stood a little unsteadily, gaining her footing.

Gabriel could not take his eyes off this mesmerizing wraith. She seemed born of water as the rivulets and drops caressed and painted her slender form. The moonlight and shadows played a foreign melody on her pale skin.

He wanted her again.

Although she still sputtered around in the water, she soon felt heat from an unexpected source. Gabriel swam up behind her and wrapped his arms about her waist, pulling her bottom against him while he kissed her neck in search of his favorite fruit called Madelene.

She rested against Gabriel's strong chest, feeling trapped, yet safe and wanted, but not for long because he quickly turned her around so she could feel his hot and heavy need, her erect nipples against his damp chest before he picked her up with no hesitation and wrapped her legs around his waist, searching for a warm, wet sheath for his own dagger.

Tight inside her, he looked into her innocent blue eyes. "How is it possible you destroy me, yet also give me life?" he whispered, overcome by his need and his longing for her.

She simply shook her head, for she had no answers either. Gabriel took it slowly this time, savoring their sodden, slippery union in achingly long minutes. Firmly grasping her bottom in both hands, he directed her movements to achieve the sweetest sensation for both of them. It was far easier to come together in the water, their slick bodies making it all the more pleasurable. Madelene clung to her husband's neck, pressing her wet breasts and hard nipples against his chest, creating a frisson of heat in a whirlpool of unabated passion. Lips clung, tasted, and kissed with no need for breathing.

Madelene matched his thrusts with equal ardor while taking his tongue into her mouth and teasing him with her engaging and unending innocence. The warm water made a unique bed as Gabriel delighted in his wife's fervent response as they ached to become as close as two people could get, until two bodies melded into one. No end and no beginning. The first time had only been a fragment, a sparkle, a longing, a single star. This time the blanket of stars enwrapped the lovers in a new world of knowingness and never-ending.

Gabriel delighted in the feel of the bathlike water lapping against his skin as he floated in the calmness before swimming strong strokes from one side to the other. He lazily watched Madelene as she rose gracefully from the water, reinventing Venus Arising, her lean pale form glistening in the late night. Would she ever cease to amaze and delight him? He didn't plan on finding out.

Madelene walked over to their makeshift blanket and pulled on her night rail, lost in what she had learned, what she had become. Gabriel's wife. Truly.

While this night changed everything for them, it changed nothing for her brother. She still needed the dagger.

Surreptitiously, she gathered the dagger in the folds of

her nightwrap along with the remaining fruit. Looking for Gabriel, she watched him climb from the lake and approach her, dripping wet, in all his nakedness, with a big grin on his face.

He reached down and grabbed his discarded pantaloons, climbing into them with little difficulty. Gabriel had never felt so free, unencumbered. As he watched her start the walk back to the house, he realized in surprise he had never planned for this to happen. He could never have taken her innocence without her willingness. When the wager's demands had been fulfilled, a year's span or a lifetime, he wouldn't be able to let her go. She enlivened his soul, where before there had only been his need for revenge and mourning for his sister.

What lay before him was continuing to build his inheritance from his uncle and finding a willing woman to wed and bear his children. He had never understood that there was more to life than planning sea routes, a good hunt, a fine wine, and preparing his sons for their destiny.

Gabriel smiled. Sons. Yes, indeed, he wanted lots of them, with Madelene as their mother.

Although much between them remained unresolved, including the dagger. And last night.

He stepped in front of her, blocking her progress. "Mrs. Lavishtock found this in the drawing room and gave it to me. It is from the count."

She looked down to see the note in his hand. Gazing up at him, she asked, "Do you believe me?"

"Of course. I should have believed you last night when you mentioned the count. However, my anger won over my reasoning. If I had understood the true circumstances, I would have searched for his foreign hide and made it unmistakably clear to him not to come anywhere near you. It will not happen again."

Noting her hands full, he told her, "Please, allow me," easily divesting her of her treasures. He immediately felt the hardness of the dagger within her thin wrap. "Ah, my dagger. I did wonder what I had done with it." He watched her with a pleasant look on his face.

She lifted her chin and told him simply, "I gathered everything to carry into the house. It wasn't as if I was going to steal the dagger." She hoped she didn't sound guilty.

But nothing could dampen his good humor. "Of course, because I would know you were the one who had taken it." He returned the dagger to its sheath, took a bite of the nectarine, and wrapped Madelene's nightwrap around her before taking her hand to walk back to the house, using the same path they had taken earlier. "If I gave you the dagger, what would you do with it?"

Madelene paused. She shook her head and sighed. What did it matter, for time was running out.

"My brother needs the dagger because the owner is demanding it and has told Matthew in no uncertain terms of the consequences should he fail to deliver it." She couldn't stop the tears in her voice, such was her worry for her brother. "But this count wants it, too. I don't know what to do." No matter what, Matthew was her only family. She had to help him and could never forgive herself if she didn't, and catastrophic events resulted.

"I have no doubt, if your brother has the dagger, it will solve many things," he told her matter-of-factly.

She stopped to stare at him in the lifting gray dawn, haze already drifting over the fields.

"You'll, you'll give me the dagger to give to my brother?" Surely, this was too much to hope for. This would fix everything. Almost everything.

"Not entirely. I'll take the dagger to your brother, and if

I'm correct in my speculation, the count will be waiting there as well," he replied, walking backward toward the house before turning to walk forward.

Madelene hurried to catch up to him and grabbed his arm. "You would do this? But what about Alec? And Matthew is expecting me. He might be, ah, unwilling to meet with you. It would be best if I took the dagger to Matthew."

Gabriel stopped, turned and took her chin in his hand, raising her troubled eyes to meet his. "Don't worry your head over Alec, I'll have a talk with her. As for your brother, you have no choice. Either I meet with him or he won't have the dagger. Trust me to see this through and to protect your brother from harm."

At that moment, gazing into his determined brown eyes, she believed him capable of anything, even making their marriage out of a loaded wager.

When she nodded her acquiescence, he took her hand, and they strolled back to the house together in quiet companionship.

Someone watched the lovers from the window in complete annoyance. *So that is the way of it. Enjoy tonight, for there will be no more.*

Chapter Eighteen

Alec surprised Gabriel with her appearance midday while he worked in his study on plans for acquiring new shipments from the West Indies.

"Mr. Westcott, may I speak with you?" Her Italian accent caught him unawares, and he looked up to find her in the entryway wearing a lovely white gown with a simple blue ribbon. He frowned, wondering why the change in dress, but thought no more on it because he was glad she had sought him out. They needed to have a conversation.

He stood and walked over to the door. "Please, come in. I wish to speak with you as well." Gabriel escorted her to a wing chair before pulling the matching one near hers. "We have much to discuss. What is on your mind?"

The young woman smiled a shy smile and fluttered her fan. Expertly. When had she— This young lady was full of surprises. He'd forgotten her real name, Alessandra, and hadn't called her by that name since their time together in Florence.

He thought about the young woman who had befriended him in Italy. Alec had been quite solicitous during his sister's illness and final passing. Although surprised when she asked to accompany him to England, he had agreed. He had even promised to keep her secret about her gender and her understanding of English, to better hide from her uncle.

For the first several months, in Westcott Close and in London, he had treated her like a young sister, and she proved to be of much assistance preparing the nursery. The young woman was adamant about earning her keep, so he had Windthorp take her under his wing.

Her dramatic change occurred when they stayed in London while he completed his plans to marry Madelene. About a week before the hasty marriage was arranged, she turned a sour tongue and vanished for a day or two at a time, returning with no explanation as to her whereabouts. He had trusted her even after she showed a reluctance to travel with him to Shropshire. Indeed, the woman was more puzzlement than the sphinx.

"Mr. Westcott, I, I hope you can understand my English, but I am most grateful you have allowed me to stay here. You have been most welcoming, but I think perhaps I should return home. If you no longer have need for me." She continued smiling at him.

A sense of relief swept over him. Alec could return to her life, and he and Madelene— "I know it was difficult to live with your uncle. Although I haven't seen him in some time, do you have any reason to believe he has changed?"

Alec cast her eyes to the floor and shook her head. "I do not believe he has changed, but everything has changed with *us*. After you brought her here, to Westcott Close." Her voice sounded different, almost angry from the soft tones she used moments past.

His brows knitted, he replied, "Mrs. Westcott? I told you about her in Florence and my plans to marry her." He sat farther back in his chair to study the young woman. *Does she have feelings for me? But why?* I have never encouraged her that our friendship would be more, only offering her a place to stay while she decided her future. He was indeed grateful for the assistance and friendship she gave him while caring for Lucinda. But there could never have been more between them.

Alec leaned over to press her hand over his, resting on his thigh. "I remember our time in Florence together. I had hoped I had come to mean more to you. You would forget about these plans to marry that English girl. We could be happy with the dagger."

A knock on the door prevented his response. "Mr. Westcott, I wanted to speak with you—" Madelene stopped inside the door, her eyes widened at seeing Alec with Gabriel. *In female clothing. With her hand on my husband's hand.*

"My dear, we were discussing our time in Italy together." His explanation only fueled her temper.

"Yes, Mrs. Westcott, your husband and I have shared a lot together."

Madelene watched the young woman slowly remove her hand from her husband's. Redirecting her attention, Alec said to Mr. Westcott, "We'll complete our conversation later," then rose from her chair to walk to the door.

Madelene gritted her teeth, Alec's complete change in appearance not lost on her. She would be a fool to not think the young girl flirted with her husband. But what did the young girl want more—the dagger or her husband?

Madelene and Gabriel ignored the young woman's departure.

"Mrs. Westcott, what was it you wished to see me about?" he asked while returning to his desk.

A nearby chair presented Madelene with welcome

support, which she fell into. And deliberated about the little scene she had witnessed. "Mr. Westcott, you never have exactly explained your relationship with Alec or whatever her name is."

Gabriel cleared his throat. "Her real name is Alessandra. And as for our relationship, nothing untoward at all. She was simply a friend to my sister and me during our stay in Florence."

"I see." She didn't, but an idea occurred to her to judge his sentiments of the girl. "It seems quite a time has passed since she was home in her own country. Perhaps it would be an excellent time for her to return?"

Leaning back in his chair, he studied Madelene and shook his head. "What a coincidence. Alec was actually here to advise me she is planning to return to her home as soon as this other matter can be settled."

"You mean the dagger?" Madelene interjected.

"Yes, there is still much to sort out about this business."

"It, it doesn't alter anything for tonight? You haven't changed your mind about giving my brother the dagger?"

"No, but something tells me that we are all pursuing the same end."

Frowning, she inquired, "You mentioned this previously. Whatever could you mean?"

"I hope to better explain after tonight."

"Where could she be?" Matthew asked himself again as he paced the small clearing off the road to Ludlow, only a mile from Westcott Close. Brelford, like a good chap, waited back at the inn for Matthew to return. Once they had the dagger, they planned to head for London as fast as the fastest carriage could convey them.

Hardly able to believe his luck, he felt great relief upon

receiving Madelene's note to meet him here tonight. She had the dagger in her possession. Matthew could finally leave this small village for the excitement of Town and more wealth in his pockets, after he returned the meddlesome sharp stick. He couldn't estimate its value.

It must be close to one o'clock in the morning. The moon acted as a beacon, brightening the night. Why his sister had chosen a different location, puzzled Matthew. *But I guess one cannot be too careful.*

Even earlier this evening, the innkeeper told him that the village had had many more visitors than usual around this time of year. Since Matthew couldn't trust the count, it could very well be Taglioni's men here looking for the dagger.

Growing impatient, Matthew noticed a long, broken limb near the outline of the trees and sat down to wait. It seemed like an hour, but in truth, only twenty minutes had passed. A gentle breeze disturbed his hair. Not uncomfortably warm, Matthew still felt perspiration on his brow.

Alert to any and all sounds, he presumed Madelene had found a way to arrange a horse and carriage to meet him. Any moment now, he expected to hear a horse's hooves and carriage wheels on the road.

His own borrowed dappled horse, King, tied to a tree, moved about restlessly. Could the horse sense something amiss? What could happen? In short order, he'd have the dagger in hand, then ride back to the inn. A beer would be very welcome taste on his palate along with the taste of success.

His hands clasped in front of him, propped on his thighs, he imagined the scene with Madelene. She would probably plead for him to take her with him again, perhaps even use tears for effect. But he could do nothing more for her. She was married. He still could not believe

Gabriel Westcott had actually taken his sister for his wife, but so be it. She seemed well looked after. Truly, everything had turned out better than he had planned.

What was that? Very faint, almost like horse's hooves, but no sound of carriage wheels. Matthew rose from his hard seat and pulled his pistol from his belt. If it wasn't Madelene, it could be a highwayman. Who else would be traveling the road this late?

A lone horse and rider. Too far away to discern the identity. Matthew hid behind a thick bush near the clearing until he could be confident of whether this person meant him harm or not.

The moon shone on Gabriel Westcott's face. Matthew frowned. What could this mean? Where was Madelene? Before he could contemplate further, he heard his name.

"Matthew Colgate. Are you here?" Westcott called. Matthew watched as his brother-in-law halted his horse and leaned across the pommel, searching the clearing.

Matthew hesitated. Westcott must have the dagger. Otherwise, why had he come and not Madelene? Was his enemy still in pursuit of some kind of revenge for his sister? If it was some type of trick, he would make Westcott pay. He stepped out from the tree. "Over here, Westcott." Not trusting his sister's husband, he kept his pistol steady in front of him.

Westcott dismounted, ignoring the pistol aimed at him, and led his horse to a nearby tree to tie him. He glanced over his shoulder at Matthew and shook his head. "No need for weapons."

Impatient to get this meeting done, Matthew demanded, "Where is my sister? Why is she not here?" He remained in his stance, watchful of any sudden movement from his foe.

Shrugging, Westcott told him, "You wanted the dagger.

I have the dagger. I decided it would be best if I meet you and give it to you. I thought it would be safer for your sister."

Taken aback, he almost spewed, "Safer? I'm her brother. She couldn't be safer in my presence." Matthew replaced his pistol.

"I beg to differ. She is with me because of you and your wager. I've heard of some of your other schemes, too, from which, no doubt, she helped you avoid any uncomfortable consequences.

No, Madelene is definitely well protected back at Westcott Close. She is now my charge and no longer any concern of yours. And because she loves you and worries, like a sister does, she wanted to make sure you received this dagger." He withdrew the silver-hued dagger and leather sheath from his coat pocket.

Although Matthew might have been affronted by Westcott's words, they were quickly forgotten at the sight of the long sought-after dagger. He started toward it but stopped when Westcott spoke.

"I can only imagine you are planning to return this dagger to Count Taglioni."

Matthew opened his mouth to speak but no words issued forth. How did he know who owned the dagger?

With a thin smile, Westcott informed him, "It wasn't difficult to learn the owner's name. I presume the count has also offered a sizable purse for its return." Westcott stepped closer to Matthew, his hand outstretched with the sheathed dagger.

"On your sister's behalf, I ask you to agree never to involve Madelene in any further schemes you might create for whatever reasons—most likely funds, I forecast." His words sounded harsh, like a vow. "Do I have your promise Madelene will no longer be distressed over any future antics of yours?"

Before Matthew could reply, he saw movement over Westcott's shoulder. His eyes widened in alarm. What was *he* doing here? In astonishment, he watched as the count hit Westcott with a heavy stick and knocked him to the ground, where he lay still.

"What, what are you doing here?" Matthew asked, his voice shaky. Why had he not insisted Brelford accompany him? It should have been so simple.

The count leaned down and picked up the dagger, which had fallen from Westcott's hand to the leafy clearing. "You've been a piece of trouble," he said to the dagger, pulling it out of its sheath and admiring the dull shine.

The night still held surprises. Matthew watched in amazement as the count twisted the hilt apart from the blade. He soon realized it wasn't the dagger the count wanted but something in the handle.

Taglioni turned it upside down and shook it, holding his hand beneath to catch—what? Nothing fell out. He turned to look at Matthew, his lips thinning.

The look in the count's eyes scared Matthew, frightened him as if he could read his own death in those black eyes. Matthew stepped back fumbling for his pistol and tried to determine how long it would take him to run to his horse.

"You betrayed me. I want the diamonds. What did you do with them?" The count walked toward Matthew, screwing the hilt and the knife back together again.

Backing up slowly, Matthew shook his head. "I, I don't know about diamonds. I agreed to meet, meet, Westcott there with the dagger." His heart beat rapidly. Matthew was flustered, seeing the look of pure evil and mercilessness on the count's face.

"I want the diamonds."

Madelene stood at the second-floor window, which afforded her a view of Gabriel on horseback as he rode down the lane toward the main road, circled the lake, and continued onward. She could see the faint outline of a horse and rider, but the dark left everything else to the imagination.

After his departure, she grabbed a thin shawl and left the house, having determined to meet Gabriel by the lake on his return home. She would wait for him there, since she dared not try to find their meeting place in the dark and on foot.

The wait back at the house had only served to make Madelene fretful and worried. She had to do something, and not even her guard, Alec, could stop her. Although truth be told, Alec appeared to have no interest anymore in Madelene's whereabouts. Perhaps she and Gabriel no longer worried about her fleeing back to London and her brother.

With a lantern to guide her, Madelene found the path they had taken only the night before. A wonderful night that had ended in his bedchamber where they slept locked in each other's arms.

Earlier in the day, Gabriel had tried to quell her fears, assuring her nothing could possibly go wrong, but Madelene remained unconvinced. After Matthew received the dagger from Gabriel, what might happen? Would Matthew want to hurt Gabriel for past grievances? She didn't want to consider any other outcome but that both men would return to their homes safely.

Madelene brushed a lock from her forehead and sighed. All she wanted was to know that Matthew had the dagger and could finally return it to its rightful owner. It would be a great burden lifted off her shoulders to know he was not in danger, and hopefully, out of trouble for a time.

A slight breeze tickled her nose as she gathered her shawl around her and continued up the path and through the notch of trees. She heard the bullfrogs in the lake, the comforting chirp of the summer crickets, and the leaves restless and rustling. The night wrapped her in its near stillness, and yet she shivered. It was a peaceful summer night, like any other night. But it wasn't, and she couldn't say why she felt differently.

The lake came into view, the water calm, the cattails on guard. It was their special place, and she felt welcome, like she belonged to this present moment. Fanciful thinking indeed.

The mirrored-moon lake tempted her to dip a foot in and test the waters, but she refrained. Safer to remain on the bank, admiring the view.

With little to do but wait and worry, Madelene held her lantern high and continued to stroll along the lake, wanting its peacefulness to steal over her and protect her from her cares.

Snap.

She whirled around, her heart in her throat, unable to breathe. Was someone nearby? Madelene stopped to listen.

Nothing.

"Is anyone there?" she called, not expecting an answer. She must have imagined she heard something. After all, who would be out this time of night, near the lake, following her? She certainly knew how to frighten herself.

Maybe it would be best to wait back at the house, she thought.

Another sound right behind her. Before she could turn or scream, someone pushed her hard, right into the lake.

Warm water hit her face and arms, stunning her, before she realized it was deeper than before. Her shoes couldn't touch the bottom. Quickly, she sank into the dark lake, swallowing mouthfuls of water, her arms ineffectively pushing the water aside and her gown pulling her farther down to the deepest end.

Madelene kicked hard to push herself to the water's surface. Coughing and sputtering, she called out feebly, "Help, help," before she went back under, swallowing more water.

Did she hear a dog barking?

Frantic, she pushed at the water, again breaking the surface. Flapping her arms on top of the water, she tried to keep her head from submerging.

And went back under a third time. Her strength began to fail her. If only she could move her legs to pull her closer to the edge of the lake, it might be shallower, and she could find purchase.

With one great kick, Madelene wrenched every part of her body above the water one last time to gain breath and scream for help. Then the water dragged her gown and her back under.

In a weakened state, but still flouncing in the water, she wouldn't give up, although her mind began to dull. Her arms began to ache.

Strong hands wrapped under her arms and pulled her up against a hard chest, where a hand cupped her chin to hold her head out of the water. She snatched valuable deep breaths, her heart still frantic in its fear.

She gasped breath after breath as her rescuer swam

toward the edge of the lake, which was closer than she realized. The water swirled and pulsed around them, as if wanting them to keep them, but the man who held her proved indefatigable. He grabbed her by the waist, lifted her out of the water, and pushed her onto the side of the bank before he dropped down beside her.

"Ruff, ruff." *Falstaff? What was he doing here? And who had saved her?*

Falstaff ran over to Madelene, who lay sopping wet with her hair hanging in drenched strands around her face, and eagerly licked her face, glad as she was that this stranger had happened by.

The stranger, when she swept the wet curtain of hair from her face and out of her eyes, was their neighbor, Mr. Bush. He lay beside her, breathing heavily, too. A few long minutes, neither could speak.

Madelene, still in shock, could not comprehend why one moment she stood by the lake waiting for Gabriel, and the next, she had been saved from certain death by Mr. Bush.

She bent over and coughed up more water before she reached over to shake Mr. Bush by the shoulder. "Mr. Bush, Mr. Bush, can you hear me?" She couldn't bear to think anything terrible might have happened to him.

"Yes, Mrs. Westcott? Is that you? Are you, will you, how are you feeling? I'm terribly sorry I wasn't here sooner." His handsome face turned toward her, as if he could see her and assure himself she would be fine. He leaned on his side to catch his breath, wiping his face with his hand before sitting upright.

"What matters is that you were here soon enough," she told him, before hiccuping. Then shivering. Then the tears fell, and she couldn't prevent them.

Mr. Bush, sitting quite close, reached and gathered her

in his arms as she sobbed on his shoulder. "My shoes, I lost my shoes," she managed between tears.

"I don't think it would be worth the effort to retrieve them," he told her ruefully, while rubbing her back.

"I hated those shoes," she told him, sniffing. "They were the wrong color of mauve." Her weeping continued on Mr. Bush's already wet shoulder, sending a thankful prayer to heaven that their neighbor took late-night walks past their lake. Falstaff sat next to Madelene and every now and then brushed his nose against her arm, reminding her of his presence.

When longer moments of quiet occurred between her subsiding cries, Mr. Bush told her gently, "I think I should get you home. Rather, if you could help me, I could perhaps help you. Between the two of us, we can ensure no more baths in the lake tonight, hmmm?" His sense of humor went awry because Madelene started sniffling again. It was some time before they could stand, collect the lantern, and make their way back home.

Mrs. Lavishtock soon had Madelene and her savior, Mr. Bush, sitting by the hearth in the kitchen, enjoying a spot of brandy for what the housekeeper claimed was medicinal purposes. She bustled around them, moaning and gasping, as she heard their almost tragic tale.

Her face white, Mrs. Lavishtock was indeed worried, first over Madelene and Mr. Bush's nearly drowned conditions, then the missing Mr. Westcott. She kept claiming her heart and her feet couldn't take this shock. In her anxiety, the housekeeper would sit heavily at the table, then rise to waddle around the kitchen. She couldn't find solace in either sitting or walking.

Falstaff, who had first raised the alarm to Mr. Bush,

Madelene had learned, lay by her bare feet. From time to time, he would lift his head, to see if anyone had food to share.

Mr. Bush finished his brandy and stood, ready to take his departure. He insisted he needed no help returning home, a path he had taken many times before.

A sudden noise broke the quiet when the kitchen door swung open. All eyes turned to see Mr. Westcott's grim face and a body slung over his shoulder.

Chapter Nineteen

"Matthew?" Madelene leapt from her chair by the hearth and ran to her husband, her heart in her throat. *Please, God, let it not be Matthew.* Eyes bright with unshed tears, she looked for comfort or answers or something from Gabriel, who shook his head.

Her husband walked slowly into the kitchen, a bit unsteady with his burden. "It's Matthew. He's lost a lot of blood." Directing his attention to Mrs. Lavishtock, he told her, "I need a room nearby. Please send Cappie or one of the other groomsmen to fetch the surgeon. He needs immediate attention."

Mrs. Lavishtock, fast on her feet despite her size, led the way. "Follow me, Mr. Westcott. We shall put him in the old butler's room."

Madelene felt overwhelmed and thankful her brother's life might yet be spared. She hurried behind Gabriel, resolute to not be a burden of sorrow. Her husband, with the heavy weight of her brother, climbed up the short flight of stairs to the servants' hall. Following her husband, she leaned on Mr. Bush, unaware of the tears slipping down her cheeks, her heart quite heavy with worry.

Gabriel hadn't spoken a word to her since his arrival. Indeed, when she caught a glimpse of her husband, his visage appeared pinched and white. Madelene determined that as soon as her brother was seen to, she'd have the surgeon look at Mr. Westcott.

At the butler's former rooms, Mrs. Lavishtock waited for them with the bed linen rolled back. "Easy now," she instructed as Gabriel laid Matthew on the bed.

In the center of the narrow bed, Matthew, of average size, looked as if he was melting into white snow, his face pasty white, his breathing labored. Much blood painted his right chest and continued to seep out. Madelene dashed her tears, refusing to believe her brother could be beyond saving.

Fanny must have heard the news because she arrived soon after with a handful of white cloths, followed by Hazelby and Windthorp with pitchers of water. They all stared at the patient, not knowing how to minister to Matthew.

In the small, serviceable room, lit by only two candles, Madelene sat at the head of the bed and pressed cool compresses to her brother's brow. She watched Mrs. Lavishtock and Mr. Westcott try to stanch the flow of blood from the wound to what looked like his upper right shoulder. Why was there so much blood?

The pale, sickly look on Matthew's face frightened Madelene. She could only help in a limited capacity, and prayed with all she had Matthew would make it through this dreadful time. Perhaps if she promised to be a good and obedient wife, God would answer her prayers. She always kept her promises or tried to.

The surgeon Longhorn finally arrived to the relief of everyone crowded into the small room. Upon entering the room, he ushered everyone out except Madelene, Mrs. Lavishtock, and Mr. Westcott.

Longhorn worked competently and intently on the patient as the night turned into the wee hours of the morning. He was able to stop the bleeding and sew the wound with several stitches. Confident Matthew would pull through, he still kept vigil like Madelene until he rest assured nothing more needed to be done.

Wiping his brow and straightening his tall form from the bed, he turned to Madelene waiting by the window and gave her the good news. When they both turned to speak with Mr. Westcott, they found him slumped in a chair.

Eyes widened in horror, she rushed across the room to her husband. What was wrong? Had he fallen asleep from exhaustion or had he been hurt as well? Guilt welled up inside her; all this time worrying about her brother, she had forgotten about her husband.

Kneeling beside his chair, she took his hand, looking into his face to see if she could discern his condition. "Mr. Westcott, Mr. Westcott." She looked up at Longhorn standing nearby. "Doctor, please, my husband. You must do something." Concern and fright weighted her words. As Longhorn went to the door to call for assistance, Madelene put her husband's hand to her cheek. "Please wake up," she whispered. "Please forgive me."

The surgeon called urgently to Mrs. Lavishtock to find two footmen to help move Mr. Westcott in order that he could better examine him. They left Fanny to watch over Matthew sleeping soundly from the laudanum given him.

Because Longhorn didn't want Mr. Westcott to endure the long climb to the first floor, the two footmen carried Mr. Westcott to the study on the ground floor. In the study, Madelene found Mr. Bush and Windthorp waiting for news of her brother, and quickly informed them of Matthew's condition and of Mr. Westcott's present state.

Windthorp waited in the corner of the study, constantly sending dark looks toward Madelene, who ignored him. Somehow she knew Gabriel's man believed she had something to do with her husband's injury, but she couldn't fret about the valet's feelings, so worried was she about her husband.

She stood next to Mr. Bush's chair, waiting as Longhorn examined her unconscious husband. Madelene felt comforted by Mr. Bush holding her hand tight, not realizing how much she needed a friend.

Swallowing hard, Madelene had no tears left to shed, surprised by her sudden and fierce concern over this stranger who overnight had become her husband. With her jaw set, her sentimentalities set aside, she would do whatever it took to make her husband well.

After the examination, the surgeon relieved everyone's worries. The footmen, Mrs. Lavishtock, Madelene, Windthorp, and even Falstaff waited in the study to learn of the diagnosis.

"It appears, Mrs. Westcott, that your husband received a hard blow to the back of his head, which must have knocked him unconscious. I felt a large lump on the back of his head, but no further injuries. I can only assume that when he awakened, he found your brother and carried him home. The ordeal exhausted him beyond measure, and Mr. Westcott simply collapsed. He needs his rest but will recover nicely in a day or two."

The surgeon paused. "Since this looks to be attempted murder, I'll need to contact the constable."

Madelene's eyes widened. "Not yet, Mr. Longhorn. Please wait until we can speak to my brother or my husband about what has happened this night. Then we'll do what needs to be done."

Longhorn nodded and leaned to pick up his bag. No matter what the surgeon's news, he could not prevent Madelene from worrying. She walked over to sit near the settee where her husband lay and clasped his hand to her breast, willing him to awake. The surgeon must have realized she needed more convincing because he leaned over to pat her shoulder.

"Mrs. Westcott, your husband will wake up tomorrow with a pain at the back of his head, but otherwise, he shall suffer no ill effects from this evening."

Madelene looked up at him and smiled faintly. "Doctor, how can I ever repay you for saving both the men I love tonight?"

Longhorn chuckled. "My repayment would be one of your lovely smiles."

Madelene tried her best to do as he asked.

It must have worked because the surgeon nodded and told her, "I'll look in on the patients tomorrow." He shrugged on his coat Graham handed him and left the room.

Since the surgeon said it would be safe to move Gabriel to his bedchamber, the footmen once again picked him up and gently carried him to the first floor.

After she saw to her husband's needs and comfort, persuaded she could help him no further, she returned to the ground floor to find Mr. Bush collecting his greatcoat and hat, prepared for his departure.

Given the lateness of the hour, Madelene convinced Mr. Bush to accept a ride home. They walked together, arm in arm, down to the hall, after she sent one of the footmen for Cappie and their carriage.

A warm breeze rustled her hair as they stood outside on the porch. A lone footman held a candle for light.

"Mr. Bush, I cannot begin to thank you for what you have done. Your heroism will long be known to me and my husband, realizing it is a debt we can never repay."

Mr. Bush patted her hand. "I don't think I'm much good for many things without my eyesight, but I've always been a good swimmer, which served me in good stead tonight. I can only thank God I was in the vicinity when I heard your little dog barking. He led me to you. I was glad I could reach you in time."

"Your humility is all goodness, but we shall always know the right of it. Please come again and often. I believe my husband will want for company in the coming weeks and to speak to you of his own gratitude."

Madelene kissed Mr. Bush on the cheek and pressed his hand. "Addle-pated that I am, I did not inquire after your health from an unsought bath earlier this night. I hope saving me from a watery grave has done you no lingering harm."

He turned his handsome visage toward her voice. "You certainly have been through quite a lot this night. *You* need to rest. As for me, have no fears. Other than no eyesight, everything else seems to be in good and working order."

"I am quite relieved to hear this. You know, Mr. Bush, you are indeed an amazing man. I doubt there would be many men with sight who would have jumped in the lake to save me."

Mr. Bush allowed himself to be helped into the carriage by Cappie. "Ah, Mrs. Westcott, there are many good men like your husband. I choose to believe that there is more kindness to be had in the world than naught."

"Mr. Bush, you are too generous and a philosopher at heart. Safe journeys."

The coach jerked off down the lane, and Madelene smiled

in the dark, yet on the verge of tears from exhaustion, worry, fright, and especially kindness from a man she knew too little.

Collecting herself, she returned to the house. After seeing her brother slept undisturbed and receiving Fanny's assurances she would awaken her should any change occur in his condition, Madelene headed to the first floor. She had another patient to see.

Inside their bedchamber, Gabriel slept soundly, and although Madelene wanted to crawl into bed with her husband, she needed to change from her damp clothes. She returned to his room to watch over him after acquiring dry nightclothes.

Afraid to disturb him, she chose a large, soft chair for a bed and fell asleep with Falstaff at her feet, dreaming of her husband, sitting in a tree. Had she really spoken the word "love" in referring to her husband? This thought scared her. What was to become of them?

"Sleeping Beauty, awake, fair maiden," the voice called softly to her.

"Ruff, ruff, ruff."

Madelene blinked awake and saw Falstaff on his hind legs, trying to climb onto the bed with Gabriel. As Gabriel leaned over to pick up Falstaff and plunk him on the bed, his flexing muscles distracted her. She remembered those strong arms holding her and wanted to crawl back into them and feel safe again.

The events of the previous night came whirling back to her, and she wondered if she would ever again know well-being. First, someone tried to kill her brother, then someone else or the same person pushed her into the lake. She wasn't exactly confident of the order of the catastrophes.

What did it all mean? She didn't know whom to suspect, but it couldn't be her husband. She wanted to tell him what happened at the lake, but thought it best to wait until he was on the mend.

Falstaff distracted her thoughts with his movements, as he had to circle several times before settling down at the edge of the bed.

She turned her attention to Gabriel. "Good morning. How are you feeling today?" She hoped her tone sounded more cheerful than she felt, pushing her reluctant body into a sitting position. Her neck pained her from using the chair as a bed, but she cared more about Gabriel's condition.

He appeared pale and winced when rubbing the back of his head. She frowned, distracted when noting he laid on his side, facing her, with a simple sheet covering the lower half of his body. Sometime in the night, he must have arisen and discarded his clothing, because they had definitely put him to bed still dressed in his outer clothes.

It would not do, it simply would not do to consider what he wore underneath the sheet, which in all probability was nothing.

Perhaps he sensed the direction of her thoughts, because he held out his hand to her. "Why don't you join me? I can assure you this bed is more comfortable than the chair." His warm brown gaze put her mind at peace. He seemed like the Gabriel from before last night's near tragedy.

She hesitated, rubbing the sleep from her eyes. "I'm terribly glad to see you are feeling better, however, I should check on the other patient, Matthew. Everyone was very worried about both of you last night, causing such a fright. I still cannot fathom what actually occurred. Do you remember what happened?"

Gabriel winced again, then rolled over on his back, looking at the ceiling. "I don't remember very much. Matthew and I had a conversation about the dagger. I had the dagger in my hand, and then I felt a sharp blow to the back of my head. I awoke and found Matthew unconscious and bleeding. I patched him up as best I could, placed him on my horse, and walked him home."

Madelene shook her head. "Did you see or hear anyone? Can you think of anyone who might have known of the meeting and wanted the dagger?"

Gabriel closed his eyes. "Perhaps. But I didn't see or hear anyone."

She could hardly believe his words. "Who do you think hurt Matthew and you? You know of someone?"

He turned his head to look at her. "I believe your brother wanted the dagger for Count Taglioni. If you had gone last night to meet your brother instead of me, I don't want to think what might have happened." His words were soft and low, his steady look unmistakable in his conclusion.

Madelene swallowed and nodded. The count wanted her *and* the dagger. "But if the count has the dagger, perhaps he'll return to wherever he came from, and we'll hear no more from him."

On his side again, facing her, he shook his head. "We can't assume he won't return. For you."

Her eyes widened at the threat, then she smiled, ready to toss off the darkness of last night. "I have no fear of the count because I know you'll protect me." Madelene rose from the chair and walked to the bed. "And my prayers were answered last night that you and Matthew are safe. That is all that matters."

Before she could protest, he grabbed her hand and pulled

her down on the bed with him, slightly jarring Falstaff, who growled and moved to the other corner of the bed.

Leaning on his elbow, he looked down at her and said, "You mean you actually prayed I would live? I thought you might have felt well rid of me, your husband, and already on your way back to London."

His words mocked her, and if he meant to tease, he drew tears instead.

She looked up at him. "I do not find your words very amusing."

If someone could look contrite and surprised at the same time, it was Gabriel. Could he have realized how deeply he wounded her with his words?

She frowned and pushed him away, fighting him to leave the bed. "This cannot be good for your head."

"Ah, I think it would be a perfect thing for my head and other parts that ache." He had a certain glint in his eye. And if she shifted more in his direction, she would feel those aching parts to which he referred.

She thought he needed more time to recover. Until the surgeon gave his opinion Gabriel was infinitely better, she would allow those parts to ache and hope the pain would go away on its own accord.

"Don't leave. Tell me more about your prayers."

"What more is there to tell?"

Without looking at her, he stroked her arm. "Tell me how worried you were about me. I like hearing it."

Such audacity. Madelene had to chuckle. "There is nothing more to tell. I think my heart stopped beating until Mr. Longhorn informed us that both you and Matthew would survive. I don't ever remember being so frightened before, and for both of you, except when my father had taken ill."

"I like knowing you were worried about me. Maybe I

should be hit on the head more often," he mused with a smile.

"You should be careful for what you wish for. I may have to hit you on the head for all the aggravation you cause me. Now, no more frivolous talk," she told him sternly.

He leaned farther over Madelene, his arm around her waist, until his lips almost touched hers.

She stopped him with a hand to his chest. "Wait."

He blinked, obviously surprised. "Wait for what?"

"Did you marry me for the wager?"

"What? The wager? Where did this come from? How you fritter from one subject to another I can scarcely fathom. We can talk later. How about—"

"I need to know. Did you marry me for the bet?" He couldn't possibly know why she asked, and she would tell him someday. Right now, she only wanted his answer.

He sighed and rolled onto his back. "No."

"No? But surely you needed the funds?"

"No."

Astonished, Madelene sat up and turned to look at her husband. "You didn't need the money?" She couldn't keep the incredulity from her voice.

When Gabriel turned his head to look at her, all amusement had left his eyes. "Madelene, I planned to win the bet, one way or the other. When I heard your brother was to marry you to that fop Brelford, I knew I had to put a stop to it. I concluded I could have you as my wife and win the money on top of it."

"Hmmm." She laid back on the bed. "I'll have to think on this more."

"Yes, you do that. Later. At the moment, I have something else in mind."

A knock on the door disturbed their conversation.

It was Fanny. "Ma'am, your brother is asking for you."

"Oh! Fanny, tell my brother I'll be there directly. Thank you."

This time, Madelene leaned over her husband to kiss him softly. "We shall continue this conversation. I want to learn more about why you desired me for a wife."

She popped off the bed and hurried out the door to change before he could deter her with his winsome ways.

Madelene found her brother lying on his side, his eyes half open, watching her enter the room. She swept over to his bedside and sat in a chair next to his bed. "Matthew, how are you feeling this morning?"

Matthew closed his eyes and shook his head. "Mad, it hurts to breathe. When is the surgeon returning?"

Fanny, standing near the doorway, answered him. "Sir Colgate, I heard the doctor tell Mrs. Lavishtock he would be here before noon."

"I wish it would be sooner," he said to no one in particular.

Madelene took his hand. "Can you try to sleep? It might help, and you won't feel the pain."

Jerking his finger in Fanny's direction, he demanded, "You, girl, get me something to drink. Whisky, brandy, whatever is handy."

Fanny, wide-eyed, looked at Madelene for direction.

In consternation, Madelene bit her lip, then nodded. "Fanny, please check with Mrs. Lavishtock and bring some spirits to my brother."

The maid quickly curtsied and fled the room.

Madelene sat quietly by her brother's bed, and before Fanny could return with any liquor, she heard his snoring.

She leaned her head against the wall. Although relieved

Matthew was safe, she worried for how long. Did the count still pose a threat to her brother? How could she help him? Of course, there was no question but that he continue here at Westcott Close for rehabilitation.

Then there was her own safety to worry over. Someone had deliberately pushed her into the lake. Reflecting on her short stay at Westcott Close, she thought she remembered the surgeon saying something about poison when she had fallen so ill.

"Is he dead?"

Madelene looked up to see Alec in her usual garb in the doorway. "No, he is not. The surgeon has told us his recovery will take some time, but he is not going to die." She stood and walked out the door, closing it behind her. "Where were you last night when all this happened?"

The young woman took a step back in the hallway, looking both ways, as if trying to decide how to answer or which way to go. "I went to bed early and didn't learn what happened until this morning when Mrs. Lavishtock told me. I'm glad Mr. Westcott was not hurt." If Madelene didn't know better, she'd think her words had an almost defensive tone to them, but she had no idea what it meant.

Alec turned and fled in the direction of the kitchen, leaving Madelene staring after her, very puzzled. *I bet that girl knows something. And I plan to discover what it is.*

Chapter Twenty

Days passed as both patients continued their healing. Gabriel mended much faster than Matthew, considering his injuries were not of such a severe nature. Mr. Bush visited nearly every day to both Gabriel and Madelene's delight, for she was becoming increasingly fond of their neighbor.

Madelene and the rest of the staff spent many hours in Matthew's room, changing his bandages and keeping him entertained. He even had Hazelby play whist with him.

Another change in the household was Madelene and Gabriel sleeping apart for those days. He couldn't convince her that his head didn't pain him, and it would heal much faster with her next to him in his bed. Concerned she might disturb him while he slept, she disagreed, knowing her husband indeed did not have sleep on his mind. She told him she thought it best if he had the bed to himself a little longer.

Madelene also felt rather strange sharing a bed with a man, and her brother lying wounded on the lower floor. To be sure, her brother expected her to share a bed with her husband, but the notion still rested uneasily with her.

And what about their future together? Gabriel had never spoken any affection for her. If she remained here as his wife, Madelene would have to give up her dream of returning to London and designing fashions for the *haut ton*. Not being dependent on any man for her livelihood. But they couldn't divorce, and they couldn't get an annulment. The only solution Madelene could imagine was remaining married but she living in London, and Gabriel living here at Westcott Close.

She'd need to have a talk with her husband about their future, and soon. Madelene wanted everything settled.

Gabriel recovered but spent much of the time reviewing his accounts with his steward, who oversaw holdings for him in Shropshire as well as in London. With all the happenings lately, he informed Madelene he had been neglecting his financial matters.

After supper, a week after that dreadful night, Madelene and Gabriel went to see Matthew and hear from the patient himself how his progress fared. Gabriel had not seen Matthew since the night he brought him home.

They sat in chairs at the end of Matthew's bed as Matthew slouched in bed with a disagreeable look on his face. Smiling brightly, Madelene told her brother, "Mr. Longhorn is quite pleased with your recovery. However, he does think it will take a month or so before you'll be well enough to endure the journey back to London."

Gabriel added, "Matthew, consider our home, your home. There is no hurry to leave. We simply want you to be strong enough for whenever you're ready to depart."

Madelene turned her attention to Gabriel with a fond

smile. How considerate of her husband to make such an offer, after all that had passed between her brother and him.

"I can't wait to leave here. I'd like to be on a coach tomorrow." Matthew made no apology for being aggravated and impatient.

"Matthew, please." She walked over to his bedside. "Say no more. We can't have you unwell and unfit to travel. You may further exacerbate your wound."

His mouth remained in a thin line. "I find it rather difficult to remain in a home where the master of the house has grievously injured his guest."

Madelene backed away from her brother, her eyes wide in disbelief. "Matthew, I'm sure the medicine the surgeon gave you must give you thoughts you would otherwise not entertain."

Her brother stared unrelenting at her. "Why don't you ask your husband why he didn't kill me the other night?"

Madelene shook her head, trying to understand the enormity of his words. How could he be saying such things? Surely, he couldn't believe Gabriel had—no, it wouldn't bear thinking about it.

Before Madelene could begin to defend him, Gabriel interjected, already having left his chair to approach Matthew and his suspicions. "I don't care for your brand of humor. For surely, that is what this must be. I do not know who did you harm the other night, but it certainly was not me. I found you and brought you home. If I wanted you dead, I would have left you where you lay." His voice grew colder with each word.

Both men warred silently with each other as Madelene stared helplessly. Who should she believe?

Matthew responded defiantly, "Perhaps you had a change of heart and decided I held some purpose after all.

Perhaps you wanted to hurt my sister with my death on your hands. Any number of reasons will do."

"Matthew, stop. You don't know what you're saying. Gabriel couldn't, he simply couldn't." Tears clawed into her throat and into her voice, until she could no longer stand the sight of her accusing brother and her silent husband.

She needed to find solace, a sanctuary. Madelene ran outside and down the terraces until she found the little pond gracing the lawn. A flat stone provided a seat where she could rest and wrap her arms around her legs. She refused to shed any more tears for her brother or her husband and the predicament in which she found herself. But her head did ache. Did she have to choose between them? One of them lied, but who?

If Matthew lied about who tried to kill him, why? What could his motive be? Or was it possible Gabriel could have tried to finish what he started over a year ago on the dueling field?

"Madelene." She heard the voice call softly.

She looked up to find Gabriel standing on a rise near her, then bowed her head, afraid he might notice the hesitation in her eyes.

A few minutes passed before Gabriel descended the last few steps until he could join Madelene on the large boulder overlooking the pond. He sat down and took her hand in his. Madelene felt his gentle touch under her chin, lifting her head to gaze at him. In his warm brown gaze, she saw a man known for his honest dealings and sincerity, and something more.

"I would hope you believe me when I say I could never hurt your brother. Not now."

She wanted to believe him. The earnest look he gave her almost broke whatever part of a heart she still possessed.

"I don't understand, why would Matthew lie?" she asked him miserably.

He could only shrug. "I cannot say I understand your brother's motives."

"But you were hit on the head. Perhaps you did still have the dagger and maybe you did stab him, but didn't mean to." She knew she grasped at the strings of a wildly dancing balloon of fancy.

He gave her a peculiar look. "Do you believe me capable of injuring another when I am unconscious?"

She shook her head and looked away. "Truly not one of my more rational thoughts."

Gabriel took her hands within his own. "Madelene, believe me. Hold on to me. If you give me the chance, I'll find out if it was the count or another who wanted your brother dead."

Madelene closed her eyes, shuttering at the word "dead."

Before she could respond, they heard a voice calling.

"Mr. Westcott! Mr. Westcott! There's someone here, you must come!"

They both glanced up in time to watch Mrs. Lavishtock appear over one of the stoned terraces. Madelene frowned, completely drained of all emotions save curiosity.

She turned to Gabriel. "What could Mrs. Lavishtock have on her mind that she must come and not send a footman to retrieve us?"

He easily rose and drew her up with him. "I think we shall discover presently."

When Gabriel and Madelene arrived back at the house, they found many of the servants gathered in the hall, watching a foreign woman with a babe in her arms chattering in

Italian to Alec. Nearby, a strange man hopped about, doing his best to avoid Falstaff's sharp teeth. The little dog seemed determined to take a bite out of the stranger's ankle.

Gabriel worked his way through the group gathered to hear the conversation. Although he knew a smattering of Italian, he would need Alec to translate.

The realization suddenly dawned on him.

The baby! Lucinda and Matthew's baby.

How could he have forgotten the date? Had it already been eight months since his birth? George Matthew Westcott. In preparation for his plans to marry Madelene and all the events which followed, he had forgotten the tenth of June was the agreed date for little George's Italian nanny to bring him to Westcott Close.

Before Gabriel had left Italy, he arranged for Donna Bella Vincenzio and her brother, Carlos, to bring Lucinda's son to Westcott Close, since Gabriel planned to raise George as his own. He neglected to realize the time he needed to prepare Madelene for this addition to their household.

Although concerned about his wife's reaction, first he had to see to the baby. He held up his hand to stop the conversation between the two women. "Alec, let's move this discussion to the front parlor," he directed.

Gabriel dismissed all the servants save Mrs. Lavishtock and Windthorp. The two foreigners, Madelene, Alec, the housekeeper, and the valet joined him in the sea green–draped room.

Even with all the loud chatter, the baby continued to sleep swaddled in his basket at Donna Bella's feet while she sat on one of the matching green settees. He remembered the Italian woman, a little slip of a woman with a plain sad face and small black eyes. Her gray color already outshone her original deep black hair.

Donna Bella's brother, seated next to her, was more animated, with a big smile and even bigger laughter, although his frown indicated he understood little, if any, English.

Alec sat at the end of the settee, across from Gabriel and Madelene. "Donna Bella says she brought the baby as promised and the baby is well. She would even like to stay on and care for the baby since she has become quite taken with him. Her brother would remain here for a time before returning to Italy. They would like you to find work for him here."

With his wife at his side, remaining speechless, Gabriel nodded. "Tell Carlos we will find a place for him." He looked at Donna Bella but spoke to Alec. "Alec, tell Donna Bella I am pleased with the care she has taken of the baby."

Alec and Donna Bella and Carlos all exchanged words, then brother and sister smiled brightly at Gabriel and Madelene.

"Alec, do they, either of them, understand or speak any English?"

Alec frowned and turned to her compatriots again. Another conversation ensued, then the young woman looked at Gabriel and shook her head. "Very little."

He brushed his hands through his hair before he said to Alec, "Will you consider staying longer, until everyone is more comfortable?"

Alec shrugged. "*Sì,* if you request this of me."

He nodded and told her, "I think that would be best." In surprise, he watched Madelene leave his side to walk over to Donna Bella and kneel to look at the sleeping baby.

"May I hold him?" she asked Donna Bella softly, breaking the silence. To illustrate her request, she folded her hands into a cradle position and rocked them back and forth.

When the older woman smiled at Madelene and nodded, Madelene carefully picked the baby out of the basket and placed him against her chest, folding his blankets around him. She stood in the middle of the room and gently swayed with the baby, leaning her head against the child's.

She flabbergasted Gabriel. Why would she want to hold a stranger's baby, not her own? Why hadn't she asked any questions or at least shot accusing and angry glances at him?

However, she did nothing but give all her attention to the infant. His wife seemed perfectly content to coo and watch the baby's face, touching his cheek with the back of her finger. It shouldn't possibly be this easy. He sighed and relaxed inwardly. Perhaps Madelene could save the situation.

The baby's sudden crying interrupted his thoughts.

"Oh! Oh dear!" Madelene looked helplessly to Gabriel, then to Mrs. Lavishtock. She tried jiggling him, but he wouldn't stop, his cries grew louder and louder.

Mrs. Lavishtock hefted herself out of her chair. "I've raised my sister's children. I know what needs to be done. Let me have him." Quick as a blink, Mrs. Lavishtock plucked little George from Madelene's arms and ambled out the door. "It's either one end or t'other!" she shouted over her shoulder.

When Gabriel jumped to his feet, everyone else rose as well, assuming the discussion at an end.

Madelene walked over to him and placed a hand on his arm, her expression unreadable. "I need to speak with Mrs. Lavishtock about the arrangements for the new houseguests." Before she left, she went to the brother and sister and said quietly to them, "*Grazie,* Donna Bella and Carlos, for bringing the baby to us," then gracefully departed the room.

Gabriel continued to stare after his wife. The woman was a complete puzzlement to him. He silently thanked fate or whatever deities had handed him a compassionate and understanding wife.

He gestured to the door. "Come, let's go to my study, where we'll discuss what needs to done."

Alec jabbered in apparent translation to the couple who nodded over and over, then followed Gabriel out the parlor door.

"I hear we have a new member in the household. How does the little brat fare?" Matthew reclined on his bed, holding his right side.

On the opposite side of the room, Gabriel, with his fists resting on the chair's armrails, watched his brother-in-law, his eyes narrowed. Surely Matthew must have wondered what Gabriel could possibly want with him, other than to learn how soon he would be taking his leave of them. How soon could he travel where Madelene would not worry about him? Probably never, he thought to himself grimly.

Gabriel gritted his teeth. "Please refer to the baby as George or not at all."

Matthew shrugged his shoulders. "In the hospitality of your home, I can honor that request."

Inwardly, Gabriel winced hearing Matthew actually use the word "honor," since Madelene's brother appeared to possess so little of it himself. He was surprised Matthew actually understood the meaning.

"Pray tell me why you are visiting my sickbed, because

the time is ripe for my afternoon nap." Matthew yawned, either weary from Gabriel's presence or his own discomfort.

Gabriel perused his subject, wanting Matthew to spin in the wind, imagining what his sister's husband could possibly want with him. "While I am extremely interested in your estimation of when you might be departing our home, I do have a question only you can answer." Gabriel saw Matthew stiffen, almost as if he knew what would be asked of him.

Matthew gave him a thin smile. "Let me not keep you guessing any longer. Ask away." He fluttered his hand, looking bored.

Gabriel stared hard at his brother-in-law, convinced if Matthew prevaricated, he would know immediately. "Why have you lied to your sister about what happened the night you were stabbed?"

Matthew's eyes widened. Obviously Gabriel's question had caught him unawares. "To what are you referring exactly?"

"You told your sister I tried to kill you. Why did you create such a falsehood? You and I know it was not how you described. The only logical explanation would be the count. He hit me and stabbed you. Enlighten me as to your reasoning."

"I'm not convinced it did not happen as I said. The events of that night are playing strange tricks on my memory. It was a grievous wound, as you know, and I almost died." He sighed. "What difference does any of this make? You have Madelene and a new babe to care for. I'll be leaving as soon as Longhorn says I can travel. Not to darken your door any longer." Matthew slumped farther into his bed, signaling their conversation at an end.

But Gabriel shook his head. "I know you to be a liar. I

do not bandy that word about lightly, especially regarding my own brother-in-law. However, you have lied to your sister that I tried to kill you, and before you leave, you will confess the truth to her. Or at least, if your memory does not serve you well, you will tell her you cannot be sure it was I behind your intended demise."

Gabriel rose from his chair, anger stirred in him. He had been unable to convince Matthew the necessity of telling everyone, especially his sister, the truth of that night. More and more, Gabriel had concluded Madelene was best left in his care, and not her brother's. He understood all too easily that family blood and connections meant little to Matthew. Difficult to believe Madelene and Matthew were full-blooded siblings, for they were so different in nearly every way.

His wife, Madelene. She possessed as much of the honor and love for her brother as he lacked for her.

A knock on the door interrupted Gabriel's leave-taking.

Hazelby's head appeared around the edge of the door. "Pardon my knock, but there's a Mr. Brelford here to see Mr. Colgate." He waited at the door for a reply.

Matthew sat up with great exaggerated pain, but his body remained alert. His weariness seemed to have vanished.

"Please show him in. I would like to talk to my friend." Matthew looked over at Gabriel to explain. "He is a friend from London and must have heard of my misfortune."

Gabriel considered his next move. Matthew wasn't planning to impart any new information, since his direct verbal attack had done nothing other than put him on his guard.

Wait. *Brelford.*

The name of Madelene's intended bridegroom. Gabriel's

suspicion was immediately aroused. Perhaps Matthew wouldn't tell him anything further, but Brelford might be enticed to do so.

Gabriel spoke to Hazelby. "By all means, please welcome Mr. Brelford into our house and show him to Sir Colgate's room." He looked at Matthew as he walked toward the door. "I hope you have a pleasant visit with your friend. But I warn you. Our conversation is far from over."

After he departed Matthew's bedchamber, Gabriel sought Windthorp immediately. He gave instructions to his valet to learn as much as he could about the relationship between Brelford and Colgate.

"Whatever are you doing here?" Matthew demanded of his friend. The last he had seen of Brelford was at the inn with a tankard in his hand.

Brelford sat in the same spot Gabriel had occupied earlier, wringing his hands. "Oh, dear. Oh dear. I didn't know what to do. I stayed at the inn waiting till the time was right. When the dust settled, I figured it would be safe to come around."

Matthew shook his head. "You should have stayed at the inn till I sent for you."

Brelford lowered his head, his shoulders slumped. "I was concerned about you," he said meekly.

Impatient, realizing this conversation would get nowhere, Matthew changed the subject. "Did you see anything or hear anything the night I was to meet the count?" His mouth turned grim. "He owes me. For the dagger and *this,*" he said, pointing to his bandaged wound, which had incapacitated him.

Brelford nodded. "I thought to stay hidden, but I worried over you and drew closer." He shuddered. "I saw the count stab you, and fearful he might find me cowering beyond the tree, I escaped, not wanting to be his next victim."

Matthew stared hard at his friend. "You didn't stay to discover if I lived or died?"

Brelford couldn't look him in the eye. "I truly thought you were done for. It was terribly upsetting," he ended in a whimper.

Waving his hand in disgust, Matthew remembered the diamonds. "Do you know why the dagger was of vital importance to the count?" When Brelford shrugged his ignorance, Matthew continued. "Apparently, there were diamonds in the dagger's hilt, but they were missing. The count, in his anger, stabbed me, believing I had tricked him and stolen the diamonds. Of course, I had no knowledge of those gems, but I know who does."

At Brelford's blank face, Matthew scoffed. "Why, Westcott! He must have found the diamonds and removed them from the dagger. At our meeting, he had the dagger with him and was on the point of handing it to me when the count sneaked up behind him and hit him on the head."

Matthew struggled to sit up farther and pinned Brelford with his hard look. "I must find those diamonds, or Taglioni might decide it is not necessary for me to continue breathing. Unfortunately, if I attempted to declare the count an attempted murderer, his cohorts would dispatch me, and quickly."

Sitting at the edge of his chair, Brelford turned pale, and he shook his head. "What can we do? Have you thought of anything?"

"Yes, what if I asked Colgate to make room for you here? Since I am tied to this bed, you might be able to search the house for the jewels."

Lips twisted, his friend frowned at the suggestion. "I

don't think that will do. Westcott and your sister would not likely welcome me with open arms."

Matthew reluctantly agreed. "Yes, probably not." He tapped on the counterpane for a lingering moment. "Why do you not go back to the inn and await word from me? I'll arrive at a plan that will get us the diamonds and heading back to London."

Madelene could not help staring at little George as she held him in her arms. He slept peacefully, his cherubic mouth opened slightly. How could she love this child in such a brevity of time? Oh, how she wished he was hers. She wanted to remember his every sigh, his every smile, and attend his every waking moment. Most mothers' wish, she imagined. She smiled, feeling foolish. That could not be possible.

Who was his mother? And why had his mother let him be taken from her to be sent here to Shropshire? Maybe George's mother thought he'd be taken better care of by his father, Gabriel.

Madelene wanted to believe she jumped to conclusions in assuming her husband was the father. But what other explanation could there be? And she could hardly contain anger toward him, after he brought such a sweet one as George into their home. Sometime today, she promised herself, Gabriel would explain everything. The thought saddened her that Gabriel had known another woman, and this woman had given birth to his child.

Her attention turned back to the little one she held in her arms, amazed how immediate the world had changed. In the flicker of a candle, her heart had turned topsy-turvy, first with Matthew injured and accusing Gabriel of the foul deed, and now this tiny soul, who needed a mother and father. Death and life, so unchartered.

She decided to find her husband and placed George in his cradle, looking around the lovely apple green room, her favorite color. Her sojourn at Westcott Close brief, she never knew this room existed in the opposite wing of the house, the same floor as her own bedchamber.

She had been astonished when Mrs. Lavishtock had shown her this nursery, already filled with a cradle and toys, clothing, an assortment of accessories the little boy would need.

Her husband must have been planning all this time to welcome his son home, but why had he never mentioned the child to her? What other secrets did he have? Did he not trust her?

Their future together now seemed more hazy than vivid.

Once Matthew left for London, where would that leave her? With a motherless child, missing diamonds, and someone trying to kill her.

She had to share her concerns with her husband. He would know what to do. Although she had dismissed the broken gig wheel as accidental, Madelene could not forget about the poisoned soup or the push into the lake, which almost became her watery grave. She shuddered, remembering the warm water and being unable to catch her breath. It was the most frightful experience, and one she wouldn't soon forget.

Mrs. Lavishtock burst into the room to interrupt her musings. Indeed—Madelene smiled—their housekeeper had no quiet way about her. "I'll watch the young one, dearie. Why don't you take tea? Fanny has arranged the parlor for you and the master."

Madelene thought they were fortunate to have such a

kind soul in their household. She always seemed to know how to make things right. "But George—"

But Mrs. Lavishtock tsked her out of the room. "I'll have Fanny watch him a bit later. You can visit tonight, when he's sure to be awake."

After one long last look at the child who had fallen into her life and already stolen her heart, Madelene sighed and walked down the stairs toward the parlor.

Gabriel stood when she walked into the room. He smiled at his wife, admiring her loveliness, her pretty pink cheeks and shiny blue eyes. He thought her quite handsome in her robin blue morning gown.

They hadn't spent much time together lately, and he missed her. Missed her soft voice and her warm smile. The look only she could give him when something he said or did exasperated her, a combination of a frown and smile.

Time had been their enemy; now he intended to reclaim it. There was much to discuss between them. He opened his mouth to speak but she started first.

"Mr. Westcott, I feel an urgent need to speak with you about something uppermost on my mind."

Of course she would want to know about the child, and he had every intention of enlightening her.

Gabriel ushered her into the comfortable rose Chippendale chair near the serving table, then sat across from her on the brocaded divan. "Madelene, I would know what disturbs you." He knew very well it could be a number of things, like her brother, or the baby, or the dagger.

As he waited for her to begin, he noticed her hands gripped the rails of the chair for support.

"I hope this doesn't sound insupportable to you, but I believe someone here might be trying to do me harm."

Chapter Twenty-One

He thought himself prepared for anything. But this.

My God. He should have known. No one had alerted him of any new happenings with his wife to cause him concern. Then with the incident the other night and George's arrival—

Gabriel couldn't contemplate, didn't want to give much credence to her words. However, he had to admit, there could be a spark of truth behind them. He had so much on his mind of late. The doctor's words about her poisoning flew back to him.

"I was hoping the poison was simply an accident," he tried to reassure her.

"But the push into the lake wasn't," she replied, much too calmly.

Gabriel leapt to his feet, placing his hands on his hips. "Whatever are you referring to?"

"I haven't had the opportunity to tell you," she began and leaned back in her chair. "But that night, I waited by the lake for you to return from your meeting with Matthew. As I waited, obviously too close to the lake's edge, someone came from behind me and gave me a very hard push, which sent me into the lake."

Pacing the room and listening to her story, Gabriel could hardly believe it. No one had mentioned this. He thought he had kept her safe, having all those he trusted to watch over her. Someone hadn't done their job. He kept his expression calm, belying the raging anger and guilt welling inside.

He looked over at his wife, who had turned a chalklike white. "Pray continue, although, thank God, I do know the happy ending."

"It was Falstaff. He was with me and began barking when he saw me in the water. You know I can't swim . . ."

He swept over to her chair and knelt next to her, grabbing her hand. "My God, I had no idea. I should have been there."

Madelene smiled at him and touched his cheek. "But Mr. Bush, on his way home, heard Falstaff barking and followed the noise. He heard me calling for help and jumped in the lake. Luckily for me, he is a good swimmer and was able to pull both of us from the lake."

Shaking his head, completely astonished by this news, he rose and walked back to the divan. "I must thank Mr. Bush when I see him again." He turned his gaze back to her. "I wish you had spoken to me sooner."

As her husband, he had not done a good job protecting her, and he planned to fix his oversight immediately. He determined to speak to all the servants to learn whether anyone had seen or heard anything untoward that night. Even with everyone's vigilance, someone had gotten to Madelene. Could it be someone within the house? He'd ask Windthorp to make discreet inquiries.

When considering all Madelene had said, Alec came to mind. His young Italian friend had been acting strange lately, as he thought more on it. Disappearing into the night with nary a word of her adventures or her destinations, or at least that was what the butler Graham had relayed to him. She still dressed as a young man, assuming she would be safer, he concluded. What could she be about?

Could Alec possibly be involved with the attempts on Madelene's life? And if so, he believed himself to be the reason.

What about the count? He was obviously still in the vicinity, and while he might want to do harm to Madelene, the night she was pushed into the water, he had been hunting Matthew and the dagger.

"Whatever should we do?" He heard the unmistakable worry in her voice.

"Madelene, you have my word I will look into this matter. Until I can be assured of your safety, you will need to remain within sight of either myself or Windthorp," he said, hoping to lessen her fears.

Madelene's deep blue eyes begged for answers, but she would have to be satisfied with his solution. "I cannot fathom it could be one of the servants. While I might be able to find a plausible answer for the poison, I *know* someone pushed me into the lake. I have no doubt on it."

Gabriel sat near her and reached across the serving table for her hand. He needed to touch her, reassure her that all would be well. He'd stake his life on it. *No one will take Madelene from me.*

"Mr. Westcott." Gabriel and Madelene turned to see who intruded on their conversation. Windthorp.

"Forgive the disturbance," he said in his dry tone, "but I have information I believe you need to hear, immediately. I will await you in your study." He left as quietly as he had appeared in his own ghostlike manner.

Gabriel knew Windthorp would only seek him out if his news was of the utmost urgency. He nodded to Madelene. "Please finish your tea. I'll send Fanny to you for company."

Madelene rose from her chair, clasping her hands together. "Gabriel, I, I would like to take dinner in the nursery. It would bring me a measure of comfort."

Her request surprised him. "We do need to speak of George, perhaps later today. Donna Bella and the young lady, what is her name, Charlotte, whom you hired as his nurse, can see to him. I would prefer you take dinner with your husband, as we have much to discuss."

Madelene had directly ignored his orders. Well, perhaps not exactly an order, more of a request to join him at dinner. Gabriel smiled to himself. Could he be jealous Madelene wanted to spend time with George and not him? Sighing, he returned to his meal in the large dining room with only Hazelby for company.

After dinner, Gabriel stood at the nursery door, waiting for her to answer.

Madelene opened the door to her husband, knowing he was bound to appear at some time and not a little disturbed she had not attended him at dinner.

"Ah, so this is where you are hiding," he told her, entering the room.

She closed the door behind him, waiting for his irritation to show itself. "I told you earlier I wanted to take dinner with George. Charlotte and I fed him, and he fussed a bit before falling back to sleep." She felt a bit defensive upon his intrusion into the nursery.

Gabriel walked over to the sleeping baby and tucked the blankets more closely about the little boy. His tenderness should be no surprise, she supposed, given the babe was his.

Looking at her in the dim candlelight, her husband murmured, "I see. There's always tomorrow night."

He wasn't annoyed with her? She still didn't know her husband well enough to understand his moods.

"I see you have already changed into your nightclothes." He took a step toward her. "Shall we repair to our room? It has seemed like a year since we last slept in the same bed." His voice warm and seductive while he reached for her.

Madelene backed away, although she yearned to walk in the opposite direction. She wanted to recapture what they had lost in such a brief time but they still had many things to sort out between them.

She had had all afternoon to ponder their situation and decided she needed more information on Alec and the baby. And even more important, she needed to know who she could trust.

"Gabriel, I, I need time. We need to talk before—"

"I know. We have to return to our own lives. You deserve answers, and I'm quite prepared to give them to you."

She stared wide-eyed at her husband, surprised, yet relieved at his forthcoming candor. "Not here, not now."

He nodded and gave her a quick smile. "We'll sort everything out in the morning. I have new information about your brother and that night. I thought perhaps—"

George's crying interrupted further conversation. Madelene swept past Gabriel to gather the babe in her arms, trying to shush him and talk to her husband at the same time.

"Tomorrow morning," she whispered, then her attention returned to little George.

Gabriel gave her a curt nod and left the room. He knew she would need time to adjust to these new arrangements.

Alone in his bed, he waited a long time to see his wife, but she never appeared. Disgruntled, he'd simply have to be patient awhile longer.

The next morning found Gabriel on his way to London. He had received an urgent message from his man of affairs at his Town office that one of his ships had sunk off the coast of the Canary Islands. Although he knew this was the absolute worst time to leave Madelene and the baby, he had to answer to his customers expecting their supplies and see to insurance arrangements.

Before he left, he met Mrs. Lavishtock in the front parlor and demanded she prepare every plate for Mrs. Westcott. It was only when the housekeeper promised vociferously she was already handling the matter that he felt satisfied.

In the yellow parlor, Gabriel gathered those he knew he could trust—Windthorp, Mrs. Lavishtock, Fanny's brother, Graham, Fanny herself, and Hazelby—and demanded that one of them would always be near Mrs. Westcott and protect her and the baby at all costs. He would return as soon as he was assured matters had been seen to in Town.

As for who posed a danger to Madelene, there had to be a connection with her brother. Trouble followed him like rain after dark clouds.

After everyone had left, he requested Mrs. Lavishtock to remain. The housekeeper eased her bulk onto one of the settees and gave him a sparkling smile. Could she know what he intended to ask of her? His housekeeper seemed to know a lot about what happened around here, even before it happened. Then he shook his head for his imagination. Impossible.

"Mrs. Lavishtock, I need your assistance. I'm planning a special introduction for Mrs. Westcott."

She eagerly nodded, her turban perched precariously on her head. "Och, I think it a brilliant idea!"

Gabriel frowned. "But I haven't told you what it is yet."

She smiled a knowing smile. "Oh, but Mr. Westcott, whatever you have planned will be brilliant!"

"Oh, right. Well, I don't have time to go into many details. I'll leave it to you. Use whatever resources are required. I'd like to open the house in a week or so to introduce my wife to whoever might be residing in the county at this time. It will have to be a small, informal affair since many acquaintances are enjoying the Season. The Derby's next week. You know, we haven't had a soiree here since before Lucinda—"

"Yes, yes, magnificent! I've already started planning the menu. You don't need to worry, Mr. Westcott, I'll see to everything. You get to London and get back here to your beautiful wife and nephew." She wobbled out the door, seeming intent on continuing the preparations.

What? How? When he returned, he would definitely have to look into Mrs. Lavishtock's history. She couldn't be some sort of seer or witch, could she? How did she know who George was, unless Donna Bella or Carlos had told her? However, since neither party spoke the other party's language— He shook his head. He had more pressing concerns.

He took one last look of Madelene sleeping peacefully in her bedchamber. It was harder to leave her than he realized.

* * *

Madelene came to breakfast in her rose morning gown and learned from Fanny that her husband had gone to Town. Why did he not take her with him? London. How she missed Town during the Season. Now was about the time for the Derby. And the dances. She sighed. What she wouldn't give to go to a dance. But she was no longer a young girl seeking fun and frivolity, but married with a husband and babe to care for.

On her mind was also her fledgling business, which she had left in the most capable hands of Mrs. Quantifours. She wondered how the older seamstress fared. Even though they had maintained sporadic correspondence, Madelene urgently wanted to return and help with the new planned fashion plates. Mrs. Quantifours assured her all was well, and she had hired a businessman to see to the numbers. Still, Madelene would have preferred hearing the news directly and not through the post.

"Ruff, ruff, ruff."

She looked down to find Falstaff at her feet. That little terrier was never far from her side, either from affection or the realization Madelene almost always had a biscuit in her pocket.

"Greetings, fair sister."

Madelene looked up in surprise to find her brother in the doorway, leaning heavily on a borrowed cane. She pushed back her chair and hastened to the door. "Matthew! Should you be up and walking around? Has Longhorn been consulted?"

Her brother waved her off. "Mad, I'm perfectly capable of standing on my own. And I'm famished." He limped over to the sideboard. "What do we have here? Scrambled eggs and lox? Delicious! You do have a good cook here at Westcott Close." He piled his plate and hobbled to the table where Madelene waited for him.

While she would always worry over him, Madelene had been trying to determine the best time to speak with her brother about returning to London. She could only persuade him if she was assured he would suffer no more ill effects from the journey.

"Matthew, I am terribly delighted you have left your sickbed. You may be able to return to Bloomsbury soon, I hope," she told him, brightly, hoping he would believe it would be best for him, and not necessarily in *her* best interests.

"But, Mad, I thought you liked having me here. This is a good place for a person to mend and have plenty of time to think."

This did not bode well, she thought. "Oh, and have you come to any conclusions?"

He continued eating and did not answer her directly. "I shall be on my way soon, I hope, but I need your help. I want you to get those diamonds from your husband."

Madelene frowned, completely taken aback. "What are you speaking of? I have no notion of diamonds. I only knew you sought the dagger. What makes you think Mr. Westcott has diamonds in his possession?"

Before replying, he drained his coffee cup and patted his mouth with his napkin, probably trying to gather his thoughts to compel her to assist him. She knew all his wiles.

"My dear sister. The dagger held no great value, but the diamonds were the true commodity. And your husband has them." He proceeded to tell her of his speculations and convince her to find the diamonds for him.

Deciding she did not want to hear any more, she rose from the table. "I think there could be more than one logical solution, but I refuse to discuss this further." She leaned her hands on the table and looked at her brother. "Matthew, I think it would be best if you would make plans to return home."

The irony was not lost on Madelene, considering it was only a short time ago that she had begged her brother to take her home. Now she wanted him gone, and she would remain behind, willingly.

Matthew leaned an elbow on the table and held his right side. She noticed he had always shown a weak side before he was attacked. Shaking his head, he told her, "Mad, I'm surprised at you. I would have believed you would want someone on your side here in this house, although I am in no condition to defend you."

Madelene started, her mouth dropped. "Defend me from whom?"

"It is no secret there are goings-on here and someone means you harm. Perhaps your own husband?"

She couldn't have been more astonished and affronted. "However can you believe such a thing, and even more, speak on it? I will not have you slander my husband in our own home. I want you to seriously consider a departure from here at the earliest opportunity." Afraid she might sound too harsh to her own brother, she relented, "It would be best for all of us. You need to get on with your life, as do we here."

"Dear sister, this can be easily resolved. I will inquire one last time. Will you or won't you speak to your husband about the diamonds?" Like an inebriate with his liquor, he wouldn't let go.

What else could she do? "If it will hasten your departure, I will have a word with him. If he has nothing more to say on the subject, than neither will I. Are we agreed?"

Matthew shrugged, then nodded. With a slight curve

to his lips, he told her, "You may be surprised at what he knows."

"Matthew, you do weary me. I'll leave you to your breakfast and see to George." She headed for the door for respite from her onerous brother.

"Madelene, I find it hard to believe you are eager to care for another woman's babe," he said to her with a most innocent look on his countenance.

At the door, she closed her eyes and bowed her head. "He's a mere babe. *George* belongs here." She didn't turn around but left her brother. As she climbed the stairs, she wondered if he had always been so selfish and ill-tempered, and she had never realized it before.

Finished with breakfast and her brother, Madelene decided to look in on George, then go for a walk. Perhaps a walk would clear her head.

She met Charlotte at the door of the nursery. Charlotte, the nurse from Town, smiled brightly, a small little thing, with red hair and blue eyes, who originally hailed from Ireland. She had made immediate friends with most of the staff, from what Fanny had told her. Except for the fact she and Donna Bella had sparred once or twice.

Madelene returned the smile. "And how is our boy today, Charlotte?"

"Very well, madam. Oh, look at the babe with those big eyes. Wide awake, he is! Come, little one, let's see to you." Charlotte picked the babe up and walked over to Madelene. "Mrs. Westcott, would you like to hold little George? He's ever such a good baby. Don't hardly cry at all, except when he's hungry. And mistress, he has such an appetite. Donna Bella and I wonder where he puts it all."

Not having spent much time in her presence before,

Madelene was surprised at the nurse's loquaciousness. When Charlotte handed the baby to Madelene, little George looked up at her and smiled, then giggled. He yawned, but his eyes never left hers. Eyes that were either green to light brown or light brown to green.

"Oh you are a precious one, you are," she whispered to him and kissed him on the forehead.

She spent the morning in peaceful company with George and Charlotte before venturing downstairs.

Outside the library, Alec stood waiting for her. Madelene's eyes widened in surprise, since Alec had returned to female clothes again. Why the change? Madelene reluctantly thought the young woman very attractive, with her large blue eyes, pale skin, and even with her short curly blond hair. And wherever had she found the pale yellow dress she wore that fit her form so well? Was it possible she continued to hold an attachment to her husband?

"Mrs. Westcott, I would, I think you should know something about your husband. Perhaps if we could talk in here?" The woman gestured to the library doors.

Madelene started. Why would Alec want to speak to her? Sighing, she nodded and followed the young woman into the library.

One of the maids had opened the burgundy drapes earlier, letting the sunlight stream into the room in dusty rays. Bookcases from floor to ceiling covered every wall, but most of the books were hardly ever touched, Gabriel had told her. These bookcases contained mainly law books from his uncle's work and his hobby of ornithology.

When they were seated across from each other in the center of the room on the divans, Alec looked at Madelene, her face emotionless. She would not make a very good actress, Madelene thought.

"It is difficult to tell you this. I have thought a long

while before I decided it best to present you with this information."

"Indeed. Pray tell, why the urgent need at this time?" Madelene could not quite keep the irritation out of her voice.

"I believe it safe now that Mr. Westcott is gone. And you need to know what he is capable of."

Madelene closed her eyes and shook her head. "You have insinuated these lies before, what makes you think you could convince me, that you could speak the truth?"

Alec continued in her monotonous tone. "I had my reasons earlier. You should know I met Mr. Westcott and his sister in Florence where I lived with my uncle. I made the acquaintance of the Westcotts through mutual friends at a baptism for the youngest child.

"When I realized the Westcotts understood only a little Italian, I offered to explain to them. Over the months, I slowly turned to Mr. Westcott for comfort because my Uncle Giovanni is very demanding. I wanted to spend little time with him, and Mr. Westcott offered his home. He was very kind to me. When his sister became sick, I could help him."

Madelene could hardly contain her impatience. "Indeed, that was very gracious on your part to help care for his sister. But what particular news do you have which would be of import to me?" This young woman's story was beyond tedium.

Alec hesitated briefly. "We fell in love."

Madelene's jaw dropped. She jumped from her seat. "Impossible. I cannot believe you. I know Mr. Westcott would not have you remain in this house with myself as his wife. When Mr. Westcott returns, I will request you leave our house immediately." This woman's declarations were a complete figment of her fanciful mind.

As Madelene headed to the door, she heard Alec say, "I know you believe someone is trying to kill you. It is your husband." The young woman had risen and followed her, calm and collected, as if they merely discussed the weather.

Taking a deep breath, Madelene turned to confront the young woman and knew she lied. With narrowed eyes, she told her harshly, "I don't believe you. I don't believe any of your banbury story. You have taken advantage of my husband's hospitality and his kindness toward you. I can assure you, you *will* vacate our home the moment Mr. Westcott returns."

Alec looked nonplussed. "Whose baby do you think lies upstairs in the nursery? You may be surprised to learn Mr. Westcott will not be as anxious for me to leave as you are." The young woman slipped out the door Madelene unwittingly held open for her, in mute disbelief.

Surely, this cannot be true. Unfathomable. Could she actually be caring for her husband and Alec's baby?

Madelene stood in the doorway biting her nails, an old habit she thought long ago conquered. She had a choice to make. She could either spend the rest of the week in her bedchamber and the nursery or continue her daily routine and confront her husband upon his return.

On her way to the kitchen to speak with Mrs. Lavishtock, she determined no one would take George from her.

Chapter Twenty-Two

Still annoyed from her recent interview, Madelene finally composed herself when she learned Gabriel had left a brief note for her with Mrs. Lavishtock, which explained his sudden departure and eased her mind. He hadn't left without thinking about her.

She decided one of the first conversations she'd have with Mr. Westcott would entail Alec. Madelene refused to consider that he had or ever could harbor any affection whatsoever for that little Italian girl, the moniker she secretly gave Alec.

Luckily for Alec, she didn't approach Madelene again that week, or Madelene would surely have forgotten her manners and boxed the young woman's ears.

In Mr. Westcott's absence, Madelene and Mrs. Lavishtock kept busy planning the house party for the ensuing Tuesday night. Invitations were posted and those still in the country accepted, probably due to both curiosity and boredom.

Excitement skittered through the servants and extra help from the village, although the number of acceptances numbered only old Mr. and Mrs. Tottencott; Squire

Jones and his daughter, Rachel; the Vicar Caring; Mr. Bush; and the ladies, Hyacinth, Rose, and Lavender Mc-Martin, apparently named after their mother's favorite flowers, or so the story went. Many renowned families still enjoyed the London Season and could not attend.

Relieved it would be an intimate gathering, Madelene and Mrs. Lavishtock planned a fine menu of several removes. After dinner, Madelene thought they could play whist or faro, and perhaps one of her neighbors played the pianoforte.

If asked, she would not have relayed how nervous she was in meeting her neighbors. She understood to curry positive favor with Lavender McMartin and Mrs. Tottencott would grant opened doors throughout the county for her.

Any hope of making a fine wife to Mr. Westcott in the eyes of the Shropshire gentry depended on her success as hostess for the evening. Madelene had finally admitted to herself, perhaps her future lay here with Gabriel and George, and it was what she wanted, her own family.

If only she could be more sure of Gabriel. Of his reason for marrying her, what Alec meant to him, George's history.

Fanny pleasantly surprised Madelene when she informed her mistress of her aptitude as a seamstress. Upon hearing the news, Madelene requested Fanny make her dress for the evening, only after the maid assured her she would have enough time to complete it.

When Madelene wasn't spending time with George or seeing all arrangements continued on schedule, Fanny fitted her with a new, white, silk gown. Madelene had received several of the latest patterns popular in Paris to study. Fanny, a few weeks earlier, had become Madelene's lady's maid and loved handling all the fine dresses

Madelene had brought from London, even if they weren't the latest designs.

As a few days passed into the week, Madelene caught the servants staring at her at various times and pondered the reason. She had also noticed someone in the household lurked—she amended, *lingered* within calling distance. It didn't take long to realize no attempts had been made on her life, with her husband gone.

Preposterous. Inconceivable. It meant absolutely nothing.

Upon the eve of the anticipated arrival of Mr. Westcott, Madelene heard a noise from her husband's bedchamber. Could Gabriel have sneaked into the house without apprising anyone?

Her heart beat faster. She had missed him and was willing to admit she missed his presence, his voice, his touch, and his kiss. Hardly daring to breathe, she opened the door, calling out, "Gabriel, are you home sooner—"

Matthew stood by one of the opened white cupboards. "Mad, you startled me. I was borrowing one of Westcott's cravats for the soiree—"

Madelene bustled into the room. "I hardly think our gathering is the right entertainment for you, in your condition."

Her brother leaned on his cane before settling into a cushioned chair. He broke into one of his famous Matthew smiles, the one he thought captivated everyone.

"Mad, I feel much better. Indeed, I hope to go home in a few days. I'll take you with me, if you want to go. I know how you long to return to Bloomsbury and our home."

Madelene's jaw dropped. Not now. Bloomsbury was no longer her home. Something was happening here. She soon comprehended he gave her the words she wanted to hear to distract her. Distract her from—

"What are you doing in here? I don't believe you are looking for a silly cravat. And how could you dare to intrude into my husband's own bedchamber to possibly steal those jewels?" She crossed her arms and tapped a finger, waiting for his answer.

Matthew rubbed his brow and dropped his head. "Mad." He looked up at her again, standing near the edge of the bed. "Mad, I need the diamonds. I've got to find them." His eyes pinned on her. "Mad, I promise, if you give the diamonds to me, I'll leave you both and never worry you again."

Sighing, Madelene sat on the bed, overwhelmed, and shook her head. Those diamonds again! She was exceedingly tired of hearing about the jewels.

Matthew leaned forward on his cane. "Mad, if I don't deliver the diamonds to the count, he may, hc may, try to hurt me again."

"The count? This count is the one who drew me to the Pickled Goose looking for you. Do you mean this count hurt you the night Mr. Westcott brought you home and not my husband? You lied? How could you do such a thing, to me?" Madelene sputtered for words to express her outrage. "This is unforgivable. From the beginning, this whole marriage farce was your idea. You put me in this predicament."

"Yes, yes, I know. But I thought it might be best. If you suspected your husband could be capable of hurting your brother, you would want to return home with me. Wouldn't it solve everything?"

She closed her eyes, unwilling to look at her deceitful brother. Could she have been wrong all this time, doubting her husband? She should have known her brother capable of anything, only caring for his own affairs.

She bit her lip and sighed. Opening her eyes, she told him, "Matthew, if you stopped looking out for your own interests, you might have asked me about the status of my health and marriage. Much has changed since that night when you wouldn't take me with you. I have a home here now. This is where I belong."

"How noble you are, Madelene Colgate. A finer saint I have never met." His sarcasm was wasted on her.

"If your intention is to stir me to anger, I do not have the inclination. I will tell you that I'm happy, and I wish you could find the same peace, too."

"It seems my plan has worked out exceedingly well for you. You have benefited more from this marriage than I could have ever foreseen." He paused and looked her in the eyes. "You say you want me to be happy. Then help me find the diamonds." His brown eyes looked cold, unrecognizable.

"I've already promised you I will talk to Mr. Westcott and inquire about the diamonds. If indeed he has them, I shall try to convince him to give them to you, but I cannot promise anything. If these diamonds are stolen, then they don't belong to you or the count, but the magistrate needs to be informed. This is probably why, if Gabriel has them, he might be waiting to learn more information about their ownership."

Matthew managed to get to his feet. "Mad, they do belong to the count. He has convinced me of this. Sister, I know you'll do this for me. You'll ensure everything comes out tolerably well. You always do."

He walked a few feeble steps to the door. "I think I may have overtaxed myself. I think it a good idea if I take dinner in my room." A grim smile on his face, he wobbled out of the room, leaving Madelene shaking her head as he departed.

How could her father, an honest, respected, and dignified member of society, have raised a son like Matthew? Indeed, she found it difficult at times to believe Matthew was a seed from him, so unlike were they in many ways. When Father had been alive, he knew how to manage her brother and to keep him on the straight path. Without Father, Matthew had become a brother she hardly knew.

She returned to her bedchamber, thoughts of her disappointing brother faded, supplanted by Gabriel. Her heart actually felt lighter. She knew Gabriel could never have hurt her brother, not then and not now. But what other lies had her brother told her? She was almost afraid to discover.

Chapter Twenty-Three

"I hear you are on the mend, brother-in-law. Very good news indeed," Gabriel drawled as he stood inside Matthew's bedchamber.

Matthew pushed himself into a sitting position, surprise written on his face. "Westcott. I didn't expect, we—yes, I am doing ever so much better. Perhaps another week—"

"Tomorrow would be a perfect day for travel to Town. I have arranged a carriage for you and Brelford, assuming he is still here in the vicinity." Gabriel remained near the door while he watched Matthew squirm upon hearing of the change in plans.

"See here, Westcott, tomorrow is too early. Longhorn comes again in the morning, and he may not think it best I should travel. And the soiree is tonight. My sister would want me to attend her."

Gabriel heard the pleading in his voice, but remained unmoved. "I'll have a talk with Longhorn myself to receive reassurance you can make the journey. As for your sister, with the baby and the upcoming festivities, she is feeling taxed."

He leaned against the wall and crossed one ankle over

the other. "On another matter, Colgate, I know you seek the diamonds, but they are not yours to have, nor the count's." At the look of shock from Colgate, he confirmed what Gabriel had already expected.

"Those diamonds were stolen by the count in Florence from the Countess Rocusco. I'm aware the count wants you to retrieve them and will pay a hefty sum if you are able to do so." He stepped away from the wall and closer to Colgate's bed.

"I also know it was the count who stabbed you that night, not I. And I plan to tell Mrs. Westcott today of this aberrant lie. Because of your deceit and untrustworthiness to me, and in particular, to your sister, I want you to leave in the morning. I would prefer you have no further involvement in your sister's life, but that is her decision to make and not my own. Are we in agreement?"

Colgate glanced around the room as if the answers could be found in the corners. He sighed. "Yes. I'll leave in the morning. Would you permit me to say my farewells to my sister?"

Gabriel eyed him curiously, for this seemed an abrupt change of heart. It could only indicate trouble brewing; like the witches of *Macbeth*, what did he plot? He would speak with Windthorp and Graham and ask them to watch Colgate closely, until he finally left their home and Shropshire.

He gave a curt nod. "Be prepared to depart at seven o'clock." Gabriel turned to leave when he heard his brother-in-law speak.

"Westcott, I, I've made a muck of things, but could we have peace between us, for Madelene's sake?"

He almost sounded contrite, Gabriel thought. "A discussion to have at a later time. Until tomorrow."

* * *

His unpleasant business behind him, Gabriel ran up the stairs two at a time, anxious to speak with Madelene and see her beautiful smile. He hoped she had arrived at agreeable terms for their marriage.

He found clean water in his bedchamber and washed the travel dust from his body. Somewhat sore from the long and hasty trip, Gabriel wanted nothing more than to lie beside Madelene. He left Falstaff sleeping under his bed, a favorite place of late.

At her bedchamber door, he hesitated, then knocked softly.

No answer. The hour still early, she probably slept. He quietly pushed the door open and discovered, indeed his wife asleep, lying on her side. Locating a chair near the poster bed, he sat down across from her. He wanted to gaze at this woman.

This woman who had mysteriously breathed life back to his heart, desolated after the loss of his sister. He would never allow anyone—friend, family, acquaintance—to know him in an intimate manner of the heart, but his sister. Although there had been other women, none could light his days and his nights.

Until now. Until Madelene.

Somehow, she had to forgive him for the terrible beginning of their marriage. They would start all over again. Perhaps, back in London—

"Gabriel," he heard her say sleepily. "I'm terribly glad you're home." She smiled with her eyes closed, looking as content as, hmmm, as a woman well loved. And she was indeed. She must know that.

Rounding the bed, he joined her and gathered her in his arms, breathing in her lavender-scented hair. His hand almost shook as he stroked her long, dark hair. His woman, his wife, awed him. He kissed her forehead in the softest of caresses.

She pressed her face close to his lawn shirt and clutched him around the waist. "I've missed you. Has it only been a week?" she whispered into his chest.

He tipped her head up to meet his kiss. What began as a gentle kiss of sweet restraint blossomed into something more desperate than he could have imagined. Their lips met again and again, and it wasn't enough. He had to have all of her, all at once.

He wanted to take it slow and mark her as his only. A morning she would always remember. A new beginning. He would show her how much he loved her by paying homage to her sky blue eyes, and her pink cheeks, and her soft dark hair, and that was only the beginning.

But his wife surprised him, more awake than he realized. His Venus came to life. She unbuttoned his shirt and slid her hands around his hard waist, playfully biting his nipples.

His plans were for naught, because she wanted him as much as he wanted her. He only wanted to please her and allow him to show her what she needed. He could believe this was their very first kiss and thought her most beautiful in the morning.

In no time, he pulled off her night rail and rolled her on top of him. Only his pantaloons remained between them. He knew the sweetest ache as he pressed his hardened manhood between her legs and cupped her bottom. When she teased him with her hair, dragging the dark tresses over his chest, then with her wet tongue, and finally with her breasts, he became undone.

The taut peaks of her breasts within his dreams and reach, he grasped them, molded them, fondled them, until she moaned for more. When she leaned down to lick his lips, her quickly learned skill of blazing mouth and hot tongue surprised and delighted him. He thought this lady was no lady. Not here, not now. Where had she learned such pleasurable skills? Innate and intuitiveness were his only conclusions, but it didn't matter.

Before he realized what she had planned, she had already reached between them, undone his buttons, and found his hard need. Her hand nearly set him off before he was ready. Both eager to be joined together, Gabriel slid his hand down her soft, undulating body until he found her wet folds.

As soon as he touched her, she jumped and muffled a squeal in his shoulder.

Madelene loved the hardness of him. He was hard wherever she was soft, and their bodies fit so well together. She began moving against his hand, pleasure racking her body, all thought retreated. Sensation after sensation flowed through her. She wanted more. She needed more.

When she almost reached the mind-numbing precipice, he pushed himself inside her welcoming wetness. As she moved her hips to match his strokes, he teased her nipples, sending frissons of delight throughout her body. Every part of her quivered and glowed with his possession, a satisfying custody of her body and soul.

It wasn't enough. He had to have more of her. Now. He grabbed her shoulders and pulled her over and under him, never losing a stroke, and continued pushing into her wet center again and again, as if it was their first and last time together. He could see the desire building in her lovely blue eyes, widening with every deepening thrust.

When he reached between them to add his caress to the top of her heat, he watched her body quiver and her eyes become a deeper blue. Together, lost in the heated throbbing moment and each other, he pulsed into her with all his strength, and she clung to him, pleasure shooting through her as their bodies and lips pressed together, in a final surrender.

Exhausted, their hearts slowed. They fell asleep in each other's arms.

"I have been unable to have coherent thoughts when you are near me. When you went away, I had time to reflect upon everything. I knew you couldn't have hurt my brother. Matthew finally confessed to me last night you didn't try to kill him." She looked up at him as he stared down at her, Gabriel leaning on his elbow next to her.

Awake after a deep sleep, Gabriel knew the time had come to talk of many things and give Madelene answers to her questions, answers he had wanted to give her long ago. It finally felt like the proper time. Before he began, he held her close against him, reveling in the feel of her and knowing she was his.

"I saw Matthew this morning, and we discussed that night." He hesitated and ran his hand through his hair. "Madelene, I have asked your brother to return to Town." He waited with bated breath for her response.

She nodded. "I think it best." The look in her eyes took her many miles away, and he wondered where she was and how to bring her back to him.

"Madelene, are you sure? I don't want this situation with your brother to affect our life together." He couldn't find the words to tell her how much her happiness and contentment meant to him.

She returned his gaze. "But there are the diamonds. He needs them and has asked me to obtain the diamonds from you. I told him—"

Gabriel pulled her closer, their bodies entwined like rose vines, yet thorns remained. "We had a chat about the diamonds as well. I told him the diamonds didn't belong to the count but rather a countess from Italy. I have to give the diamonds to the magistrate in London, who will see they are returned to Italy and their rightful owner."

She raised herself supported on her elbows, fear reflected in her eyes. "But what about the count? Matthew told me he feared for his life if he didn't hand over the diamonds to him."

"I've spoken to a good friend of mine on my recent trip to London. He planned to look into the affair and have a word with the count. After Count Taglioni learns he won't be receiving the jewels, and the magistrate wants to speak with him, we believe he'll make urgent plans to return to Italy."

He felt the relief fall from her shoulders as she returned and melted into his side. "Thank you for interceding on my brother's behalf. I worry so about him. You see, he can't take care of himself. My father always looked after Matthew, but with Father gone—"

"Perhaps your father didn't allow your brother to stand on his own often enough. He appears to be struggling to become a man, a long overdue change."

"That is so."

Enough talk of her brother. The situation would soon resolve itself once Colgate had left Westcott Close and returned to his own home.

Their reunion had consumed much of his thought on the journey to and from Town. He wanted her to know something very important, and he had to find the words to tell her.

Reaching for her hand, he said quietly, "Madelene, I

must tell you something. I have wanted to tell you for a long while."

He felt her stiffen, not knowing, obviously, if he carried good news or bad, and held her even tighter.

"I have to tell you about George."

"I don't want to know. Please, I don't want, I can't. I love the little fellow, and I—" Her voice shook with tears.

Whoever said there was a fine line between tears and laughter must have known his wife. He placed a finger under her chin and raised her eyes to look at him. "Madelene, there is no reason to be in such a state. He is your nephew."

If possible, her blue eyes became bluer and bigger. She sat up abruptly and stared at him, as if she could measure the truth in his eyes.

Gabriel nodded and smiled. "Little George is our nephew."

Tears surfaced in her hopeful eyes, her face still pale. "But how? I—" She frowned, carefully assembling the news. "Little George is *my* brother and *your* sister's child?" She could barely speak the words and shook her head. The information must have been too much for her to absorb.

She wrapped her arms around her legs, needing time to sort the implications and presenting him with a lovely view of her satiny back, which he had to touch, more than once, and which, to his slight annoyance, she ignored.

After moments passed, she focused again on Gabriel. "The news that George is my nephew is joyous indeed, but Matthew . . . he doesn't know he has a son?"

The truth and his decision rested uneasily with him, but she needed to know his plans—plans and promises he had made eight months ago to his sister. "No, I haven't told him, and I don't intend to. It was my sister's wish.

You know he cared little for my sister. He wanted nothing to do with her. Even told her he had but a few months to live, in hopes she wouldn't want to marry him."

His anger grew at the remembrance of her suffering to bring a man's child into the world who had not given her more than a night of bedding and thought, and who had nothing more to give to his beloved sister. "Colgate doesn't want a son, and when my sister knew she wouldn't survive, she made me promise to raise him as my own. Somehow, in the brief two hours she lived and held George in her arms, she managed to give him all the mother's love she had to serve him for a lifetime."

He willed his wife to understand. "I must ask you. Your brother can never know."

Madelene, a rapt listener to the story, shook her head, her mouth turned down. "His shocking behavior has grieved me in the past. I fail to understand his behavior, but never more so than at this moment. I ache at the pain he caused your sister." She held his hand tightly. "I wish I had known, but he flippantly informed me it was none of my affair."

She paused and pressed him. "He must know," she whispered, and Gabriel's heart echoed her pain at the thought of losing George.

"I am not willing to discuss this at the moment. I need more time to think on the situation and what is best for George. You must consider your brother is barely able to care for himself, never mind another living creature. I fear what might have become of you if I hadn't learned of the wager."

"Not that I can condone any of my brother's actions, but the marriage was to be only temporary and solve our financial straits."

He stared into her pained eyes and knew she would

have a difficult time forgetting her brother's actions, and the right and wrong of it. "My dear, it would have been very difficult to obtain an annulment, no matter what your brother might have told you."

Madelene lay back in bed and pulled the white linen to cover herself, although the room was warm. "Perhaps someone gave him erroneous information. Do you truly believe my own brother would wish me ill?"

Reclining on his back, Gabriel sighed. "I can answer your question with my own instincts. He probably didn't give the whole arrangement much thought. Your brother tends to display an appalling lack of farsightedness."

They lay quietly together until Madelene put a hand to her forehead. "My goodness. What must the time be? We have guests arriving tonight, and I must dress and talk to Mrs. Lavishtock." She shoved her husband's arm. "Go, go. We cannot dawdle any more in bed."

"How easily my wife turns from lover to shrew," he told her with a smile, but he did rise to pull on his clothes, telling himself this conversation was far from over.

"Mr. Westcott, you will please leave my room. And I wouldn't bandy the word 'shrew' about, because you might just deserve one."

He saluted her on his way to the door. "Touché. But as long as she was the beautiful Madelene, I would have her any way that I could." He jiggled his eyebrows lasciviously.

"Go, you hedonistic heathen!" she mocked him and threw a pillow in his direction.

Only after his departure did she realize they still hadn't discussed Alec. At least she was more than relieved to learn Alec was not George's mother.

* * *

"Oh, ma'am, if I must say so, you look lovely this evening. Mr. Westcott will be hard-pressed to take his eyes from you," Fanny told Madelene breathlessly after putting the last of the baby's breath in her hair.

Madelene smiled at her reflection in the looking glass as she sat in front of her vanity. "If this is true, it is due to your fine work. Fanny, I am very delighted with this gown you made. I should have you make all my dresses, for your skill as a dressmaker is incomparable. You would put my former mantua-makers in Town to envy."

Blushing, Fanny replied, "For sure, ma'am, you are kindness itself. Not many such as yourself would trouble themselves with a beginner."

"You give yourself too little credit. I'm sure I will not know what to say should any of the ladies tonight inquire about my seamstress. I may have to create a fib. If Ludlow heard about your accomplishments, you might not wish to remain as my lady's maid."

"Oh, Mrs. Westcott, I do not think of such things. I am fortunate to be in your employ."

Their eyes met in the looking glass. "I'd say we both had good fortune. I better hurry with these earrings or Mr. Westcott will wonder why I dally."

Fanny had prescient sight at Gabriel's admiration of the picture Madelene made as she joined him in the rich burgundy drawing room.

"You are a confection of brilliance, and I hunger for your sweetness," he murmured in her ear, giving a care to the distance between them. It wouldn't do to create talk as they waited to welcome their guests in the drawing room. Before he knew it, gossip would be stirred as the country folk spoke of Mr. Gabriel Westcott as quite besotted over his new wife. Even though, of course, he was.

Before meeting Gabriel to receive their guests, Madelene had checked on dinner with Mrs. Lavishtock, made sure Falstaff had been fed, and looked in on her brother. She thought it strange Matthew was dressed for the soiree, although he had no intention of attending and had not been invited.

"I'm leaving in the morning, Madelene. Your husband has kindly arranged for a coach to return us to Town. I don't know when I shall see you again." His face looked rather morose, alarming Madelene.

Us? He couldn't possibly mean the baby? "Who—"

"Brelford has been waiting for me in Ludlow until I can return home. He has certainly been a steadfast friend, which I have sorely needed."

Madelene relaxed slightly. He didn't refer to George. But . . . hoping her husband would understand and on the verge of telling Matthew, she heard Falstaff barking and excused herself to see about the commotion.

In the kitchen, Madelene had found Alec standing next to the outside door, her clothes disheveled and dirty, Mrs. Lavishtock shushed Falstaff while inquiring where Alec had been.

"Mr. Westcott asked me go to the village and collect a package for him."

"That surely does not explain your appearance. You're as filthy as a chimney sweep," the housekeeper told the young woman, who couldn't have looked more disinterested in the berating.

When Alec noticed Madelene in the kitchen, they stared at each other, distrust mirrored between them before Madelene turned to the housekeeper and smiled. "Mrs. Lavishtock, please see Mr. Westcott receives his package. Our guests will be here soon. Please see to Falstaff and anything else that comes through the *servants'* entrance." She left the kitchen, determined to discover where Alec had been this evening.

Gabriel and Madelene stood together near the entrance to the drawing room while Hazelby held a tray of Madeira wine and Graham announced the guests as they arrived.

"Mr. and Mrs. Tottencott," Graham intoned, sounding far older than his youthful appearance allowed. Fanny told Madelene he had been practicing his introductions to have that certain quality of elegance in his voice, befitting his master and mistress.

In a brief history of the county, Gabriel had informed Madelene earlier in the day that Mrs. Tottencott was related to Princess Caroline's Lady-in-Waiting, the Countess Willins, by marriage, six or seven times removed, he could never quite remember. The countess at the time held court in London with her husband, the Earl of Fieldsforth. Since her sister could claim a royal connection by a whisper of threads, Mrs. Tottencott believed herself an important cog in the society circle of Ludlow.

Madelene smiled at Mrs. Tottencott as she wobbled into the room, leaning on her gold-tipped cane to the left, all dressed in gray from her shoes to her gloves to the top of her head. Her husband, Mr. Tottencott, followed close behind his wife, apparently to ensure she didn't tip over, although he could hardly claim equilibrium himself from the gout he suffered on his left foot. Madelene watched them parade into the room, and decided if he leaned right and she leaned left, they could walk as one, with ne'er a worry of tumbling. She hid her smile at the thought.

"Mr. and Mrs. Tottencott, we are honored you have

joined us this evening. May I present my wife, the former Miss Madelene Colgate, now Westcott." Gabriel performed the introductions.

The older woman peered at Madelene through her quizzing glass from top to bottom, scrutiny unmistakably on her mind. So intently was she examined, Madelene felt confident the woman could detect sugar specks on her lip from a plum cake she had eaten earlier. Ever gracious to this bastion of presumed power, she endured the perusal, well aware Mrs. Tottencott could be a powerful friend or a powerful foe in the country. Madelene did not wish for the latter.

"Mrs. Tottencott, may I echo my husband's sentiments in welcoming you to our home?" Madelene wished to sound sincere but was becoming increasingly uncomfortable under the old woman's glare.

"I didn't hear your wedding banns announced, Mr. Westcott," she informed the couple in her staccato voice, when she deigned to clip a few words.

Although Madelene started at this unexpected pronouncement, Gabriel gave Mrs. Tottencott the warmest of smiles. "Ah, I see, we cannot put anything past you. You are far too clever. I am sincerely regretful. The oversight is none but my own." He took Madelene's hand in his own and kissed it. "You see, Mrs. Tottencott, as I was quite determined to marry Miss Westcott, I didn't allow time for any of the usual formalities or traditions."

Her sharp eyes scanned back and forth between Gabriel and Madelene, intent on missing nothing. "So, Westcott, this is not the arranged marriage your uncle wished between you and Lady Shillmont. He would be most unhappy. Her father's lands adjoined to your property would have made an immense acquisition to the

Westcott fortunes." She had to stop her unsought and unpleasant diatribe, overcome by a coughing spell.

Lady Shillmont, Madelene thought. *Hmm, another story to learn.*

"Please, Mrs. Tottencott, let me help you to a chair. You must be weary on your feet." Gabriel showed the couple to the closest settee and assisted in making them comfortable by offering a glass of Madeira, which they both declined.

"Ah, Mr. Westcott—" Mrs. Tottencott continued but it was interrupted by new arrivals.

"The Misses Lavender, Lilac, and Rose McMartin," Graham announced loudly from outside the drawing-room door.

"Hyacinth, I told you! *Hyacinth.* Wherever did you get the name Lilac?" A small blond woman stood before the butler with hands on her hips. "My name is Miss McMartin," she informed him in a shrill voice.

"Terribly sorry. I knew the other name to be a flower, but lilac was the only one come to mind." Graham nodded to Madelene and Gabriel before making his escape.

Hyacinth, a tiny birdlike woman, flew into the room with her two sisters close behind, her small hands and mouth flapping together about rude butlers, or at least that was what Madelene thought she heard. The woman spoke without breath, making it difficult to discern actual words.

By way of introduction, she pointed to a tall, pale female, rather nondescript in appearance, and called her Rose—surely a gross mistake in nomenclature from her parents, Madelene couldn't help think. Lavender stood next to Rose and was easily the prettiest of the three. As Hyacinth was short and Rose tall, Lavender fit somewhere in the middle. She had light brown hair, big brown eyes, and a very serene shy smile.

The boldest of the three, Hyacinth claimed dull blond hair, unimaginative brown eyes, and a small mouth constantly in motion. All three wore pale flowered frocks with a variety of colored sashes, perhaps not of the latest fashion, but not unbecoming.

Madelene guessed the sisters to be within a year or two of each other and just on the outside of marriageable age. She didn't know enough of the family's circumstances, but had never seen or heard of the McMartins in London during the Season. If the notion few bachelors resided in Shropshire could be presumed, these young ladies would need to seek farther afield for matrimonial conquests. The three latest arrivals found a seat and accepted the offered Madeira while the Vicar Caring was announced and introduced to Madelene.

Madelene took a step back from his booming and overbearing presence. She thought he would do well as the Master of Ceremonies in a circus, so loud was his voice. "Mr. Westcott *and* Mrs. Westcott. I finally have the privilege to meet the newest resident of Shropshire. *Delighted, delighted.*"

The eager vicar bent over Madelene's hand and kissed it, holding on to it as he continued his monologue. "I was saying to Mrs. McMartin, the girls' mother, the other day, I had not yet had the pleasure to make the acquaintance of Mrs. Westcott but hoped to do so in the near future. And can I believe it? Here I am. A lucky man, yes, a lucky man, indeed."

He finally gave Madelene her hand back and turned to the rest of the occupants. "How fortunate to have such a delightful group for this evening's gathering. Honored, that's what I am, honored."

Gabriel, in the end, had to actually shove him into a seat and hold him down, when he would have popped up like corn in hot oil, Madelene mused. When she had an opportunity to view the vicar, she noted his small pock-scarred face, small black eyes, and mouth, mostly open for talking. Oh dear. With the vicar, Hyacinth, and Mrs. Tottencott, Madelene hoped the others would be permitted a word here and there.

She delicately sniffed the air. If she wasn't mistaken, the vicar smelled of mold. In his costume, he looked every inch the part of a parson from his broad-toed shoes to his black clothes and white neckcloth. Why ever did it appear vicars had an obsequious nature? She wondered if it was a requirement of the job.

Inwardly sighing, Madelene was relieved to see an old acquaintance, Mr. Bush, enter the room, cane in hand. Both Gabriel and Madelene greeted him warmly, trying to be heard over the vicar's posturing to Mrs. Tottencott.

Gabriel walked Mr. Bush to the center of the room and informed his friend of the current occupants as Mr. Bush nodded at the chorus of welcomes.

Lavender surprised Madelene by leaving her chair and walking to Mr. Bush's side to offer her own personal respects. In a low voice, she said, "I am so pleased you are part of the festivities, Mr. Bush. I fear it has been too long since you have stopped for a visit."

"Miss Lavender McMartin," he said, then turned in the direction where he understood the other sisters were seated. "Miss McMartin and Miss McMartin. I must say I'm glad there are only the three of you." His audience laughed politely, and he assured the three sisters he would take the earliest opportunity to stop on his next visit to Ludlow. Madelene thought she saw Lavender press Mr. Bush's hand and looked with raised eyebrows at Gabriel, who shook his head imperceptively. No matchmaking skills would be needed here, Madelene smiled to herself. And didn't her friend, Mr. Bush, deserve such a sweet and well-bred young lady?

The last invited guests, Squire Jones, a large man of middle years, and his young daughter, Rachel, no more than twelve, arrived and greeted everyone. The squire proved a pleasant addition to the crowd, providing comment when warranted and silence when not sought for contribution, while his daughter looked mostly down at her clasped hands and probably wished she was elsewhere.

After a few pleasantries were shared, Graham called everyone to dinner. Gabriel and Madelene led the way, followed by the teetering Tottencotts, the vicar and Hyacinth, the squire and his daughter, Mr. Bush and Lavender, and Rose on her own. Given the acceptances and declines for the soiree, Madelene had wished for an even number at the table, but there was nothing for it.

Madelene beamed as their friends greatly admired the lavish chandelier and the well-laid table. Even the summer blooms of white and pink carnations added a pleasant ambience. After being seated, Hazelby and the other three footmen served the first remove, a delicious cucumber soup, a leg of pork boiled with peas, pudding, and greens and roots. The second remove consisted of roasted turkey, tarts, and fruit.

The small party enjoyed more removes, each one more delicious than the last, until even the squire had to beg off, exclaiming he was more well fed at Westcott Close than his very own pigs, at which Rachel scowled and sank farther into her chair. Rachel reminded Madelene of herself at that young age, although she had to admit she probably hero-worshipped her father more than Rachel did her own.

Distracted once again by Mrs. Tottencott, since they sat next to each other, Madelene nodded and smiled at the older woman's reminiscing over her years in London, her first Season quite a success, her sister's connection to the royal family, she vaguely remembered Madelene's father, and wasn't her brother in some trouble years back over a kidnapping?

Madelene felt the color drain from her face. How far news traveled even after all these years. Matthew had been five and ten years of age, and little more than easy prey for a trio of criminals promising guineas to drive a carriage. The trio had neglected to mention it was a kidnapping. All had ended well, and no charges or conviction were ever laid at her brother's door. Still—

Gabriel must have sensed her consternation because he interrupted their conversation before she could find her voice to reply.

"Mrs. Tottencott, have you had the wonderful opportunity to hear Rachel sing? She has sung for many fine families in the county, and I wonder if she would grace us with a selection this evening?" Gabriel turned to the young girl with a warm and hopeful expression.

The squire's daughter returned his smile shyly and nodded.

"Delightful," intoned the vicar, overhearing the request. "I have heard Miss Rachel sing in church, and I may tell you, no one nearly breathes until she finishes her recitals."

The squire humpfed. "Vicar, I think you have much imagination. My daughter sings well, but time will tell if it will come to aught."

"As long as it gives pleasure to the listener and the performer, surely, that is success in itself," Madelene looked at Rachel and smiled. "How fortunate you are to have such talent. I look forward to your performance later."

With dinner over and cigars and port enjoyed, the men joined the women in the drawing room. The squire, Rachel, Hyacinth, and Rose played whist while Gabriel, Madelene, and the others listened to Lavender play the pianoforte. The young woman played extremely well and appeared agreeable to everyone's ears, in particular to Mr. Bush's, if Madelene divined correctly.

They would make a sweet couple, and after all, Lavender did act the part of a lovelorn young woman. Only Madelene could not ascertain in which direction Mr. Bush's ardency lay.

During a break while Rachel prepared to sing and Lavender to accompany her, Mrs. Tottencott interrupted the silence. "Tell me, Mr. Westcott, I have heard an unusual rumor in the village, which I find hard to give credence to."

Madelene closed her eyes briefly, agitated as to what Mrs. Tottencott could possibly ask. However, her husband sat beside her in perfect comfort and humor and cocked his head at his guest. "Pray tell, whatever does this rumor have to do with our household?"

Mrs. Tottencott cleared her throat. "Ahem. Could it be possibly true that there is a babe in this house? I understood you to be married a short amount of time, hardly time—"

"I am pleased you have asked the question of me, for it would be displeasing for you to learn the truth from any other source." He smiled cordially at his audience, and Madelene tensed beside him, concerned how he would present the situation.

"During our sojourn in Italy, I, that is, my sister and I, befriended distant cousins on my mother's side. Before we were to return to England, my sister became terribly ill. One of our cousins, Gemma Madroni, assisted with my sister's care.

"As I planned to return to England with Lucinda, an acquaintance informed me Gemma had been overcome with a grave illness, and would we raise her child, a boy, because Gemma thought so highly of our family. There were no other relatives to look after the boy, so I arranged for him to be brought here, when he reached a year or nearly a year.

"Little did I realize my sister's health would soon take a turn for the worse, and she would not be here with me. But I am committed to raising the boy as my own, and due to my good fortune, I have my wife by my side." He looked to Madelene for reassurance. He had decided many months ago he would never besmirch his sister's name, no matter the cost or falsehoods they would have to tell.

Madelene smiled and nodded. "There is no more story than that."

Before she could continue, the vicar added, "What kindness! What generosity! How noble you both are to want to raise the boy as your own. Oh, Christians, we are indeed in the home of saints. You will be blessed in heaven—"

Mrs. Tottencott must have sensed a sermon ensuing and quickly interrupted. "Yes, Vicar, that is very generous of Mr. and Mrs. Westcott. Certainly a surprise, assuming they will have their own children some day."

Gabriel opened his mouth to reply, but a knock on the door prevented him.

Madelene looked to the door and saw Charlotte, her face pinched white, motioning to her. She excused herself and hurried over to the nurse at the door.

"Mrs. Westcott, ma'am." Her voice shook, indeed her whole body trembled.

Something was terribly wrong. Madelene left the parlor and closed the door behind her. She didn't want their guests to be disturbed and privy to whatever worried the young woman.

Concerned over Charlotte's state, Madelene laid a hand on her shoulder. "Charlotte, please calm yourself. Whatever can possibly have happened to put you in such a vexed condition?"

"It's George."

Frozen, Madelene could only stare; her heart seized tight, and she felt a cold fear never known before. "What is wrong with George? Tell me!" She could barely think, waiting anxiously for a reply.

She didn't want to hear. She didn't want to know.

Charlotte, with tears in her eyes, told her mistress. "I only left the nursery for a moment. I thought George wanted milk, and I couldn't find Donna Bella—"

Her eyes widened and she knew a dreadful foreboding. "You left George? Did he fall? Is he hurt?"

Charlotte shook her head several times. "No, no, Mrs. Westcott. He's, he's gone."

Her brow furrowed, Madelene looked more closely at the nurse. "What do you mean, he's gone?"

"Someone has taken him."

Chapter Twenty-Four

Gabriel asked to be excused from his guests to determine what had become of his wife. Outside the drawing-room doors, Graham advised him the nurse and Mrs. Westcott had headed in the direction of the nursery, and they both appeared most agitated. Gabriel ran the entire way, unsure of what he would find.

Bursting through the opened nursery doors, he found his wife sitting on the floor with Charlotte sitting next to her. He watched in confusion as Madelene stared at the floor and the nurse held her hand, patting it, while stuttering and weeping at the same time.

Whatever could have happened? Gabriel rushed to kneel next to his wife, his heart thudding in his ears. "Madelene, what is it? Please tell me what is wrong so I can make it right."

Madelene kept shaking her head, and he knew.

He looked at Charlotte. "Where is George?" he demanded. He didn't have to search the nursery to know he wasn't here, the babe wasn't in the house.

At that moment, Mrs. Lavishtock bustled into the room and froze when she saw her prostrate mistress.

"Oh, it's happened. My dear girl. I couldn't stop him." She pressed her hands to her lips in dismay.

Gabriel, with his arm around Madelene, looked up in astonishment. "What is going on and where is George? Will someone please tell me? Who couldn't you stop?"

With Charlotte blubbering, only Mrs. Lavishtock answered. "It's the mistress's brother, Mr. Colgate. He took George."

"Mrs. Lavishtock, are you confident of what you are saying? How can you accuse Mrs. Westcott's brother?"

The housekeeper shook her head. "He is not in his room. I have heard rumors among the staff of Mr. Colgate's displeasure here, and that he might be capable of dark measures."

Gabriel did not want to believe Mrs. Lavishtock, since she had no concrete evidence. But the more he pondered on the likely suspect, he knew. He knew Matthew Colgate was capable of such a devious affair, though he couldn't fathom the reason Colgate had kidnapped George, unless he planned to use the babe in some nefarious manner. Perhaps in exchange for those damnable diamonds. He wished the gems and thieves had never interfered in his home.

Fury alighted inside him. He should have known and kept better watch. Perhaps if he told Colgate about the child— Little good it did now to change the outcome of events already on course in a terrible and unexpected direction.

No time for lingering longer. He helped Madelene stand, and holding her in his arms, lifted her chin so she could look at him and believe what he said. "We will get George back. I promise you. Believe me. As soon as I can determine what direction your brother headed, I'll go after him. I'll bring little George back. Madelene?" He was afraid for her until she spoke.

Her beautiful blue eyes focused again on him, "I believe you, Gabriel. I know you'll bring him back. But Matthew?"

Hardly able to contain his anger at her brother, he narrowed his eyes and clenched his jaw. After hesitating, he replied, "I cannot make a promise which I may not be able to give you." He gave her a brief kiss. "I'll have Mrs. Lavishtock and Fanny stay with you, and I'll leave shortly after I talk to the others."

Before he left the nursery, he questioned Charlotte about the timing of when she left George sleeping and returned with the milk. She couldn't be quite sure but thought it was an approximation of thirty minutes, editing the version where she stayed longer to gossip with Fanny.

Gabriel didn't want to waste time determining responsibility. He only wanted to find George safe, then he would make Matthew regret he ever played this dangerous game. The stakes this time were too high. Colgate had involved a helpless child, and that could never be forgiven.

He prayed for George's safe return, realizing with irony that praying was not a habit of his. If it was in his power, George would soon be back with them, enjoying his goat's milk and his favorite toy, a stuffed mouse named Baba.

Downstairs, he instructed Windthorp to offer apologies to their guests for the abrupt halt to the evening, but Madelene had taken ill. The less explanation, the better. Any more detail, and Mrs. Tottencott might call on her distant connection to the Crown for help, which certainly would not do.

As ordered, Windthorp saw their guests to their carriages and received their well wishes for Mrs. Westcott's speedy recovery, but Mr. Bush refused to leave. He told Gabriel's valet, "I want to help. I'd like to see if there is anything I can do for Mrs. Westcott. Please let me stay."

He could not be convinced otherwise and remained in the foyer where Gabriel found him several minutes later. Stopping to have a word with his friend, Graham called to him.

The butler hurried over with a vellum in his hand.

Gabriel scanned the contents, and his rage burned even brighter. Exactly what he had feared, in Colgate's own handwriting: "Bring the diamonds to London and you'll get the boy back."

He closed his eyes and took a deep breath. He'd get the boy back, and in the same condition as he was taken, or Matthew would not have only the count to fear for his health.

Graham told him that Cappie had mentioned a carriage and two horses were missing.

With a baby and perhaps a stop in Ludlow for Brelford, assuming Matthew's cohort still lingered in the area, a one-horse rider should easily overtake them. Based on what he was able to glean from the staff, Colgate had about an hour start. A fleeting thought pursued him. Who cared for little George while Colgate held the reins?

Time now measured in heartbeats, Gabriel changed into traveling clothes, looked in on Madelene one last time, and promised to send word as soon as he had George or returned with him. Windthorp stood at the top of the staircase, small satchel in hand, ever prepared for his master. Gabriel grabbed the bag and ran down the stairs. He was committed to finding George and Matthew in the swiftest time and thought to head first to Ludlow, and then the main road to London.

Before he left, he issued strict warnings Madelene should be watched at all costs, still worried over her safety.

On his way to the stables where Cappie was to saddle Mars, he saw Mr. Bush, still waiting in the hall. "Bush, there are few I can trust. I need to get to London immediately or at least on the road to Town. Since I do not know how successful I'll be in locating Madelene's brother and our charge, George, I'll send word for Madelene and the others to join me, if necessary, at the town house."

"I'll remain here to help any way I can," Hayden told him, holding his hand out for Gabriel's grasp.

Gabriel smiled. "You are indeed a worthy friend. Watch over Madelene, for I fear for her health. She loves George."

Bush nodded. "Yes. Godspeed."

Shrugging on his coat, Gabriel glanced around and whistled.

No Falstaff. He walked toward the kitchen, still whistling. No black-and-white terrier tore down the hall at him, and he didn't have time to look in his bedchamber.

"Bush, one thing more. Remember to have Madelene bring Falstaff. It is of the utmost importance."

If his friend thought it odd to travel with the little dog, he kept his thoughts to himself.

One last matter. Gabriel called to Graham. "Have you seen Alec? I need her to—"

"She's gone." Graham stood steadfast with only bad news to deliver this night.

"Gone where?" The night became blacker and blacker.

"Cappie told me a few minutes ago. Alec accompanied Mr. Colgate."

Why would Alec go with Colgate to London? For what

purpose? And the answer was too ready. Colgate needed Alec to care for the child. He felt a brief flicker of relief before he remembered another possibility.

Alec had always planned to return to her uncle, the Count Taglioni, and back to Italy. With the diamonds, of that he could not be more certain.

When he found her, he thought, she had better have feared for her life than gone willingly with the master perpetrator, taking their child from them. They would have a long talk when next they met.

Entering the stables, Gabriel found Cappie had saddled Mars, whose tail twitched as he moved restlessly, his ears pricked up. He was ready to run. Gabriel grabbed the reins, swung himself up onto his horse, and headed out into the tarnished night.

After she ensured Mr. Bush was settled in for the night, Madelene stayed up for hours having tea with Mrs. Lavishtock, Fanny, and Charlotte in the kitchen, hoping to learn of word about George.

Talk came round to Alec, and to Madelene's surprise or perhaps not so surprising, Mrs. Lavishtock had learned that on the young Italian girl's journey from the village to Westcott Close, she had fallen off her horse and had been set upon by a wild dog, or so she would have them believe, the housekeeper added.

Then Mrs. Lavishtock showed Madelene the package that Alec had delivered to Mr. Westcott, who indicated the package was actually for Mrs. Westcott.

Halfheartedly, Madelene unwrapped the brown paper to discover the latest French fashion plates and pale pink muslin material. How terribly thoughtful of her husband. If the situation was different, she would have been thrilled at the present. At the moment, she could only concentrate on the joy to be had when Mr. Westcott brought George back safely.

At half past three in the morning, Mrs. Lavishtock shooed all of them to bed. Although Windthorp stood guard outside Madelene's bedchamber, none of them could have known the danger had passed from Westcott Close and headed in the direction of London.

Chapter Twenty-Five

There was no sign of the carriage on the main road to the village or to London. They must have been farther along than he'd originally estimated. Gabriel headed toward Town, riding hard for five, then ten miles, the moon providing a shallow light. As he rode, the warmth of the night soon wet his brow.

If he had given the diamonds to Colgate, if he had told him about George— It made no difference, for Gabriel would never have altered his course, given the chance to change the past.

Weary mile after weary mile he pushed himself and Mars onward, convinced he would soon overtake the carriage, but this late at night, he passed no one on the road. Exhausted beyond measure, feeling soreness in his limbs, something caught his attention farther down the road, which he could barely discern.

Growing closer, he saw it was a carriage and breathed in new hope by clicking Mars into a gallop. Thirty yards from the site, he saw it was his carriage, but the horses were gone. Not willing to take chances with Colgate or the life of George, he slowed down prepared for a defensive attack from the rash young man and his companions.

Nothing.

Gabriel jumped off Mars before the horse came to a full stop and ran to the carriage. Upon closer inspection, he saw the carriage rested on its side with a broken shaft.

Grimacing, his first thought was, had anyone been hurt in the accident? But he simply had no way of knowing and had to rein in his wayward thoughts. Nothing would convince him that there would be any different outcome to the situation other than returning George unharmed to Madelene and his home, Westcott Close.

But where were they? He found nothing and no one in the carriage or in the surrounding area. Where could they have gone?

He swallowed his unease and mounted Mars again, riding up the road while studying the tracks in the road. Tracks of horse hoofprints and large wheels furrowed the churned-up dirt. Another carriage must have stopped to assist them.

This was the only possible solution. Unfortunately, Gabriel knew in his condition and his horse's, he couldn't catch up to them this night. They were farther ahead and probably traveling much faster.

"We are grateful to you for helping us in our hour of need," Brelford told the stranger, who called himself Simon Cumberlane, the Earl of Bevondard. Ensconced in this fine carriage, Brelford looked with casual interest at Lord Bevondard, but knew his preference to be for the fairer sex.

Luck had played a great part in their adventure this night. After their carriage broke down, the baby crying without hesitation, everyone shaken but unhurt, his lordship's carriage came upon them, and the earl offered them assistance by taking them to London with him.

Brelford reflected on what Matthew had whispered to him before they climbed into the carriage. His friend knew his lordship for all the wrong reasons and wanted to remain unknown to him. Matthew instructed Brelford to introduce him as Brelford's brother, which his friend easily accommodated.

It appeared years earlier, young Colgate had taken part in a plot to kidnap the earl, in one of his more youthful indiscretions. The earl had forgiven them all, but Matthew had hoped never to see the man again. And here they were, accepting his hospitality to London.

The child began to cry softly, distracting Brelford's thoughts. In close confinement, there was little to do but watch Alec rock the baby in her arms, but he wouldn't stop crying and wouldn't go back to sleep. Matthew drew his hat down over his forehead and slumped in his seat, presumably to make himself as unseen as possible.

However, the disturbance seemed not to bother the earl. He smiled easily, surprising Brelford with his handsomeness. "The babe has healthy lungs. I have two fine sons of my own, but it is my wife who knows what to do when one of our children is in distress. Madam, you look too young to have a child, are you his guardian?"

Alec and Brelford stared at his lordship before Brelford provided a quick solution. "Yes, she is the baby's aunt. My brother and I agreed to take the babe to Town, where his parents are waiting for him. Friends of the family." He pointed to Matthew. "He is joining us in Town for the baby's christening."

His lordship nodded. "What are the parents' names? Perhaps I am acquainted with them?"

Brelford answered, amazed at his own glibness. "I would highly doubt my sister and her husband would travel in your circles, but their names are Mr. and Mrs. Roger Marchibroda."

Bevondard considered the names but momentarily. "No, the name has no familiarity." Fortunately for Brelford, the earl ceased his questioning.

It was another half hour before the baby went back to sleep. In the silence, all the occupants finally found rest, if not a peaceful one.

"How foolish I am, Mr. Bush." Madelene had admonished herself several times the next morning to her companion when she learned he had remained at the house. "I was of no help to Mr. Westcott last night. I simply could not believe my brother—" She could not finish her thought.

"Your concern is for the child, and of course, your brother. I am sure he means the child no harm. He must know how much the boy means to you and Mr. Westcott. I gather the diamonds you mentioned must have driven him to desperation."

Unable to sleep the last few hours of the night, Madelene had waited and hoped and prayed. This morning, with no word from Gabriel, she had to resign herself to the fact their quest remained unfinished. She stepped back from her wardrobe, handing another gown to Fanny to pack in her trunk. Windthorp had awakened the household early to apprise them they needed to pack for London, where they would meet Master Westcott.

"I never thought my brother capable of this. I am at a total loss to explain my brother's behavior. His desperation has turned him into a stranger, a man I don't know. I don't know how to help him. But he's taken George. If anything were to happen—" She lost the tears she was determined to keep to herself.

Mr. Bush rose from the chair and slowly walked to Madelene's voice. She held out her hand to him and reached for his when he drew near. "You must believe your husband will find George and protect him," he assured her while squeezing her hand.

"Yes, but who will protect my brother from my husband's wrath?" she asked sadly, knowing there was no answer.

Gabriel lost no time after arriving in London to arrange a meeting with a private detective, Mr. Oberstein, an elderly wiry man, known among society's elite for finding lost relatives with the utmost discretion. Unprepared to wait to hear from Colgate, between Oberstein and other acquaintances, Gabriel would search every lodging, from the London docks to the London Tower, every inn, every physician who cared for children, markets, orphanages, until he had exhausted every possibility.

Then he would start all over again. While he would have preferred to hand little George to Madelene on her arrival in a few days, he knew he couldn't accomplish such a feat in so short a time, unless Colgate contacted him. Reminded of his wife, he hoped Bush had remembered to send along Falstaff.

If Colgate had returned to his town house in Bloomsbury, Gabriel would soon know. However, he doubted Madelene's brother would make it too easy for him to find the child. He'd be afraid Gabriel would steal the baby back without the exchange of the jewels. And Gabriel had to play cautious with any dealings since he didn't have the diamonds in his possession. Not yet.

His next item of business had been to find Rascal, a young man who knew many nefarious scoundrels in Town, and who could ferret out information like a dog hunting the fox. The young orphan in his late teens had big ears, long black hair, and nine fingers. The curse of Rascal's life was to have been born with one finger shy of his left hand. Whenever Gabriel wasn't in London, Rascal usually disappeared, and no one knew to where.

His mother had left him in the St. Augustus Home for Unwanted Children many years ago because she had little interest in raising a deformed son. From the young age of seven, he had learned many useful habits, such as how to blame another for his misdeeds, how to avoid work by intimidating the younger boys to do his share, and how to live on the streets, when the time came, and he would be forced into the drudgery of factory working.

He had escaped the orphanage by his fifteenth birthday and lived by his wits, running errands when he wasn't stealing, which he considered an art and figured to be one of the best. His life changed when he made the mistake of—or was fortunately caught at—stealing Mr. Westcott's horse. What he planned to do with a stolen horse, no one ever quite understood, since it would have been impossible to sell the animal in Town.

The night Cappie caught Rascal, Gabriel, instead of calling the magistrate, hired him on at the town house and gave him a room over the stables. By showing Rascal a kindness never known to him, Gabriel earned the young boy's devotion.

Over a month ago, Rascal had trailed Colgate to Brelford's lodgings to learn of the wager. Only the other day, the boy had jaunted over to Mrs. Grecian's boarding room and reported back there was a new lodger in Brelford's old rooms, an unsurprising development.

Another likely culprit in this drama was Count Taglioni. Gabriel thought it highly unlikely Alec would turn to her uncle for assistance, but taking all precaution, sent Rascal to observe the town house in Mayfair. He returned with news the house was closed, all the occupants gone.

The next day, before Gabriel and Mr. Oberstein started planning their search and strategies, Gabriel instructed Styers, the butler, to detain anyone delivering messages. He knew the only sensible action Colgate could take was to send a message to the house with directions on where to meet to deliver the diamonds and retrieve George. It might be a long shot, but they could possibly learn something from the messenger.

After Gabriel had spoken to the local magistrate, Mr. Thomaskin, he would have to turn over the diamonds for their return to Italy, and Madelene's brother to court. Thomaskin knew of Count Taglioni and believed him to be an imposter. If Colgate gave the gems to Taglioni, he had no doubt they would all be on the next ship headed out the Channel.

What to tell Madelene? That he intended to have her brother arrested for kidnapping and stealing? That Matthew would be sent to prison because of him? Could she, would she, ever be able to forgive him? He knew if her love for her brother was as great as his love for his sister, Lucinda, they might not have a future together.

A few days later, Cappie assisted Madelene and Fanny down from the carriage and, with the help of the other coachmen, began unloading their luggage. Madelene had no time to appreciate Gabriel's town house as she quickly made her way up the stairs, anxious for news about George and her brother. Gabriel and Styers greeted her and Fanny in the small but ornate white-and-black-trimmed foyer.

"Mrs. Westcott, my dear." Gabriel, dressed in black pantaloons, white lawn shirt, black waistcoat and coat, went to her side and took her outstretched gloved hand and kissed it, his gaze warm and concerned.

"Mr. Westcott." Madelene, dressed in a deep blue traveling coat and matched feathered poke bonnet, smiled at her handsome husband, wishing her heart bore no burden. Although happy to see her husband, she watched his face for any sign. "Have—"

Gabriel shook his head. "Not yet, but I am hopeful— "

"Woof, woof." Falstaff pranced on his back paws, trying to get someone's attention.

Madelene shook her head and knelt to pick up her dog. "You certainly have been a good little one on our journey. Perhaps the cook will have a tidbit for you in the kitchen."

Falstaff jumped out of her arms and trotted down the corridor, presumably acquainted with the location of the kitchen.

She rose and looked at her husband. "I daresay I found it strange you requested Falstaff to come with us. But I'm sure you have your reasons."

Her gloved hand in his, Gabriel said to Madelene, "Let us go to the front parlor. We can talk better there, and I can explain."

She handed Styers her cloak, gloves, and bonnet and followed Gabriel into the front parlor, which overlooked Mayfair's Park Lane. The palest of rose and green decorated the warm and welcoming room. Gabriel ushered her onto a mint green brocaded chaise longue and sat next to her, gathering her hands in his. Only four days had passed since the soiree, but the time seemed longer.

Madelene stared into his handsome face, aching for

him to hold her and assure her George was safe and this whole horrible affair was over. But she could see, those were words he couldn't give her.

His intense look encompassed her entirely, as if to memorize her features or to see how she fared from her journey. He needn't look too closely to see the tiredness in her eyes and the quivering of her lips.

His hand reached over to stroke her cheek. "Madelene, are you well? Your face has lost some of its color. Are Fanny and Mrs. Lavishtock looking after you?" His genuine concern mirrored in tone and look.

"I, I have been unable to eat. I have been so very worried."

Madelene did not hide her great anxiety from her husband. She did believe in him and trust him that he could make everything right. But would he hurt her brother by doing so?

"I wish I could give you the news we both desperately seek, but I've not heard from your brother. We're searching all parts of Town for any sign of him and George. I'm sure your brother is seeing to George's needs and will soon send him back to us."

He thought to be reassuring, but Madelene could only imagine George crying because he was hungry or scared in a dark place somewhere in London. The pain she felt at her baby's welfare was akin to the pain she felt at losing her father.

She couldn't bear the thought of losing George, too. And what about Matthew? How could she help him? She knew she had to be strong and reserve all her energy to do something. But what, exactly?

Finding her voice, she told him, "I know you're right. We *will* find George and Matthew." She gave him a cockeyed smile. "I just need something to eat, and I'll help you any way I can. Was Millie able to provide any information at our town house in Bloomsbury?"

Gabriel stood, placed his hands in his pockets, and walked over to move the rose-and-green drapes aside to look out onto the street. "No, Millie has not seen or heard from your brother. I have a Mr. Oberstein, a private investigator, working for me, who has checked your old home and is following other avenues of your brother's acquaintances."

"And Millie, how is she faring?"

"From Oberstein's accounts, she is well and handling the household matters." He gazed across the room at her. "I do expect Colgate will send a note to us shortly, informing us where and when to meet him with the diamonds."

"And the diamonds. Where are they? Do you have them here?"

Gabriel returned to the chaise and leaned over the back. "I will show you later. You'll be surprised. You've had them with you all the time."

The journey must have knocked some sense from her because she couldn't think to what he referred. Why would the diamonds be in her possession?

At the look she gave him, he told her, "Do not worry, I don't intend for you to remain long in the dark. First, food. I find myself, like Falstaff, needing a bit of nourishment."

At the door, she forestalled him with a hand on his arm. "Gabriel, whatever shall we do about Matthew?"

His mouth tightened when she mentioned his name.

Afraid of what he might say, she implored him, "Gabriel, I know Matthew won't hurt George. If he returns George to us, and we give him the diamonds, then Matthew can give the diamonds to the count and everything can go back to the way it was."

His eyebrows arched at her question, but with no

hesitation, he told her what she feared most. "Madelene, it cannot be. Everything has changed." He seemed to choose his next words carefully. "I've contacted the magistrate, Mr. Thomaskin, whom I saw the last time I was in Town. He had to know about the diamonds."

She could only stare at her husband and shake her head. "You would send Matthew to the magistrate, then to King's Bench Prison? I've heard only terrible things about the prison." Madelene took a few steps away from her husband to examine the enormity of his words.

She pressed a hand to her lips. "That was how all this started. Our marriage to win the wager, to pay his debts, to save him," she whispered.

He walked over to her. "Madelene, the count does not own the diamonds. They have to be returned to the countess. But I will see if I can use my influence to prevent your brother from seeing the inside of a gaol. Come, let's go to the dining room."

Madelene shook her head. "Please have Styers show me to my bedchamber. I need to lie down. Perhaps if you could have Fanny bring some tea." She opened the door to the parlor and stood in the foyer, awaiting her husband.

After he pulled the bell for Styers, he followed her. In mere moments, Styers with his whiskered face and jolly blue eyes appeared.

Gabriel watched his butler escort his wife up the main staircase, disheartened he could not give Madelene the peace of mind she sought.

"Duckins, I promise, it shall only be for a short time," Colgate told his acquaintance.

The bachelor Duckins lived in a comfortable town house, near Covent Gardens, which he had purchased with his winnings from the wager. Arnold looked over at Alec, bouncing a baby in her arms, and another man who stood slightly behind Colgate.

"I don't know. How can we keep it quiet? As soon as that baby starts to wail, my neighbors will suspect something."

Colgate clapped him on the back and pushed Duckins back into his neat but plain foyer. "Have I misled you before? I've told you, it's for a short time. We need a place to wait while I make arrangements."

Arnold smelled the untruth. "What arrangements? I know you have a house in Bloomsbury. Why can't you all wait there?" Not ready to have trouble sitting on his doorstep, Duckins was rather anxious for the little group to leave.

"The town house is being renovated. No place for a baby. By week's end, we'll vacate your house." He paused. "You owe me."

Duckins sighed. He thought his debt had been paid. But it was only four days.

Colgate must have sensed his surrender because he motioned for Brelford and Alec to follow him into a nearby parlor. "Four days." He pointed his finger at the young woman called Alec, who for some strange reason dressed in boy's clothing. "You, you make sure the babe keeps quiet, or you'll be on the street."

Duckins followed them to the door, watching as Brelford and Colgate sat on the new dark green settee and bent their heads together. He noticed the strange young woman chose a comfortable wing chair by the window for herself and the babe.

Strange, the last time he had seen Colgate, he was more chipper and relaxed. Something had changed him. This new Matthew looked desperate and lean. Duckins, who had befriended the young baronet many years ago, found himself actually afraid of him.

Shaking his head, he left them to it. He wanted nothing to do with a babe or the nefarious plan he caught in Colgate's eye. The look did not bode well.

Chapter Twenty-Six

Madelene paced her blue-and-gold-striped bed-chamber, determined to find George and save her brother. But first, she had to learn where Gabriel hid the diamonds. The next step would be to get word to Millie that Madelene would meet Matthew at the house in Bloomsbury tomorrow night with the diamonds. The timing would be late, when everyone slept and few people traveled the streets.

The person she trusted most to deliver the note to Millie was Fanny. She'd send her lady's maid to her old home tomorrow morning. Her arrangements were simple enough, except for one caveat: If Matthew was not at their home, how would Millie know how and where to send the message? She shrugged away obstacles to her plan. Millie had to have some knowledge of how to contact her brother.

Madelene stayed up later than usual, finding herself unable to sleep. Her thoughts jumbled, she could find no uncomplicated answer. She wanted to tell Gabriel, but he seemed determined to send Matthew to prison. Would her husband ever forgive her if she helped Matthew escape to the Continent? In her heart, she realized sadly that whatever the outcome, she might never see Matthew again.

His predicament reminded her of another time, several years ago. Her brother could have only been about fifteen, and she a few years younger. Youthful and reckless, he met up with a trio of ne'er-do-wells, fresh off their ship at a tavern in Covent Garden. They convinced Matthew to join him on a lark. A handsome sum would be shared among all of them, and the motley crew convinced him no one would be hurt.

As Madelene recalled, the story did have a happy ending. The man they kidnapped was the Earl of Bevondard, and the person behind the deed, none other than his soon-to-be-wife, Lady Evangeline Buchanan. Lady Buchanan astonished the *haut ton* by her unique type of courting, Madelene hazily remembered her father telling her. Luckily, the Lord Bevondard thought it high enterprise and paid the handsome sum to all for their assistance in bringing the betrothed couple together.

Their father, Sir Colgate, was most displeased with his firstborn and withheld his allowance for one month. If only her dear father were here. He could talk to Matthew, convince him to return George and give up the hunt for the diamonds. Her father could make everything right.

She walked over to one of the two windows facing the small yard behind the house, adjacent to the stables. Lost in thought, Madelene moved the pale blue drapes to the side and found Gabriel sitting outside her window. Precariously, it seemed.

Thankfully, it wasn't raining.

"Gabriel! Whatever are you doing outside my window? Are you confused about where you are? We are not at Westcott Close and there is no tree."

Her husband, who sat on a narrow shelf outside her

window, leaned back against the side of the house, showing no fear of falling. He smiled and bent his knee, bracing his arm across it.

"Nice evening, isn't it?" he said, referring to the warm early summer night. "If I closed my eyes and listened to the stars and not the carriages and voices from the street, I could imagine I'm home."

Madelene pushed the curtains to the side and perched on the inner opposite side of the window. "This does seem a strange place to hold a conversation, but I should be accustomed to your choices for conversation and other things in odd places." She was reminded of a night not too long in the past, when they both sat in a tree.

"Ah, yes, unfortunately, there are no trees close to the house, and we wouldn't have the privacy we savored at our home in the country."

He looked at her keenly and shrugged his shoulders. "We appear to be at a stalemate. I must either remain outside your window this night or you can invite me in."

While Gabriel offered his dilemma, Madelene drew up her knees, braced her arms on them, and rested her chin on her arms. Her periwinkle blue dressing gown pooled around her bare feet. She cocked her head and thought. And then did some more thinking.

She wanted to keep him wondering what her answer would be. She loved him. Oh goodness, she actually thought of that word again. She was in serious trouble. She loved a man who wanted to harm her brother. Well, maybe that wasn't exactly right. But how could they forge this abyss between them?

To interrupt or hurry her consideration, Gabriel pretended to start to fall. It was a puerile, amateur move at best, which could fool no one. He couldn't hurt himself by falling more than a floor, the distance not great to the ground.

But there he was, clinging to her ledge.

She took pity on him. When Madelene grabbed his hand to help pull him over the ledge, he swung his feet up and over and easily hoisted himself into her bedroom. He stood there staring at her, probably wondering what she planned to do next.

Madelene backed away from the window, then deliberately headed around the bed, then to the sitting room door. At the door, she turned around and found him lying on her bed. He looked very comfortable, as if he planned to spend the whole night there.

"Gabriel, I think it would be best if we—" she began.

"I concur wholeheartedly. Come join me here. We shall both be more content than sleeping separately." He held his hand up as an invitation.

An invitation to *her* bed. Honestly. If he thought for one moment they'd do more than sleep—

"Madelene, come, lie here with me." He closed his eyes, continuing to talk. "I find I can rest better with you beside me. I have no intentions on your body tonight." He opened one eye, probably to gain her reaction.

His voice did sound soothing and inviting, and she did want to lie beside him. She did miss him. She missed his even breathing, the way he'd pull her to him and sleep with his arm over her hip, possessively, lovingly. She wondered if he loved her. Could he love her as much as she loved him?

All these complications. Nothing mattered but getting George back and making sure Matthew was safe. She had to remember that.

Madelene slipped off her nightrobe and, dressed in only her thin blue night rail, tentatively climbed into bed. Wanting him but afraid to want him.

He reached over and pulled her against him. Like he

had always done. As if this was the only place in the world for her. Next to him. She stiffened, waiting for that moment when he would brush her hair aside and kiss her shoulder, then her neck, then—

"This is quite pleasant, isn't it? I know it must seem strange to appear outside your window, but I wanted to look in on you without bothering you, in the event you were asleep," he murmured into her shoulder. His arm tightened around her waist. "I miss her."

Madelene lay on her side and wondered to whom did he refer? Perhaps he had drifted off to sleep, dreaming.

But he hadn't. He stroked her arm as he spoke. "I wish you had known Lucinda. Did you ever meet her at an assembly or country dance?"

Starting to relax, yet feeling the unanswered heat between them, Madelene had to think hard to follow his questioning. "Lucinda? I believe I saw her at a few dances. I remembered thinking how petite she was, almost like a china doll with light brown hair."

"Yes, that's a fair description. She was rather small for her age. They say our mother was also of short stature." He rolled away from her and onto his back, leaving her backside cold. Before she could decide what to do, Gabriel used his right arm to pull her to his side, so she could rest her head on his shoulder. He still had his shirt and pantaloons on, having removed his boots earlier.

"I look for her sometimes."

Madelene frowned into his shoulder.

Gabriel sighed deeply. "When you lose someone who has always been in your life, I sometimes wonder if you don't spend the rest of your life, or part of your life, looking for them."

She thought of her father and knew what he meant.

"When I've walked to the lake to fish, I look for her

sitting on a blanket reading the latest book from the lending library. There's something about my memory of her that won't let go. It's difficult to explain. It's as if there was a piece of my heart cut out when she left me.

"I'll never be the same. I want to go back to the way it was, but I can't. Sometimes, I wish I could see her one more time, tell her I will raise her son to be a fine man. Tell her I forgive her all those times she told Aunt Adelphia I ate the blueberries out of the blueberry pies."

Madelene settled more firmly into his side, listening to his calm tenor voice as he told her stories about Lucinda.

It was too soon. He had only lost Lucinda seven months ago. It had been over a year and a half since her father. Gabriel had such strength in him, and she felt so weak. Whenever she thought of her father, her heart pained her, like it was broken and wouldn't work again. It couldn't be repaired, like a clock with the little hand missing.

She shared thoughts about her father, told him things she had never told anyone because they wouldn't understand. Hadn't even told Matthew. If he felt the loss of their father, she had never seen evidence of it. She was willing to give him the benefit of the doubt, since she knew everyone had their own ways of grieving.

In a faltering voice, she told Gabriel, "I've looked for my father, too. When I walk past White's Club and remember how he enjoyed a game of whist with his friends, I imagine he's in there at that moment. It somehow brings me comfort.

"I remember him describing the Sleeping Mermaid tavern near the docks. He said they served the best liver and onions anywhere in Town. And a very good beer." She smiled to herself but couldn't separate the happy memories from the loss of his death.

She braced a hand on Gabriel's chest and pushed herself up, looking down into his brown eyes. "How do we ever become whole again?"

Gabriel brought her gently down to his chest again and pulled her even closer. "I wish I had a good answer for you. We owe it to your father and my sister to build a life together. They would want to know we are happy."

Madelene wanted a better reason, but knew none could be had. She asked him, emotion caught in her throat, "How can we be happy, when it was my brother, who, who—"

Her husband kissed her forehead. "I cannot be content unless I forgive him."

"Can you?" she whispered.

"I have because he brought you to me."

They fell asleep soon after, finding contentment in each other's nearness.

Over breakfast, Madelene and Gabriel lingered in the dining room enjoying sausages, tomatoes, and herring. Madelene had just poured another cup of tea when they heard a knock on the door.

They looked at each other before Gabriel jumped to his feet and met Styers at the door. Styers handed him notes and told him that after close questioning, neither of the two delivery boys could describe in any detail the person who had sent them.

Gabriel glanced at both of them and handed the first one to Madelene, who opened it and discovered an invitation to a ball given by Lord and Lady Londringham. A scribbled note at the bottom indicated Lady Londringham had only just learned the Westcotts had arrived in Town.

She looked up to watch Gabriel surveying another missive, and tried to wait patiently to learn of its contents.

Standing next to the table, her husband glanced at the note from Matthew Colgate.

"This evening. At eleven o'clock at the Sleeping Mermaid Tavern, near the docks. Bring the diamonds and no one else. You'll get the babe back."

Chapter Twenty-Seven

"What is it? The note, is it from Matthew?" Madelene asked anxiously, trying to read her husband's thoughts.

Gabriel stared at her for a moment before shaking his head. "Ah, no, just word from one of the insurance companies I need to address."

Madelene sat back in her chair, dismayed. When was Matthew going to contact them?

"And your note?" he inquired after stuffing his message in a top coat pocket.

She showed him the invitation. "What do you think, Mr. Westcott?" she asked her husband, who perused the note.

"Hmm?"

"The ball tonight. It is awfully short notice." *What to do,* she thought. At any moment, they could hear from her brother, so it would be best not to leave the house. However, she did intend to meet him at the town house tonight. If they attended the ball, she could slip away, provided she had the diamonds in her possession.

She could see his mind pondered something far different from her question. He looked over her and smiled. "It must have been some time since you attended a society event. Why do you not consider going? I don't know the earl and his wife. It is kind of them to invite us or more particularly, you, since you are the sister of a baronet."

Madelene nodded. At any other time in her life, she would have loved to attend the gathering and view the latest Paris fashions and visit with old friends. Indeed, it seemed a superficial desire, considering all else.

Lady Patience Londringham. She had last seen Lady Londringham over a year ago. A lovely, vivacious, and daring woman, if the stories were true about how she and the earl, her husband, stopped a band of French spies intent on invading England on the southeast coast many years ago.

She decided to send a note to Lady Londringham accepting the invitation for her husband and herself. Later in the evening, she could claim an illness and slip away from the ball to meet Matthew.

"If it is my decision, then we shall attend."

Gabriel nodded and, with a smile, turned to leave.

But Madelene was not through with her husband just yet. "Mr. Westcott, please do not keep me in suspense any longer. Where do you keep the diamonds?"

Her husband raised his eyebrows. "Oh, yes. Falstaff. Has anyone seen Falstaff?"

"Ruff, ruff." The little dog, who lived under the dining-room table waiting for a careless diner to drop a tidbit, heard his name. Madelene felt him brush by her morning dress, unknowing Falstaff had been under the table all this time.

"Here, boy." Mr. Westcott swept up Falstaff and placed him at the edge of the table, which was covered with a dainty petal pink tablecloth. Gabriel looked at Madelene. "Have a care Mrs. Lavishtock does not learn of this recklessness on her linen tablecloth. But it is all for the good."

Madelene watched wide-eyed as Gabriel unhooked the little dog's collar and held it up. "Mrs. Westcott, I made incisions in this leather collar, inserted the diamonds, then sewed the holes tight. The jewels have been in Falstaff's collar ever since."

Madelene fell back in her chair. Simply amazing. No one, not her brother, not the count, not Alec would have thought the dog kept them safe. She smiled at her husband's cleverness and watched as he took a knife and sliced open the leather stitches.

One by one, the diamonds fell onto the tablecloth, ten stones in all.

"I understand from the investigation handled in Florence, Italy, these diamonds were part of an earring and necklace set belonging to the Contessa Rocusco. Count Taglioni, for a time, was the contessa's lover, and given his greed, stole the set from the contessa. The local constabulary found the London jeweler, who had been paid handsomely to pluck the diamonds from their setting."

From his buff waistcoat pocket, Mr. Westcott pulled a small leather bag and gathered the diamonds, dropping them into it. "They will be safe with me until we can locate Colgate and George." He returned the bag to his pocket. "After we find George, we can hand over these diamonds to the London constabulary, who will see they are returned to the rightful owner."

During the revealing, Falstaff had wandered across the table, sniffing the air and inching ever so close to the finished plates.

"Oh, no you don't, you little scavenger!" Madelene leapt from her seat to collect the sneaky would-be thief and plopped him on the floor, where he promptly ran out the open dining-room door.

"I have errands this morning I must see to," Gabriel told Madelene as he excused himself from the dining room.

Madelene smiled, already deep in thought how to get her hands on that leather pouch.

In the front parlor, Madelene hastily wrote a note of acceptance to Lady Londringham and a note for her brother to be delivered to her old home. She said a prayer Matthew would receive the note and bring George to their town house in Bloomsbury. Wouldn't Gabriel be surprised when she came home this night with George? Indeed, he might be greatly disappointed she had to give the diamonds to Matthew, but she could discern no other satisfactory solution. She spent the rest of the morning putting a plan together.

Madelene lay on her favorite deep blue chaise waiting for word when she heard a timid knock on her door.

"Madam, it's me, Fanny."

"Come in, Fanny," Madelene called and sat up, anxious to learn of her maid's success. "Well? Do you have news?"

The young woman entered the room and shut the door before replying. "Yes, madam, but it was not easy. I had to be ever so clever so as Mr. Windthorp would not know what I was after." Fanny held up the buff waistcoat Mr. Westcott wore earlier in the day. "This is what you wanted."

Madelene sprang from her lounge and over to Fanny, grabbing the piece of material and rifling in the pockets. She held up the leather bag.

"Madam, what is it? Is it very important?" Fanny asked.

"Quite." Madelene hurried to her dressing table for her reticule and dumped the contents out. Untying the leather string, she opened the bag and dumped the glittering stones into her hand.

"Oh, madam," Fanny gasped, her jaw dropping.

"Promise me you don't know what I am about, in case anyone asks you," Madelene instructed her maid before pouring little soap balls into the leather bag, then shaking the bag. "Yes, it appears to be the proper weight."

Stuffing the leather bag back into the waistcoat, she turned to face Fanny. "Fanny, please return this waistcoat to Mr. Westcott's room and ensure no one sees you."

Fanny nodded, a frown crossing her brow, obviously puzzled by these latest events.

At the door, Madelene called to her. "I need to prepare for the Londringham ball. If you could obtain a light refreshment for me, we'll start the task of beautifying me."

"Oh, madam, if it to be called a task, let it also be called terribly effortless to make you even more beautiful," loyal Fanny told her.

Their eyes met in the looking glass as Madelene sat down at her vanity table. "Why is it you are only a few years older than I, but somehow you appear younger? Perhaps it is the optimism you carry with you. You are a treasure, dear."

Fanny smiled, curtsied, and hurried out the room to do her mistress's bidding.

"Rascal, do not ask any questions," Mrs. Lavishtock instructed the young man severely. The housekeeper sat at the table in the kitchen below stairs eyeing Rascal, who sat nearby eating a pudding cake, one of the bribes given him.

The young man sighed. "Wot is it you'd 'ave me do? Steal from the master? Steal from Mr. Westcott? No, I'd never do such a thing."

Mrs. Lavishtock gritted her teeth and pushed her royal blue turban back on her gray-haired head. "Besides the money I've promised you, what if I told you it was a matter of life or death?"

Rascal cocked his head and looked at her with narrowed eyes. She could tell he was becoming interested in the subject. "'ose life and 'ose death? As long as it's not mine, don't matter."

"Come, come, 'tis quite serious. Even though it might seem like you're stealing from the master, you'll actually be doing him a favor." She pushed a star confection in his direction. "Here, have another."

"I don't know. It does seem furtive, if I say so myself," the young man told her in earnest.

Mrs. Lavishtock sighed, never realizing it would be this difficult to convince the young groomsman. It was like trying to part Falstaff and a biscuit. And the word "furtive"? Wherever could he have learned— Cappie, of course. Not only was the elder coachman teaching Rascal how to read and write, he was also trying to improve the young man's vocabulary.

Unwilling to give up, she appealed to his vanity. "Rascal, the reason I'm asking you to do this is because I trust no other to get the job done," she told him.

"Well, 'ow do I know, when Mr. Westcott learns of my doings, 'e won't send me off to the work 'ouse or even the gaol?" Rascal folded his arms in front of him and waited.

"Because I'll tell Mr. Westcott this was all my doing and you did this under my direction."

Rascal brushed the hair out of his eyes and stood up, first grabbing the confection, and nodded. "Keep these sweets at the ready, and I'll take a wander up to Mr. Westcott's room to look for this leather bag."

"Wait, young man." Mrs. Lavishtock pulled her roly-poly body away from the table and stood, pulling a small fabric bag from the voluminous folds of her skirt. "All that needs doing is to replace the leather bag in the master's waistcoat with this one. He'll never know the change. Think it can be done?"

In reply, Rascal rolled his eyes at the effrontery. In total insouciance, the young man left the kitchen.

She looked after her young cohort and shook her head. She would make this right for her mistress and master. Satisfied she could do no more, she turned her attention to tea.

At the punctual hour of nine o'clock that evening, Mr. Westcott, refined in white waistcoat and white neckcloth, black dress coat with long tails, and breeches, escorted Madelene down the arched center stairway in the Londringhams' large town house on Berkley Square.

Madelene was most pleased with her pale lemon muslin dress with capped sleeves, a dark blue ribbon tied under her bosom, white gloves, and daisies in her dark curls. Walking down the elegant staircase, Madelene smiled, remembering the dark and possessive look Mr. Westcott gave her before they climbed into their carriage. Especially when he whispered in her ear that he wanted to find the ties to her silk hose later. Did he know he caused her to quiver at his suggestion? In all likelihood, indeed.

A number of dancers already crowded the floor to the music of an English country dance. Having known her husband for a brief span of time, she knew not whether Gabriel could dance. She loved to dance, and many a partner had delighted in her gracefulness, or so they had complimented her.

Madelene might be inclined to dance with her husband, but she must keep in mind her part in the drama to unfold later. She would be hard-pressed to enjoy the evening with the worry that surrounded her like her own cashmere shawl.

They walked through crowds enjoying libations or waiting to dance along the gold-trimmed walls of the ballroom, while acknowledging acquaintances on the way toward a row of chairs when they heard their names called.

"Madelene Colgate. Oh goodness, Mrs. Westcott! I am not accustomed as of yet to your new surname!" Lady Patience Londringham floated across to greet them.

"She was a phantom of delight—" Wordsworth's words came unbidden to Madelene. Surely he had composed those words to describe Patience, Lady Londringham. With deep green eyes and rich reddish brown hair, her face bright, dressed in the palest of greens with feathered green headdress, she was a vision. The warmth and generosity in such lovely proportions could seldom be found in London's *haut ton*.

Lady Londringham had befriended Madelene last year at one of the masquerades. Patience simply couldn't credit Madelene had created her own costume of the fairy Tatiana from *A Midsummer Night's Dream*. It was at the ball when Patience admired her costume that Madelene had confided in the older woman her talent and fascination to adapt French patterns for British fashion.

Because Madelene was concerned about society's acceptance of her trade as a modiste, Lady Londringham had named herself Madelene's patron in secret. She found a Frenchwoman on Bond Street who would sell Madelene's designs under the fictitious name of "Madame Quantifours."

Her infant business continued despite her father's passing only a few months later, which left Madelene bereft and unsure about her shop. She had been on the verge of sharing her success with her father, although not quite confident of his reception of her work. Without her father, she had thought to retire her yearling business.

"Lady Londringham! It seems quite a time since I've last seen you, but surely, not so long," Madelene greeted her friend warmly.

The friends embraced before Madelene turned to present her husband to Patience. "Mr. Westcott, I'd like you to meet Lady Patience Londringham, the Earl of Londringham's wife."

Gabriel took the gloved hand Patience presented and bowed over it. "It is a pleasure to meet someone of such renowned fame. Some years have passed, but tongues still linger over Miss Patience Mandeley's adventures to save her brother."

Unwittingly reminding Madelene of her own current dilemma.

Patience blushed, not realizing her husband had joined the trio and slipped his arm about her trim waist. Lord Londringham added, "Would there be more daring women in the world, we men would have little time to rest." He stepped forward to bow to Madelene and greet her husband. "Mr. Westcott, I'm sure you realize what a wonderful lady you have married."

Before Gabriel could reply, Patience added, "Madelene, my dear, we were very surprised, not only by your hasty nuptials but that you married *Mr. Westcott.*" The last statement was made for Madelene's hearing only when

Lady Londringham took her arm, and they walked over to one of the empty gold sofas. Their husbands followed, probably believing they had much gossip to share.

Madelene smiled and looked at her friend, their gloved hands still clasped together. "Patience, it is quite the drama."

"Oh, I can only imagine. You married the man who dueled with your brother." Patience fluttered her dark green-tinted fan to hide her words from those who would read her lips. "I have been worried for you. First you went missing, then no one heard from Matthew Colgate for some time. No one knew what to believe."

"I know, I wanted to tell you, my friend, but it happened so quickly. I had little time to prepare myself for it as well." Madelene hurried on the conversation before their husbands could reach them. "Patience, I need your help. It is of the utmost importance and concerns my brother *and* my husband. Please don't ask any questions, and later, I'll enlighten you about everything."

Patience smiled and pressed Madelene's hand. "You don't need to tell me anything other than what I can do to help you."

Madelene saw Lord Londringham and Gabriel stop to chat with the Duke and Duchess of Gloucester. Breathing a sigh of relief, she told her friend, "I plan to be ill about eleven o'clock this evening. I want you to have a footman obtain a carriage for me."

Patience nodded but frowned. "Your husband will not allow you to leave without him by your side. Your feigned illness will worry him, I have no doubt."

Biting her lip, Madelene asked, "Perhaps your husband could distract him with a card game and port?"

Patience looked over and smiled at her husband, who happened perchance to be looking at her and returned her smile. "Consider it done. Hmm, I guess there is more than one adventurous lady in London?" The older woman patted Madelene's hand.

But Patience's kindness and assistance did little to ease Madelene's mind on what the night would bring.

"What shall I tell the mistress if they return and you are not here?" Styers asked of Mrs. Lavishtock as she pulled herself into the hired hackney at the back of the house.

Seated in the carriage, the housekeeper leaned out the window. "They'll not return before I do. But if they do, tell them I've retired to bed. They need not know I've gone out for the evening. Keep this to yourself, young man. I go about on urgent business for Madame Westcott."

Styers shook his head, watching the hack turn the corner and continue out of sight. Something was up for sure tonight.

Chapter Twenty-Eight

Matthew Colgate glanced around the darkened tavern's great room where dockers and sailors became acquaintances sharing a beer and a story about the latest press-gangs or a trip to the Far East. All was quiet; no one should bother them or give them much mind. Distant yelling could be heard beyond the door as stevedores unloaded newly arrived ships. The oily, moldy smell lingered inside the tavern as well as outside.

He hoped this transaction would be brief, already determined to hand the diamonds over to Taglioni at his town house afterward and head to the Continent. His trespasses were too great to be forgiven by his sister, and especially by Westcott. He wanted to be through with this entire affair.

Based on the time, Westcott should appear at any moment. He kept watch at the entryway from the wooden seats across the room, every time and again returning his gaze to the contents of his tankard. His shoulders slumped, he wondered how he had fallen so far. But soon it would be all over.

Madelene would understand; she always had before.

And he *had* warned her. Told her if she didn't give him the diamonds, the count might see Matthew didn't have heirs.

She'd been a good little sister. Always told him she loved him, and proven her loyalty on more than one occasion.

Except when it came to the diamonds. She had stood by her husband. What choice did she leave him but to take George as barter? Although it had been his only solution, the babe had been much trouble. He had been quite surprised Alec offered to travel with them and care for George, but she had started complaining about the babe almost from the moment they had left Westcott Close.

Alec's motives smelled suspicious to Matthew, who knew he couldn't trust her. Which begged the question, why had Westcott trusted her and permitted her to live in his home? Didn't he know she was the one who stole the diamonds from her uncle originally? Both he and Alec had reason to fear the count.

Matthew shook his head and downed his beer. His fob watch indicated almost eleven o'clock. He glanced over at the door yet again to see a few more men straggle in and wander over to a table, looking for libation.

Later, he planned to sell the town house and move to France. The situation between France and England appeared to be easing. Now Madelene was cared for, nothing here in London prevented his departure and starting a new life on the Continent.

So intent was he on his appointment with Westcott, he forgot the note Millie had given him earlier in the day. He had sneaked into the back of the house to obtain a change of clothing, aware that without a doubt the count or Westcott had someone watching the house.

In a hurry to leave, he had thrust the note into his coat

pocket and promptly forgotten it, his thoughts on keeping an eye open for anyone looking for him, so that he would not be followed.

Matthew fumbled in his pocket and produced the note. He had to squint in the squalid candlelight to read it, and drew back in surprise. Then he crouched over it again.

It was Madelene's handwriting. "Meet me at our house in Bloomsbury. I have the diamonds. Bring George. Half-past eleven, tonight."

Flabbergasted, he read the note another time and another. If Madelene had the diamonds, why had Westcott agreed to meet him here? Who had the gems? He scratched his chin, then decided he'd best meet his sister. Perhaps there had been a change of plans, and the notes were ill timed.

He started to rise when he saw the door open and West-cott strolled in. Nothing to do but wait to see what his brother-in-law had to say. Matthew could only trust the outcome of this meeting would prove to be more advantageous than previously.

Madelene instructed Patience to give the note explaining her sudden return home to Mr. Westcott when Madelene's carriage had departed and it would prove too late for him to stop her.

On the way to her old home, she settled back into the squabs and felt for the smooth leather of the bag in her reticule, comforted to know she would soon have George back and her brother could do whatever he wanted with the diamonds. Madelene hoped her husband would not be angry with her for replacing the diamonds with the little round soaps, but he must understand. She did it for them. For George. Tomorrow morning would start their new life.

The night grew late as the carriage drove closer to Bloomsbury Square, a place she knew as well as her own features. Her mouth dry and heart pounding, she anticipated finding Matthew at their home. And once again holding George in her arms.

Concerned the count or one of Gabriel's men might see her and guess her mission, she told the driver to round the corner and stop two blocks from the house. She assumed the driver must have heard these strange requests before from a well-dressed woman seeking discretion, for he did not look in her direction, but did as instructed.

A hurried few minutes later, Madelene knocked on the servants' entrance. When Millie opened the kitchen door, Madelene walked in and threw back the hood of her cloak.

"Oh, miss, it is glad I am to see you. I saw the master earlier today and gave him your note. He does not look well." She stopped for a moment as Madelene removed her cloak. "You don't look so well yourself. You're awfully pale, miss." Millie continued jibbering at Madelene while the maid shooed her into the parlor. "What you need is a bit of sponge cake, the kind you like so well? I'll just put the kettle on."

"I won't be here—" Madelene began, then realized Millie had hastened back to the kitchen. She looked over to the mantel clock. Ten minutes after eleven. Not too much longer and Matthew would be here, probably entering in the same inconspicuous manner.

As she waited for the kettle and Matthew, Madelene walked around the little back parlor, touching favorite pieces, lost in yesterday's memories. She anticipated the sharp pain she had known before whenever she looked at her father's portrait over the fireplace, but, strangely, the hurt did not seem as sorrow-bearing.

Millie interrupted her memory tracking and served tea

in the candlelit parlor. Madelene took a measure of the room and found the drapes faded yellow, the Oriental carpet worn, and the mahogany wood needed bright polish. It seemed as if she hadn't been at her home in years, rather than a month. So much had changed in such a short amount of time. Looking about, Madelene appreciated she had outgrown this place, once a home she could never bear to think of leaving.

Eleven thirty and still no Matthew. The more minutes ticked by, the more anxious Madelene became. Millie had assured her that she had delivered the note into her brother's hands. Then where could he be?

Mrs. Lavishtock waited outside the door after she knocked. She wasn't familiar with this area of Covent Garden and didn't want to linger on the porch step in the dark.

Little Arnold Duckins. Although not little any longer and still a bachelor, and still beyond redemption. She always knew he'd end up in prison, always skirting the law. When she heard he fell in with Matthew Colgate, well, Colgate had a reputation, which was quite tarnished.

But the young girl, Madelene. She needed protection from her brother's machinations. And all had been well, until Sir Colgate had stolen the baby.

She would fix it. Mrs. Lavishtock planned to rescue George and uncover why her nephew gave lodgings to Matthew Colgate and that little Italian girl, Alec. The news Arnie was involved with a kidnapping and stolen jewels had surprised her little.

While waiting, she glanced back at the dark street where the hackney remained. The jarvey had promised he'd stay to drive her back to Bloomsbury Square, where Fanny had told her she would find Mrs. Westcott. If her nephew Arnie had allowed any harm to fall to the babe, she would make him regret they were related. The child had always got himself caught up in mischief in his earlier years. But her sister, Martha, would want her to keep her son out of gaol.

Duckins finally opened the narrow wooden door and gazed at her, his mouth dropped open. Gathering his composure, he stuttered, "Aunt, Aunt Mabel, what, what a surprise! Why, why are you here? It's rather late for a visit." He scarcely had spoken the words before she pushed past him and squeezed into the doorway.

"Where is he?" She drew herself up to five feet one and looked up at her nephew. "I want the babe," Mrs. Lavishtock told her nephew firmly.

"What, what—what babe?"

"This one," Alec said, walking down the stairs, holding George in her arms. "Take him, I can't handle him. I want no more part in all of this." She thrust the swaddled babe into Mrs. Lavishtock's very relieved and welcoming arms.

Mrs. Lavishtock unwrapped the blankets to see for herself the child was as right as rain.

She heard Alec intone, "The *bambino* is fine. Maybe a little hungry, we have no more goat's milk." With arms crossed over her chest, the young girl raised an eyebrow. "Where are the diamonds? I assume you brought them with you?"

Duckins stared at Mrs. Lavishtock and Alec and shook his head, as if he didn't know what to make of this exchange.

But Mrs. Lavishtock understood the young woman. The housekeeper rooted in her large skirt pocket and her fingers touched on the leather pouch. She pulled it out and threw it to Alec. "I want you and you," she pointed to Alec and Duckins, "to stay far away from the Westcotts, whether they be here in Town or in the country. You have put them through too much, especially with taking the babe. Near broke their hearts."

Before she finished speaking, Alec had opened the bag and dumped the gems into her hand. Her lips curved into a smile as she looked at the glittering stones. Totally absorbed in her newfound wealth, she paid no notice to Mrs. Lavishtock or her nephew, and ran up the stairs.

Mrs. Lavishtock waddled to the door with her precious bundle, who slept with a contented smile on his ruddy face.

Her nephew hurried after her to open the door. "Aunt Mabel, I wanted no part of this. They came to my door, seeking my help. I couldn't turn them away, with the babe and all."

But Mrs. Lavishtock paid him no heed, determined to return George to his parents without any further delay.

When Gabriel had learned from Lady Londringham that Madelene had fallen ill, he immediately planned to return home, until the countess assured him it was of a slight nature. Relieved, he thought about tonight and what he had to do.

Soon after, he took his leave of the ball and the Londringhams for the London docks. In the carriage, he shrugged on an older greatcoat and hat, the better to blend in than his evening wear.

Gabriel swung open the door to the Sleeping Mermaid tavern and strolled in, catching sight of Madelene's brother. He gave his brother-in-law almost an imperceptible nod, then walked around the mismatched tables as if he was in no hurry, had no particular place to be, no one particular to meet.

With a casual glance around the large room, he calculated how many men filled the bar and the nearest exit from the tavern. He liked to plan for all contingencies, aware he could not underestimate Matthew Colgate. When Gabriel could assure himself no accomplices lingered near Matthew, he approached the back table and slid onto the bench.

He wanted this business to be dealt with swiftly, but how could he trust Colgate to produce George after he handed over the jewels? And what had Colgate been thinking—to bring a babe here?

Gabriel studied the man before him. His old adversary. For Madelene's sake, he wished— It would not matter. This leopard would not change his spots. Matthew still held his left side with his right hand, and in the dull light, his face appeared very pale, quite sickly. It was obvious he hadn't washed in a few days, and he had a desperate look about him. Gabriel was glad Madelene would not see her brother like this.

The constable would soon be on Colgate's coattails for the kidnapping. As for the outcome of the diamond theft, Gabriel couldn't determine because it remained to be seen what part the count might play in this act. Indeed, the count was the master puppeteer, and Gabriel was determined to cut his strings. All of them.

Chapter Twenty-Nine

Millie began snoring. Madelene sighed and wrapped her arms around her chest while pacing the small room. Matthew was an hour late. She couldn't think, could hardly breathe. The fire kept the room quite warm, but Madelene could only feel the coldness in her heart.

Something felt terribly wrong. Every time she looked at the mantel clock, the hands seemed to stand still. The whole house slept silent, except for Millie's snoring. Madelene was on the verge of waking the maid and telling her to go to her room, when she heard a knock at the servants' entrance.

Scarcely knowing what to expect, she rushed from the back parlor to the kitchen. Gulping, she suddenly thought of the danger she might be in if it wasn't her brother or Gabriel. Before she could grab an iron from the fire, the door opened.

Mrs. Lavishtock appeared on the other side, holding a bundle in her arms. In stunned amazement, Madelene went to her side and closed the door.

"Mrs. Lavishtock, how—" she began before the house-keeper stopped her.

"I have George," she announced softly.

A huge burden seemed to lift itself from Madelene's shoulders. She could breathe easier. *George is safe. He is with me.* In no time, the sleeping baby was in her arms, and Madelene could not look at his small round face enough, tears brimming in her eyes. She noted all the little features she had fallen in love with while kissing his little hands, unconcerned he might wake.

And he did. His big green eyes stared up at her; he blinked a few times, then fell back to sleep on her shoulder. Holding him close to her heart, knowing they would never be separated again, Madelene walked into the back parlor where Millie had begun to stir. Mrs. Lavishtock followed Madelene and found the nearest chair she could fall into.

Comfortable in her old favorite rocking chair, George clutched tight, Madelene looked over at her housekeeper. "Mrs. Lavishtock, I must admit you were the last person I would have expected through the door. However did you find George?" The last she whispered.

"Ooh, I could use a cup of tea. Would—" she replied, fanning herself with her hand.

"Certainly. Millie, would you please heat up the kettle?" she asked the sleepy-eyed maid, who nodded and made her way back to the kitchen, too sluggish to even notice the sleeping babe.

"I won't keep you waiting to hear of how I retrieved George. I finally remembered hearing about a Mr. Arnold Duckins making a wager on Miss Westcott marrying within three days. I thought if your brother needed a place to hide with the baby, maybe he would stay with my nephew, Arnold."

The housekeeper stopped to clear her throat. "Yes, so

I went to see my nephew tonight and sure enough, there was George with the Italian girl, Alec."

At the name of her nemesis, Madelene's eyes narrowed. After all Gabriel had done for the young woman. Mrs. Lavishtock continued on, breaking through her deliberation.

"I had no difficulties retrieving the babe. And when she gave me George, I looked at him to make sure no harm had come to him."

"Did they ask about the diamonds? I cannot believe they simply handed George to you." Madelene frowned, knowing Mrs. Lavishtock did not have the diamonds in her possession.

Mrs. Lavishtock bowed her head. "It only mattered to me to somehow rescue our baby, George." The housekeeper couldn't quite meet Madelene's eyes.

"Yes, certainly, but what did you give her? You could not have given her the diamonds." Her tone was more harsh than she realized.

"Yes, Mrs. Westcott. I had Rascal steal the bag of diamonds from Mr. Westcott's chamber. I didn't know what else to do." The housekeeper implored her, "Please say you forgive me. I thought George was worth more than the diamonds."

Madelene couldn't think and wearily rubbed her brow. How could Mrs. Lavishtock have the gems when she had them in her pocket, ready to give her brother? Mystery to be solved later. It only mattered George was safe and back where he belonged.

Her lower lip quivering, she told Mrs. Lavishtock, "Do not think more on it. I do not know how I'll ever be able to repay you for finding George. I am terribly grateful, and I know Mr. Westcott will be as well."

At that moment, Millie entered the parlor with a steaming cup of tea.

"A great relief, to be sure. This will do nicely. Thank you, miss." Mrs. Lavishtock eagerly reached for her refreshment.

A banging on the kitchen door startled them.

Matthew. Madelene sighed in relief. He was finally here, and they could make amends. She could persuade him—

Crash. Thump.

Madelene, the housekeeper, and the maid all rushed from the parlor into the kitchen to see what had caused the commotion.

It was indeed Matthew. He lay facedown on the floor, looking as if he had fallen into the house. Madelene handed George to Mrs. Lavishtock before rushing to her brother, who muttered intangible words and moaned.

Kneeling beside him, she turned him over and saw the blood. It trickled from a cut on his forehead, but the worst flow came from his stomach, which he clutched with his hands, apparently to stop the bleeding.

She had to think quickly. "Millie, please go for the surgeon, Dr. Riley, on Millhouse Street. It's only a few blocks from here." The housemaid caught up her cape and flew out the door. The sight of all that blood might have unnerved her and winged her heels.

Madelene reached for several kitchen linens to place over her brother's hands and pressed down with her own. They had to somehow stop the blood flow. How could this have happened yet again? Mrs. Lavishtock, holding George, hovered nearby, intoning she had been concerned something like this might happen.

"Mrs. Lavishtock, please. What should we do? Should we move him? I don't think I can lift him by myself." Her tears began to slide down her cheeks. Matthew kept coming in and out of lucidity. The pain must have been unbearable. After all he had been through, Madelene knew he couldn't beat death a third time.

She kept shaking her head, sure her own heart had stopped. When Madelene checked for his pulse, she could feel it, but it was faint and slow. There had to be something she could do. She couldn't fail him now, not when he really needed her.

Gabriel! He would know what to do, but how to get word to him at their home in Mayfair?

Despondent, Madelene cradled her brother's head in her lap and continued pressing the linens to his wound while talking to him. "Matthew, everything will be fine. George has been returned to us. Please, don't." She didn't know what words to use to comfort him, to make him try to stay alive. After dashing her tears on her shoulders, she leaned down to kiss his cheek. "You must try, Matthew."

The wind whipped Gabriel through the door, and it banged against the wall. He stopped and stared. "Madelene! What— Matthew! I thought he might come here."

She lifted her tear-streaked face to his strained visage. "What happened? How did you know?"

He ignored her question. "Let me help Matthew. I'll put him on the kitchen table." He collected the wounded man off the floor and carefully placed him on the table in the center of the room. Madelene stayed by Gabriel's side, continuing to administer comfort. All she had.

With shadowed eyes, she looked at her husband. "What more can I do? We do? Is there anything?"

Gabriel sighed heavily and rubbed his chin, watching Matthew's pale face and flickering eyelids. "Have you sent for a surgeon?" he asked her in hushed tones.

She nodded, then realized he didn't notice her gesture.

"Yes." She cleared her throat. "Yes, Millie went to fetch Dr. Riley nearby. She should return any time with him."

Grabbing Madelene's shoulders, he asked roughly, "I heard blue vitriol in water might help stop the bleeding. Would you know if there is any in the house?"

She shook her head. "I don't know. I wouldn't think so." Madelene tried desperately to think of any type of medicinal cures they might have.

"Something to relieve his pain. Any laudanum, perhaps?"

"I believe we have anodyne draught, which might help."

"That will do," he told her, turning back to Matthew, whose motions seemed slower, almost as if he was falling asleep.

While Madelene was handing Gabriel the draught, she heard the front doorbell ring. Moments later, Millie and the surgeon bustled into the kitchen, followed by Rascal.

Madelene felt drained, exhausted, yet calm. A surgeon at the bedside of a patient must bring some relief to the worried relatives of the patients. If anything could be done for Matthew, Dr. Riley could make it so. Riley was renowned for his studies on bleeding and leeches. Not that bleeding was needed in Matthew's condition.

The surgeon asked everyone to wait elsewhere because he needed room and quiet. He glanced at the occupants and requested Gabriel to assist him. Madelene begged to be allowed to stay in the room, in a chair in the corner, so she would not disturb their work. She couldn't leave her brother now.

Matthew's moans filled the room, aching Madelene's hearing and heart. She wanted to block out the sounds, but there was no relief. Alcohol and a metallic smell wafted over to her corner, underlining all her fears. Madelene looked to the servants' entrance where she could escape. But she remained fixed in her chair.

After an hour of working with Gabriel and trying tinctures, hot balsams, and agaric of the oak to stop the bleeding, the surgeon's shoulders slumped. He backed away from the table.

Looking at Gabriel, he shook his head. "There is nothing more to be done." Then he turned to Madelene and looked at her with eyes full of sadness. All was hopeless.

Her arms wrapped around her chest, she rose unsteadily to her feet and walked the few steps to her brother's side. He had not yet left her. She put her arm around his head and leaned down to whisper. "Matthew." His breathing was shallow and slow. His eyes flickered open. "Matthew, George is your son." Her brother stared at her, and she saw a small smile fall over his face. A few minutes later, he was gone.

At first, she couldn't believe it. Didn't want to believe it. Her husband and the surgeon left her alone in the kitchen with her brother. Time didn't matter, and if asked what consumed her thoughts, she would have been hardpressed to say. Taking leave of a loved one is not for the faint of heart. No matter the choices he had made, she had forgiven him everything, knowing she would never understand his reasoning.

She actually smiled thinking of her brother and father together again, where they belonged. When she finally remembered to cry, Gabriel returned to the kitchen and silently took her in his arms and held her, holding back the demons threatening to devour her.

Chapter Thirty

The coroner and mortician were called as Madelene and Gabriel waited in the back parlor. When George awakened, she took him from Mrs. Lavishtock's care and fed him, absorbed in his cherubic, innocent face.

After the mortician prepared the body for burial with Mrs. Lavishtock and Madelene watching, they moved Matthew's body to the front drawing room, where Madelene's father had lain upon his death.

A few hours before dawn, it was decided Gabriel and Mrs. Lavishtock would return to the town house in Park Lane with the baby. Madelene insisted on remaining alone by her brother's side throughout the rest of the night and morning. Rascal agreed to keep her company, and Gabriel promised to send Windthorp to the town house.

Gabriel didn't want to leave her, but she convinced him she needed to be with her brother, alone, this last time. He understood and departed, albeit reluctantly.

An hour stroked by as she sat near her brother's body in his burial clothes. Her companion, Rascal, would walk into the room to check on her and the fire to keep it burning, although the early morning hours were not very cold.

After he checked on Madelene, he would return to his place in the back parlor and try not to fall asleep.

While Millie retired for the night, Windthorp sat in the kitchen, wanting something to occupy his time, but all he could do was count the hours till he could return to Mr. Westcott's side. Madelene, though thankful for the close company, continued to reflect upon the day that began with her brother alive and ended with him dead.

She was still mystified by the events of the night, for Gabriel had not had time to apprise her of what he knew or saw what happened to Matthew. Somehow she knew Count Taglioni and Alec played a part in this tragedy, and she determined to make it known to the constabulary.

Her own eyelids becoming heavy, she had begun to nod in her chair when she heard a raspy foreign voice behind her. "The beautiful Madelene."

Madelene jerked awake and felt cold, smooth steel against her throat.

"I wouldn't move if I were you, but simply listen to what I have to say. Perhaps you will prove more amenable in assisting me than your brother could."

She didn't turn around. The count. "What do you want? Are you not satisfied with the death of my brother that you seek mine as well?" She didn't know where she found the courage to answer him.

Taglioni chuckled behind her and removed the knife to walk in front of her. The silver blade blinked in the candlelight.

"My dear Mrs. Westcott. Your brother disappointed me for a number of reasons. Earlier this evening, he ran into my knife." He continued, ignoring her gasp of pain and his admission of murder.

His eyes gazed coolly on her, reflecting the ice in his soul. "I only wanted the diamonds and you. And Matthew

Colgate could deliver neither to me. He, in fact, refused me again tonight, when I mentioned your name. Since he no longer had the diamonds, he ceased to have a purpose."

Madelene stared at this hollow shell of a man, refusing to believe he could utter any more venom that would sting any crueler. She gritted her teeth, her jaw throbbing. "I regret the day my brother and you ever crossed paths. He has paid the price, and you soon will also."

"*Tsk, tsk,* Mrs. Westcott, a threat from a lady?" He looked at her with disdain. "This affair has wasted much of my time and my patience." Walking closer to Madelene, Taglioni sheathed his knife with effortless aplomb. He clearly thought he had no need for a weapon in handling her.

Madelene glanced toward the hallway that led to the back parlor and kitchen.

"I suggest you not consider the valet or young boy as your champion. They both sleep peacefully at the moment, I let them live." He walked over to the window and pushed the drapes aside, looking out into the street.

She rubbed her forehead, trying to gain time and think how to thwart the devil in gentleman's clothing. It looked as if she would have to save herself.

"Pray tell me, if you have the diamonds you so ardently pursued, why are you here?" She surreptitiously studied the room, awaiting his response. There had to be some type of weapon to be found.

He wandered back over to her side and chuckled. The sound made her want to retch, as he unexpectedly reached over and touched her cheek before she could turn away. "If I were you, I wouldn't play the game the way your brother did. He lost."

Madelene sat still in the wing chair, almost as if she were tied down, though she wanted to leap from the chair and strangle the smirk from his face. If she wanted to gain advantage, she needed to tamp down her firelit anger.

"How tiresome you English are. When I confronted your brother outside the tavern, he handed me a bag with nothing but fake stones. I have held the real ones in my hand. Surely I could tell the difference, even in the miserly light in the alley."

He sat down at the edge of the settee, skirting the table and Matthew's body. Indeed, he barely gave it a notice.

"I found the note from you to your brother. *You* have the real diamonds." He paused deliberately. "I want this affair done. Now, I want you to tell me where the jewels are."

Madelene slowly eased out of her chair, trying to look as if she needed to stretch her legs. "Mr. Westcott plans to turn the diamonds over to the magistrate. I don't have them."

The truth finally made the count less careful. He leapt from his perch and started toward her. "Let us hope your husband still has them. It would make everything so much simpler."

Madelene retreated from Taglioni and backed toward the fireplace. "What would you have me do?"

His threatening presence nearly made her lose her composure.

"I need to return to Italy, and you'll be going with me. Since your husband will want you back, he'll need to deliver the diamonds, the real ones, to me at the docks before we sail."

Her eyes wide, she wet her lips. *Think. Think of a distraction.* She told him in a quavering voice, "Mr. Westcott will not exchange the diamonds for me. He has been preparing to divorce me."

His eyes gleamed black. "That's not what Alessandra has told me."

One step, then another. He was almost near to reach out and touch.

Someone coughed from the back of the house.

Taglioni turned around, prepared for defense, but not for an offense. In the breath of a moment, she grabbed the heavy gold fire tongs and swung it toward his head.

The resounding thud rattled the house when he fell to the floor. Unconcerned whether he lived or not, Madelene rushed past his outstretched body and to the kitchen, where Windthorp sat rubbing his head.

"Mrs. Westcott? What happened?"

When she heard another noise behind her, it gave her a fright, but it was only Rascal walking stiffly into the room, rubbing his eyes, as if he had only awakened.

"Windthorp, Rascal, I've killed Count Taglioni! He must have hit *you* on the head," she told them, pointing to the valet. "And you were probably fast asleep." She looked at Rascal.

The young man and the older man looked at each other before leaving the room to run to the front parlor. She heard them calling to her. Count Taglioni still lived; her blow had knocked him unconscious but not delivered death.

Her heart still beating fast, she could finally breathe, having forgotten how when she heard the count's voice behind her. She went to wake Millie and send her on another errand, this time for the constable.

The next day sobbed great raindrops, graying the day, like Madelene's heart. She had returned to Mr. Westcott's home after ensuring her brother's body was looked after and now sat in the front parlor, wanting to rest and find peace. Stretches of time seemed to pass before the window as she stared without seeing.

The door opened and when no one entered, Madelene turned to discover Falstaff at her feet. She gathered him on her lap and watched as he sniffed her pockets for the usual biscuit but came away empty-handed. Disappointed, he jumped off her lap and went to hide under a nearby table. "You little traitor. I thought you came to provide me comfort, and all you can think of is your next meal." Her words were said with such softness, Falstaff could only assume he had pleased her and banged his tail on the floor. She shook her head and smiled briefly, forgetting.

Madelene wanted to know what happened the previous night. With all the commotion, she had not had an opportunity to ask Gabriel. Although she knew the knowledge couldn't change the future without Matthew, she needed to know.

Another knock on the door and this time, Gabriel himself did enter the room, dressed in a dark coat and pantaloons. He walked across the room, sat down in a chair next to hers, and reached for her hand.

She focused her eyes on her husband's beloved face, memorizing the details to plant in her heart.

Gabriel pointed to Falstaff. "I presume he is not providing you much in the way of companionship."

"True. He wanted nothing more to do with me when he found no biscuit in my pocket."

They sat together in quiet harmony for a time.

"Madelene—" He turned to her, but she held up her hand.

"Gabriel, I, I want you to tell me about the tavern and the count."

Her husband looked at her and shook his head. "Not now. Another time."

Madelene pressed her hand to his, her words tumbling after the other, surprising herself she could even voice them. "Please, I feel this need to understand what my brother's last minutes were. Why this had to happen."

Folding his hands together, he bent his head, perhaps trying to remember or trying to forget. A minute passed, then another. With a long sigh, he turned to Madelene and clutched her hands tightly. "I went to the Sleeping Mermaid tavern to meet your brother after the ball last night. I was to bring the diamonds, and I planned for your brother to advise where I could find George. I could only hope your brother would honor this agreement."

He hesitated, then continued, "After a few brief minutes with your brother, I gave him the bag of diamonds, but before I could learn anything further, Rascal rushed into the tavern looking for me. He blurted out he found George by following Mrs. Lavishtock. We ran out and found a hack to take us to this fellow Duckins's home, but when we arrived, Mrs. Lavishtock and George had already departed.

"We returned to the town house, but you were missing and Mrs. Lavishtock and George were yet to be seen. Fanny informed me of your destination, which is how Rascal and I ended up in Bloomsbury and found you and Matthew.

"After I left your brother, Taglioni must have found him." He stopped and looked into her eyes. "I couldn't give your brother the real gems and have the count possess them again. I had planned between your brother and me, that we might oppose the count together.

"I had a Bow Street Runner waiting outside to take Taglioni into custody and warned him to watch for the count before I left to find George." Gabriel paused. "I keep reliving last night and wondering what I could have done differently—"

Madelene stared at him, shocked at his words. *If only*

Gabriel had given the real diamonds to Matthew, he might be alive. Was Gabriel indirectly responsible for my brother's death?

In ignorance, Gabriel halted her accusing thoughts. "Madelene, when your brother became involved with the count, there was only a small possibility Taglioni would have let him live. The count couldn't have trusted your brother wouldn't alert the magistrate, and he would not have had to pay your brother for delivering the gems to him."

Her lower lip trembled. She swallowed hard. *All he said was true.* Could she ever forgive herself for not helping Matthew this one last time?

Madelene finally nodded. "You could have done nothing more." She placed his hand to her cheek.

She gave him a measure of comfort he had not known he needed.

Chapter Thirty-One

On June 28, 1812, they laid Sir Matthew Colgate to rest next to their father, the last baronet, in St. George's Cemetery. Engraved on his tomb were the words, "Matthew Nathaniel Colgate, 1784–1812, Beloved Son, Brother, and Father."

From the upstairs window, Madelene had watched the carriage taking her brother to the cemetery, followed by Gabriel and other family friends in another coach. A beautiful sunny, almost perfect day. So many tears shed over the last few days, Madelene knew this ache in her heart would lessen, but never truly go away. All those times, she and her father had whisked him out of trouble. *I guess I couldn't keep saving him indefinitely.*

She remembered earlier at the church service as Gabriel took her hand in his when the rector finished the blessing and delivered the twenty-third psalm, which they all recited. Madelene looked over the small crowd and noted, of course, Mrs. Lavishtock, a funeral weeper by the look of things; Arnold Duckins, who stood nearby his aunt; and Mr. Brelford.

Matthew's friend, Mr. Brelford, appeared to be taking

her brother's death particularly hard. His face was white and drawn. Even from across the church, she saw his hands shaking and clutching a white handkerchief. Perhaps this Mr. Brelford truly loved Matthew as the dearest of friends, which brought a smile to her lips. She wanted someone to love Matthew besides herself, and George, well, someday, she would tell him about his father and his mother, with Gabriel's help.

They planned to leave London the next day and journey to Westcott Close, a place she now thought of as home. After the last fortnight, Madelene wanted to mourn for her brother in private and take solace from those who surrounded her, particularly Gabriel and George. Those two men whose very being made her heart beat fast, for very different reasons. How she loved them both, and surely they knew.

August. Fall would come too soon. Madelene looked out her first-floor window at the trove of trees near the lake that would slowly lose their leaves, no longer to provide hiding places for lovers until next year.

Had it only been late last spring, when she and Gabriel had first been together? It seemed longer, as if she could never remember him not being in her life. But that seemed like an odd thought. Perhaps by becoming his wife and George's mother, she had shed her other life as daughter and sister.

Madelene waited anxiously at the window, looking for her husband's return. He had spent much time in Town looking after his shipping ventures and seeking a partner. A Mr. Conkhorn, an elderly lawyer who lately had come into an inheritance, decided to invest with Westcott Shipping

Enterprises. Together they planned to use new routes to the West Indies.

She remembered how excited Gabriel became as he spoke about the ships, the cargo, and the future. Indeed, he hadn't mentioned *their* future, but it was all one and the same.

Whenever he returned to Town, Madelene would spend more time in the nursery with the baby and Charlotte. Donna Bella and Carlos had decided to return to Italy, which meant Madelene had to find a new governess. Gabriel promised to look into the matter while he was in London and possibly bring back someone who might be suitable for the position.

Two months. Two long months since she and Gabriel had been together. Since she was in mourning and with the matters of the estate to settle, and her husband's business affairs, circumstances had schemed to keep them apart, or so it seemed.

Tonight would be different. She promised herself and Gabriel a surprise or two, which might actually compel him to admit he loved her. Three simple words. Three easy words. But he had never said them to her.

She took dinner in her room, still waiting for the master of the house to return. Her constant companion, Falstaff, lay nearby, his stomach, for once, satisfied—at least temporarily. Dressed in white night robe and rail, she looked and felt the picture of health.

Lying on her chaise longue, Madelene prayed they could start again and put the past and how they got here behind them.

Heavy footsteps thumped down the hallway and past her bedchamber. She flew to the door to peek, and there he was entering his own room. He probably wanted to remove the road dust.

This was it.

* * *

What was that noise?

Gabriel, naked after washing, heard something at his window. Unperturbed at his state of undress, he approached the window, thinking maybe a wild branch knocked on the glass.

However, to his delight, the noise was indeed his wife, looking beautiful and luminous and slightly damp, for a drizzle had begun.

She stood on the sturdy branch outside his window, grasping a top branch for support. Blinking sweetly at him, she said, "I know this might seem a bit unladylike for courting—but could I possibly come in?"

"No." His answer was short and quite confounded.

"No?"

"I'm coming out."

"Oh, but it's raining and—" She noticed. "You don't have on a stitch of clothing." Her eyes widened as she watched her naked husband climb out his window and back her slowly into the well-worn familiar knot of the old tree.

Standing together with leaves to hide their embrace, Gabriel gathered Madelene in his arms and swept in for the longest kiss of his life. Of her life. He pressed her damp body close to his so that there was not even air between them that they didn't share.

Catching his fingers in her long, wet hair, he knew how to warm her in all the right places. Even knew how to set her on fire—first with his tongue, then continuing his onslaught down her cheek to her neck and then farther. Her night robe slipped off and drifted down to the ground before either could catch it.

They both stopped for a moment to look where the robe

had fallen and laughed. If they didn't pick it up tonight, there would be stories bandied about in the morning.

"Ruff, ruff." Falstaff growled, then barked again.

They stopped, frozen in their embrace.

Something was wrong.

Gabriel turned to Madelene and put his finger to his lips before he walked down the branch and looked in her window. He vanished in a thrice into her room.

Waiting a moment to see if he would return, she heard talking, both Gabriel's and someone else's. The someone else sounded like a woman, and quite familiar.

Alec.

She was back. All this time, Madelene had thought she had returned to Italy, after her uncle was jailed for robbery, murder, and other crimes both in England and his homeland.

Madelene climbed through the window and exclaimed, "What— "

"Stop there," Alec told her, pointing a gun at her.

Gabriel stood right inside the window, also apparently stopped by the gun the young woman held.

Although Madelene felt wound as tight as a clock, she sensed a calmness in her husband, but couldn't understand it. What was his plan? Surely he must have a plan. Heroes always had plans.

"Gabriel, where are the diamonds? You may have given my uncle a banbury story, but I know you still have them."

Madelene took a closer look at the young woman who had haunted them from the beginning. Her eyes were as sharp as ever but her hand shook slightly—from exhaustion or distress? Madelene wondered.

With hands on his hips, Gabriel shook his head. "Give it up, Alec. I don't have them. I've been informed the gems have been returned to the Countess Rocusco in Florence."

Alec's eyes narrowed. "No, I don't believe you. I didn't steal the diamonds from my uncle in Italy only to have them returned there." She stared at Gabriel. "We could have had the diamonds and each other. You didn't need *her*." She jerked her head at Madelene but kept the gun steady.

Before Madelene could bristle at this affront, Gabriel stepped in front of his wife. "Alec, I told you in Italy, and I told you again when we arrived in England. There has never been anyone for me but Madelene Colgate."

Madelene could see that as Gabriel continued to talk, Alec's face turned brighter, her breathing came faster. This young woman, possibly mad, could shoot them at any time.

Holding out his hands, he told her calmly, "Alec, put the gun down and we can talk. If you return to Italy, we won't speak to the magistrate about kidnapping charges." He took a step closer.

Alec took a step back. On Falstaff's tail. The little dog yelped and tried to bite her ankle. Somehow, Alec managed to keep the gun on her target while avoiding Falstaff's teeth. Gabriel sprang toward her, but Alec stopped him.

Pointing the gun at Falstaff, who still growled at her feet, she ordered, "Stop, or, or, I'll shoot the dog!"

Madelene steamed until she boiled over. Alec could threaten her or Gabriel with a gun, but not Falstaff! Unthinking, hoping surprise would be her weapon and asset, she stepped from behind Gabriel and rushed across the room. Madelene knocked the gun to the floor, then turned and hit Alec in the chin. The blow sent the young thief tumbling in stunned submission.

The gun lay on the floor out of reach until Gabriel walked over and picked it up.

Another knock on the door. Almost before Gabriel had a chance to throw on his robe, Mrs. Lavishtock burst through the door. "I thought I'd find you here!"

In surprise, Madelene looked at the housekeeper. *Did she mean Falstaff?*

"Alec Taglioni, the magistrate is downstairs waiting to ask you questions." Her voice, normally strong, sounded winded, probably from climbing the stairs.

Alec had risen to her feet, still smarting and angry, her fists clenched with no release.

Gabriel smiled at their housekeeper. "Mrs. Lavishtock, I've already told Alec she can return to Italy. We have George back and that is what is important."

Mrs. Lavishtock kept shaking her head. "No, Mr. Westcott, this woman is wanted for attempted murder."

Madelene, holding Falstaff to her chest, couldn't help but enter the conversation. "Attempted murder? Whose?"

The housekeeper turned to her. "Yours, I'm afraid, madam."

Unable to keep the astonishment out of her voice, Madelene shrieked, "Mine?" Whatever— *The poison, the push in the lake, when I almost drowned.* She started toward Alec before Gabriel caught her at the waist from behind.

He looked at Alec, who had sidled closer to the door and possible flight. "I trusted you. I brought you into this house, and you put my wife and child in danger?"

He waved his hand at Mrs. Lavishtock. "Please take her downstairs, and here." With the gun in his hand, he walked across the room and handed it to her. "I don't think you'll have any difficulty with her. As soon as I dress, I'll join you directly."

Mrs. Lavishtock took the gun, a little too readily, Madelene thought, hoping the gun wouldn't "accidentally" go off before Alec made it to the parlor where the magistrate waited, considering their housekeeper's wrath emanating from her turban.

Graham opened the doors to the terrace, permitting a warm breeze to dance into the breakfast nook. He laid the hot repast on the sideboard before returning to the kitchen for coffee and tea. When he returned, the butler hid a smile, watching Mr. and Mrs. Westcott walk together into the nook. They were a delightfully happy couple. Fanny had told him they couldn't be more blessed. He missed her, his silly sister.

As brothers would be, she annoyed him when she was here, but he missed her when she was gone. Left in London. He couldn't imagine her luck. Miss Fanny Dushorn from Ludlow running Mrs. Westcott's mantuamaker shop, Madame Quantifours. He shook his head. She would be fine. He should stop this woolgathering and serve the coffee.

"Mrs. Westcott? Mrs. Westcott?" Millie called before she entered the breakfast room.

Madelene looked up, her brows raised. "What is it, Millie?"

"What do you think of the deep blue gown for tonight's soiree? I must make it ready for you." The maid stood at the door waiting for her answer.

"The blue would be just the thing. Thank you for your thoughtfulness. It is of great pleasure to have you with us now. You are a treasure to me." Madelene smiled fondly at her lady's maid as Millie curtsied and flew out the door.

Mrs. Lavishtock rolled in the door with something in

her hand. "Och, Mrs. Westcott, I wanted to show you this recipe for starched corn for dinner tonight."

Bemused, Madelene looked up at her housekeeper. "Thank you, Mrs. Lavishtock, but I am sure whatever you serve us will be perfectly prepared and perfectly presented."

Gabriel smiled at his wife. "Such alliteration, have you a desire to be a poet?" He gently teased her.

"None whatsoever. What trips off my tongue even amazes me at times."

"Yes," he agreed, imbued with sardonacism.

Cocking her head to one side, she wondered, "And, your meaning, sir?"

"Only that I find you amazing. And lovely in gray this morning. I find you lovely in anything and nothing." The latter said sotto voce.

"Shameless flatterer. You may woo me anytime with such lavishments."

"I'd like to lavish you," he leaned toward her to whisper. "Mrs. Lavishtock." He straightened and looked at the back of the housekeeper heading in the direction of the kitchen.

"Och, yes, Mr. Westcott. Is there something—?"

Gabriel dropped two leather bags on the lace cloth. "My intuition tells me that one of these bags is yours—the currant and stone mixture?"

Mrs. Lavishtock appeared to not quite understand his meaning by her frown and puzzled look. "Oh, sir, I do believe you are mistaken. But I'll take care of ridding it for you."

Gabriel looked at her closely. "Perhaps you are correct. It certainly was a brazen attempt to rescue George with the fake gems I had contained in the original bag, which someone switched." He ignored Madelene's gasp.

"Yes, brazenly good luck." She reached over to retrieve the bag and retire to the kitchen with her dignity intact.

"I must check with Mrs. Lavishtock on the dinner seating tonight. Since the same guests will be attending, I thought it might do well to change it slightly. Perhaps place Lavender McMartin next to Mr. Bush?" Madelene explained to her husband while rising from the table.

He caught her by the hand before she could make good her escape. "I assume this other bag is yours? You are the only one in this household with the special scented soap balls, which could never have fooled me for the real gems. Do I look so easily duped? Fortunate I am, I had bags made with false gems."

To answer him, she returned her gaze to his. "I was desperate and had nothing else which might do for this purpose."

He looked at her with those devastating brown eyes. "Amazing."

Their guests had departed at the ripe hour of eleven o'-clock after a lovely evening of cards and music. Even Mrs. Tottencott exclaimed the event and Madelene to be a success. Leaving Graham to extinguish the candles, Gabriel and Madelene made their way up to the first floor and down the hall to their bedchamber.

Leaning on his shoulder, Madelene asked, "Who is Lady Shillmont?"

He gave her a puzzled look before the realization dawned on him. His reply was full of mirth. "Why, she was Lord Shillmont's first wife, Isadora, and a good ten years my elder. We had little in common other than we were neighbors, until she moved to Brighton to live with her sister and bequeathed her property to a distant nephew, I believe." They stopped in the hallway, and Gabriel turned Madelene to face him, placing his hands on her shoulders.

"My love, Princess Charlotte would have had an easier time trying to catch my eye. No, my heart would have no other, not after a certain young woman faced me with a pistol on a dueling field."

Madelene's jaw dropped. "I might have killed my future husband! I am so very terribly sorry. Could I dare hope you have forgiven me?"

His hands slid down her back to bring her closer for his kiss. "Yes, as soon as you said, 'I do.'" She stretched her arms around his neck and leaned in for his kiss. One kiss couldn't last long enough, which meant another and another.

"Wife, I do believe we should continue this conversation where others cannot overhear, especially when we stop talking."

Gabriel removed his clothes and slipped into bed with his welcoming wife already waiting for him. He began his homage to her body by kissing her shoulder, her waist, her hip.

"We must talk."

He looked at his wife in astonishment. Surely whatever she had to say could wait. No, her expression showed sincere stubbornness.

"I don't know how to begin," she began and rapidly began to lose his attention as his hand found one full breast for fondling. "Gabriel, I love you." Now she had his attention, momentarily, until he found her nipple with his mouth.

She punched him in the shoulder, ever so gently. "Did I not make myself clear?"

"Perfectly, my dear, but I already knew that." He did stop to gaze into her shimmering eyes. *Was she about to cry?*

"How could you know? It was my surprise." Her bottom lip quivered.

I must have said something wrong.

Perhaps he should try again. "You're right, my dear. I was not absolutely certain, but I hoped. A man can hope his wife will love him, can he not?" *Was that as sincere as it needed to be?*

She smiled indulgently at him. "I have another surprise as well."

Through with the conversation, he placed her hand on his hardened member. "As do I." He leered at her.

She sat up, unabashedly, her naked glory on display. "Yes, that is a nice surprise, but I have a different kind. I'm, we're going to give George a brother or a sister."

Stunned, Gabriel sat up next to her. He thought about the family they had made together and how it was going to continue to grow. To show his infinite love, for that is what he called it, he leaned over to kiss her gently. It was not one of passion but rather a forever-kind of kiss, a promise they would keep to each other.

Epilogue

3 November 1812
Three Months Later
London, England

Madelene frittered with her white lace gloves while Fanny and Millie perfected her slight train. Fanny had designed Madelene's wedding dress, only needing a slightly bigger waistline to accommodate her belly, not quite showing.

Today was Gabriel and Madelene's wedding day. Indeed, second wedding day, she thought, but the one that meant so much more. It was Gabriel's gift to her, one of many he had lavished on her over the past few months, content with their lives, the coming babe, watching George struggle to stand, and Falstaff looking a little more blubberly. She smiled, thinking they both ate for two, but between the two of them, the little dog had no good reason.

All the wishes and dreams couldn't bring her father or brother to her side, but she would always savor their memory. She whispered, "Father, I am happy. I found a man who wanted me for his wife and not for the dowry I could bring him."

And Matthew. Unintentionally, he had had a direct hand in finding her a husband, to love for all time.

She closed her eyes to remember many nights ago, when they walked to the lake, now chilled with cool air. Gabriel had reached over and pulled her cloak closer under her chin, to warm her where he couldn't.

"This will always be a special place for me."

She smiled at him. "Yes, for me as well." Something seemed wrong. He didn't look happy, and he sounded very serious.

"Madelene. I want you to marry me. Will you spend the rest of your life with me?" His warm hands held hers tightly.

"Of course, but I cannot believe you have forgotten we are already married," she gently chided him.

"I want you to marry me again. We'll do it the proper way this time, and I will leave you in no doubt as to the love I have for you. It is beyond knowing. It is beyond feeling. It is beyond forever." His voice sounded gruff.

Teary-eyed, Madelene replied, "Yes, I'll marry you, for I know the same love."

If one had asked him, Gabriel could not have thought of one single more thing he could want in this life. With Madelene, he had everything.

More by Bestselling Author
Hannah Howell